'*An old wooden ship, I'm certain. Its masts gone. Just the stumps, all coated in ice. And the helmsman, frozen to the wheel. The ghost of a man and the ghost of a ship, all draped in white. And then it was gone . . .*'

These were the last scribbled notes of a glaciologist found frozen to death on the shifting ice of the Weddell Sea – notes that became the fragile clues to a gruesome mystery, shrouded from the world by the ice and storms of Antarctica.

The enigmatic Scotsman, Iain Ward, was the one man with the nerve and the courage to pursue the truth behind the dead man's fateful words. Despite the questions they asked about his mysterious wealth, a man brave enough to purchase a rusting hulk called *Isvik* and set sail from Punta Arenas into the frozen unknown . . .

Could a ship remain locked in the ice for centuries? Or was there a darker, more sinister secret buried in Antarctica's frozen wastes . . .?

Also by Hammond Innes

Hammond Innes has now written twenty-seven hugely successful novels. He has also written two travel books, a history of the Conquistadors and a fictional history based on Captain Cook's last voyage. He was awarded the CBE in 1978 and more recently Bristol University has awarded him the honorary degree of Doctor of Letters.

A Scot born in England, he wanted excitement and he wanted to write. He had both during the Battle of Britain, writing *Attack Alarm* while a gunner defending Kenley fighter station. It was in the early fifties, with books like *The Lonely Skier*, *Campbell's Kingdom*, *The White South*, all of them filmed, that he achieved international fame. His work developed steadily with such books as *Atlantic Fury*, *Levkas Man*, *The Big Footprints*.

New editions of every book he has written are constantly appearing in various countries.

In addition to his life of writing and travelling, Hammond Innes is deeply committed to forestry. His knowledge of the sea, so evident in his books, comes from his very considerable experience of ocean racing and cruising. He lives in Suffolk.

HAMMOND INNES

Isvik

PAN BOOKS
in association with Chapmans

First published in 1991 by Chapmans
This edition published 1992 by Pan Books Ltd,
a division of Pan Macmillan Limited,
Cavaye Place, London SW10 9PG
in association with Chapmans
Associated companies throughout the world
3 5 7 9 8 6 4 2

ISBN 0 330 32176 5
Printed in England by Clays Ltd, St Ives plc

To the memory of
DOROTHY
who was only able to travel
the first half of this book with me.

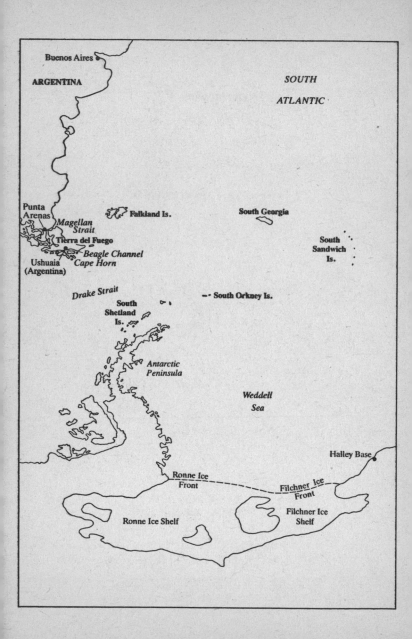

CONTENTS

I

THE POOLS WINNER

ONE

January, and East Anglia under a mantle of snow. It was still falling, tiny flakes driving across the flatness of the airfield, hangars edged with icicles and only the cleared runway cutting a black swathe through the bitter cold. I had left the guardroom till last, knowing they would have kept it warm. There was damp rot in the floorboards under the reception window, worm in door lintels that were beginning to rot at the base. I completed the entries on my clipboard and stood there for a moment checking back through my notes.

The Admin Sergeant, who had been escorting me round the various messes and quarters, returned from answering the phone. 'Station Commander would like you to join him for a drink before you leave.'

I didn't say anything, my mind concentrated on the job in hand, wondering whether I had missed anything. Twenty-three pages of notes and tomorrow I would have to cost it all out, produce a report, and an estimate, of course. It was an old station, mostly built in the war years, the quarters patched again and again, windows and doors largely of untreated wood protected only by paint. There were huts, too, that were beginning to crumble. It would be quite a big job, and whether Pett, Poldice got it would depend on my figures, as would the profit they made, and this was my first big survey since the company had been taken over.

I closed my clipboard. The Sergeant repeated the invitation and I asked him, why the Station Commander? I had done RAF stations before and it was the Wing Commander Admin who had always looked after me, never the Station Commander.

'Couldn't say, sir.' He glanced at the clock over the desk. 'He's

11

waiting for you in the officers' mess, so if you've finished I'll take you across.'

It was past one and no sign of a rise in temperature as we walked along the frozen roadway past the main gate where the security men huddled for warmth in their glassed-in box. The sound of engines warming up was loud on the freezing wind and our breath smoked. The Great Ouse would be edged with ice today right down to King's Lynn, and my little yawl, lying in its gut on the Blakeney salt marshes, would be frozen in.

The Group Captain was waiting for me in the main bar, a tall, dark man with an aquiline nose and a craggy face. There was a wing commander and a squadron leader with him, but he didn't introduce me and they drifted away as he asked me what I would have to drink. When I said a whisky mac, he nodded – 'Good choice, but I'm flying this afternoon.' He was drinking orange juice.

The bar was dark, the lights on, and as soon as I had been handed my drink he took me over to a table in the far corner. 'You know a good deal about ships, I believe. Wooden ships.' He waved me to a chair.

'Do you mean sailing ships?'

He nodded.

I told him I had been on a few. 'Sail training ships.' The grateful warmth of the drink seeped down into my stomach. 'And I've a boat of my own,' I added. 'Wood, not fibreglass. Why?'

'Old ships,' he said, not answering my question. 'Square-riggers.' He reached into the buttoned pocket of his uniform and pulled out several folded sheets of paper. 'This time last year I was in the Falklands.' He was silent a moment, looking down at the sheets. His mind seemed to have drifted back to his period on the islands. 'Strange place,' he murmured. 'The most extraordinary command I ever had.' He lifted his head, his eyes focussing on me again. 'How long do you reckon a wooden ship would last in the Antarctic, in the sort of icy conditions you get down there?'

'I don't know,' I said. 'Depends on a lot of things – the type of timber used in the construction of the hull, its condition, the latitude you're talking about and the range of temperature.' And I added, 'It's also a question of how many months of the year it's subjected to freezing, and particularly whether the timbers are immersed all the time. If the air has been allowed to get at them . . .' I hesitated, staring at him and wondering what was in his mind. 'So many variables, it's impossible to say without knowing all the circumstances.'

He nodded, opening out the folded sheets and smoothing them against his knee.

They were photocopies of what looked like pages from a notebook, very creased and the scribble illegible from where I was sitting. 'You're thinking of the hulks still lying around the Falklands, are you?' I asked him. One of our directors had gone out there at the time they were preparing the SS *Great Britain* for the long haul back to the original graving dock in Bristol where she had been built. He gave slide shows locally of the pictures he had taken, and since wood preservation was still the company's main business, many of the pictures were close-ups of the wrecked and abandoned ships he had seen around the islands. 'If you want information about the Falkland hulks, you'd better ask Ted Elton,' I told him.

'No, not around the Falklands. I don't know where, that's the trouble.' He tapped the sheets he was holding. 'These are pages from a glaciologist's notebook. They were found on his body and I had them copied before sending his things back to London.' He passed them across to me. 'He was probably on the flight deck waiting for his first sight of the Ice Shelf, otherwise he wouldn't have seen it.' And he added slowly, 'Or did he imagine it?'

'What?' I asked.

'A ship. A big sailing ship. Locked in the ice.'

'An old ship? You said something about an old ship, a square-rigger.'

He nodded. 'Read what he says.' He passed me the sheets and I held them up to the light.

There were three of them stapled together and the first words that caught my eye were: *Masts gone, of course. Just the stumps, all coated in ice. The deck, too. All I could see was the outline. An old wooden ship. I'm certain. Unfortunately my camera was back aft with my gear. Three masts and what looked like gun ports, the deck a clear*

13

stretch of ice bounded by battered bulwarks, and aft of the wheel . . .

I turned to the second page, the writing suddenly very shaky, almost illegible, as though the aircraft had hit turbulence. . . . *a figure. The helmsman, frozen to the wheel. That's what it looked like. The ghost of a man, and the ghost of a ship, all draped in white, snow or ice, only the outline showing. And then it was gone, my eyes blinking in the ice glare. I almost didn't believe what I had seen, but this is what it looked like* . . . And on the third page he had drawn a rough sketch of the vessel.

'Have you shown this to anyone with a knowledge of old ships?' I asked the Group Captain.

'I haven't personally,' he said, 'but the National Maritime have reported on it. They say it looks like an early nineteenth-century frigate. But of course that's largely guesswork. The sketch is too rough for anybody to be certain, and the question they raise is the same that everybody has raised who has read those pages – did Sunderby really see it or did he hallucinate? His name was Charles Sunderby.' He paused, tugging at the lobe of his left ear. 'He had been home on sick leave, his trouble apparently requiring psychiatric treatment.' He said it hesitantly. 'The effect of a winter at McMurdo. He had done several Sno-Cat journeys to icebergs out in the pack, examining the heavy layering that apparently takes place when new ice is forced up over older ice.' He turned his head, looking suddenly straight at me. 'So, back to my original question: could a wooden vessel of the late 1700s, or early 1800s, survive almost two centuries in that part of the world? I know in Alaska and the north of Canada, where there are no termites, wood can last almost indefinitely. The gun carriages at Fort Churchill, they go back to the formative years of the Hudson Bay Company.'

'It depends very much on the degree of humidity in the summer months,' I said. 'But even if the timber could last, would the ship?'

He nodded. 'Knowing what the winds are like down there you're probably right. But I met the man. We had a drink together the night before he left.' He sat there for a moment, staring down at his glass, lost in thought. 'The odd thing was he was scared. That's why it sticks in my mind so.' He spoke slowly, reminiscing.

'A glaciologist and scared of the ice. That's why he'd been home on leave, to sort his problem out. Or did he have some sort of premonition? Do you believe in that sort of thing?'

He looked up at me, his grey eyes wide. Not the sort of man who'd know about fear, I thought. And then he said, 'Poor bugger. I nearly lent him my amulet – the one given me by an Ethiopian just before he died. We were on the grain run from Djibouti. Grain and rice, and I had pulled him aboard at the last minute, thinking to hell with regulations, I'd save one of the poor bastards. But I didn't succeed and he gave me this . . .'

He put his hand inside his shirt and pulled out a face like a sunflower carved out of some pale-coloured stone. 'Worn it ever since.' And he added, 'We all of us have moments when we need to grip on to something – something that will reassure us that the luck hasn't run out. So I never gave it to him and his plane disappeared into the ice.' He slipped the amulet back inside his shirt, silent again.

'When did it happen?' I asked him.

'What? Oh, the plane. Let's see. I've been back almost six months now and it happened just before I left MPA. Funny thing, you know, it was only by chance that he caught that particular flight. He had been flown out from somewhere in the States in an Argentine Air Force plane. He was Argentinian, you see. At least, that's what his passport said. But he was an Ulsterman really. His nature, I mean – very puritan. He landed up at the Uruguayan base near Montevideo, then hitched a ride to Mount Pleasant on one of our aircraft that had been diverted to await an engine replacement. All chance – haphazard airlifts that were like stepping stones to oblivion, the final step when he hitched the ride on that American plane. It landed in my bailiwick because of an electrical fault, and as soon as my engineers had sorted it out it took off, and that's the last anybody saw of it.'

'How did you come by the notebook then?' I asked him.

'A big German icebreaker found the bodies. They were lying out on a layered floe of old ice about thirty miles north-west of the Ice Shelf, not far from where Shackleton's *Endurance* was crushed. No sign of the plane, no flight recorder, nothing to

15

indicate what happened, just the bodies lying there as though they had only had time to scramble out onto the floe before the plane sank.' His hand was fingering the lobe of his left ear again. 'Very strange. The whole thing is very strange. The only written record we have of anything that happened on that flight is there in Sunderby's notes on ice conditions and his sighting of that extra-ordinary *Flying Dutchman* of a vessel.' He sighed. 'Could he have imagined it? He was a scientist, very precise in his speech . . .' He hesitated, shaking his head. 'Well, it's past history now and it all happened a long way away. A very long way away.' He repeated the words thoughtfully as though he needed to remind himself that time had moved on and he was back in Britain.

He glanced at his watch and got to his feet. 'I've got to go now. A young pilot who's a wizard in the air, but can't handle money, or women it seems.' And he added, 'Expensive boys, fighter pilots. Cost the taxpayer a hell of a lot to train them. And after I've done my best to sort the poor devil out . . .' He smiled at me, a sudden flash of charm. 'One of the joys of flying is that you leave everything behind you on the ground. Including that muck.' He nodded at the tall windows where the light had almost vanished as snow swept across the flatness of the airfield. 'At fifteen thousand feet I should hit blue sky and sunshine.'

I handed the notes back to him and as we went towards the door he said, 'It was the AOC reminded me of it. Had a visit from him last week. He'd just come back from Chile where they had flown him down to Punta Arenas, that base of theirs down in the Magellan Strait. There was a lot of talk apparently of an old frigate with an Argentinian crew and flying the Argentine flag having been sailed through the Strait just after the war en route to their base in the far south of Tierra del Fuego. Apparently some woman, a relative of one of the crew, had recently been making enquiries.'

He paused as we reached the big carpeted foyer at the front entrance of the Mess. 'You all right for transport?' And when I told him my car was parked behind the building he took me down a corridor that led past the cloakrooms and showed me a short cut through some offices. 'Strange,' he said as we parted, 'the way that episode stays in my mind. Those bodies lying out on the ice, and Sunderby's notebook recording ice conditions in the Weddell Sea, nothing else, and at the end of all that scientific stuff, those three pages describing the glimpse he'd had of a sort of ghost ship locked in the ice.' He shook his head, his features dark and sombre as though the man's death was something personal, his memory a physical hurt. 'Drive carefully,' he said as he opened the door on to a brick passageway. 'Everything's freezing out there.' His hand was on my shoulder, almost pushing me out, the door shutting abruptly behind me as though in talking to me he had revealed too much of himself.

At the end of the passage I walked out into the bitter wind that whistled across from the open space of the airfield to find my car with the windscreen iced over. I sprayed it, but even so I had to run the engine for a good five minutes before I had even a peephole I could see through, and all the way back the roads were icy as hell despite the salting, the weather conditions so bad I didn't reach King's Lynn until past four.

The factory was in the industrial estate on the flats down river, but the Pett, Poldice offices were where they had always been, close by St Margaret's and the old Hanseatic 'steelyard' that had been a sampling yard before the 1500s. The building was cold and strangely silent. Everybody seemed to have been sent off early. The office I shared was empty, my desk clear except for a letter typed on a single sheet of K.L. Instant Protection notepaper.

I picked it up and took it over to the window, shocked and unbelieving as I stared down at those two brief paragraphs, two paragraphs that told me I wasn't wanted any more.

Dear Mr Kettil,

This is to inform you that the Pett, Poldice operation will be closed down as of today. All manufacturing will thereafter be concentrated at the KLIP factory at Basingstoke, the whole Group being administered from Instant Protection's Headquarters at Wolverhampton. Your services being no longer required, you will kindly vacate your office forthwith as both the office building and the factory have now been sold.

The terms of your employment will, of course, be met, and our

Wolverhampton office will be in touch with you at your home with regard to redundancy pay, pension, insurance etc.

A man describing himself as 'Personnel Executive' had scrawled a faceless signature at the bottom.

I think I must have read that letter through at least twice before I finally took it in. Redundancy, like newspaper disaster headlines, is something that happens to others, never to oneself. And we were such an old-established company.

I stared out at the brown brick of the warehouse opposite that had been converted into flats, the narrow gap between it and the next building showing a cold glimpse of the river. A mist of light powdery snow fell out of a pewter sky. It was typical of our firm to have held on to these offices for so long. The directors had thought the antiquity of the building an asset, for Pett, Poldice went right back to the days when ships were built of wood. They had been timber merchants then, and as the vessels coming up the Great Ouse to King's Lynn changed from wood to iron, younger generations of the Pett family had diversified into importing tropical hardwoods, and later still into the preservation of timber, particularly the oak-framed and oak-roofed buildings of East Anglia.

It was only when men we had never seen before began poking around the various departments asking questions about cashflow and cost ratios that we learned the Pett family had sold out to Instant Protection, a subsidiary of one of the big chemical companies and our keenest competitors. I should have realised then what was going to happen. But you don't, do you? You bury your head in the sand and get on with your work. And there was plenty of that, for we had a full order book, which made it all the more tragic.

I put my anorak on again, scooped up the few things that belonged to me and shut the door on almost five years of my life. Nobody even to say goodbye to, just an empty building and a security guard I'd never seen before on the door.

I had never been forced to look for a job in my life. I had never been unemployed. I had simply followed in my father's footsteps. He had worked for Pett, Poldice ever since the Navy released him from national service in 1956, and because I had always known there was a job there for me, most of my spare time was spent sailing out of Blakeney exploring the Wash and the Norfolk coast. That was after we had moved from the North End part of King's Lynn to Cley, and when I had finished school I volunteered for one of the Drake projects, then crewed on a Whitbread round-the-worlder.

I was lucky. I could do that because the certain prospect of a job with Pett, Poldice gave me a safety net from which to launch myself at the world. Now, suddenly, that safety net was gone and I discovered how harsh a world it could be. I had no qualifications and in the field of wood preservatives everybody seemed to be cutting staff – 'streamlining' was a word I heard all too often so that I met others who had been declared redundant, and quite a few of them did have the qualifications I lacked.

Only the sales staff, the younger ones in particular, seemed able to shift jobs with relative ease. I discovered this about a month after Pett, Poldice was shut down. Julian Thwaite, an ebullient extrovert from the Yorkshire Dales, who had been our sales manager and lived quite near us at Weasenham St Peter, suggested we all meet for a drink in the centre of King's Lynn, 'to exchange experiences, information, contacts and aspirations'. It was a nice idea, done out of the goodness of his heart, for he himself had apparently had no difficulty in switching from wood preservatives and special paints to lubricating oils. Almost fifty, out of a total workforce of seventy-nine, turned up at the Mayden's Head in the Tuesday Market Place, and of those only fourteen had found new jobs. It was the workers at the factory and the specialised staff at the old Pett, Poldice office that were experiencing the greatest difficulty in adjusting.

Within a week of being declared redundant I began toying with two possibilities, both of which excited me and had been in my mind for some time. The first was to sell my boat, borrow enough cash to get me a big 35–40 foot motor-sailer and set up as a charter skipper. The other was to set up my own wood preservative consultancy. Both these possibilities were exciting enough to have me lie awake at night planning, and as often as

19

not fantasising. It was that evening at the Mayden's Head, talking to those other poor devils who had lost their jobs and hadn't got another, that finally decided me.

I started looking at the charter skipper possibilities first, for the very simple reason that it had always been something of a dream of mine and I knew my way about the sailing world of East Anglia, the people to ask. But I soon discovered that the cost of borrowing the money to buy the boat meant that at least two months of my chartering would disappear in interest payments before I even started meeting all the other costs: maintenance, equipment replacement, stores, expenses, etc.

It just wasn't on, not unless I could finance it myself. And so I set myself up as a self-employed wood consultant, and instead of writing to possible employers, I started offering my services to companies and institutions I had been in touch with during the five years I had been at Pett, Poldice.

One of those institutions was the National Maritime Museum at Greenwich. We had once done some rather specialised work for them on a newly discovered figurehead. I got a nice letter back from the Deputy Director, but no offer of work. He saw no prospect of requiring the services of anybody outside of the Museum staff in the foreseeable future.

It was what I had expected, so I was a little surprised, about six weeks later, to receive a further note from him to say that, though he couldn't promise anything, he thought it might be worth my while if I could arrange to be in Greenwich the following Wednesday when he had a meeting fixed with somebody who needed advice on the preservation of ships' timbers. *Not really my province*, the note added, *but the ship itself is of great interest to the Museum, and the circumstances are intriguing. I thought of you in particular because of your sailing experience. You will see why if you can attend the meeting which will be on board the Cutty Sark at 11.00.*

It was a curious letter, and though I could ill afford the time, and indeed the expense, of going up to London, Victor Wellington was too important a figure in the world I was now trying to establish myself in for me to ignore his invitation.

That Wednesday morning I took the early inter-city express,

which got me into the bedlam of reconstruction that was Liverpool Street station shortly after nine. The sun was making bright bars through clouds of dust and picking out the network of new iron columns and girders towering above the boarded alleys that channelled the rush-hour traffic through big machines grabbing at the foundations of old buildings. Outside, by contrast, the City seemed bright and clean. I had plenty of time so I stopped for a sandwich and a cup of coffee at a small café by the Monument, then walked on to Tower Pier and caught a boat down to Greenwich.

Twenty minutes later we were turning into the tide in Greenwich Reach, crabbing across the river to snuggle up to the pier. Beyond the pier buildings, the masts and yards of the *Cutty Sark* stood high against a blue sky, varnish and paintwork gleaming in the clean bright slant of the sun's light. To the left, as I stepped ashore, I could see the green of grass between the pale grey stone of Wren's riverside masterpiece. I glanced at my watch. It was not yet ten-thirty.

The *Cutty Sark* stood bows-on to the river, her great bowsprit jabbing the air midway between Francis Chichester's *Gypsy Moth IV* and the pier entrance. I walked over to her and stood for a moment leaning on the iron railings, looking down into the empty dock that had been specially constructed for her. Stone steps led down on either side so that visitors could look up at the sharp-cut line of her bows and the figurehead with its outstretched arm and flying hair. There was a walkway all around the inside of the dock to a similar set of steps at the stern. A gangway and ladder on the starb'd side led up to the quarterdeck, but the main entrance to the interior of the vessel was to port, almost amidships between the first and second of her three masts. It looked something like a drawbridge, as though it had been lowered from the tumblehome of the ship's hull to lie flat on the stone edge of the dock.

I still had twenty minutes to wait and I strolled across to *Gypsy Moth*. Looking at the slender racing lines of that Illingworth thoroughbred, I marvelled that a man in his mid-sixties, keeping cancer at bay on a vegetarian diet, could have sailed her single-handed, not just round the world, but round the Horn. By comparison with the *Cutty Sark* she looked tiny, of course, but standing there, close by the wind-vane steering, gazing up at the main mast standing against the sky, she looked one hell of a handful for an elderly man all alone.

I thought of my own boat then, the beauty of the June morning making me long to have her back, to be sailing out of Blakeney, north down the gut, seabirds white in the sunshine, and out by the point seals basking on the shingle, their heads popping up to look at me out of limpid brown eyes ... And here I was in London, the boat sold and myself urgently in need of work.

I glanced at my watch again as I walked back to the *Cutty Sark*. Sixteen minutes to eleven. I would have liked to go on board to refresh my memory of the ship's layout, but somehow I felt it would be wrong to be more than fifteen minutes early. If Victor Wellington heard I was on the ship, he would almost certainly send for me. It would give an impression of over-eagerness. Pride, of course: I didn't want him to know how desperate I was for some sort of a contract from the National Maritime, however small. If only I could get that, then I felt other business would follow.

The sun was already striking warm off the stone surround of the dock as I wandered down the starb'd side, the Gypsy Moth pub shining gold on brown beyond the ship's stern, its sign painted with Chichester's yacht on one side, his plane on the other, and there was a youth standing alone on the concrete viewing platform. His back was against the railings, a slim, lounging figure in light blue cotton trousers and a loose-fitting gold blouson with a brown sweater tied round his neck. He had a camera slung from his shoulder, but somehow he looked more like a student than a tourist.

I noticed him because he wasn't looking at the *Cutty Sark*. He was standing very still, staring intently at the Church Street approach where one of those little Citroëns was trying to squeeze in between a delivery truck parked outside the Gypsy Moth and the row of five chain-secured crush barriers separating the roadway from the brick and concrete surround of the dock.

A young woman got out of the car after she had parked it, her black hair cut very short, almost a crew cut, so that it was like black paint gleaming in the sun, the bright silk of a scarf tied loosely around her neck – and something in her manner, the way she stood there looking up at the *Cutty Sark*, her head thrown back, her body tensed . . . It was as though the tea clipper had a special significance for her.

By then I had reached the stern of the *Cutty Sark*. I walked past the student, then stopped, leaning my back against the railings, watching as she reached into the car, pulling out an old leather briefcase and extracting a loose-leaf folder, which she rested on the bonnet. She stood there for a moment, turning the pages. The student shifted his position. He was short and dark, a gold ring catching the sun as he unslung his camera, opening it and checking the setting. Like his clothes, the camera was an expensive one.

There were plenty of tourists about, but they all seemed to be at the bows of the ship or gathered around the entrance amid-ships, so that at the moment when she locked her car and started walking towards us the student and I were the only people standing at the stern of the *Cutty Sark*.

She moved slowly, stuffing the folder back into the bulging briefcase. Her manner seemed abstracted, as though her mind was far away and she saw nothing of the beauty of the morning or of the tea clipper's masts towering against the blue sky. She was of medium height, not beautiful, but striking because of the firm jut of her jaw and the curve of her nose. It was a strong face, her cheekbones sharply etched in the morning light, the forehead broad, and the eyes, which caught mine for a moment as she approached, were brightly intelligent under straight black brows.

She was then only a few yards away and the student had his camera to his eye. I heard the click of it as he took a picture of her. She must have heard it, too, for she checked, a momentary hesitation, her eyes widening in a sudden shock of recognition. But there was something more than recognition, something that seemed to leave her face frozen, as though with horror, and behind the horror there was a sort of strange excitement.

It was a fleeting expression, but even so my recollection of it remains very vivid. She recovered herself almost immediately and walked on, passing quite close to me. Again our eyes met, and I thought she hesitated, as though about to speak to me. But then she was moving away, looking down at the heavy watch on her wrist, which was of the kind that divers wear. She was stockier than I had first realised, quite a powerful-looking young woman with a swing to her hips and strong calf muscles below the dark blue skirt. At the entrance to the ship she had to wait for a group of school children, her head thrown back to gaze up now at the *Cutty Sark*'s masts. Then, just before she disappeared into the hull, she half paused, her head turned briefly in my direction. But whether she was looking at me or at the student I couldn't be sure.

He had his camera slung over his shoulder again and had turned as though to follow her. But then he hesitated, realising I think that it would be too obvious. I was standing right in his path, and now that I could see his face, I understood something of what had perhaps affected her so strongly. It was a very beautiful face. That was my overriding impression. A bronzed face under a sleek black head of hair that beneath the beauty of its regular features was touched with cruelty.

It was only a few seconds that we stood facing each other, but it seemed longer. I nearly spoke to him, but then I thought perhaps he didn't speak English. He looked so very foreign, the eyes dark and hostile. Instead, I turned away, walking quickly the length of the dock. I would give it another five minutes before going on board. As I reached the bows the student was crossing the entrance gangway. He glanced quickly in my direction, then disappeared into the hull, and my mind went back then to the meeting ahead, wondering again what would come of it. That note from Wellington, the reference to a ship that was of great interest to the National Maritime, and that bit about the circumstances being intriguing. What circumstances?

As I passed under the bowsprit and the maiden with the outstretched hand and flying hair, a car came through the barrier and parked against the Naval College railings. Three men got out of it, all of them dressed in dark suits, and one of them was Victor Wellington. They were talking earnestly amongst themselves as they made their way quickly across to the ship and up the gangway to the quarterdeck. They stood there for a while, looking for'ard at the rigging, still talking with a degree of concentration that suggested perhaps they weren't looking at the ship or at anything in particular, but were entirely engrossed in the subject of their conversation.

They were there about a minute, an incongruous little gathering in their dark suits, then they moved to the after end of the coachroofing and disappeared down a companionway. I rounded the stern of the ship and headed for the entrance. There is a ticket desk on the left as you go in and when I told the CPO on duty my business, he directed me to a little cuddy of an office on the far side, where one of the *Cutty Sark*'s captains was seated at the table drinking a mug of tea.

'Mr Kettil?' He glanced at a typewritten note on the table in front of him, then got to his feet and shook my hand. 'The meeting is in the after cabin. Do you know the way?'

I shook my head. 'I've been here once before, but I don't remember the layout.'

'I'll show you then.' He gulped down the rest of his tea. 'The others have arrived, all except one.' He then led the way to the deck above, up the ladder to the quarterdeck and aft till we were just above the wheel position. Brass treads led down into a dark-panelled interior. The beautifully appointed dining saloon ran athwartships, taking up the whole after part of the officers' living accommodation.

As soon as I had ducked my head through the doorway I remembered it, the superb quality of the woodwork. The panelling was of bird's-eye maple and teak, all of it a dark rich reddish colour. So was the refectory-type table that ran athwart the saloon, plain planked seats like pews either side with backs that folded up for easy stowing, and aft of the table a magnificent dresser with a mirror back and barometer set into it as a centre piece. There was a skylight over the table with a big oil lamp gleaming brassily below it, and just behind the for'ard pew was a little coal grate set in what looked like a copy of a cast-iron Adam fireplace.

There were four men seated at the table: Victor Wellington, the two who had boarded the ship with him, also a somewhat gaunt individual, and at the far end was the young woman I had been so conscious of as she walked from her car to the ship. She looked up from her loose-leaf notebook as I entered, and again I was aware of her eyes and the look of appraisal; also something else, something indefinable, a sort of recognition, not quite animal, but certainly sexual.

The ship's duty captain had taken his leave and Victor Wellington was introducing me, first to a very slim, live-featured man, an admiral, who was Chairman of the National Maritime Museum, then to the young woman who was sitting next to him – 'Mrs Sunderby'.

She smiled at me, a quick lighting up of her features. 'Iris Sunderby.' She pronounced it 'Eeris'. The eyes were very blue in the electric light beamed down from the big brass lamp above her head. 'I'm the cause of all these kind gentlemen giving up so much of their time.' She smiled at me, but very briefly, her English careful now and her eyes on the door.

The other two men were the Chairman of the Maritime Trust and, next to him, the almost legendary figure who had saved the *Cutty Sark* and then gone on to form the World Ship Trust. Victor Wellington waved me to a seat opposite Mrs Sunderby, and as I manoeuvred my body into the position indicated, I was remembering why her name was familiar. I hesitated, then leaned across the table. 'Sorry to ask you this, but are you still married? I mean, is your husband alive?'

Her eyes clouded, the lips tightening. 'No. My husband's dead. Why?'

'He was a glaciologist, was he?'

'How did you know that?'

Hesitantly I began telling her about the strange conversation I had had some weeks back with a station commander who had served in the Falklands, and all the time I felt the need to tread delicately, not sure if she knew about her husband's psychological state, his fear of the ice. I was skating round this when the discussion about presentation of a World Ship Trust International Heritage Award was interrupted by the arrival of the man we were all apparently waiting for.

His name was Iain Ward and everybody at the table rose, no easy feat I found, the polished plank edge of the pew catching me behind my knees. I think it was innate good manners rather than respect for wealth, though the fact that he had suddenly found himself presented with a cheque for over a million probably made some difference. It was the Chairman of the National Maritime Museum who said with a friendly smile, 'Good of you to come all this way, Mr Ward.' He held out his hand, introducing himself with no mention of a title.

It was as they shook hands that I realised the man's bulging right sleeve ended in a black-gloved hand. He had paused in the entrance, his head slightly bowed as though in anticipation of contact with the deck beams. He was about my own age, tall and heavily built with long sideburns and a slightly diffident smile. 'Sorry if Ah'm late.' He had a very strong Scots accent.

Iris Sunderby stepped out from the restriction of the pew opposite and moved towards him. 'Do come in. I'm so glad you could make it.' And the Museum Chairman, still with that charming smile of his, said, 'You're not late at all. We were early. We had other business to discuss.'

She introduced him to the rest of us and he went round the table, shaking everybody very formally with his left hand. Clearly his gloved hand was artificial, but what the bulge in the sleeve was I could not quite figure out. When she had finally ushered him into the vacant place beside her, she handed everybody a typewritten sheet of paper, a memorandum setting out very briefly the reason for this meeting. Iain Ward glanced at it momentarily, then lifted his head to gaze round the table. He was seated right opposite me, his big frame squeezed into a loud check sports jacket, his shirt open at the neck to reveal a heavy gold chain round a thick bull of a neck. There was also a gold signet ring on one of the fingers of his left hand.

An awkward silence was broken by Victor Wellington saying, 'Now that we're all here I think we can get started.' He waited until we were settled, then went on, 'To go back a bit, Iris first got in touch with me about this *Flying Dutchman* of a ship shortly after her husband's death. Since then she has been very busy trying to raise money and, at the same time, making enquiries in Buenos Aires and Montevideo, and more particularly in the far south of South America, at Punta Arenas in the Magellan Strait and at Ushuaia in the Beagle Channel. As a result, we have, all four of us, come to the conclusion that if her husband did in fact sight the wreck of a square-rigged ship in the ice of the Weddell Sea before the plane he was in crashed, then it has to be the frigate *Andros*.' He looked across at the World Ship Trust representative. 'You have some photographs, I believe?'

The other nodded. 'Two in fact. One taken just after she was raised from the mud of the River Uruguay in 1981, the other after she had been restored and purchased by the Argentine Navy. Both are from the World Ship Trust's *International Register of Historic Ships*.' He had several copies and these he passed round the table. When we had all looked at them, Wellington said, 'Speaking for the Museum, and the Chairman is in full agreement, we would support any effort on anybody's part to obtain for exhibition in Britain a fully-rigged Blackwall frigate. That's what we believe it to be. It would be one of the earliest frigates on display anywhere in the world . . .'

'You support the idea,' the Chairman of the Maritime Trust put in, 'but you're not prepared to put your money where your mouth is – that right?'

Wellington glanced at his Chairman, who said, 'Moral support, yes; money, no. We've none to spare at the moment, as you well know, but we'll help in any way we can if and when restoration is in progress.' He looked across at Iris Sunderby with a lift of his eyebrows. 'Perhaps Victor will let you have the floor now. And you, sir,' he added, turning to Ward. 'If the ship is there, and if it can be recovered, and presuming it really is the *Andros* . . .' He gave a quick shrug, the smile back on his face. 'A lot of ifs, I'm afraid.' He stared at the man. 'You're serious, are you? About financing the search for the vessel, and its recovery if found?' Then he added, speaking slowly, 'Expeditions, my friend, do not come cheap. It's a hell of a lot of money for one man to put up.'

'Ye doubtin' Ah've got it? Is that it?' Ward leaned forward across the table, his tone suddenly belligerent.

'No, of course not. That's not what I want to talk to you about.'

'What then?' He didn't wait for an answer. 'Look, just in case ye didn't believe it, Ah brought these along to show ye.' His left hand, delving into the breast pocket of his jacket, came out with a bundle of press-cuttings. He almost threw them across the table. 'There ye are. There's even a close-up of the cheque. Y'see what it says – one million tae hundred an' thirty-six pounds, seventeen pence. But understan' this: Ah'm only interested in the search, no' in the restoration.'

The Admiral nodded. 'Of course. We understand that. And I'm sure, once we have a full appraisal of the ship's condition, and what remains of the hull is berthed in a proper port so that an appeal can be launched, there will be no difficulty in raising the necessary money.'

'Mrs Sunderby has included a memo . . .' Wellington's voice trailed away as the Admiral's grey eyes turned suddenly frosty.

'A memo is not the same, Victor. Mr Ward here needs to be assured that his commitment ends with the arrival of the ship's remains in say Port Stanley or even Grytviken in South Georgia. Just as we need to be assured, before we lend our support to the project, that he has a proper idea of the cost. And the dangers,' he added, turning back to Ward. 'That's what this meeting is all about. Now –' and his eyes fastened on the Scotsman – 'if I can put a few questions to you: as I understand it, or –' and he glanced quickly down at a sheet of paper in front of him – 'as you have given Mrs Sunderby to understand, you're prepared to commit up to half of what you've apparently won on the pools to the search and recovery of this icebound ship, and apart from being consulted regarding type of vessel to be used in the search and the make-up of the crew, the only proviso you make is that, whatever the circumstances, you will be included in the search team. In other words, you're buying into the expedition. Correct?'

'Aye, but ye've got to understan' –'

'One moment.' The Admiral held up his hand. 'You have a handicap. And here I'm going to speak to you man-to-man as a naval officer. In fairness to the others, who will be risking their lives with you on the edge of the Ice Shelf in areas where the pack is continuous throughout the year, I think you should reconsider the condition you've made –'

'No!' It exploded out of him, his body bending forward across the table, the left hand clenched so tight the muscles showed in knots and his eyes levelled at the Admiral. 'This is what Ah want. Ah've had a wee bit o' luck, see. Ah've won the pools, got mesel' a bloody great cheque, an' now the house Ah live in is inundated wi' beggin' letters, postbags of it, all the usual charity professionals trying to get their snoots in the trough, an' callers too, a lot o' no-good villains an' half the dropouts an' cranks in Britain. First thing Ah got was an incinerator. Ah burn the lot in the backyard. Ah know what Ah want, see. The reason Ah'm here is that Ah asked the OYC – that's the Ocean Youth Club, Ah sailed on one o' their boats once – an' they suggested Ah contact the World Ship Trust.'

The words poured out of him, a dam breaking. 'It's no' the ship Ah'm interested in. It's the excitement, the sense o' somethin' worth while. Ah wanted somethin' Ah'd have to fight fur, somethin' that'd take me sailin' half across the world. And then –' He turned his head, smiling suddenly, his eyes gleaming – 'Then Ah saw Mrs Sunderby's ad, in one o' the yachtin' mags. She wanted crew fur this Antarctic ship search, crew that could pay their way an' contribute to the cost. So here Ah am.' He had turned back to the Admiral. 'Me condition stands. If Ah finance the expedition, then they got to take me wi' them. Understan'?'

There was a sudden silence round the table, the young Scotsman and the grey-haired Admiral staring at each other. Finally the Admiral said very quietly, 'I've never been to the Antarctic, but as a youngster I was on an Arctic exercise. We were marooned in the ice for two weeks. I know what it's like. You don't. Fitness is everything. And if we support Mrs Sunderby's expedition –'

'*My* expedition,' the other cut in harshly. 'If Ah'm payin' fur it, then it's *my* expedition. The Iain Ward Antarctic Ship Search. That's what it'll be called.' He suddenly grinned. 'Ye got yer place in history, sir. Ah want mine. Even if it kills me. See.'

30

'And if it kills the others?' The Admiral paused, the grey eyes hard as they stared at Ward. 'How would you feel then?' And he added, his words coming slowly so that they carried weight, 'Speaking for the Museum, I cannot agree to supporting an expedition that's saddled with a fundamental weakness.'

'Meanin' this?' Ward patted the gloved right hand.

'Yes. Meaning just that.'

'And that's yer only objection?' Ward's face was flushed. 'Ye're goin' to damn the whole thin' just because o' me participation, wi'out the slightest knowledge o' what the poor wee hand God gave me can doe, wi'out even botherin' to test it out?' He scrambled out of his seat, came round to where Victor Wellington was seated opposite the Admiral. 'Shift over, will ye.' His gloved hand reached out, fastening on the man's shoulder and pulling him sideways. Then, bending to avoid the deck beams, he scrambled out of his jacket, sliding his long body into the space that had been made for him. 'Right.' He rolled up his shirt sleeve to reveal a withered claw of a hand set high up on the arm, wrist and elbow seemingly all one, the joint merging into the muscles that bulged below the shoulder. The hand was fastened round a plastic grip that activated the artificial hand through a bright metal connecting arm. 'Now, ye just take hold o' me artificial paw an' we'll test it out, ye an' me, an' Ah'll bet ye a fiver ye've no' the grip or the muscles Ah've got.'

The Admiral hesitated, staring at the withered mockery of a hand and the gloved fingers that had opened ready to clasp his own. Slowly, almost unwillingly, he nodded his head, reached forward and gripped the gloved hand, wincing as the steel fingers closed on his own flesh and bone.

'If it's too uncomfortable Ah'll drop the artificial extension an' ye can test out the grip this claw o' mine's got. But then, o' course, it will have to be elbows off the table.'

'No, we'll try it this way. I've seen artificial limbs like this before and I'll be interested to check the efficiency of it.' He was smiling now. 'Haven't played this game since I was a middy.' He planted his elbow on the table. 'Say when.'

Ward had placed his own strangely-shaped elbow-cum-wrist

in position, the muscles above beginning to swell as he said, 'Okay, let's go.'

Squared up to each other, their faces tense and set, they began to strain, arms literally trembling with the effort. The theatricality of it was almost ridiculous, an expedition into the Antarctic apparently depending on the outcome. Ward was like an actor slipping into a well-worn part and I knew he had done this before, a sort of party trick. He was enjoying himself. You could see it in his face. So, in his different way, was the Admiral. Socially, and probably politically, they were poles apart, yet in their personalities there was something remarkably similar. Seeing them face-to-face like that, the good hand locked with the gloved steel, muscles straining, the blood pulsing, they were like two gladiators – one could almost hear the crowd baying.

And then in a flash it was over, the Admiral's arm bending outwards, his whole body being pressed sideways until his arm was flat on the table.

Ward released his grip on the artificial forearm and the gloved fingers let go the Admiral's hand. 'Would ye like to try it wi'out the gadget?' The metal extension fell with a dramatic clatter on the table-top. 'It'll have to be standin' up, elbows free, o' course.'

The Admiral shook his head, flexing his fingers.

'Ah was born like this,' Ward said almost apologetically. 'Ah've been learnin' to cope wi' it ever since Ah were shoved out into this wicked world, an' gradually Ah've built the muscles till Ah've a lot o' strength here.' He tapped his shoulder as he got to his feet. 'Ah've even got a black belt. Karate.' He was putting on his jacket again. 'Does that set yer mind at rest or d'ye want me to run up the *Cutty Sark*'s riggin' and scramble over the futtock shrouds or whatever?'

The Admiral laughed. 'No. I think my objection has been very conclusively overridden.' He turned to Mrs Sunderby. 'What about crew? I presume you've given some thought to that.'

She nodded, pulling another file from her briefcase. 'I contacted the Whitbread people, the RYA, the STA and the RORC. Out of a list of over a hundred names for which I had some biographical and performance details, I narrowed it down to just over twenty who might have the time and the inclination to join this sort of expedition. As a result I have seven possibles.' She hesitated. 'If you have somebody in mind, Admiral . . . ?'

He shook his head slowly. 'Alas, those that leap to mind are all too old for this sort of a lark, myself included. Now if I were forty years younger –' He gave a little shrug. 'What's the total complement you have in mind?'

She glanced down at the typed sheet in her hand. 'Apart from myself and Mr Ward here, I'll need an engineer, an experienced navigator, a sailing master, a deckhand with Arctic experience and a cook who is also a sailor – five in all. I think that should be enough, though we could do with one extra in case of injury, and I'll need somebody who is a competent radio operator.'

'You've got them lined up, have you?'

'Yes, I think so. Four of them anyway. The hardest to find will be a deckhand with actual experience of working with sledges on ice. A man who is available and has a great deal of experience on North Polar sea ice is, in my view, too old; also he has a wife and three kids and his fee is commensurate with his family responsibilities. There was an Irishman who had done all sorts of things, half of which I didn't really believe, and an Australian who ran a radio shop in Perth and had worked for a year at the Australian Antarctic base largely as stand-in radio operator. He claimed to have done quite a lot of sailing and to have been a member of the reserve crew for one of the America's Cup contenders when the race was run in Perth. Unfortunately he recently married a veterinary graduate and didn't want to leave his wife. She had sailed the coast of Western Australia in her father's boat, so I suggested he bring her along. A vet isn't quite the same as having a doctor on board, but at least she would have been able to stitch up wounds, set bones and dish out the right pills. But in the end she said, No, it would ruin her chances of becoming a partner in the firm she had recently joined. A pity. They sounded ideal, particularly as he says he's a ham radio enthusiast. The others . . .' She gave a dismissive little shrug. 'It's not easy trying to get crew when you still haven't solved the financial problem. They've got to be the right people. They've got to have the right temperament as well as the experience. And we do need somebody to handle the radio side. It's our lifeline to the outside world.' She glanced at Ward, adding quickly, as though afraid she might have discouraged him, 'I've still got feelers out, of course, and I am sure, once I have the boat, and support for the expedition is guaranteed, I will be able to attract the right people.' Her eyes looked nervously round the table. 'Anyway, that's the crew situation at the moment.'

The Admiral nodded and turned to his Director. 'You agree, Victor? We give moral support.'

Wellington hesitated, his eyes searching his Chairman's face. 'The one thing the Museum lacks, apart from money, of course, is a full-size ship to complement our superb building. Something like the *Cutty Sark* here, so that visitors can walk straight from historical exhibits on to the deck of the real thing. It's something that the Friends of the Museum, and quite a few of the staff, have been pressing for over the years. If this Blackwall frigate really exists, if there really is a ship like that down there in the ice . . .' His eyes gleamed and his voice changed, taking on a sudden note of almost boyish enthusiasm as he told Ward what it was that made this particular type of frigate so special.

Apparently they were not naval vessels at all, but large East Indiamen built at Blackwall on the Thames just downstream of the Navy Yard. By then the Company, and also the Dutch, needed faster vessels, ships that could outrun or fight off any attacker, so they began building to the lines of the naval frigates and the first of the Blackwall-built vessels was the *Seringapatam*. 'This was in 1837, in the last days of the East India Company, so not many of them were built.' That first vessel had been of 818 tons, almost half the size of the largest they ever built, which was 183 feet long with a beam of 40 feet and a tonnage of around 1,400. The *Andros*, he thought, was about 1,000 tons. 'Most of these ships were later used as emigrant transports; they also went south round the Horn for the Californian and Australian gold rushes.'

While he was talking I had become increasingly conscious of the sound of voices from beyond the door that led for'ard to the officers' galley and cabins, children's voices mainly. And then a

34

movement caught my eye above the hanging lamp, two small faces peering down at us from the skylight. As soon as they realised I had seen them they vanished and in their place was a young man's face, dark, intense, the eyes slightly protuberant and a thin spoilt mouth, the dull gold sleeve of his blouson flattened against the glass. He was looking down at Iris Sunderby, a strange glint in his eyes. Was it lust? Hatred perhaps? I couldn't be sure. All I knew for certain was that the sight of her sitting there, her head bent over her papers, had sparked off some violent emotion.

He must have sensed I was watching him for he suddenly turned his head and looked straight at me. I could see his eyes more clearly then, very dark and full of malevolence. Or so it seemed at the time. But it was such a fleeting glimpse, then it was gone and I thought he smiled at me. A second later I was staring up at an empty rectangle of blue sky. 'Tourists,' Wellington said. 'They get all over the place.'

I glanced quickly across at Iris Sunderby, wondering whether she had seen him and what her reaction had been, but her head was now turned towards Victor Wellington as he described more fully the *Andros* frigate; dimensions, masts, rigging, all the construction details so dear to a curator contemplating a prize exhibit.

I don't remember much of what he said, for the face in the sky-light had made an extraordinary impression on me. It sounds ridiculous as I write about it now, just the glimpse of a face through a ship's skylight, but I knew then, in that instant, there was something between them, something that linked him to Iris Sunderby in a way that was both personal and frightening. It was such a startling impression to form in the photo-flash moment of his staring down at her. But there it is. That face conveyed something, the very intent, very concentrated expression of it sending a chill through me that even now I cannot entirely explain.

'If the expedition – your expedition – were successful and you found the remains of the *Andros* in the ice, with Peter Kettil here to advise you on its preservation . . .' That mention of my name jerked my mind back from its wild imaginings. It was the first indication I had of the real purpose of my presence here at this gathering.

'Are you suggesting I advise them – out there?' My voice sounded small and uncertain.

Victor Wellington's sharp little eyes fastened on me. 'Of course. It's essential to have an expert on the spot to assess what is necessary for preservation of the ship's timbers so that it can be flown out, together with the appropriate technicians. Then, when the salvage boys have cut a way out for her, the hull can be towed north into warmer seas without fear of it disintegrating.'

'But –' I hesitated. The possibility of my being a member of the expedition hadn't occurred to me.

He smiled. 'Why do you think I asked you to attend this meeting?'

'But I'm not qualified,' I said. 'Timber preservation, yes – but sailing in the Antarctic . . .'

'You know about ships. You've sailed, and you have a boat of your own.'

'I had. But on the Norfolk coast. You're talking about the Antarctic.'

'Nelson,' the Admiral cut in. 'Burnham Thorpe. He was brought up on the edge of the saltings there. And the north of Norfolk is sometimes referred to as the Arctic Shore. It's cold and it breeds a certain type of man. You'll fit. Won't he, Mrs Sunderby?'

I turned my head to find her looking at me very intently. Clearly she hadn't been ready to make a decision there and then. But suddenly she smiled. 'Yes, of course. The Admiral's right.' And she added, 'If we do find the ship, we'll certainly need the sort of specialised knowledge you can provide.'

Nobody asked me how I felt about a voyage into the Antarctic. They just seemed to take it for granted I would go along with them, the talk turning to the availability of a suitable search vessel that would be within the budget Ward was offering. And like a fool I just sat there and said nothing. If I'd had any sense I'd have got to my feet and walked out, for the boat the Sunderby woman had in mind was a sixty-foot motor-sailer with a quarter-inch steel hull and a powerful diesel auxiliary. It was lying in the Chilean naval port of Punta Arenas on the north side of the

Magellan Strait and had been strengthened and equipped for a Norwegian prospecting expedition in Queen Maude Land that had run out of money before it had even started.

Mrs Sunderby had been down to Punta Arenas, had seen the boat. Its name was *Isvik* and it had been left in charge of one of the expedition members, a Norwegian named Nils Solberg. The boat was for sale and she thought Solberg, who was an engineer and whom she regarded as highly competent, would go along with any new expedition.

The discussion then turned to the feasibility of wintering over in the ice. The name David Lewis was mentioned. Apparently he had wintered a vessel of very similar size in the ice in Prydz Bay in the Australian territory of Queen Mary Land with a crew of only six, including two girls. Clearly it could be done, and the meeting finally broke up with Ward agreeing to meet the initial cost, including purchase of the vessel, which Mrs Sunderby thought could be acquired for a figure well below the US$230,000 the bankrupt Norwegian expedition were asking.

The object of the meeting in the *Cutty Sark* after cabin had clearly been to influence Ward's decision. But once she had his agreement, she also had the backing of all the three institutions represented there. As she put it, 'Now all we need is about thirty hours in every day, the right weather and a hell of a lot of luck.' She rose to her feet, looking round the table. 'Thank you, gentlemen – for your time, and for your help.' She was smiling, her eyes shining, and she added, 'You've no idea what this means to me – personally.' The way she said it conveyed an extraordinary sense of excitement. And as the maritime heritage men said goodbye and ducked out through the after door beside the dresser, leaving just the three of us there in the cabin, the thing I was chiefly conscious of was her vitality. Now that she had got what she wanted, she seemed packed full of energy, so that just being there with her gave me an extraordinary lift, my feeling of depression quite gone.

'Did you come by car?' She was speaking to Ward.

'No. Water bus.'

'Can I give you a lift then?'

He shook his head. 'Ah'd prefer to go back the way Ah came. There's a lot to see on the river here. Also, Ah've a wee bit o' thinkin' to dae, ye understan'. Ah've never before had anythin' to dae wi' this sort of an outfit – Ah mean admirals an' directors o' museums an' maritime trusts. It's all new to me. An' there's the wee matter o' what Ah'm lettin' mesel' in fur. Ah mean, six months, maybe a year if we're locked into the ice, searchin' fur a vessel Ah'm no' at all sure really exists.'

'But you've read the notes Charles made.' The voice was crisp and sharp. 'You know very well that he must have written that description of the ship within minutes of having sighted it. We've been over all this on the phone and I've explained to you that I have a navigator in mind, a man I'm convinced has actually seen what my husband saw.'

'Aye, but ye haven't produced the man. Ye haven't even told me his name or where Ah can contact him.'

'No.'

They stared at each other, hostility building between them so that the atmosphere in that panelled saloon was almost frigid.

It was Ward who finally broke the heavy silence. 'Och hell!' he muttered. 'What's it matter?'

'How do you mean?' Her eyes blazed.

'Just that Ah don't care very much one way or t'other. Whether the ship exists outside o' yer husband's imagination is no' all that important to me. Ye say this nameless navigator o' yers has also seen it?'

'I think so.'

'Okay then. But Ah want to see him before he joins us as navigator. Where can Ah meet him?'

'At Punta Arenas. That's if he agrees.'

'Where is he now?'

'Somewhere in South America.'

She turned away, the movement and the expression on her face making it clear she was unwilling to answer any more questions.

Ward hesitated, then gave a little shrug. 'Okay, if that's the way ye want it. But understan' this, girl, it's *my* money an' ye don't ship crew wi'out Ah check them first. Okay?' And he added almost waspishly, 'If we find the ship, good – but Ah'll no' lose any sleep if we don't set eyes on her. It's like Ah was sayin'. Ah've made some money an' now Ah want to use it to dae somethin' Ah've always wanted to dae. The ship is merely an objective.' A sudden smile lit up his features. 'If it's there, fine. But it's the challenge o' the thin'. That's what's important to me.'

His manner, his whole bearing, the way he faced us, was pure theatre. He was playing a part and we were the audience. 'A challenge,' he repeated. And then he smiled that attractive smile of his, held out his left hand and said, 'Ah'll be thinkin' about it all the way back to Glasgae, Mrs Sunderby. O' ye, too. Let me know when ye've fixed the boat, an' the price – then Ah'll talk to the lawyer men Ah seem to have acquired. Also the accountancy laddies who check the figures.'

He left us, his mouth stretched into something near a grin as he ducked through the after cabin doorway like an actor going off stage at the end of his big scene.

Iris Sunderby's reaction was similar to my own. 'God!' she breathed, tossing her head back in a gesture of irritation as she listened to the sound of his footsteps on the deck above. 'Much more of that man and I'd –' She checked herself with a wry little smile, then snatched up her briefcase and began stuffing her papers into it. 'Do you think that accent of his is real?' She turned and looked at me. 'Well, do you?'

I shrugged. 'Does it matter?'

'Yes, it does.' There was a note almost of desperation in her voice. 'If it isn't, then the man's far too complex, has much too much imagination. And if I can't stand his play-acting here, how the hell am I going to manage in the close confines of the boat. It could be for month after month, you know. If we get locked into the ice, per'aps for a whole winter. *¡Dios mio!*'

She stood there, staring at her reflection in the dresser's mirror. The silence for that moment was absolute. 'Trouble is,' she went on slowly, 'that man is just about my last hope.' She snapped the lock of the briefcase shut and moved towards the door. 'I've been knocking on big company doors till I'm sick of the sight of men trying to avoid telling me outright my husband was a nutter.

And the endless letters . . .' She shook her head. 'If it hadn't been for the Admiral –' She turned and looked at me again, holding out the bulging briefcase. 'All these notes and memos of mine,' she said angrily. 'All wasted on him. An ego a mile high and that Glasgae accent of his . . . The Admiral saw it at once.'

'Saw what?' I asked.

'Ward's reluctance. That it was all just a game to him. He'd only come down from Scotland out of curiosity. A Glaswegian truck driver – *Ah've never before had anythin' to dae wi' an outfit o' this sort*.' It was a fair imitation and she repeated, 'The Admiral saw it at once. Clever, the way he handled the man.'

'You mean that man-to-man stuff about his disability endangering lives?'

'Of course. You don't think the Admiral behaves like that normally? Not in his nature. But he saw Ward's reluctance, realised he wasn't going to throw his cash around, so he go straight for the jugular.' She was excited, her English slipping as she moved towards the door again. 'Where are you going – Liverpool Street station, is it?' And when I nodded she offered to drop me off. 'I've got to go through the City anyway. I need to visit the Argentine Embassy, Cadogan Gardens.'

It was while we were saying goodbye to the *Cutty Sark*'s Captain that I saw the student again, standing by one of the pictorial display panels. He lingered there until we moved towards the exit, then he started walking casually down the length of the deck. He emerged into the sunshine just as we reached the ship's stern. 'I see your boyfriend is still keeping you in his sights.'

I said it as a joke, but she didn't take it that way. 'He's not my boyfriend.' There was a sudden tension in her voice, and she didn't turn her head to see who I was referring to.

'You know him, don't you?'

She didn't answer and we walked in silence until we reached her car. As she unlocked it he passed us, running along the upper walk that led past the big square flower tubs to the kiosk and on to Chichester's *Gypsy Moth*. He kept on the far side of the platform, and since we were at a much lower level, I only caught a glimpse of his head and shoulders until he came off the raised level and ducked down to the right, towards the underground car park run by the British Legion.

She was leaning into the back of her car, rearranging her things, and she hadn't seen him. A family of tourists stood near us, talking to an old man who had just come out of the Gypsy Moth pub. 'They call it Church Street now,' he told them. ''Cos of the church there, St Alfege. But way back, afore they brought that ship 'ere an' knocked all the buildings down to build a dock for 'er, this was a street of shops an' 'ouses, right down to the pier. Billingsgate Street. That was the name of it.'

They passed out of earshot, a child's voice raised, demanding ice-cream. We got into the car and she drove off. Looking back as we turned into College Approach, I saw a bright red open sports car shoot out of the street opposite the Gypsy Moth, a man at the wheel, and no passenger. It followed us as we turned right by the entrance to the Royal Naval College and right again on to the main road.

When I told her he was following us, she didn't say anything, but her face had a set look, her eyes on the rear-view mirror.

'Who is he?' I asked. 'What's he want?'

She didn't answer, and when I repeated the question, she shook her head.

'Is he a student, or just a visitor?'

'A student, I think.'

We drove in silence, heading down river till we joined the motorway and turned north. Several times I looked back, but it wasn't until we were dipping into the entrance of the Blackwall Tunnel that I caught the flash of that red sports car weaving through the traffic behind a big cement truck. She had seen it too and she changed lanes, putting her foot down till we were nose-to-tail with the car ahead.

'Do you think he's following us?' I had to yell to make myself heard above the noise of engines reverberating against the wall of the tunnel.

She nodded.

'Why?'

41

She turned her head. 'Why do you think?' she yelled. Her mouth was a thin line, her eyes blazing with anger.

I shrugged. It was nothing to do with me. But I had an uneasy feeling it might be if I landed up crewing that boat of hers down into the Antarctic. 'Who is he?' I asked again as we came out into the relative peace of the above-ground traffic.

'His name is Carlos.' She banged the wheel again. 'He send that fucking little sod. One of his boys, but he's some sort of a cousin, too. He even looks like him.'

'Like who?'

'Ángel.' She looked at me out of the corner of those extraordinary blue eyes and laughed. 'Oh, you'll love him.'

'Who is this Ángel?' I asked.

Still looking at me, she almost ran into the vehicle ahead. 'You really want to know? He is half my brother, wonderfully handsome, like that boy. And he's a devil,' she added viciously. 'Fucks any girl he can get hold of and sodoms them too. Nothing he likes better than having them crawl on their hands and knees with their rumps in the air, then he has . . .' She glanced at me, the flicker of a smile. 'I see I have shocked you, but that is the sort of man he is.' She swerved suddenly, cutting across the front of a lorry as she changed lanes. '¡Dios mio! I should know.' She was silent for a moment, then she said, 'It's the Italian in him, a legacy from a bitch of a woman named Rosalli Gabrielli.' She swung abruptly left on to an intersecting cut-off. Another glance, and a funny little laugh, her eyes alight with a strange excitement. 'Don't look so worried. The libido don't thrive, I think, down in the ice of the Weddell Sea. You will be safe enough.' Again that little laugh, a soft, throaty chuckle now.

A road sign indicated that we were in the East India Dock Road. She slowed for some lights. 'I'm sorry. I should have kept quiet about the family. We are not always very nice people.' She shrugged. 'But perhaps that goes for a lot of the human race.'

The lights changed and she swung left into a side street. 'You ever travel the Docklands Light Railway? It's rather like riding the El in New York before they build any skyscrapers. I'll drop you off outside the *Telegraph* building. The train will take you to the Tower, and from there it's only a short walk to Liverpool Street station, or you can take the Circle Line.' She turned left again, a mean, shabby little street with a view of water ahead, then right and more water as she doubled back on her tracks. Another glimpse of the river, and then we were crossing the entrance to some docks.

I glanced back. No sign of the car. 'Where are we?' I asked.

'Isle of Dogs. West India Docks.'

'You seem to know your way around.'

'I live here.'

'Why?'

'Because it's cheap. I have a couple of rooms in a house that's due for demolition.' We turned up on to what was the raised quay of the South Docks, two massive buildings of glass and granite-like cladding, and beyond them, seen through the piers supporting the overhead railway, a litter of developers' high gantry cranes. 'There'll be nothing left of the old Tower Hamlets streets in a few years' time.'

'There must be other parts of London just as cheap,' I said. 'What made you pick on this?'

'You ask too many questions.' She swung under the round pillars of the railway and stopped outside the second of the glass-fronted buildings. 'I like water and here the river and the docks are all around me.' She nodded to the iron stairway painted in Docklands Light Railway blue that led up to the little station poised overhead. 'I have your address and telephone number. I'll be in touch. Hopefully in about two or three weeks' time.'

I thanked her for the lift and got out. She drove off then, and that was the last I saw of her till the police brought me down from Norfolk to identify the body of a woman they had fished out of the South Docks. When they slid her body out and pulled the plastic sheet away it looked at though she had been battered to death with an axe.

TWO

I had only met her that once and the appalling mess they uncovered for me in the hospital mortuary was quite unrecognisable. The body was about the same build. That was all I could tell them. Concentrate on the clothes, they said, and that ring on her finger. But I didn't know what clothes Iris Sunderby possessed and she might have had any number of rings. I certainly had not noticed one when I sat almost opposite her in the after cabin of the *Cutty Sark*, or when her hands were on the steering wheel as she drove me through the Blackwall Tunnel and on to the Isle of Dogs.

I asked them why they thought I could help and they said that divers had dredged up a handbag from the bottom of the dock. In it they had found the remains of several letters, one from Victor Wellington, another from me, the others from addresses in the Argentine. 'Have you any reason to think she would commit suicide?' The Inspector threw the question at me almost casually as we walked out into the damp atmosphere of a day that was hovering between drizzle and rain.

'Quite the reverse,' I said. 'She was full of plans for the future.' And I told him briefly about the ship in the ice and the vessel waiting for us in Tierra del Fuego. But he already knew about that. 'Mr Wellington said the same thing and I've spoken to a man named Ward up in Glasgow. I gather he was willing to finance the expedition.' He nodded, leaning his body into the wind. 'So it's murder.' He turned his head, a quick, searching glance. 'Have you got any views on that, sir?'

'No, why should I?' And I told him again that my visit to the *Cutty Sark* was the first and only time I had met her. But then I

44

remembered the student, a cousin she had said, and I explained how I had seen him watching her park her car by the Gypsy Moth pub, how he had looked down at us through the *Cutty Sark*'s skylight and had then followed us in his bright red sports car.

'Did she give you his name?'

'Carlos,' I said.

'His surname?'

But I couldn't tell him that and in the end he thanked me for my co-operation. 'If you hear anything else . . .' He hesitated. 'I think I should tell you the state of the body is not indicative of the cause of death. The pathologist is quite satisfied she died by drowning.' And he added, 'The wounds to the head and neck were probably caused by her body being sucked into the swirl of a ship's propeller. We checked with the Maritime Trust vessels and one of them regularly runs up the engines, usually at slow ahead to lubricate the prop shaft. The watchman did that the night before the body was reported to us.'

'It could have been an accident then?'

'It could.' He nodded. 'Seems she'd formed a habit, ever since she'd rented the room in Mellish Street, of taking a walk in the evening, usually with her landlady's dog. Quite late sometimes. She liked to walk round the docks. So yes, it could have been an accident, particularly as the night she disappeared she had already taken the dog out.' But I could see he didn't think it likely. 'She was last seen down by the river at the end of Cuba Street by the South Dock Pier. Perhaps I should say that two men saw a young woman of her description on her own and without a dog. They had been having a drink together at The North Pole and though they couldn't give the exact time, they both said they had stayed in the pub until it closed.' We had reached the police car and he paused, the keys in his hand. 'Originally she was going to drop you off at Liverpool Street station, you said. It was on her way. Do you know where she was going, her original destination before she changed her mind?'

'I think she said Cadogan Gardens, something to do with the Argentine Embassy.'

'And then, when she found she was being followed, she swung off the main road and headed back towards her lodgings on the Isle of Dogs. Was she scared?'

'I don't know,' I said. 'Maybe. But it didn't show in her face. More annoyed than scared.'

'Did you get the number of his car?'

I shook my head. 'He was three vehicles back.'

'A Porsche, that right?'

'It looked like a Porsche, but I can't be certain. All I am sure about is the colour and that it was an open sports car.' Once again I went over the description I had given him, the boy's face dark and tense behind the wheel, the black hair streaming in the wind as we came out of the Blackwall Tunnel still vivid in my mind. 'We'll have a Photofit picture circulated, but it's not much to go on. The car is a better bet. Not too many open top Porsches around in this country.'

He offered me a lift to the nearest tube station, but I said I would rather walk. I was feeling slightly sick. I had never seen a dead body before and I needed to come to terms with the memory of that battered, half-decapitated corpse, the pale marble of her skin and the open wound along her thigh.

He nodded. I think he understood. 'I'll be in touch,' he said as he got into his car, adding, 'We're not revealing the cause of death, not just yet. Understand?' And he drove off eastwards, while I turned and headed towards Limehouse and the Docklands Light Railway. I wanted time to think, and a sight of the environment in which she had lived during the time she had been in England might help. The line ended, I knew, at Island Gardens at the southern tip of the Isle of Dogs. From there I could walk through the foot tunnel under the Thames to Greenwich. If I was lucky I might be able to have a word with Victor Wellington. We had both seen the body and between us we might remember something that would make identification more positive.

But it was the motive that was nagging at my mind. If that young relative of hers had done it, then there had to be a motive, something personal, and remembering the violence of her reaction when she realised he was following her, I wondered whether

46

I ought to have passed on to the Inspector the exact words she had used.

The Docklands Light Railway was still relatively new, the blue-painted, glass-domed station glistening in the wet. There was a train already in, two box-like glass coaches painted blue and a warning to say that their operation was automatic. It left almost immediately, and sitting up front with a gaggle of tourists and no driver, it was like travelling on a toy railway. As it swung away from the Fenchurch Street line and headed south on an elevated track parallel to the West Ferry Road, the whole of the Isle of Dogs opened up ahead of us. The drizzle had turned to rain, the water in a succession of docks we crossed dark and mottled, and in between them construction areas that were glistening islands of yellow earth criss-crossed with the tracks of heavy vehicles out of which rose a forest of gantry cranes.

At South Quay station we were right alongside the *Telegraph* building, swinging east, then south through an area of new construction, the buildings brash and for the most part architecturally appalling. Crossharbour, Mudchute, a view west beyond Millwall Dock, almost every building knocked flat and the streets boarded up, and across the river the pinnacles of Greenwich and the masts and yards of the *Cutty Sark*.

I had tried to get a glimpse of Mellish Street between the newer buildings, but there were very few of the old houses still standing and it was difficult in the midst of all the construction to picture what it must have been like for her living down there, walking the dog at night, her mind all the time on the Weddell Sea and the abandoned expedition boat waiting for her at Punta Arenas.

From the Garden Islands terminal it was only a few minutes' walk to the park entrance and the glass-domed rotunda that houses the lift to the Greenwich Foot Tunnel. The sky was beginning to lighten over Blackheath, the beauty of Wren's architecture on the far side of the river standing in perfect harmony above the darker grey of the water. I stopped at one point because a shaft of sunlight had suddenly pierced the gloom. It picked out the Royal Naval College and a ferry angling across the river. There was a Thames barge, too, motoring up Blackwall Reach, the whole scene suddenly Turneresque. How many times had she come down here to the southernmost tip of the Isle of Dogs? A pointless question since I didn't even know how long she had been in England. I should have asked. So many questions I should have asked her, remembering that sense of awareness I had felt at first sight of her.

The lift was for up to sixty passengers and there was a TV monitor by the gates showing the northern half of the tunnel with tourists moving up and down it. A notice said it had been opened in 1902 at a cost of £127,000, that it was over twelve hundred feet long and between thirty and fifty feet below the water according to the state of the tide. There were quite a few kids in the tunnel when I entered it, the high-pitched scream of their voices resounding in the long lavatorial tube-train-sized passage – two hundred thousand white tiles, the notice had said.

I think Victor Wellington was as glad to see me as I was to see him, for when I asked for him at the Museum I was shown straight into his office. 'Bad business,' he said after he had greeted me. He must have said that three or four times during the quarter of an hour or so I was with him. 'No, I've no doubt at all.' This in reply to my question asking him whether he was certain the body was that of Iris Sunderby. It was the ring, he said, and he went on to describe it, an eternity ring of unusual thickness and banded with what he took to be thin rectangles of ruby and emerald. 'On the left hand,' he said. 'Very striking.'

I shook my head. I hadn't noticed any ring.

'A bad business.' His hands were locked together on the desk. 'It's not nice seeing somebody, anybody, in that condition. But somebody you've met, a strong, characterful young woman – very striking, didn't you think her?'

'Yes, very striking,' I agreed. 'Great vitality.'

'Vitality, yes. It hit you straight away, a sort of sexual energy.' There was a sudden gleam in his eyes, his small mouth slightly pursed so that I wondered whether he was married and if so what his wife was like. 'She wasn't raped, you know,' he added. 'It wasn't that sort of killing.'

48

'You asked?'

'Yes, of course. It's the first thing that comes to mind.'

'And you're convinced she was killed.'

'That's the Inspector's view. What else? It was either that or suicide, and she wasn't the sort of person to kill herself, not when she'd just got the backing she needed. And it would be odd if she fell into the dock by accident. Sky clear and a nearly full moon. Now if she'd had the dog with her . . . But she hadn't.' He got to his feet. 'Her brother was one of the Disappeareds. That may explain it.'

'How do you mean?'

'The Disappeareds. Don't you remember?' This over his shoulder as he walked across the room to a bank of filing cabinets. 'All those silent women holding a weekly vigil in that square in Buenos Aires. There was a lot about it in the press two or three years back. A mute accusation for the loss of their loved ones. About thirty thousand of them. Just disappeared. Surely you remember?' He pulled open one of the drawers. 'Connor-Gómez. That was the family name, her name before she married, and her brother was Eduardo. She talked about him briefly when she first came to see me. He was a scientist. Biology I think she said.' He found the file he wanted and lifted out a sheet of notepaper. 'Here we are. Just an ordinary thank you letter for arranging that meeting on board the *Cutty Sark*, and then at the bottom a PS.' He handed me the letter. 'I gave a copy of it to the police, of course.'

It was a typed letter, short and to the point, with a wild flourish of a signature sprawled across her name typed at the bottom, and below that the postscript, hand-written and difficult to read: *Other people are after the ship. Don't let them discourage Ward please.* The *please* was heavily underlined.

'Have you been in touch with him?' I asked.

'Ward? No. What's the point? Nothing I could do about it and he'll know she's dead. The media gave it full coverage, all the gory details.' He held out his hand for the letter. 'So ironic, just at the moment when she'd found a backer, and an interesting one, too. He came and saw me here the day after our meeting,

49

wanted to know a little more about her.' His glasses caught the light as he turned back to the filing cabinet. 'I couldn't tell him much, but I learnt a little bit more about him, enough anyway to realise he could contribute quite a lot to the expedition. He's not just a truck driver, you see. Not any more. He has his own business now and runs a small fleet of those transcontinental monsters they use on the Middle Eastern run down through Turkey. That's the modern equivalent of the old silk road.' He paused, searching for the folder he had taken the letter from. Then, when he had found it, he said, 'I asked him about the cargoes he was running, but he wouldn't say much about that, or their destination. I don't imagine it was drugs. He didn't seem that sort of man. But it was certainly profitable. Arms most likely, and the destination probably Iran or the Gulf States.'

He pushed the drawer to and returned to his desk. 'A pity,' he said again. 'She had been trying unsuccessfully for over six months to raise the necessary funds in South America and the States. Finally she came to England and got herself a room in Mellish Street, where she'd be close to the Museum here and at the same time handy for the City where she hoped to fund the expedition. Then, when the institutions turned her down, she began advertising in a few selected magazines. That was how she landed Ward. Rather similar, the two of them – wouldn't you say? Both of them with a lot of energy, a lot of drive.'

Wellington had resumed his seat and he leaned across the desk, staring at me as he said abruptly, 'How do you drown a woman?' He didn't wait for an answer. 'I asked the Inspector that. You hold her head under water, of course. But to do that in the South Docks you'd have to be in the water yourself. How do you get out? And when you have found the ladder, or whatever it is, you're sopping wet as well as scared. Somebody surely would have seen the man. I mean, you don't forget a sight like that, do you? At least, that's what the Inspector is banking on.'

'She could have been drowned in her lodgings, in the bath, something like that,' I said. 'Then driven to the dockside and dumped there.'

We were still discussing the various possibilities when his

50

secretary came in to say the Admiral was waiting for him and all the members of the ship model group were assembled. He nodded and got to his feet. 'Bad business,' he said again as we went to the door. 'And bad luck on you. Could have made your name on a project like that. But perhaps you're best out of it.'

'How do you mean?' I asked. And when he didn't immediately reply I added, 'Because of that postscript to her letter?'

We had paused in the corridor outside. 'No, because of Ward.' He seemed to hesitate. Then he said, 'There was no pools win, you see. He came by his money some other way.' And when I asked him how he knew, he gave a little deprecating laugh and said, 'Simple. I just phoned a couple of the main operators.'

'You mean he hasn't got a million?'

He shrugged. 'Can't answer that. All I know is, if he's got that sort of money, it didn't come to him through a pools win.' The words hung in the air as he stood there smiling at me. 'Too bad it turned out this way.'

He had nothing else to offer me, of course, but before he went off to discuss ship models he was kind enough to say he'd continue to bear me in mind if he heard of anything that required a wood preservative consultant.

I had a sandwich and a cup of coffee in the Museum cafeteria, then walked back through the foot tunnel to the Isle of Dogs. I didn't take the train. Instead, I decided to walk along West Ferry Road until I reached Mellish Street. There were houses at first and a few trees, but at the Lord Nelson, on the corner of what the developers had left of East Ferry Road, the hoardings began. From then on it was all hoardings, dust and heavy machinery, and all that was left of old Millwall were the pubs. They stood, solitary and splendid, waiting for the coming of the yuppies – the Ship, the Robert Burns, the Vulcan, the Telegraph, the Kingsbridge Arms. By Cyclops Wharf and Quay West a long stretch of hoardings advertised Greenwich views, gymnasium, restaurant, swimming pool, running track, squash, water sports, leafy squares, cobbled streets, bakery, the Island Club, the river bus – a you-name-it, we've-got-it development.

And then I came to Tiller Road and the vestige remains of

Tower Hamlets' cheap-looking post-war housing. Mellish Street began like that, too, breeze-block two-storey tenements with rusty metal windows and concrete slab porches, and behind the tenements several tower blocks climbing the sky. But halfway up the street, from Number 26 on, it was the old original terraced houses with front parlour windows that jutted out into front garden patches.

The house in which she had lodged was one of these, right at the end of the street by a solitary tree.

I don't know what I expected to learn from this visit, but though I rang the bell several times, there was no answer. A black kid was trying out a skateboard down by the tenements, otherwise the street was deserted, a few parked cars, that's all. I hammered on the door. There was no sound, not even from the dog, but a curtain twitched in the house next door and I had a glimpse of a cotton dress and a sharp, lined face with eyes full of curiosity.

She must have been waiting for me there behind the door, for she opened it as soon as I rang the bell. 'Good morning.' I hadn't thought what I was going to say and we stood there for a moment facing each other awkwardly in silence, her eyes grey and slightly watery. 'I was wondering about the dog,' I said hesitantly.

'Mudface? She took it with 'er, ter Poplar ter stay with 'er brother. You the perlice? She got fed up wiv the perlice.'

'No,' I said. 'I know Mrs Sunderby.'

Her eyes brightened. ''Er as was murdered?' She was a real East Ender.

'How do you know she was murdered?'

'Well, I don't, do I? But that's what I 'eard. The papers, they don't *say* it were murder, but that's wot they bin 'inting at. An' all chopped up like that, makes shivers run down yer spine just ter think aba't it. Wot yer want then?'

I started asking her about Iris Sunderby, what time she normally took the dog out at night, whether she had had any visitors, and I described the student I had seen at the *Cutty Sark* that day. I didn't say he had followed us and I didn't mention the name Carlos, but I did tell her he had had a red open sports car and as soon as I said that she nodded. ''E parked it up beyond the tree there. I was a't the front talkin' ter Effie Billing an' this little red car turns a't of Mill'arbour an' stops right there.' Her description of the driver fitted. He hadn't got out. He had just sat there as though waiting for somebody.

'When was this?' I asked.

She couldn't give me the date, but it was a Wednesday, she said, about a fortnight ago. And it had been in the late afternoon, about tea time, which meant he had picked up her trail again after she had dropped me off at South Quay station. Or maybe he had managed to keep us in sight all the time. 'Did he talk to her?' I asked. 'Did he call at the house?'

She shook her head. 'Not that I saw, an' I was watching on an' orf for more'n an hour I'd say. Then she came out an' drove orf in 'er little car. An' as soon as she's inter Mill'arbour 'e whips that little red beast of 'is round an' roars off after 'er.'

'Did you tell the police?'

She shook her head. 'Didn't ask, did they?' To her the police were clearly something to be avoided.

I thanked her and walked away, past the house Iris Sunderby had lived in for what must have been at least a fortnight, past the tree, turning left up the main Millharbour road towards Marsh Wall and the *Telegraph* building and the dock where her body had been found. Away to the left was the slender, box-shaped indicator of the *Guardian* newspaper. I was in an area now of brash new construction and for the first time I became conscious of the Development Corporation's obsession with flattened gables that seemed to me remarkably ugly. A feeling of depression came over me, this frantic development I had walked through, and all for what? A few years of London air and diesel fallout and it would be completely in tune with the tattiness of the rest of the Borough of Tower Hamlets. The image of the body lying in that dock with the head and upper torso chopped to bits seemed a sad vignette that matched the mood of the strange dockland tongue hanging out in a great loop of the river.

Why? Why? Why? Why had she been killed? All that effort to prove her husband right, to prove he'd really seen the ship and hadn't hallucinated. I was thinking about the irony of it, the waste, as I walked towards the overhead railway and South Quay station.

To the west of the *Telegraph* building a narrow walkway led to the dockside and the gangway leading to Le Boat, a restaurant occupying the upper deck of a vessel called the *Celtic Surveyor* and incongruously roofed in a sort of plastic reproduction of a big top. A journalist going on board at the stern told me the ship belonged to his newspaper and had been moored there to act as the staff canteen. He was critical of the management for letting off the upper part to a commercial outfit and said they had had quite a fight to get the restaurant to repaint the original name on bows and stern. 'It's bad luck to change the name of a ship, isn't it? Le Boat!' There was a lot of expression in the way he said it.

The drizzle had started again, a fine, wet mist. The sun had gone and the water of the dock was very still and very black. The *Telegraph*'s patch was fenced off from the next development, but by clinging to the barbed wire wrapped round a stanchion I was able to swing my body out over the dock and on to the other side. An open gravel expanse led to a neat brick array of office and residential accommodation facing a dockside walk along the line of Maritime Trust vessels, which included the tug *Portwey*, and beyond that the coaster *Robin* with the *Lydia Eva* moored outside.

The water between these vessels was foul with accumulated filth, the surface of it some six to eight feet below me. Vertical iron ladders, rusted and overgrown with weeds, were set at intervals in the dockside. This was where her body had been fished out of the water, right under the tug's bows where a scum of plastic cartons, old rags and pieces of wood lay congealed in a viscid layer of oil. I should have asked that woman in Mellish Street whether anybody had visited her the night she had been killed, whether she had seen a car parked outside, for now that I had seen the dock for myself I was even more convinced her body must have been dumped there.

I walked back through the new development to Marsh Wall. A construction worker in a hard hat was pile-driving steel rods that protruded from around the base of one of the round columns supporting the overhead railway, the machine he was using kicking up dust and making a noise like a compressed-air drill. I tried to picture this place at night, no construction workers, everything quiet. There were street lights and the development had some exterior lighting of its own. There would be shadows, deep shadows, and nobody about, the alleyways between the buildings like black shafts. He could have knocked her unconscious, then pushed her in, the place deserted and nobody to hear her cry out or the splash of her body as it hit the water. A train ground at the rails overhead and I wondered how late they ran. Could somebody in one of the carriages have seen her standing there with Carlos?

A sign almost opposite me indicated the top of Lemanton Steps. I crossed the road and found myself looking down two flights of new brick that led off the high green bank built to retain the water of the dock. The steps led down into Manilla Street, past a timber importers, 'Lemanton & Son, Established 1837', and right opposite was a pub with the improbable name of The North Pole. By then I was tired and hungry. Inside, I found it full of construction workers and for a moment I thought it was just a grog shop, but as my eyes became accustomed to the gloom, I saw one of the girls come out from behind the bar with a plate of sandwiches. She was a big, dark girl with skin-tight black pants and a seductive swagger to her bottom that matched the big-toothed smile and the come-hither black eyes.

I got myself a lager, and when she brought me my thick wad of a ham sandwich, I asked her if she'd ever served the young woman whose body had been found in the dock. 'Did she ever come in here?' I asked. 'Did you know her?'

She checked, the plate still in her hand, her eyes gone dead and the smile wiped from her face, all the flounce gone out of her so that she suddenly looked old and worn. She half shook her head, banging the plate on the table and turning quickly away. I hadn't expected such a positive reaction from what had been no more than a random enquiry and I was left with the certainty that my question had scared her.

I watched her while I ate my sandwich and she never smiled once after that, and she didn't come near me again. It was the other girl who collected my money, but as I left the pub I was conscious that she was watching me furtively.

It worried me all the way back to the City and Liverpool Street station, the certainty that she knew something. But what? In the end I pushed it to the back of my mind. She would deny it, of course, so no point in telling anybody. But when the police finally caught up with Carlos and began to build up their case . . .

That girl, and his carelessness in letting her bag fall into the water, nagged at my mind again that night. It was in the small hours, lying awake and thinking of her stretched out naked in that refrigerated tin box, that I remembered how she had suddenly referred to what I now knew to be the Disappeareds. It was just after we had come out of the Blackwall Tunnel and she could see young Carlos following us. 'So many killed,' she had murmured, staring into the rear-view mirror.

'What's that got to do with it?' I had asked her and she had turned on me. 'Eduardo is one of them,' she had said. 'Eduardo is my brother. My younger brother. And that little bastard –' She nodded at the reflection in her rear mirror – 'Why is he here? Why does Ángel send him?' And she had gone on about her half-brother, how evil he could be.

Something else she had said came back to me then. 'He hated Eduardo.' And when I had asked her why, she had said, 'Because he is a good man, a Connor-Gómez. Not Sicilian. My father has told him Eduardo –' Her mouth shut tight on whatever it was she was going to say. 'That is before they burn down the store.' She swung across the truck we were passing into the left-hand lane and then made the sharp turn left where it was signposted Isle of Dogs.

That was when we had lost sight of the car behind. Her mood had changed then, the tension gone. I should have mentioned all this to the Inspector, but I hadn't remembered at the time. I had been too shocked at the sight of her body, everything else blotted out. And then Victor Wellington reminding me of it. Had she meant her half-brother was one of those responsible for what had happened to the Disappeareds? Or was she simply saying he had been a supporter of the Junta, the military regime that had caused the terror, or at least condoned it? I knew very little about it, only what I had read in the papers after the invasion of the Falkland Islands, and anyway it was no concern of mine – except that I had met Iris Sunderby and had been brought down to London to try and identify her body.

To get it out of my mind I took the following day off, borrowed a friend's boat and sailed it out to Blakeney Point, anchoring under the shingle there. It was one of those cloudless East Coast days, the sun blazing down and a bite in the wind, which was north-east force 3 to 4, the sort of day when even visitors from hot climates suffer from sunburn. I stayed out overnight, caught some fish, and after making a splendid breakfast of them, sailed back in the dawn to find that Iain Ward had phoned in my absence.

The message on my Ansaphone said he had seen the papers that morning and would I phone him urgently. And he gave his telephone number. By 'that morning' he obviously meant the previous morning's papers. I didn't take any papers myself, but my next-door neighbour let me have a look at his *Express* and there, under the heading 'DOCKLAND KILLING', I found my name referred to as one of those who had been called in to identify the body. Inspector Blaxall was quoted as saying that positive identification would probably depend on dental evidence and as a resident of the Argentine it might be some time before the police in Buenos Aires were able to trace her records. Even then the condition of the body would make it difficult to check the dental information. There followed the names of those who had been called in to identify the body, among them mine: *Peter Kettil, a wood preservative consultant, who had also talked to Mrs Sunderby at the conference on board the* Cutty Sark *last week, seems to have been fairly sure the body in the dock was hers.*

The report went on to give something of Iris Sunderby's background. Her father, Juan Connor-Gómez, had been head of the family department store in Buenos Aires. He had committed suicide just before the Falklands war, his business having failed following a fire that gutted the main building and destroyed something over a million pounds' worth of stock. Her brother, Eduardo, a bio-chemist, had disappeared at about the same time. *According to the police, the possibility that this is a political killing cannot be ruled out. 'It may be that it goes back to the period when people all over the Argentine, but particularly in cities like Buenos Aires, were disappearing. A report on the family background from the police in Buenos Aires is urgently awaited. Until our people have that report the purpose behind this brutal killing will not be known.'*

I phoned Ward at once, but got no answer, and it wasn't until evening that I finally got through to him.

'Are ye all set, Peter?' Those were his opening words. And when I asked him what he was talking about, he said, 'Are ye all packed an' ready to go, 'cause Ah've booked tae seats fur Sunday on a flight to Madrid. We stay overnight, then fly Iberia direct to Mexico City. Meet ye at the BA check-in desk at 13.00. That all right?'

I couldn't think what to say for a moment, the abruptness of it taking my breath away. 'You mean you're going ahead with the expedition?'

'Och aye.' He said it quietly, a matter-of-fact statement. 'Why not? The boat is there. We can sail as soon as we get to Punta Arenas.'

'But . . .' It was now Wednesday evening. 'Are you serious? I mean . . . well, you can't leave for a sail in the Weddell Sea just like that. We'd need stores, gear, clothes. We'd need to plan ahead, to plan very carefully.'

'All taken care of.'

'But . . .'

'Ye just listen to me. Ah'm used to organisin' things at short notice. Ah've cabled that Norwegian to have the boat stored an' ready to sail within a week and Ah've transferred the necessary funds to a local bank wi' instructions to settle all accounts. Ye've got a passport, have ye?'

'Yes.'

'A valid passport. Ye've no' let it run out?'

'No. It's fairly new.' My thoughts were running away with me, my imagination too. It was one thing to sit in on a meeting like that in the *Cutty Sark* theorising about whether or not there was an old frigate locked in the ice of the Weddell Sea, talking vaguely about an expedition to recover it; quite another to have somebody say we leave in four days' time, destination Antarctica. 'Visas,' I said. 'I'd need visas. And money – traveller's cheques. Another thing, what do we wear? For an expedition like that you need special clothing.'

'All taken care of,' he said again. 'Ah provide the money, an' the special clothing, the very latest in protective gear, that's being flown out, Ah hope tonight. 'Fraid Ah had to guess yer size. Visas will be dealt with by me travel agent. His office is in London.' He had me write down the address, which was in Windmill Street. 'Have yer passport there by 09.00 tomorrow mornin' and Jonnie Crick promises to hand it back to ye wi' all the necessary visas in time fur us to catch the plane. Okay?'

'No,' I said. 'Not okay. This is Norfolk, not London, and it's already past eight in the evening.'

'Of course. Ah should have told ye. A motorcycle courier from a delivery firm callin' itself the Norfolk Flyer will pick yer passport up at 06.30 tomorrow mornin'. And see that there's a full-face picture of yerself with it fur photocopying. And when ye pick yer passport up on Sunday mornin', pick mine up as well.' For the moment his voice seemed to have lost almost all trace of an accent. 'Windmill Street,' he added, 'is just to the north of Piccadilly Circus, a turning off Shaftesbury Avenue. Ye'll find Jonnie's office on the third floor. Don't forget, will ye? Ah need to be on the plane to Madrid with everythin' sorted out and Ah've still a lot to dae. Hold on a minute now and Ah'll give ye the flight number.'

'Look, this is crazy,' I said. 'Nobody planning an expedition leaves it to the last minute like this, certainly not an expedition to the Antarctic. You haven't even got the boat yet.'

'Ye're wrong there, laddie. Ah bought *Isvik* last week, two days after we met at Greenwich. What shall we call her, the *Iain Ward*?' The way he said it, the fact that he was considering changing her name, the whole precipitate business of rushing off to the Antarctic made me suddenly feel I was dealing with a megalomaniac. Yet he had seemed sensible enough. Maybe it was the telephone. The telephone does accentuate inflexions in the voice, nuances of personality that are not perceptible when overlaid by the visual impact of the individual. But I was thinking of Iris Sunderby's words – *an ego a mile high* – and her view that his accent was phoney.

'Are ye there?'

'Yes, I'm still here.' What the hell did I say to him?

'Luke, d'ye want the job or not?'

'I didn't know you were offering me a job.' I said it without thinking, to gain time while I tried to find a few answers to the questions racing through my mind. If his travel agent could produce visas for two or three of the more difficult South American countries at such short notice there must either be something wrong with them or . . . 'How much are these visas going to cost you?' I asked him.

'That's none of yer business. But they'll be the real thin', not forgeries.' I could almost hear him smiling at the other end of the line. 'They'll cost a bit more, of course, but everythin' costs more if ye're in a hurry. Aye, and if it's money that's worryin' ye, Ah'm no' expectin' ye to come along just fur the ride. Ye'll be there to dae a job so Ah'll pay ye a salary. No' a very big one, mind ye, but still enough to provide fur yer funeral if we get into trouble and lose our lives. Now, is there anythin' else, otherwise . . . Och, the flight number.' He gave it to me. 'Terminal One.'

'I'm not going to be rushed into this,' I said. 'I need time to think.'

'We don't have time.'

'Why ever not?' I demanded. 'It's still winter down there. There's lots of time before the spring –'

'The time of year doesn't concern me.'

'What does then? Why are you in such a hurry?'

'Ah'll tell ye when we reach Madrid, no' before. Now, dae ye want the job or not? Ah need a wood preservative expert, somebody whose technical opinion will be accepted, but it doesn't have to be ye.' His voice hardened as he added, 'Ah'll be frank with ye. Ye're not by any means the best qualified expert available. Inside of a week Ah could have somebody with more qualifications flown out to join me. So ye think it over, okay?' The smile was back in his voice. 'See ye at the BA check-in desk 13.00 hours Sunday. And don't forget to pick up the passports from Jonnie.'

There was a click and the line went dead. I was left standing there staring blankly at the saltings, my mind in a turmoil. Slowly I put the receiver back on its rest. The sun was setting, the salt marsh illuminated in a golden glow. Glimmers of light picked out the dark ribbons of water, the hides used by the wardens and the bird-watching members of the NNT standing stiffly like pillboxes, black and white Friesians grazing with their rumps turned to the north-westerly breeze, and far away across the flat expanse of the reclaimed marsh, beyond the pale yellow line of the shingle horizon, the white of a tanker's bridge was followed by the red funnel of a freighter, their passage so distant they seemed to hang there, immobile.

My mother called from the kitchen. 'Who was that, dear?'

I didn't answer for the moment. The sound of her familiar voice seemed to accentuate the appalling choice with which I had been presented. I was in the front room of my family's semi-detached house on the coast road just east of Cley with its white-painted picture-postcard windmill. Since my father's death it had become my den. Now I called it my office.

'Anybody I know?'

'No.' I went over to the window. 'Just a client.'

'Well, supper will be ready in a moment, so don't do any more work.'

The tanker and the red funnel had repositioned themselves imperceptibly and I was looking at the view with a sense of hyper-awareness. It was a view that I had come to take for granted. But not now, not if I were going to hand my passport to that Norfolk Flyer chap in the dawn and then go down to London on the Sunday, to Windmill Street and on to Heathrow in time to meet Ward at the flight check-in desk at 13.00. And if I went with him . . . That view was suddenly very precious to me.

The Warden came out of his house near the end of our row of neat semis. I watched him as he crossed the road and took the well-worn path out to the first hide. Even in winter with the wind blowing straight down from the Arctic and the marshland all frozen solid, the waterways iced over and a dusting of snow on everything, the crystals driven horizontally against the glass of the window with a sound like the rustle of silk, even in those conditions, this Arctic shore of Norfolk had its charm. And now as I stared, I felt it clutching at my heart.

Punta Arenas! That was where he was asking me to go and I hadn't even looked it up in my school atlas. No point, I had thought. Iris Sunderby was dead. And now this Glaswegian planning to run the expedition himself.

Why?

I leaned my forehead against the cold of the windowpane. No harm in meeting him. I could always refuse to fly at the last moment. I ticked off in my mind the questions I needed to ask him.

'Supper's ready, dear. Bangers and mash, your father's favourite. Come along. I'm taking it in now.'

'All right, Mum.' And I stood there for a moment longer as I thought of my father. He had never been abroad. Incredibly he had never been to London, had barely been outside of Norfolk all his life, and when we had moved to Cley this view had been for him a total fulfilment. And yet, when I said I was going on a Whitbread round-the-worlder, he hadn't batted an eyelid, hadn't attempted to dissuade me.

'It's on the table, dear.'

Sometimes I felt the world outside of East Anglia wasn't real to him.

'A nice sunset. Your father always liked it best at this time of the evening, so long as the sun was setting in a clear sky.'

She was standing in the doorway, taking off her apron. 'Come along now.' I took the apron from her and tossed it on to the desk, where it lay like a faded flower piece sprawled across the typewriter. I put my arm round her shoulder. 'I may be going away for a bit,' I said.

'Oh, when?' She always took my movements in her stride. Thank God, she had become accustomed to my coming and going. 'Where are you going this time?'

'Punta Arenas,' I said.

'Spanish?'

'Sort of.' And I left it at that. I didn't tell her how long I might be gone. And anyway I didn't know, or even whether I would go at all.

'You're very quiet,' she said as I slashed my knife through a beautifully crisped sausage. She always was a perfectionist in whatever miserable object she was cooking. 'Something on your mind?'

'You know my mind, Mum. Empty as a returned beer keg.'

'I don't drink.' She stared at me uncomprehendingly. She was solid Saxon-and-Dutch East Anglian. Loyal as anybody could possibly be, but completely devoid of humour. My father's little jokes had just bounced off her like hailstones off a swan's back. Perhaps that's what had made them such a good match. Dad's wit sparked on half a dozen cylinders at least. He was an East Ender, pure Cockney. His father had emigrated from Stepney to Norfolk after the First World War when land was cheap. He'd sold his winkle stall in Aldgate Market and bought a few acres at Cley. I hadn't known him, only my grandmother, who had been born in Eastcheap and had a cackling laugh. She and my father were very close, and when she was gone, he had turned his attention to me. We had had a lot of fun together for we were on the same wavelength you might say.

And then he'd had that stroke. Odd, the human brain. It's everything – the personality, the bright intelligence, the humour, everything. And in a flash it's gone, a blood clot sealing off blood vessels, starving the brain cells. Suddenly they're dead. And brain cells are the one and only part of the human body that cannot repair themselves. He had never been the same again, all the fun we'd had gone. God, how I had loved that man!

I loved my mother too, of course. But not in the same way. Fred Kettil had had that something, a different sort of It to Marilyn Monroe, but still an It. The times we'd had, the laughter.

And then suddenly, nothing. Just a blank stare. Why? Why take a man like that in his prime? What the hell is God up to? 'You used to laugh at Dad's jokes, Mum,' I said. 'Why not at mine?'

'You know very well I didn't understand them. I just laughed because he expected it. But not at the rude ones,' she added archly. 'You remember a lot of them were very Clacton Pier. But he was fun. He was always great fun.' And her eyes glimmered in a very personal way so that I was afraid she was going to burst into tears. She cried very easily.

I suppose it's a question of imagination, and I sat there silent for a moment thinking about imagination and what exactly it was, as I tried to spear another of her crisp little sausages. Why should one person have it and another not? What goes on inside that skull of ours, what makes it tick? And when we die . . . ?

I was still thinking about that, and what I might be letting myself in for, when I went up to bed. And in the morning the courier arrived almost ten minutes ahead of time, a Polish kid, thin as a lath, on a big BMW motorcycle strapped round with panniers. He glanced at the envelope I handed him. 'J. Crick Esq.' And he read off the address. 'I know where. Soho.' He stuffed my passport into a pannier already bulging with packages. 'Good day, I think.' He had turned his helmeted head to stare at the distant line of shingle, bright yellow in the sunlight.

It was the sun that had woken me, slanting in through the north-east-facing side window of my bedroom and shining full on my face. 'Yes, it will be another lovely day.'

He nodded, still staring out across the saltings. 'Same where I come. Too much flat. I like flat.' He smiled at me, and added, 'London no good. A12 no good. Better here.' He pulled his visor down, gunned the big engine and with a wave of his hand roared off in the direction of Cromer and the road to Norwich.

I took a walk then, out as far as the first hide. There were curlews piping, several waders – sandpipers, a godwit, but whether black-tailed or bar-tailed I couldn't be sure, and I thought I saw a greenshank. These in addition to the ducks and swans and the inevitable gulls, the shapes and the plumage brilliant in that crystal-clear light with the sun climbing up the pale blue, almost greenish early morning sky.

Now that the courier had gone off with my passport, I felt almost light-headed. I had made the first decision. I had taken the first step towards the Antarctic. Nothing I could do now until I collected my passport from the travel agent in Windmill Street. Even then I wouldn't be able to make a final decision because in fairness I would have to deliver Ward's passport to him. That would be the moment of final decision, and standing there by that hide, watching the movement of the birds, the incessantly changing flight patterns, I fined it down to just two questions: why the haste, and how had he made his money?

If Iris Sunderby had been alive I would have found it so much easier to make up my mind. There was something about Ward . . . But I was thinking of that battered body lying in an unrecognisable mess of flesh and bone in that morgue, the memory of it suddenly so vivid that I no longer saw the geese thrashing across the dawn sky, the growing brilliance of the sun as it cleared the high ground by Sheringham. If only I could have talked it over with her.

What a dreadful way to die. Had she known who it was? I shook myself free of the morbid memory, turned abruptly and headed back home.

Two questions, and on his answers to those questions, and the way in which he answered them, would depend whether I went with him or not. Telling me on the flight wasn't good enough. I'd have to get the reason for his haste out of him before we moved into the departure lounge. Just those two questions, that would settle it one way or the other. It was out of my hands.

Freed of the need to make up my mind immediately, I went about organising such business as I had, determined that no client should feel let down if I did decide to go with Ward. I had less than thirty-six hours in which to arrange everything and I found the problem of what clothes to take more difficult than dealing with my business. Several times I tried to contact Ward. I wanted to know exactly what he had meant when he said he had arranged for cold weather clothing to be flown out. I needed a list. What about underwear? And gloves? I seemed to remember that layers of gloves were essential, also layers of leg coverings and socks, special boots. But the first three times I tried to get through to him his phone was engaged, and after that there was no reply. I would have liked to have got hold of Lewis's book. Somebody who had read it said he thought it included a checklist in one of the appendices. Unfortunately it wasn't available at Cromer and I hadn't time to drive down to the big Norwich library.

It was a very odd experience packing and organising for an absence that might be longer than the Whitbread, knowing at the same time I might be back home in Norfolk by Sunday evening. A rush of enthusiasm to get the job done resulted in its being more or less finished by midday, so that for a while I was left in a sort of vacuum of suspended animation. But then, as people realised I would be away for some time, the phone began to ring.

Even my mother, to whom time had never meant very much, got the idea that I might be away for longer than usual. 'You will remember, dear. The Flower Festival. I'm relying on you.'

Cley's St Margaret's, looking over the Glaven valley to something of a mirror image of itself at Wiveton, is a wonderful old fourteenth-century church. It was built by the men who shipped the Norfolk wool out of Cley when it was a real port to the Flemish weavers across the North Sea. The services there were always rather special to me for the parapetted clerestory has great cinquefoil-shaped and cusped circular windows through which the light pours, and when it was massed with the glorious colour of innumerable flower arrangements it really took one's breath away, it was so beautiful. 'It's one of the things I'll miss,' I said.

'Oh, but you can't. What about me?'

'I'll miss you, too,' I said, putting my arm round her thin shoulders.

'Oh, don't be silly.' She shrugged me off. She was a very independent person. 'You know I don't mean that. It's the flowers. An awful lot of them, and all in buckets of water.'

'I know,' I said. I had helped her each year since my father had died.

'And then there's the watering and the spraying.'

She said all this again when we were back on the Saturday evening from the Ledwards who ran an antique furniture shop in King's Lynn. It was his boat I had borrowed. I think she had forgotten that Maity's wife, Mavis, had arranged it at the last moment as a farewell dinner party for me. But then she saw my gear stacked in the tiny hallway and she began to cry. I told her I hadn't made up my mind yet whether I was going or not, but that in any case I'd be with her in spirit.

'Spirit's no good,' she said, 'when it comes to buckets of flowers, and now that Fred's gone . . .' She went on like that all the way up the stairs. Wine always made her a little petulant.

I said goodbye to her outside her bedroom, pushed her in and gently closed the door. What else could I do? And that old cliché jumped into my mind: *A man's gotta do . . .* Shit! I didn't know what I was going to do. I still hadn't made up my mind, and I went to sleep wondering whether I ever would, even when Ward had answered those two vital questions.

I was up and watching at the door when Sheila's little Volvo drew up at the gate. I had already humped my suitcase and the canvas bundle with my sleeping bag, oilskins and cold-weather clothing to the roadside. I closed the door gently and walked down the path. It was not yet six, a dull grey dawn with low cloud and a cold damp wind out of the north. I don't think she heard me leave. At least there was no sign of her at the windows when we drove off.

'Julian sends you his love and hopes to God you know what you're doing.' She grinned at me. 'So do I.' Sheila was Julian Thwaite's wife, a big, bosomy girl who had once been his secretary and now did the odd bit of typing for me. To keep her hand in, was how she put it, and she had refused to charge for the time she had put in during the last two days. 'He's gone fishing, otherwise he'd have driven you himself and I could have had a nice lie in.' She went through Salthouse at over sixty, nothing on the road, and we were on the A140 and driving south by six-thirty.

I was catching the 07.10 inter-city from Norwich and we

arrived at the station with a quarter of an hour to spare. 'Got your ticket? Money, traveller's cheques, passport – no, you're picking that up, of course.' She swung my suitcase and canvas roll on to the roadway.

'You'll make a good secretary yet.' I grinned at her, and she grinned back.

'Find that ship, get yourself some more clients and I'll leave Julian to do for himself and come and secretary for you full time. Okay?' She suddenly put her arms round me and gave me a hug, kissing me full on the mouth. 'You look after yourself, my boy.' She got back in the car, smiling up at me as she added, 'Just remember, the Weddell Sea isn't exactly the Norfolk Broads.' And with that, and a final wave, she was gone.

I was alone then, her words reminding me of the future, the risk and the possible reward, so that when I boarded the train the Antarctic seemed to have moved a step nearer.

THREE

All the way up to London I sat thinking it over, wondering about Ward. I knew so little about him. How *had* he made his money? And when I got to Crick's office, I found he wasn't a travel agent at all. He was a lawyer. I hadn't expected that.

The office was on the second floor of a somewhat dilapidated building at the far end of Windmill Street. There was no lift and I was sweating by the time I had dragged my baggage up two long flights of stairs. 'J. Crick & Co. Solicitors' showed black on the frosted-glass panel of the door, and it was Crick himself who opened it. I didn't see anybody else there, and he didn't invite me in. 'You're late.' He said it quite affably, his voice so quiet it was almost a whisper.

'The train was late,' I said. 'In any case, it wasn't due in to Liverpool Street till nine-forty-five and I had to queue for a taxi.'

'It don't matter.' He smiled. He was a balding, bustling little man with large horn-rimmed glasses. I don't know what race he was, middle European probably, certainly not English. 'You wait here,' he said, peering down at my baggage. 'Keep an eye on it.' And he disappeared into an inner office before I could ask him any of the questions that were in my mind.

He was back almost immediately with two stiff manilla envelopes. 'Here is Mr Ward's passport.' He handed me one of the envelopes and a form. 'You sign for it please. All the visas are there, all he asked for.' He produced a pen and I signed. 'And there is yours. Bolivia is not possible, not in the time. But I think perhaps you don't go to Bolivia. Explain please to Mr Ward. The others are difficult enough.'

I started to ask him how he had managed it at such short

notice, but he shook his head, smiling. 'You don't ask. It is done, that is all that concern you.' But he looked pleased.

'Mr Ward referred to you as his travel agent, but I see you're a solicitor.'

'Yes.' The smile had vanished, replaced by a wary look. He began to shut the door, but I had moved my canvas roll into the gap. 'You must have an interesting variety of clients,' I said. 'So many Chinese in Soho, all those strip joints and blue cinemas.'

'I deal only with ladies of the stage, ladies who are in trouble, you understand. No Chinese.'

'Prostitutes, you mean?'

'We call them ladies of the stage. They prefer that. Most of them have been in front of the footlights at one time or another.' He glanced at his watch. 'Now, Mr Kettil, if you'll excuse me. I only came in this morning because of you.' He pushed my canvas roll out of the way. 'My regards to Mr Ward please and tell him any time . . .' He nodded, smiling again as he closed the door and locked it.

Back in the street and humping my gear laboriously to Picca-dilly Circus Underground, I thought his clients probably included blackmailers as well as prostitutes, or perhaps he did the blackmailing himself. It was the only explanation I could think of that would produce visas like rabbits out of a hat. And if he was a blackmailer, what was Ward? Thinking about that as the Piccadilly Line took me out to Heathrow, I began to consider espionage as possibly his real occupation.

At the airport I had over an hour to wait, and since I had no ticket, I couldn't check in and get rid of my baggage. I bought a paper and sat reading it over a cup of coffee until it was the time Ward had said he would meet me. But one-thirty came and went, and no sign of him, the minutes ticking away relentlessly as I stood by the BA desks, watching the endless flow of passengers checking in. I began to think he might not turn up. Having geared myself to face the challenge of an expedition that might cost me my life, I suppose I was mentally on a high, for I now became fearful lest he might have abandoned the whole project.

And then suddenly he was there, with a porter and a great mound of baggage. He also had a woman with him. I hadn't expected that. 'Mrs Fraser,' he said. 'Otherwise Kirsty – my secretary.' She gave me a little nod and a perfunctory smile. She had the tickets in her hand and moved into line to wait her turn at the desk. He turned to me. 'Ye got the passports?'

I nodded. 'There are one or two questions . . .' I began.

'Later.' He took the manilla envelope I handed him, slit it open and ran quickly through the pages, turning them with the thumb of his left hand as he checked the visas. 'Good.' He slipped it into the pocket of his Norfolk jacket. His secretary was by then handing the tickets to the BA receptionist and the porter was swinging the baggage, item by item, on to the scales. 'You are overweight,' the girl at the desk said, and he grinned. 'Of course Ah'm overweight. Always have been since Ah could afford to eat well.'

The girl didn't smile. Maybe she'd had a long day already, or perhaps it was just that she didn't have a sense of humour. 'Your baggage,' she said. 'You will have to pay excess.' I don't know what nationality she was, but her English was very precise.

'Of course.' He left his secretary to deal with that. 'Must have a leak before we board. See you in a minute.'

'We haven't much time,' I said, and he waved his hand as he disappeared into the mêlée, his head, with its dark unruly hair, raised as he sniffed around like a bloodhound in search of the toilet indicator.

They were already announcing the final call for the Madrid flight when he rejoined us and we hurried along the passageway to the boarding gate. His secretary was still in attendance. Apparently she was coming with us as far as Madrid, and when I asked him why, he said curtly, 'Business.' And then, apparently thinking I was due some explanation, he added, 'Spain is becomin' important industrially. Ah've been developin' some contacts there. Kirsty's very good at that.'

She was just ahead of me, and looking at the trimness of her figure and the swing of her hips, I couldn't help it – I said, 'I can just imagine.'

He looked at me and grinned. 'It helps,' he muttered. 'But she's also a clever businesswoman.'

She turned with a quick smile. 'I'll have that in writing, please.' There was the trace of an accent, but it wasn't Scots, and though the blonde hair gave her a Scandinavian look, she was too small and it was bleached anyway. It was difficult to guess her origins and I wondered what their relationship really was. The easy familiarity between them suggested a long association, at least a close one, and when we had boarded the plane I found myself in an aisle seat separated from them by two rows.

It was the same in Madrid. I don't know where they went, but I was on my own in a hotel near the airport. 'See ye tomorrow on the plane. Fourteen-thirty take-off. Iberia.' And with a nod and smile the two of them disappeared into the crowd, heading for the exit. I had a feeling he didn't want to be alone with me, even for a moment, or was it that they wanted to be on their own, a last night together before he took off for the Antarctic?

Sitting in the hotel bar, drinking Fundador on my own, I felt as though I were in limbo, waiting for something to happen, a sense of unreality taking hold. I looked at the ticket I had been given – Madrid, Mexico, Lima, Santiago, Punta Arenas. And after that . . . ?

I had some more brandy, and that seemed to do the trick – I had a good night's sleep. And in the morning, when I got to the airport, they were already there. 'Look, I've got to talk to you, before we depart.' It was my last chance. I couldn't afford the fare back from Mexico City, and certainly not from Punta Arenas. 'Some questions -'

'Later. Ah told ye. After we take off.'

'No, now.'

But he shook his head, and when I insisted he leaned suddenly forward, his face gone hard. 'Ah said later. We'll talk later, when we're airborne.'

He was so close I could smell the stale sweat of his body. He had clearly had an energetic night and as he turned back to his girlfriend, I seized hold of his arm, my mind suddenly made up.

'I'm not boarding that plane unless you tell me where the money comes from, why you're in such a hurry.'

I'd got hold of the wrong arm and the hidden claw fastened on my fingers as he swung round on me. 'Yer baggage is already on the plane.'

'I don't care.'

The obstinacy in my voice got through to him at last. 'Very well. Ah'm in a hurry because Ah'm concerned for Iris Sunderby's safety.'

I stared at him. 'What the hell are you talking about? She's dead.'

'On the contrary, she rang me from Heathrow just before boardin' her plane.'

'What plane? When?'

'Last Thursday evenin'.'

Thursday evening, and her body pulled out of the dock on the Wednesday morning! 'You say she was boarding a plane?'

He nodded.

'Where was she going?'

'Lima.'

Iris Sunderby. Alive! I couldn't believe it.

'Come on,' he said, glancing up at the departure board, where green lights were flashing against our flight. 'Time we were boardin'. Ah'll explain later.' He turned back to Kirsty Fraser, gave her some hurried instructions about somebody called Ferdinando Berandi, then bent and kissed her. 'Take care.' And she went clack-clack-clacking away on her too-high heels.

'When she's finished here,' he said, 'she goes on to Napoli.'

'Why?' He was standing watching her, but she didn't look back. 'What's Naples got to do with it?'

He turned abruptly, peering down at me as though unsure how to answer that. 'The Camorra,' he said finally. 'Ah need to know somethin' and she has contacts there. Kirsty knows Napoli well.'

'But the Camorra is the Neapolitan version of the Mafia, isn't it?'

'Aye.' He was staring at me, not wanting to be questioned further.

'I don't understand,' I said. 'You told me she's your secretary, so presumably she's going to Naples on your behalf.'

'Ah tell ye, Ah need the answers to one or tae questions.'

'And she can get them for you? How?'

His lips twitched, a glint of sudden humour in his eyes. 'Ye don't check up on a girl like Kirsty too closely.'

'But why the Camorra?' I insisted.

'Because a lot of them come from Napoli.' And he added by way of explanation, 'Just remember this when we get to Argentina: the country was swamped at the turn of the century by a mass influx of immigrants, some three million of them Italian, mostly from the south. Full of piss and wind.' His voice was suddenly contemptuous. 'They call it braggadocio. It was braggadocio that sent Mussolini trampin' into Africa. It sent the Argentinians into the Malvinas. Galtieri was full of it.'

Another boarding announcement, a last call and he turned abruptly on his heel. 'Come on. Better board the bloody thing and get on with it.' There was a note of resentment in his voice as though he was embarked on something he didn't relish. He picked up his overnight bag, and with a nod to me, walked towards the boarding gate. I followed him. His mind was now so obviously locked in on itself that there was no point in trying to question him further.

I don't know how much was curiosity, how much the sense of excitement I was inevitably feeling at being caught up in something bigger than myself, but whatever it was I found my mind was now made up. I would see it through. And once having taken that decision, I felt strangely relaxed. With the whole flight in front of me there was plenty of time to get the answers to all my questions.

We were travelling first, something I had never done before, so that I was quite content, lying back after the meal, listening to taped music on the headphones and enjoying a brandy. I felt strangely disembodied, not sure that it was really me flying south-west in brilliant sunshine above a white sea of cloud. Another world, a world without worries, a world that had never heard of insects boring into wood, or fungi and damp rot.

'Ye awake?' The gloved steel hand pinched my arm. 'Ah said, are ye awake?' He was leaning towards me. 'Take those earphones off fur a moment.'

I did so and he smiled. It was a switched-on sort of smile that left me wondering what he was thinking. It didn't extend to the eyes. 'Ye've got some questions,' he said.

I nodded.

'Well, I've got one for you.' There was barely a trace of any accent now. 'What decided you to come before I'd given you the answers to the questions you were worried about?'

What had decided me? I shrugged and shook my head. 'Iris Sunderby, I suppose.'

He nodded, smiling again. 'Aye. She's a very attractive young woman.'

'Is?'

'Either is, or else the person phoning me Thursday evening was a very good mimic.'

I thought of the body I had been shown in the hospital morgue. If it wasn't hers, whose was it? But he wasn't making it up, no point, and his face, close to mine, deadly serious. 'Are you really Scots?' I asked him. 'Or do you just put it on as an act?'

'Och, no. Tha's me natural accent.' And he added, 'Ye want me life story?' The smile was more like a grin now as he leaned back, half closing his eyes. 'All right then. Ah was born into the Glasgae Mafia.' He said it as though it was something to be proud of. 'A Gorbals laddie whose drunken sot o' a mother was pitched out into a grand new high-rise tower when Ah was two years old. She was a whore. Ah never knew my father. By the age o' seven Ah'd been arrested twice, a real little toughie, livin' on the streets most o' the time, scratchin' a livin' round the docks an' watchin' the unions kill them off. In the end, Ah stowed away in the loo o' a sleeper to London, finished up just north o' the Mile End Road workin' fur a man who ran a bric-à-brac barrow.'

He was silent for a moment, his eyes tight closed so that I thought perhaps he had gone to sleep. But then he leaned towards me again. 'Clark was 'is name. Nobby, of course. Nobby Clark. Well known in the trade, 'e was – stolen stuff, see.'

Brought up as I had been in the East of England, I could recognise genuine Cockney when I heard it, and he had slipped into it so easily. 'Some of it was straight, nat'rally. 'E mixed it up, Nobby did, and nobody ever nicked 'im. Portobello Road, four ack emma of a Saturday, that was 'is best pitch. The boys used to bring the stuff in as soon as 'is stall was set up an' by six o'clock all the 'ot stuff was gone, 'is pitch as clear as a whistle by the time the first copper come nosin' ara'nd. Cor, stone the crows!' He was almost laughing now, his eyes wide open and alight with the fun of the life he'd led. 'The things I learned in the three years I was wiv 'im you wouldn't believe.'

He sighed. 'An' then, when I was risin' ten, an' just beginning to get the 'ang of things, the silly old sod goes an' dies on me. Gawd Christ! I loved that man, I really did. 'E was like a favver to me in the end. The only one I ever 'ad.' His grey eyes, staring past me out of the window, were moist with emotion. 'Yer know somep'n, Pete. I paid for 'is funeral. 'E hadn't made any provision, like, so I paid for 'im to be buried a't o' what I'd saved. I thought I owed 'im that. Then blow me, if a lawyer man doesn't grab 'old o' me just as I was settin' up on me own. D'yer know what Nobby gone an' done – set up a bleedin' trust for me eddication. Christ! I could'a killed the old bastard. 'Cept 'e was in his grave already.'

He suddenly burst out laughing. 'A reg'lar card, Nobby was. And so instead of gettin' meself clapped in irons an' sent to some bloody Borstal to learn new ways o' maintainin' the standard o' livin' to which I was becomin' accustomed, I found myself at a middle-class prep school learning to speak posh the way the poor cuff-frayed masters thought the Queen's English should be spoke. You ever been to a prep school?'

I shook my head. 'I was state-educated.'

'Well then, you wouldn't know what the little buggers get up to after lights out. They were on to the hard stuff, some of them, when I got there. Got themselves caught, of course, in the end, and the headmaster flogged the lot of them. This was the early seventies. The tabloids got on to it and tore the place apart. The *Guardian* even had a leader on it – hands off our poor little misguided darlings, not their fault. Blame the parents, the state, the social workers, private enterprise, down with the system. Needless to say, the school went bust. And I went to Eton.'

He stopped there and I was left wondering whether he had made the whole thing up. No trace of an accent now, and speaking copybook English. 'Why Eton?' I asked him.

'It was in Nobby's will. The trustees were to get me into Eton. Nobby didn't say how, and to this day I don't know what strings they pulled, but to Eton I went. Why?' He shook his head, smiling. 'Lesson number one, I suppose – never get caught. The trustees, they even congratulated me on keeping my nose clean – very upright behaviour, my boy, model of rectitude. Well, what did they expect? I wasn't throwing my chances away by peddling drugs in a prep school, and I certainly wasn't getting myself addicted. Seen enough of that. Anyway, I got a nice little racket going in stolen car radios. Flogged them to unsuspecting parents on match days, speech days, and through other boys at half term and end of term.'

'Are you serious?' I asked. 'You really were educated at Eton?'

'That's right. Old Nobby had written me a note, which the trustees solemnly presented to me in their Gray's Inn offices. I read it there and then, but I didn't tell them what was in it, though they wanted to know, of course. I think the best line – and the one that concerns you perhaps – was, "*I don't want you to finish up a small-time crook like me. At Eton, you'll learn to do things right. They don't get caught. Remember that. At least not often.*"' There was a smug look on his face. 'Good advice, that was. And I haven't been – not yet anyway.'

'So you never made a million on the pools.'

'Never done the pools. Waste of time when your life's as full as mine. After Eton, instead of going to a university, I decided to see a bit of the world. The trustees were far too straight-laced to switch money earmarked for university education to supporting my wanderlust, but if you've been trained at the back side of an East End antique barrow it's surprising how much you can make dealing here and there, especially across frontiers, and at that time Europe had plenty of them despite the Common Market.'

'Is that how you made it?' I asked.

'What? Oh, the million.' He shook his head, leaning close again, the claw gripping my arm. 'Know something? If I knew I was worth a million it'd mean I was too busy counting it to lash out on an expedition into the Weddell Sea. I don't know what I'm worth. I've got four mammoth great sleeper trucks running stuff through Turkey into the Middle East and the Gulf. I'm a trader, see. My money's all tied up.'

'But that cheque . . .'

'What cheque?' And when I reminded him of the press cuttings he had shown us on the *Cutty Sark*, he just laughed and said, 'Any promotion outfit with a graphics department can run up a little thing like that and get it photographed. I had to have something visual, see, something I could show them that they'd believe in and at the same time that wouldn't upset them on moral grounds. If I'd said I was running arms, wheeling and dealing with Arabs, Iranians, Israelis, all that gang, and using odd intermediaries, they wouldn't have had anything to do with me. But a pools win . . .' He winked at me, and suddenly I had a vision of him as a bookie in a loud check suit on Newmarket Heath, even a ticktack man. He had that sort of a face – battered and slightly coarse. But you didn't really notice that because the essence of the man was his vitality. Coarse-featured he might be, that big beak of a nose, but because the energy that drove him constantly showed through, it was his personality, not his features, that stamped themselves on the memory, so that after a while I wasn't even conscious of the bulge in the half-empty sleeve. And when he smiled, as he was smiling now, the battered features had a warmth and vitality that gave them quite extraordinary charm. 'Bit of a mixture, aren't I?'

He was certainly that – if all he had said was true. 'Was your mother really a prostitute?'

'Sure.'

'And you never knew your father?'

'No.'

I thought he must be making at least some of it up, and in the close proximity of an aircraft it didn't seem to matter that I'd asked him two such personal questions. 'So why have you told me this?'

'Look,' he said. 'Ah don't know where we'll land up, how long we'll be together or what will happen. But this isn't a fun ride, and one thin' is certain, if we take this boat she's persuaded me to buy down into the Antarctic, you and me and the Sunderby girl, a Norwegian engineer Ah've never met and a guy she thinks has seen the ship and is a competent navigator, all five of us are goin' to be livin' cheek-by-jowl in the close confines of a very small vessel. Ah know all about ye. Ah made a few enquiries, and anyway yer character is written all over yer face. Ah needn't have bothered. Ye're reliable and Ah know Ah can get on with ye okay. The question is, whether ye can get on with me and Ah thought maybe this was as good an opportunity as any to give ye a glimpse of my background. Just so as when the chips are down and thin's get tricky ye'll have some idea why Ah'll behave the way Ah probably will.' He suddenly grinned at me. 'Ah'm no' an easy man, ye ken. So if ye've any more questions, now's the time.'

'Well, of course – the obvious one.'

'Sunderby?' He nodded. 'Ye don't believe she phoned me, is that it?'

'No, not quite. But are you sure you've got the right day? Thursday, you said. In the evening.'

'That's right. She was flyin' to Paris, de Gaulle airport, then to Mexico City and on to Lima.'

'Are you saying the body they pulled out of South Dock that Wednesday morning wasn't hers?'

'Couldn't have been, could it?'

'But her handbag . . .'

'She must have thrown it into the water. It was the only positive evidence of identity the police had produced.'

'Did she say she'd done it?'

'Thrown the handbag in? No, she didn't say so. She didn't need to, and anyway she was talkin' about something else. About that student fellow, Carlos. She was very hepped up, excited. D'ye think she takes drugs?'

'I wouldn't have thought so.' She had seemed much too sensible.

'Nor would Ah. But the excitement in her voice –' He hesitated, his eyes staring past me at the cloudscape billowing up to the west of us, a great rampart of convoluted cu-nim towering in fantastic shapes and back-lit by brilliant sunlight. 'Was he good-looking? You saw him, you said.'

I shrugged. 'He was slim, with a somewhat serious face. Yes, he was good-looking all right in a rather Spanish way.'

'Italian, you mean. The boy's Italian.'

'How do you know?'

'His mother was Rosalli Gabrielli, a Neapolitan lady of very doubtful virtue whose one period of respectability was when she was married to Iris's father, Juan Connor-Gómez, the playboy son of a chain store millionaire. Carlos's father was a Sicilian named Luciano Borgalini. Luciano's brother Roberto used to pimp fur Gabrielli.'

So that was why he was sending Kirsty Fraser to Naples. But when I asked him what more he needed to know about Carlos, he shook his head. 'There's nothin' further Ah need to know about him. It's his uncle, Mario Ángel Connor-Gómez, Ah'm interested in. He's the issue of that brief marriage between Iris's father and Rosalli. Ah'm beginnin' to build up quite a dossier on him, but Ah need to know a whole lot more about his background. He was one of the *Montoneros. Ángel de Muerte*, they called him, and that's a nasty reputation to have. Maybe that nephew of his is no better. Maybe it's in the family. And if they're both killers . . .' He paused there, looking suddenly thoughtful. 'Some women like playin' with fire. So if she's a bit of a nympho – and don't forget this, they're related in an odd sort of way – if that vitality of hers runs to sex . . .' A lift of the eyebrow and he left it at that.

What he was suggesting was that Carlos had a fatal attraction for her and that she had got a kick out of the thought that the police might arrest him on suspicion of having dumped her body in the water. 'You think he was planning to kill her?'

He shrugged. 'Seduce her, more likely. If his uncle had told him to find out from her why she was so determined to get an expedition mounted to locate that ship. And that,' he added, 'would suggest there's somethin' more to her interest in the vessel than just a matter of proving her husband right.'

'And she was flying to Lima?'

'Yes. It's on the way to Punta Arenas.'

'But she could fly to Buenos Aires and on from there. It would be quicker.'

'Quicker, yes. But my guess is she's gone to Lima to talk to the boy's uncle.'

'Why?'

'Maybe there was seduction on both sides.' He said it slowly, the hint of an amused smile lighting his eyes. 'Maybe he let slip somethin' she needed to know. Lyin' in bed after a tumble people say things they didn't orter, right?'

The erotic mental flash produced by his words reminded me of the spark that had seemed to leap between us that moment by the *Cutty Sark* when she had been walking towards me and our eyes had met. 'I don't believe it,' I murmured. 'She didn't strike me as the sort of person . . .'

'No? Ah've often wondered,' he murmured reflectively, 'why some women always seem to fall fur the worst sort of men. It's not the size of their pricks. At least not in my experience. Ah'm fairly well endowed –'

'Good on you, mate!' A man had risen from the seat in front, hanging a lined, leathery face over us. 'But don't wave it around here – frighten the stewardesses.' He winked and nodded, then stepped out into the aisle, weaving his way with care towards the loos.

'Bloody Australians!' Ward growled. And then he said something about women having reforming natures, wanting to mould men to the image of their desires. 'It's one explanation, the motive moral as well as emotional, the drive not so much sex as the desire to exercise power, female power, over the male.'

Remembering her energy, her single-purposed drive to get backing for her expedition, I thought that a much more likely motive. But when I said so, he laughed and shook his head. 'Don't ye believe it. Oh, Ah grant ye she's obsessed with the idea of searchin' fur this ship, but Ah still reckon it's somethin' more than just the need to prove her husband right.' And he added, 'Because ye're the sort of person ye are, ye leap to the conclusion that others are as straightforward and sensible as yerself. What dae ye know of women?' And when I began to protest, he said, 'Italian women. Girls whose genes are crossed with those of a whore. Yes, a whore,' he repeated, as I asked him what the hell he was talking about.

He was silent for a moment, then he said, 'Oh well, we'll see what Iris Sunderby makes of Mario the Ángel. Either she'll eat him, or he'll eat her, and if Ah had to bet on it, bearin' in mind his reputation . . .' He shrugged. 'That's why Ah'm in a hurry to get to Lima. Ah'd like to catch her at her hotel before he does. Iris Sunderby's name incidentally, before she married, was Iris Connor-Gómez. Gómez.' He said it again, slowly, as though savouring the name. 'Same as the Ángel. I need to find out if Juan Connor-Gómez was also his father. His mother was almost certainly Rosalli Gabrielli. She was a cabaret singer at the Blue Danube in BA.'

He was silent after that, leaning back in his seat and finishing his brandy. I tried to get more details out of him, but he shook his head. 'Rosalli Gabrielli originally came from Catania in Sicily, but she grew up in Naples. She went back there after Juan threw her over. That's about all Ah know.' He leaned down to his briefcase and pulled out a paperback with the title *¿Muerto O Vivo?* in bold red print on a white background.

'Spanish?' I asked him.

He nodded. 'By a journalist.' He opened it at a marker. 'It's about the *Desaparecidos*, the Argentinians who disappeared. There are still about ten thousand of them unaccounted fur. Ye don't speak Spanish, dae ye?'

'No.'

'Pity. If ye read this . . . Ah could have got it in English. It had a big success in the States when it was first published there just after the Falklands War under the title *Dead or Alive?* But

82

Ah thought Ah'd better start brushin' up on my Spanish.' He reached into his briefcase again and got out a small pocket dictionary. 'Some words Ah have to look up.'

'How many languages do you speak?'

He shrugged. 'Half a dozen, Ah suppose. Ah like the sound of words, ye see, so languages come fairly easily to me. But my Spanish is very superficial. Ah don't speak any language fluently, not even my own. Enough to get by in business, that's all. This man –' He turned to the cover and indicated the author's name – 'Luiz Rodriguez, he's good. He's done his leg work, interviewed a lot of people, includin' Mario Ángel Gómez. Met him secretly just before he left the Argentine fur Peru. And there's even a bit about Iris's brother Eduardo, who disappeared quite late, in July 1984. He was a scientist. Biology. Incredibly, he was tae years and more at Porton Down.'

'Porton Down?' The name rang a bell. 'Isn't that something to do with chemical warfare?'

He nodded. 'It's an experimental establishment, scientists playin' around with all sorts of horrors. According to this man, it was the first of its kind in the world.' He began leafing through the dictionary. '*Podrido*. That's a new one on me.' And when he found it he nodded. 'Putrid. Ah should have guessed that.'

The stewardess bent over us to ask whether we would like anything to drink during the film. A moment later the lights dimmed and the screen on the for'ard bulkhead came alive, an old Gary Cooper western. Ward kept his reading light on and began chasing another word in the dictionary. I leaned back, watching the film, but not really taking it in. In the semi-darkness, with the blinds all down and the murmur of the engines powering us at speed above the Atlantic towards what was once the New World, my thoughts ranged free over the kaleidoscope of events in which I had become involved.

At one point I turned from the screen to look at Ward, bent now over his book, totally absorbed. He had a big, solid head, and his strong features, with that great beak of a nose and the slightly sensuous mouth, were outlined in profile by the hard white pinpoint of light beamed down from above.

Some time after the film was over and the lights were on again the same stewardess issued us with landing cards. Glancing over Ward's shoulder to see what he was entering for our address in Mexico, I saw he had put his occupation as 'antiquarian', and when I made some humorous remark about it being an odd description for a haulage contractor operating the Near Eastern run, he smiled at me almost slyly. 'Covers a multitude of sins . . .' He peered rather pointedly at my own card and nodded approvingly. 'Between us we should give them enough to occupy their minds.'

All through the flight, ever since we had taken off, part of my mind had been groping for some explanation, some sensible reason for his getting himself so deeply committed to this expedition. Altruism? But there was nothing altruistic about him, and mulling over the extraordinary mix of his upbringing, I was tempted to think that Eton may have had a far greater influence on him than he would care to admit. Either that, or else he smelt a profit in it, and since I couldn't see that there was money to be made out of the *Andros*, I was forced back once again to considering the possibility that he was in some branch of intelligence.

Why else would he be brushing up on his Spanish, reading with such concentration a book on the Disappeareds and breaking his journey at Lima? That he might have fallen for Iris Sunderby never crossed my mind.

II

ANGEL OF DEATH

ONE

The time difference between London and Mexico City is six hours, and because we had been travelling with the sun, it was still quite high in the sky as we descended into the sepia haze that hung over the whole flat expanse of what had once been a great lake. Dust! That was my first impression of a city whose disastrous birth rate has made it the largest in the world, a vast expanse of concentrated housing broken only by open spaces of baked earth where the wind-blown dust swirled, and far away to port the snow-capped volcanic hulks of Popocatépetl and Iztacci-huatl towering huge through the burnt brown atmosphere.

'We'll dump our things at the hotel,' Ward said, 'and if there's time we'll have a look round.'

The landing was a smooth one, but once we were inside the terminal building everything moved at a snail's pace, the queue at immigration long and slow moving. When it was our turn I found he had been right about the word antiquarian giving the immigration officers something to think about. They were a good ten minutes arguing over what it meant, even calling in the senior officer on duty, who spoke a little English. 'Old books? Why you want old books? You are tourist, no? In transit.'

'Aye, Ah'm booked out on the flight to Lima in the mornin'.' Ward was smiling a bright, happy, almost drunken smile, playing the innocent Scot and putting on his broadest accent. 'Dae ye no' like books yersel'? Books are me most prized possessions, ye ken. There's the binding now. An' inside ye'll find all the truth about the world in which we live. An' auld books, the woodcuts, the drawin's – dae ye no' ken the drawin's o' Leonardo da Vinci? – the beautiful illustrations, the illuminations o' the monks an' priests – it's a fabulous world, an' all there inside o' the gold-lettered covers.'

He went on like that until the chief officer nodded him through with a glazed look in his eyes. He never glanced at the visas, never looked at my passport. 'Just as I said,' Ward murmured, no trace of an accent as we collected our baggage. 'Covers a multitude of sins.'

As soon as we had cleared customs he made for a bank of telephones, and when he rejoined me he was smiling. 'That's all fixed. He got my cable and he'll meet us fur dinner.'

'Who?' I asked as we picked up our overnight bags and moved towards the exit.

'The author of that book, Luiz Rodriguez. He lives here.'

At the hotel he told the taxi to wait, and after checking in and having a quick clean-up in our rooms, we drove out to Teotihuacan. 'Ah'd have liked to take a look around the Archaeological Museum, but Ah fear we'd never make it in time through the rush-hour traffic. It's the other side of the city, whereas Teotihuacan is relatively handy.' He passed me a map and a brochure he had picked up at the hotel. 'At least we shall be able to say we've seen the Temple of Quetzalcoatl, the Street of the Dead, and the great Pyramids of the Sun and the Moon.'

Teotihuacan was some twenty kilometres north-east of the centre of Mexico City and I thought I had probably glimpsed those pyramids through the dust haze as we flew in. The brochure said that the Pyramid of the Sun was over sixty metres high, larger than the Great Pyramid of Egypt, and the Street of the Dead more than three kilometres long, but even though it contained a plan, as well as photographs, I was still not prepared for the colossal dimensions of the place.

We had barely forty minutes there, but we still managed to walk the whole huge complex, even climbing to the top of the smaller Pyramid of the Moon. Ward had his camera with him, and though he led me round at a breathless pace, talking all the time about the terrible religious cult of the Aztecs, he also took quite a few pictures, usually with myself or some other human in the foreground to give an indication of the scale of the place.

In addition to Quetzalcoatl, the feathered serpent god of learning, he talked of Tezcatlipoca, the sky god, Tlaloc, the rain god, and the name I have most difficulty in pronouncing or even spelling, and the most terrible god of all – Huitzilopochtli.

I have a picture in my mind still of endless queues of captives waiting under guard to mount the steps of the Aztec temples where the priests of Huitzilopochtli stood waiting with obsidian stone knives, hands and faces black with caked blood, their robes stiff with it, as they worked industriously to open up each human chest, extract the still-palpitating heart, offering it to their filthy god, then tossing the torn-open body back down the steps to the waiting warriors below, who hacked it into joints for the ritual cannibalism that ensured both the pleasures of the flesh and added prowess from the absorption of the captive joint into their own live bodies.

It is a picture indelibly imprinted, Ward's voice painting it in quiet words, neither excited nor repelled by the horror of it, but simply repeating information he had obtained from one of the books he had borrowed from his Glasgow library as soon as he knew the route he would be taking to Punta Arenas and the Antarctic. I have referred to it here because, to me, Mexico was a curtain-raiser to the horrors we were to uncover later.

The sun was setting in a red blaze as we drove into the centre of Mexico City. the long geometrically laid-out streets already darkening into canyons filled with the lights of cars. There were men half-hidden by piled-up mountains of coloured balloons at some of the street corners, a relic, Ward said, of the magnificent feathered headdresses of the Aztecs, and with the stillness of evening the dust haze had gone, so that the huge square of the Zócalo had a brooding sense of peace, the cathedral's twin towers still touched with the sunset's warmth and the great mass of it dominating the presidential palace.

The restaurant Rodriguez had chosen was in one of the streets behind the cathedral, a small sombre place which served only Mexican food. He was tucked away in a corner, the only man on his own, a solitary candle illuminating his face as he pored over the paper on which he was writing. It was an unusual face, the skin stretched tight across high cheekbones and of a yellowish-ochre colour like old parchment, the features themselves almost patrician with their high forehead and prominent nose.

He didn't look up as we crossed the room, his head bent and the pen moving swiftly across pages held in a clipboard. I had the sense of a withdrawn person, a loner. 'Rodriguez?' There was no warmth in Ward's voice.

The man raised his eyes, nodded, then closed the clipboard and got to his feet. 'Señor Vord, eh?' They shook hands, eyeing each other warily. Ward introduced me and we sat down.

'What's that you're drinking?' Ward asked, leaning forward and putting his big nose down to sniff the pale liquid.

'Tequila.'

'Ah yes, made from the *Agave tequilana*, the sisal tree plant.' Rodriguez nodded. 'You like some tequila?'

Ward nodded. 'I suppose so. You going to have one?' he asked me. 'It's pretty fiery stuff.' And when I nodded, he flicked his fingers at a passing waiter. '*Dos tequilas*. What about you, Señor Rodriguez?'

'*Gracia*.'

He ordered three, then sat back, staring at the man we had come to see. 'You writing another book?'

'No. An article for an American magazine.'

'About the *Desaparecidos*?'

'No. It concern the drug traffic on the Mexican-US border. Cocaine. It come mainly overland from Colombia and Ecuador.' There was a short silence. 'You want to see me about something?' It was a question, not a statement, and the man was nervous. 'What is it you want to see me about?'

Ward didn't answer. He just sat there, staring at the man.

'You say it is urgent, a matter of life or death for me.' Rodriguez spoke softly, his voice so low it was almost a whisper. 'What is it about then?'

Ward hesitated, then shook his head. 'Later.' He picked up the menu. 'We'll talk about it later, after we've fed.' But Rodriguez wanted to know right away. He still had his biro gripped in his right hand and he was fiddling with it tensely, his brown, slightly almond-slitted eyes fallen to the table, unable to meet the directness of Ward's gaze.

The drinks arrived, three thick-rimmed glasses full of a slightly syrupy liquid, rather like mead, but with a sharper, more aromatic flavour, and as Ward had said, very fiery. He ordered *sopa de mariscos*, which was crab, mussels and shrimps with *cilantro*, onions and rice, followed by *guacamole* and *chile salteados* with a *tortilla*. Rodriguez had already ordered for himself. I followed Ward's lead as he seemed to know what the dishes were.

Rodriguez was part Indian, a short man with lank black hair. 'I have a touch of the Quechua in me.' He announced this in English, an explanation of something he had said that Ward had not understood. They had been talking in Spanish. 'You must excuse,' he said. 'I am not speaking altogether correctly. My Spanish is of the Argentine. There are many variations all through South America, and of course here in Central America it is different again, particularly in Mexico.' He pronounced it *Mehico*.

Ward's excuse for talking in Spanish had been that he was accustoming himself to using it freely. The soup came and with it the three bottles of beer he had ordered. Rodriguez was starting with prawns wrapped in bacon. At this point the conversation, still in Spanish, seemed to be about politics and the Mexican economy, but when Ward had finished his soup, he suddenly reverted to English. 'Mario Ángel Gómez.' He pushed his plate away and stared at Rodriguez. 'When did you last see him?'

There was silence, the writer's eyes gone suddenly blank. Like an animal sliding away from an unwelcome confrontation, he took refuge in a displacement activity, taking the last of the little pastries hot with spice that had come with the drinks and waving the empty plate at a passing waiter.

'Well?'

'When I am finishing the book. You say you have read it. It is all in my book, everything about Gómez that I know.'

'He went to Peru, didn't he?'

'He was going to Peru. That's what he told me when I interviewed him that second time in Buenos Aires.'

'And you didn't visit him there?'

'No, I don't visit him.'

'You mean you haven't seen him in Peru? You haven't talked to him after he took up residence there?'

The man shook his head. But before he did so there had been a fractional hesitation.

'He *is* in Peru, isn't he?'

Again a shake of the head, and when Ward pressed him, repeating the question, Rodriguez said, 'Maybe. But I don't know for sure.'

The waiter arrived with the next course and they reverted to politics, talking Spanish again, Ward's tone, his whole manner softened. He was trying to put Rodriguez at his ease. But then he suddenly asked, 'Why did he leave Argentina?' He was a fast eater and now he was leaning forward across his empty plate, his English sharp and abrupt. 'Why?'

Rodriguez shrugged. And when Ward persisted, he said almost reluctantly, 'Why does any man leave? There were rumours. I have said that in my book.'

'Rumours concerning the *Desaparecidos*?'

'Per'aps.'

'But nothing ever proved?'

'No. It was just stories in one or two of the papers, the *Peronista* journals mainly.'

'And that's why you interviewed him?'

'Yes.'

'You wrote that you caught him at his flat just at the time he was leaving the country.'

'The second time, yes. That's right. He was already packing.'

'Because he was afraid if he stayed he would be arrested?'

Rodriguez shook his head.

'When Alfonsin came to power was there never any talk of arrestin' him?'

'I tell you nobody ever accuse him of anything. After the Malvinas war he is something of a hero. In Puerto Argentina his plane is destroyed on the ground. All the aermacchis are destroyed, so he takes some marines to make a reconnaissance across the island, his objective Goose Green. Shortly after he is flown back to the mainland, to the most south naval base of Río Grande in Tierra del Fuego. From there he fly a Learjet, acting as pathfinder for the Skyhawks, and I believe once for the Super Etendards. At that time they have one Exocet left.'

'Yes, but what about before the Falklands war, when he was a youngster, before he was commissioned? Was he a member of the Triple A?'

'The Triple A?'

'Aye, the right-wing *Peronistas* who destroyed the *Montoneros* back in '73 – June 20, wasn't it, at Ezeiza Airport? You mention that in your book, too.'

Rodriguez's eyes were fixed on his plate, his short dark fingers crumbling the remains of his *tortilla*. Ward leaned forward across the table, his eyes fixed on the man's face, his tone aggressive as he said, 'The Triple A was based on the ESMA, the Navy Mechanics' School.' He reminded me of a barrister I had once watched interrogating a hostile witness and I was sure his switch to English was not for my benefit, it was done to put Rodriguez at a disadvantage. 'Your book doesn't say whether or not he was at the *Escuela Mecánica de la Armada*, but the implication –'

Rodriguez was shaking his head angrily. 'What you read into my book is more what you want, I think. There was some talk, but nothing proved, no accusations.' He emptied his glass and poured himself some more beer. 'All I know is that he is with the naval air forces. At the start of the Malvinas war he is with the Escuadrilla de Ataque based at Punta Indio, flying Aermacchi 339As and he is sent to Puerto Argentina –'

'You mean Port Stanley. But that was much later. The time that interests me is before he was posted to the aircraft carrier *Veinticinco de Mayo*, before he became a flier. Also why he has now left Argentina. You don't say why in your book, so perhaps you tell me now.' Ward leaned quickly forward again. 'Come on, man – why?' And when Rodriguez did not answer him he said very quietly, 'Was it because of anything that happened when he was at the *Escuela Mecánica de la Armada*?' A pause, and then, '*Ángel de Muerte*, that was his nickname, wasn't it? And he was proud of it. He had it painted on his aircraft, that's what you say.'

There was a long silence, Rodriguez sitting there, dumb.

'Well, just tell me where he is now. Surely ye can do that. Where dae Ah find him – in Peru, where?'

'*Te digo, no sé.*' Rodriguez said it in Spanish, in an obstinate tone of voice that suggested finality. 'I don't care to talk about him – not to you, not to nobody.' He slapped his hands flat on the table and got to his feet. Then, leaning down, staring into Ward's face, he said nervously, 'Who are you? Why do you ask me all these questions about him? He is not important. Not any more.'

He was scared. It showed in his eyes, and in the way his voice had become increasingly sharp, almost strident.

'Sit down.' Ward's tone made it a command, but his voice was quiet.

Rodriguez shook his head. 'I cannot answer any more questions.' And he added, 'I don't know who you are, why you want to ask me–'

'Please!' Ward raised his left hand, a placating gesture. '*Por favor.* As your host I have perhaps been a little too brusque. Please sit down again. And please try to give me some indication of where this man can be found.'

'Why you want to know?' His voice was high-pitched, his English slipping. His short, stout body was very still as he stared down into Ward's face.

Silence then, the two of them facing each other. I could hear the talk at the next table, the staccato clatter of Mexican, and behind me the piercing voice of an American woman.

'All right, I'll tell you why I'm interested in the man.' Ward waved him back to his seat and called to the waiter to bring the coffee. '*Y tres más tequilas,*' he added. And to Rodriguez – 'Come on. Sit down, fur God's sake. Ah'm not goin' to shop ye!'

'What is shop?'

Ward frowned. He had used the word quite automatically. It expressed his intention exactly, but to explain it . . . 'Let's say that Ah'm not going to the police or anybody in authority. This is a purely personal enquiry. Now sit down and Ah will explain just why I am interested in this Mario Ángel Gómez.'

There was a further moment of hesitation, then Rodriguez suddenly made up his mind, and with a brief nod of his head, resumed his seat. 'Okay, *señor*. Why is it, then, that you are so interested?'

Ward began to explain, about Iris Sunderby and the boat waiting for us in Punta Arenas. The coffee came and with it three more glasses of tequila. 'Señora Sunderby should have flown straight to Punta Arenas, but instead she stopped off in Lima. Her name before she married Charles Sunderby, an English glaciologist, was Iris Madalena Connor-Gómez. My information is that Mario Ángel Gómez sometimes uses the double name Connor-Gómez and that they are related. In fact, they both have the same father. Is that right?'

Rodriguez shook his head. 'I never meet this woman you speak of.'

They stared at each other for a moment, then Ward said, 'All right. What about Carlos then? She told my friend here that he was some sort of cousin. Do you know who his mother was?'

Rodriguez shook his head again.

'The boy was in London, a student at the university, and according to our immigration people he gave his name as Borgalini, his address care of a bank in Lima. Why Lima?'

'I don't know.'

'Is it because Ángel Connor-Gómez is in Lima?'

Rodriguez shook his head violently. 'I tell you, he is packing up to leave Buenos Aires the last time I saw him. He don't say where he is going.'

'Did you ask him?'

'No.'

A pause then as the waiter brought the coffee and refilled our cups. Rodriguez leaned forward. 'Sometimes, you understand, is not very safe to ask questions.'

'So you did regard him as dangerous?'

'No, I don' say that. It is just that one learns to be careful, particularly if one is a writer. Look what happened to that Indian chap of yours who wrote about the Koran.'

'There is nothing blasphemous in your book. Nobody has issued a *fatwa* or put out a contract. So why are you scared?' There was a silence then, an uneasy stillness between the two of them as they sat facing each other. 'Is it because he was called *Ángel de Muerte*?'

'No, no.' Rodriguez shook his head emphatically. 'That is something that come out of his reconnaissance to Goose Green. It became a last stand, all very dramatic. His marines, suddenly faced with the British paras, took up a defensive position in some abandoned trenches and under Gómez's leadership fought very last ditch, full of courage. They were killed almost to the man. That is probably when they give him that name – the Angel of Death.' He said it in English, slowly, as though enjoying the sound of the words, and he added with a secret little smile, 'That happened just before he was recalled at the request of Lami Dozo himself. His navigational skills were required at Rió Grande and it was then he painted his Learjet with the name *Ángel de Muerte*, on both sides, so that on the radio beamed to the English they could say the Angel of Death was coming with his French missiles loaded to kill.'

'Then the nom de guerre was nothing to do with the Disappeareds?'

Rodriguez hesitated, then shrugged his shoulders. 'Who can tell? As I have said, there were rumours. That is all.'

'You questioned him about it?'

'Not directly. I tell you, it is dangerous to ask questions like that. But I make enquiries. Nobody can tell me anything that is certain. There is no record.'

'But he was at the *Escuela Mecánica de la Armada*?'

'*Si.*'

And then Ward asked him what had happened to Iris Sunderby's father, Juan Connor-Gómez.

'He kill himself. I say that in my book. He is Chairman and Managing Director of the Gómez Emporium, a big store in the centre of Buenos Aires. When it is burn down he lose everything, so . . .' He shrugged.

'You wrote that he was arrested.'

'Yes. The company was in difficulty. This is at the beginning of the Malvinas trouble. It was thought he may have set a match to it himself. For the insurance, you see. But nothing is proved, so he is released. That was about a year before he commit suicide.

The insurance people are still fighting the claim in the courts.'

'And his other son? What happened to Eduardo? You don't mention him, except to say that he was a biologist and that he went to England to work for two years at the chemical weapons experimental establishment at Porton Down. You don't say what happened to him.'

More tequila arrived and Rodriguez sat there staring down at the yellow-green liquid in his glass.

'Well?'

He shrugged. 'I don't know. I don't know what happen to him.'

'Is he one of the *Desaparecidos*?'

'Could be. I don't know. A few months after he return from England he bought a flight ticket to Montevideo in Uruguay. That is the last anybody hear of him.'

Ward switched then to the Gómez family background. They were talking in Spanish again so that I couldn't follow what was said, only the gist of it, and that largely from the names they referred to: Iris Sunderby's, of course, her grandfather, too, and the Connors, Sheila Connor in particular, and there was constant repetition of the name Rosalli Gabrielli. Suddenly Rodriguez's eyes widened. '*¿Me acusás a mi? ¿Por que me acusás? No escondo nada.*' His eyes darted to the door.

'Och, relax, man. Ah'm not accusin' ye of anythin'.' Ward was leaning forward, his gaze fixed on the Argentinian's face. 'All Ah'm askin' from ye is the man's present whereabouts.'

'I tell you, I don't know.'

Ward's left hand crashed down on the table, spilling coffee from the cup he had just filled. 'Ye're lyin'. Tell me his address –'

Rodriguez jumped to his feet. 'You do not speak to me like that. You have no right. If I tell you I don't know, then you must accept –'

'Balls!' Ward's hand slammed the table again, his voice gone quiet, almost menacing, as he said, 'He's in Peru. Ye just tell me where –'

'No. I am leaving you now.'

Ward was on his feet in a flash, his gloved right hand reaching out for the other's arm. 'Sit down! Ye haven't finished yer drink yet.'

'No, no. I go now.' Rodriguez's face was screwed up with pain as the grip of that dummy hand on his arm forced his body slowly sideways towards his seat. '¡Dejame ir!' It was almost a squeal.

'Ah'll let ye go when ye give me his address. Now sit down.' Ward pushed him back into his chair. 'Got a pen?' he asked me. His hand was still gripping the man's arm, holding him there, and when I nodded he said, 'Give it to him. And pass him one of those paper napkins; he can write the address down on that.'

Rodriguez was still struggling and out of the corner of my eye I could see the patron watching us uneasily. I thought he might phone the police at any moment. Ward was leaning forward again, his weight dragging at the arm he was still holding. Rodriguez hesitated, his eyes shifting from Ward to the silent faces of the other diners, all watching us. Then suddenly he seemed to sag back into his seat, his hand reaching slowly for the pen I was still holding out to him. It shook slightly as he scribbled an address, then pushed the serviette across the table, his body slowly relaxing as Ward let go of him and picked up the serviette.

'Cajamarca?' He passed the serviette to me, his eyes fixed on the man. 'Why Cajamarca?'

'It is where he lives.'

'Yes, but why? Why there? Why not in Lima or Trujillo or Cuzco?'

The other shook his head, shrugging his padded shoulders. 'He has a hacienda there. The Hacienda Lucinda.'

'At Cajamarca. Where's that?'

Rodriguez's face looked blank.

'All right, you haven't been there, you say. But you must have been sufficiently curious to check it out on a map. So where is it?'

There was a pause, then Rodriguez said, 'Cajamarca is in the north of Peru.' He pronounced it *Cahamarca*. 'It is inland from the coast, behind the Cordillera do los Andes.'

Ward nodded. 'Ah remember now. It's where Pizarro ambushed the Inca army, right?' He was suddenly smiling. 'Very appropriate.' He seemed to wait for his words to sink in, then added, slowly and with emphasis, 'Pizarro was a thug. An avaricious, cruel bastard.'

'He was a brave man,' Rodriguez muttered. They might have been referring to somebody they knew.

'Oh yes, he was brave all right.' He turned to me. 'If ye read Prescott ye'll get the impression Pizarro crossed the Andes and destroyed the great empire of the Incas with just forty horse and sixty foot. But it wasn't quite like that, was it?' He had turned back to Rodriguez. 'He had guns and armour, and the God of the Catholics behind him, and a whole army of dissident Indian auxiliaries in support. Still, Ah grant ye, an incredible feat.' And he added, his voice quietly emphatic, 'A brave, very determined, very obstinate man. Not a gentleman like Cortés, but a peasant, with a peasant's cunning and greed. The Mafia would have loved him.'

Rodriguez was getting to his feet again, the uneasy look back on his face. He seemed to find something disturbing in what Ward had said.

'Sit down, man. There's a little matter we haven't touched on yet.' Ward pointed to the chair. 'Sit down, for God's sake.' He leaned back. 'Here in Mexico the Spaniards topped every Aztec temple to Huitzilopochtli, every pyramid, either with a church or a statue of the Virgin Mary. Ye're a Roman Catholic, Ah take it?'

Rodriguez nodded slowly.

'A very pragmatic church. A lot of glitz.' He seemed to be talking to himself. 'Ah wonder what Christ makes of all the horrors done in his name. And now we have fanatical variations of the Muslim faith breathin' hate and venom all over the Near East.'

I didn't follow the relevance of his religious digression. Nor I think did Rodriguez, who had subsided into his seat again, a sad, dazed look on his face.

'*¡Salud!*' Ward raised his glass.

'*¡Salud!*'

'Tell me –' His tone was mild, almost conversational – 'how much did he pay you?'

The man's eyes slid sideways to the street door. '*No comprendo.*' The door was open and he started to rise.

'You understand perfectly well.' Ward was very much the old Etonian now, his manner still mild, but with something in the voice that held Rodriguez riveted, both hands on the table and his bottom half out of his seat. 'You went to Peru.'

'No.'

'You went to Peru,' he repeated, 'and you saw Gómez. He still uses his service rank, does he?'

'Yes, he is *Capitán* now.'

'So you saw him.'

The other didn't answer.

'How much?' Ward's voice had hardened.

'I don't go to Peru. I come here to Mexico City where it is not too far by airplane to visit my publishers in San Francisco.'

'You went to Peru.' Ward said it very quietly this time, but with an emphasis that made it sound like a threat.

'You cannot prove anything.'

'No?' Ward left his enquiry hanging there, smiling quietly. Then he said, 'What I need from you is not so much what he paid you, but why. You went to Peru –' He pulled a diary out of his breast pocket and checked some notes at the end – 'on March 5 this year. That is just two months before your book came out. What were you going to write into the book if he didn't pay you?'

'Nothing. Nothing, I tell you. He pay me nothing.'

Ward glanced at his diary again. 'According to my information your book has sold some eight thousand copies in the English language and the print figure in the Spanish edition was twenty-five thousand. You have two wives to keep, the one you are living with here, who is really your mistress, and I believe rather expensive, particularly as she already has a daughter, and your wife proper who will not divorce you and is living in the Argentine with your two children, a boy and a girl. You also run a big Chrysler and have two addresses, one here in Mexico City, the other in Cuernavaca. In other words, you live an expensive life, more expensive than you could possibly afford on the basis of the royalties from your two books and the articles you period-ically write for newspapers and magazines in the States. So – what is it you haven't told me about this man?'

Rodriguez didn't answer. He subsided back into his seat, staring down at his drink, while Ward watched him, waiting. Their eyes met. Then Rodriguez glanced at the door again as though seeking escape, but it was shut now. His eyes flickered round the restaurant. There were still several people watching us, conversation muted.

'Well?'

He shook his head, suddenly reaching for his drink and swallowing it in one quick gulp. He stared at the empty glass for a moment. I think he would have liked another, but instead he pulled himself slowly to his feet.

Ward had also risen, the two of them facing each other. 'You mention in your book that some time after the capitulation at Port Stanley, Gómez was given the job of testing an aircraft for its long-range capabilities, flying it out of that Argentine base at the bottom of Tierra del Fuego. You suggest he was secretly testing it for work on the Antarctic land mass, flying it south over the pack ice. How far south? Do you know where?'

'*No.*'

'As far as the Ice Shelf?'

'*No sé.*'

'It couldn't have been entirely secret since you say it was reported in the papers. You even have a picture of him taken on his return. It was a German plane, a Fokker I believe?'

'*Si.*'

There was a moment's silence, the two of them standing there and the restaurant quite still now. 'We'll be stopping off in Lima,' Ward said. 'If Gómez is not at the address you have given me I shall presume it is because you've been in touch with him, so don't phone him. Okay?' And he added, 'I will not, of course, mention our meeting here in Mexico City.'

The other nodded and turned towards the door. But then he paused, a look almost of malice. 'If you go to Cajamarca you should know *el Niño* is running.'

'So?'

'*El Niño* is the counter-equatorial current.'

'I know that.'

'Every six or seven years it overruns the Humboldt.'

'And then?'

'And then . . . per'aps you will see.' He smiled, adding, 'When *el Niño* run the fishermen don't earn nothing because fish like the cold of the north-flowing Humboldt, not the warmth of the Equatorial, and with no fish, the birds die.'

'How do you know what's happening down there in Peru? Have you been there again?'

'No. It is in the papers. The birds are dying.'

'And how's that concern us?'

'I am never on the Pacific coast in *el Niño* year,' Rodriguez said, still smiling, 'but if the rains of the Amazon slip across the Cordilleras you will maybe have a bad flight to Cajamarca. *¡Buen viaje!*' he added, not bothering now to hid his malice as he turned quickly to the door and made his escape.

Ward knocked back the rest of his tequila and called for the *cuenta*. 'Time we got some sleep. The next few days could be a wee bit hectic.'

All the way back to the hotel he sat hunched and silent in the rear of the taxi, his eyes closed. He only spoke once, and then he was merely voicing his thoughts aloud. 'That aircraft was fitted with long-range tanks. He could have got to the South Pole and back. Or he could have flown it around in the wastes of ice where Shackleton lost the *Endurance*. Nobody would see him there.' And he added, 'Ah wonder how much Iris knows?'

I failed to follow his train of thought, my mind still on the meeting with Rodriguez. 'You really think he was blackmailing the man?'

He looked at me then, a quick flick of the eyes. 'Of course. And not just Gómez. A book like that, it's a great temptation fur a journalist who knows so much he's scared to go on livin' in his own country.'

I said something about the political climate in the Argentine having changed since the Falklands War. I thought I knew that much about the country. I suppose I had read it somewhere. But he laughed and shook his head.

'That's a very naïve assessment. Nothin' has changed. Not

really. The Argentines are still ethnically the same, the population still predominantly Italian, most of them havin' their roots in the south of Italy and in Sicily. The Camorra and the Mafia are part of their heritage, violence in their blood.'

I started to argue with him, but all he said was, 'Leopards don't change their spots just because the fashion in political leadership alters. And remember, the Junta that decided on the invasion of the Malvinas, at least tae of them, were of Italian extraction. They're finished, of course, now, but there will be others – others that are lyin' low fur the moment. Rodriguez knows that. Probably knows who they are. That's why he's scared to remain in Buenos Aires.'

He relapsed into silence then, and because my mind was still trying to grapple with the politics of a country I knew very little about, I failed to ask him whether Gómez had made that flight on his own or if he had had a crew with him.

It was only later, when I was lying in my bed, with the neon lights of a bar across the road flickering on the curtains and music blaring, that I remembered Ward standing in the saloon of the *Cutty Sark* and asking Iris Sunderby who she had in mind as navigator, who the man was who had convinced her he had also seen a ship locked in the ice of the Weddell Sea. I had thought at the time she had been referring to an officer on some survey vessel, the British Antarctic Survey's supply ship perhaps, or else a pelagic fisherman or whaler, even an Antarctic explorer. But now it came back to me. She had said, *A man I'm convinced has actually seen what my husband saw*. Those had been her words, and if she was being exact, they would mean that he had seen the icebound vessel from the air, exactly as Sunderby had seen it.

I lay there for a long time thinking about that, the loud insistence of the Mexican music from across the way drumming in my ears and gradually merging into the crashing ice of layering floes as my mind drifted into a fantasy of trekking with Iris Sunderby towards the dim outline of an icicle-festooned ghost of a ship, the man at the helm towering like a giant question mark over my jet-lagged brain. Had Charles Sunderby imagined it, or had he really seen the figure of a man standing frozen at the wheel?

I woke in a daze, the music replaced by the roar of traffic and the sunrise showing like a great red orange through a gap in the buildings opposite. There was no wind, the air crystal clear. I was too excited at being in such a strange city on the other side of the world for there to be any question of going back to sleep again. I got up, dressed and went for a walk, my limbs lethargic with the altitude, my brain sluggish after the disturbed night. The shops were opening and I browsed for a while in one that sold books as well as newspapers and magazines, but I failed to find the American edition of Rodriguez's book. Instead, I came away with an old copy of Prescott's *Conquest of Peru*. It was dusty and the spine was broken, but at least it was in English. Even so, it cost me rather more of my American dollars than I expected.

By then the sun was risen above the tops of the buildings and it was hot. I walked slowly back to the hotel. No sign of Ward, so I had breakfast, then rang his room. First time I tried his phone was engaged. When I finally got through to him he said very brusquely, 'Don't phone again. Order a taxi fur ten-forty-five and hold it till Ah come down. Ah'm waitin' fur a call.'

'It's getting late,' I said.

'Ah know, but this call is important. Anyway, they'll not take off on time.'

It was almost eleven before he appeared, looking as though he hadn't slept at all. 'Taxi there? Good. Make sure it doesn't go off.' He dumped his overnight bag with mine and I went out to tell the driver we were just coming. When I got back he was at the cashier's desk settling the bill. It was in US dollars, not Mexican pesetas. 'And there is also', the clerk said, 'two hundred and seventy-nine dollars owing for your calls, *señor*.'

Ward paid with American traveller's cheques and we hurried out to the taxi. '*Aeropuerto.*' He flopped into his seat.

'That was quite a telephone bill,' I said as we moved off.

'International calls are expensive.' He closed his eyes.

'London? Or were you phoning Lima?'

I don't know whether he was asleep or not, but he didn't answer. He was equally uncommunicative when we reached the airport. His guess that the flight would be delayed proved correct.

Security, they said. Apparently there had been a bomb scare recently. The transit baggage had not been loaded and customs officials and police were insisting on all cases being opened and everything laid out on the floor. It all took time and it was past midday before we finally got away.

Ward ordered vodka, drank it straight and went to sleep with ¿Muerto O Vivo? open on his lap. The meal came. He waved it away and went back to sleep. We had just passed over a gaggle of eighteen-thousand-foot volcanoes, great slag heaps of ash with gaping vents pointed at the clear blue bowl of the heavens, when he finally shifted in his seat and leaned across me to look out of the window, blinking his eyes. 'Know where Ah'd like to be goin'? The Galapagos.' He nodded his head towards a white line of distant cloud far out over the starb'd wing tip. 'Out there. Can't be more than a thousand miles. Mebbe Ah'll dae that when Ah've extricated mesel' from the Southern Ocean an' all that ice.'

He picked up his book again, opened it at the marker and settled himself in his seat. He was back, playing the Glasgow boy and wearing his tourist hat like a hired costume. The stewardess came down the aisle, a big-breasted young woman exuding a strong odour of perspiration. He ordered another vodka and turned to me. 'What about ye? Horse's Neck?'

I nodded.

He gave the order and we returned to our books. I had become totally absorbed in William Prescott's account of the Inca civilisation, which had been destroyed by the greed of Pizarro's Conquistadores. It was a fascinating glimpse of a people who in the sixteenth century had never seen a wheel or a sea-going ship, had never faced an armoured knight on horseback or the fire power of crossbows and guns, but whose roads and lines of communication through the incredible terrain of the Andes, whose methods of agriculture by irrigation and whose whole political set-up, so close to what we know as Communism, was in some ways more advanced than that of their conquerors.

The drinks came and Ward sat back, watching me out of the corner of his eye. 'When ye've finished absorbin' Prescott Ah guess ye'll know as much about Peru as most Peruvians. Probably more.' And he added, 'This will be the first time Ah've visited the country, but havin' read Prescott myself Ah don't think Ah'm goin' to like the Spaniards and what they and the mestizos have done to it.' And then he said suddenly, 'That phone call Ah was waitin' fur – it was from the hotel Iris had given me as her address in Lima. They say she pulled out three days ago.'

'Then why are we stopping off in Lima?' I asked him.

'You don't have to. You can go straight on to Punta Arenas if you'd prefer.'

'But you're stopping off?'

'Yes. She didn't fly on into Chile. Ah checked with both Lan Chile and UC Ladeco. Also Aero Peru. In any case, she had a hire car delivered to the hotel. The assistant manager said when she left she was drivin' it herself.'

My thoughts of the night came back to me. 'You think she's gone up to Cajamarca?'

'Well, she's certainly not drivin' herself all the way down through Chile to Punta Arenas. That's well over three thousand miles and God knows what the roads are like south of Valparaíso, if there are any. It's all mountains and deep-cut fjords.' He smiled at me. 'So ye've reached the same conclusion as Ah have, that Mario Ángel Gómez is the navigator she referred to as the man who can lead her to that icebound ship. Ah doubt there's anybody else has had the sort of opportunity he's had for flyin' around at will in that part of the Antarctic.'

'There are bases,' I said. 'Half a dozen countries have survey and exploration establishments around the fringes of the Antarctic land mass.'

He nodded. 'But they fly set pattern routes on direct lines from their southern supply points to their Antarctic bases. Ah had a look at the Royal Geographical Society's latest maps, some of the charts, too. None of the supply routes go close to the point where Sunderby's aircraft ditched. And Ah had a word on the phone with a Cambridge don they put me on to – he was somethin' to dae with the Scott Polar Institute, and he confirmed that supply aircraft would not normally be overflying the area we're interested in.'

The fact that Sunderby's plane was en route for the American base at McMurdo made no difference except that the operational word was 'normally'. 'There were tae things that were not normal about that flight. In the first place, the plane made an emergency landin' at Port Stanley to have an electrical fault put right. That's how Sunderby came to be on the flight. Secondly, he was a glaciologist and it may well be that he persuaded the pilot to swin' away to the east. It would only call fur a small diversion from the direct route from Stanley to McMurdo Sound to give him a glimpse of the Ice Shelf and the area where Shackleton's *Endurance* was beset and finally sunk.'

His point was that the Americans did not normally fly supplies out of the Falklands. I asked him what Gómez's point of departure had been and he replied, 'Ushuaia, accordin' to Rodriguez. That's the Argentine base in the south-west of Tierra del Fuego, on the Beagle Channel. Not ideal, Ah'm told, but that may have been part of the test.'

'You say he was refuelled. He must have had some sort of a flight plan.'

Ward was silent for a moment. 'He was testin' a plane. It had probably been modified fur work in Antarctica. The Argentinians have a short strip airbase in the north of the Antarctic Peninsula. Visecomodorio Marambio Ah think it's called.' He spoke hesitantly as though trying to work it out for himself. 'Maybe he flew the final stage from there. And he must have been testin' in part fur flight refuellin' because Rodriguez says in his book he was refuelled somewhere over the Bellingshausen Sea, which is a long way west of the area where Sunderby lost his life.'

'What are you suggesting?' I asked. 'That as soon as he was refuelled he took the opportunity of seeing if he could locate the remains of that American plane?'

'No. The plane's sunk. Ah don't think there's any doubt about that.'

'Then what?'

'Ah don't know.' His voice had slowed again, little more than a murmur. 'Ah'm just thinkin' aloud.' He turned his head towards me. '*And Ah saw an angel come down from Heaven, havin' the key of the bottomless pit and a great chain in his hand.* D'ye recognise that?' he asked.

I shook my head. 'You're quoting from the Bible, are you?'

'The Revelation of St John.' He smiled. 'Wonderful stuff. Ye should read it.' And then, suddenly practical, he said, 'When ye've finished yer drink Ah suggest ye put Prescott away, turn yer light out and try and get some sleep. There should be a car waitin' fur us at the airport when we get in to Lima. Ye've got your international driving licence?'

I nodded.

'Good. Ye'll be drivin' when we take it over. It'll save time. There's always the chance they'll query the validity of my own licence –' He tapped the steel forearm and gloved hand resting on his lap. 'Foreigners can be a wee bit difficult about it sometimes.' Somewhat pointedly he closed his own book and tipped his seat right back, preparing himself for sleep. 'We'll go to the hotel first. Ah'd like a word with the doorman if they've got one. Then we'll head fur the coast and the Pan-Am Highway, drive right through the night. Okay?'

'Yes,' I said.

'We'll drive and sleep in turn. With luck we should be in Cajamarca in time for breakfast.' And then he switched abruptly from practicalities, quoting in a stage whisper: *'And I saw a new Heaven and a new earth; for the first Heaven and the first earth were passed away: and there was no more sea.'* He spoke it without a trace of a Scot's accent. 'Patmos,' he murmured. 'I was there very briefly a couple of years back. There's a great white fortress of a monastery crowning the top of the island. It was once full of treasures, but all I could think about as I stood on the battlemented roof, looking out over the Aegean, was that a disciple of Christ's had sat in his cell in a little monastery half-way up the hill recording the extraordinary revelations he had been vouchsafed. Was he mad? The Emperor Domitian condemned him, so he had evidently seemed so, to a Roman. But it's great reading.'

He settled himself more deeply in his seat. 'Och well, we'll see whether those lines fit when we reach the top of the pass over the Andes.' He switched out his overhead light, closed his eyes, and instantly, it seemed, he was asleep.

When we arrived in Lima it took time to go through the formalities. Again the immigration people questioned him about his occupation, even going so far as to check the word antiquarian in an English-Spanish dictionary. 'Useful, ye see,' Ward said as we went through to the baggage claim area. 'He was so busy worryin' over what "antiquarian" meant that he hardly glanced at our visas. And yer occupation of wood preservation consultant is not exactly a description he comes across every day.' He was smiling as we took our place by the baggage conveyor belt.

When we had finally retrieved all his excess baggage, it took us even longer than in Mexico to clear customs because he insisted on unrolling a big holdall right there on the bench to get at his oilskins. 'We'll almost certainly need them at Punta Arenas. Iris said it blows and rains like hell just about every day in the Strait of Magellan. Better get yers out, too. It's rainin' up in the mountains accordin' to that nice immigration laddie. He said he'd heard it on the radio this mornin'. There's floodin' too, in places. The *Niño* factor. Rodriguez was right.'

We checked all but our oilies, hand baggage and briefcases into the airport lock-ups, and after what he had said about the weather, I was glad to see, when we got to the car desk, that he had laid on a four-wheel-drive land-cruiser. While he was signing the hire and insurance papers, the girl produced a parcel from a cubby-hole at the back. 'Ees left for you this morning, *señor*. A courier from the *Librerío Universal* bring it. There is some extra to pay, plees.'

He nodded without looking up as she placed it on the counter. 'Books,' he said.

She nodded, asked for our driving licences, then took us outside to where the vehicle was parked in the shade of a tree. 'It may not be as comfortable as an ordinary saloon,' Ward said on a note of apology, 'but buggered if Ah was takin' any chances in a country like this.' He pulled open the rear door and tossed the package of books on to the back seat, together with his gear. 'Ye check the vehicle over while Ah see that we've got a manual and all the necessary papers.'

The girl was already producing the car's documents from a compartment below the instrument panel. 'What are the roads like? Bad I suppose.' I was walking round the vehicle, peering underneath to check the state of the tyres and the exhaust line.

'The coastal road is fine, macadam all the way. The turn-off to Cajamarca is north of Trujillo, so we've got about six hundred kilometres of fast drivin'.'

The speedometer read 62805, but that was kilometres, not miles. The vehicle was dusty and there was some rust. I lifted the bonnet. 'What about the mountain road?' I asked. 'We have to cross the first of the cordilleras according to the map you showed me.'

'Rodriguez said it was okay. Macadam until we run out of the coastal plain and start to climb. After that it's a dirt road, but fairly new. It seems heavy trucks use it every day, so it can't be too bad.'

I finished checking the leads and cooling pipes. 'Nothing to worry about then.' And I closed the bonnet.

He nodded, paid the deposit, again in US dollars, and passed me the keys. 'Ye're drivin'. Okay?'

'*¡Buen viaje!*' The girl flashed us a brilliant smile and took her brightly uniformed efficiency off to deal with another customer, a big American with a broad-brimmed stetson shading his leathery features.

The hotel we were headed for was in the centre of the city, a nightmare ride with everybody driving like crazy and blaring their horns. And it was hot, the humidity very high with a miasma hanging over the buildings as though the clouds were so heavy with moisture they needed to rest themselves on terra firma.

There was no doorman at the hotel where Iris Sunderby had stayed, but the woman at reception confirmed that she had left by car shortly after eight on Sunday morning. She remembered because she had seen her drive off and it was unusual for 'a *señora* of her quality' to be driving herself with no companion.

All the time Ward had been talking to the receptionist his head had been half turned to the street doors, which were wide open, framing an incessant movement of people in an iridescent haze of hot sunlight. His eyes darted from door to lift, watchful and alert, as though he were expecting somebody. It had been the same at the airport and I had thought then that perhaps he half expected Iris Sunderby to materialise out of the crowd. Now it worried me, but you can't ask a man like Ward if he's scared. I felt he was as tensed-up as that.

It was the same as we drove off, but my attention was then concentrated on the traffic. 'Turn right at the corner here.' He said it abruptly, his body twisted round so that he could look back at the hotel.

'It's straight on,' I said. I had looked up the directions for the Pan-Am Highway at the hotel.

'Ah know it is, but turn right. Turn right, damn ye – here!' A horn screamed from behind us as I swung the wheel over without indicating. 'And right again.' He wanted me to go round the block and park the car about fifty metres short of the hotel.

'Why?' There was a car close behind me.

'Just do as Ah say.'

The car was still with us as I slid into the kerb just short of the hotel entrance. It passed us then, a very battered American car with a young Indian at the wheel. He gave us a hard stare as he passed, very slowly. A moment later he also parked, right outside the hotel entrance. 'Quick! Pull up close behind him!'

Ward had his door open and was out in a flash before we had even stopped. The Indian had got out too and was coming round the back of his car. Ward's left hand shot out, grabbing him by the arm and dragging him past me. 'Drive on!' The door behind me was flung open, the man bundled in. 'Go on – drive!' Torrents of Spanish as I backed away and pulled out into the traffic. I didn't know what to do. I didn't understand Ward's behaviour, so I just concentrated on getting out of the city as fast as I could.

'We'll dump him somewhere up the Pan-Am.' Ward's voice was close against my left ear.

'What's it all about?' I could hear the Indian struggling in the back. 'For God's sake! You can't do this sort of thing . . .' A main intersection was coming up, the traffic lights not working and a policeman on duty. He waved me through so that I didn't even have to slow. 'Let him go,' I yelled. But Ward didn't answer.

111

He was talking to the Indian, sharp, barked questions in Spanish.

It went on like that all the way out of Lima, Ward's voice sometimes hard and accusing, sometimes dangerously quiet, and the Indian mumbling his replies, and sometimes answering in his own tongue. 'He's from Puno,' Ward said at one stage. 'Thirteen thousand feet up on the shores of Lake Titicaca. Says he has a woman and two boys to keep and needs money.' And he added, 'Can't blame him. If Ah lived in a clapped-out city like this with inflation at two hundred per cent, or whatever it is, Ah'd dae just about anythin' fur payment in solid US dollars.'

It occurred to me that Ward's early background couldn't have been all that different. 'What's he got in his mouth?' I had caught a glimpse of the Indian's face in the rear mirror, a flat, rather moon-shaped face with high cheekbones, blackened teeth and dark eyes that were so slitted he had a Mongol look. His hair was lank and very black and his right cheek bulged where he had something wadded behind his teeth. 'There's a smell, too,' I said.

Ward laughed. 'Nothin' to the way ye probably smell to him. But it's coke. That's what he's chewin'. The coca leaf. They all chew it. Keeps hunger at bay.' And he added, 'Ah wish Ah'd known about coke when Ah was a kid.'

'Why, have you used it?'

'Of course Ah have. But Ah was out where the poppy grows so Ah started on hashish and stuff like that. Not good. But cocaine – no, let's say the coca leaf . . . Hell, if ye know how to use the stuff it can dae ye a power of good. There was a man way back at the beginnin' of this century made an elixir of it, sent it to all the crowned heads of Europe, the Pope, too. They all loved it, thought it was the greatest thing they'd ever drunk.'

We crossed the Rimac river, which was swollen, running brown and very fast. I knew the way then, for we were back-tracking the route we had taken from the airport. 'He was following us, wasn't he?' I asked.

'Aye.'

'Why? Has he told you why?'

'To earn some money.'

'Yes, of course. But who paid him to follow us?'

'The other one, the man he was with. He doesn't know where he got his orders from.'

Directions for the great north-south coastal highway came up and suddenly we were on a dual carriageway that cut through the remains of a giant sand slide. I was doing over a hundred k.p.h. then through a miasma of mist, the Pacific glimmering opaquely away to our left and the light fading. 'Stop at some nice convenient pull-in and we'll take leave of our friend.'

I pulled over and Ward and the Indian got out. There was a hot, wet wind, but no dust blowing. It was too damp. '¿El Niño?' Ward said, and the Indian nodded. 'Si, si. El Niño.'

'His name is Palca.' Ward handed him a ten-dollar note. '¡Buen viaje!' He laughed and clapped him on the back.

The Indian looked at the note, then at Ward. His face was impassive. It showed neither surprise nor pleasure. 'Momento.' He jerked his poncho up, felt about in the pocket of his filthy jeans and produced a screwed-up bit of paper which he handed to Ward with a few muttered words. Then he turned, and with a little gesture of farewell crossed the highway and headed back towards Lima, a small, shambling figure glancing back every now and then in search of a truck that would give him a lift.

Ward opened up the paper to reveal two tiny clay figures interlocked, the woman with her head bent over the man's huge phallic erection. 'What is it?' I asked him.

'Some sort of votive offerin', Ah imagine. Ah've seen this sort of thin' in the Mediterranean, but not as erotic.' He held it out to me. 'Look at the self-satisfied smirk on the man's face. Good, isn't it? He said it was Mochica, from a grave south of Lima. It's typical of Mochica pottery – a lot of it is highly erotic. Ah've seen pictures of drinkin' vessels where the only way of gettin' at the liquor is through the penis, but Ah've never seen fellatio depicted or pictures of miniatures like this ... Maybe it's just a copy. But if so, it's remarkably well done.'

He was staring at it almost lovingly. Then he turned and stood for a while gazing out at the Pacific. 'Ah feel like stout Cortés, silent upon a peak in Darien.'

'That's a long way further north,' I said. 'And anyway it was Balboa.'

'Ah know.'

He got back into the front seat and we started up the coast. 'Ah don't like it,' he said at length. There was a long silence, night closing in fast. I switched the headlights on.

'What don't you like?' I said at last.

'He was just a driver. Ah should have grabbed the other one. Ye didn't notice him, did ye? He was waitin' fur us at the airport, a mean-faced little mestizo dressed in a pale blue suit. Ah didn't see him at first. He was standin' half-hidden among a group of American tourists.'

'Where was this?'

'In the baggage claim area. He watched us go through customs, followed us to the lock-up, then out to the parkin' lot. Remember Ah asked ye to go slowly at the start? He was running then to that old heap the Indian was drivin'. They were behind us all the way to the hotel.'

'If he was following us,' I said, 'why didn't he stay in the car?'

Ward shrugged. 'Wanted to make certain we weren't bookin' in fur the night, Ah suppose, find out what our plans were. He was lurkin' in a doorway while Ah was grabbin' the driver.'

'But why? Is there something you haven't told me?'

'Such as?'

I hesitated. But what the hell, better have it out with him now. 'Are you something to do with Intelligence?'

I would like to have been watching the expression on his face, having put the question to him so bluntly, but just at that moment I had to slam on my brakes for two gaudily painted trucks, one of them with *La Resurrección* elaborately painted in red. They loomed up ahead of me, travelling side-by-side at just over 80 k.p.h. and completely blocking the highway. I flashed my headlights and the one on the left gradually pulled ahead.

I heard Ward laugh. 'Whatever gave ye that idea?' He brushed the question aside and I realised it had been silly of me to ask it. If he were Intelligence he certainly wouldn't tell me. 'Ye have too vivid an imagination,' he said.

By then the faster truck, *La Resurrección*, had pulled over and I had a blurred impression of brilliantly painted pictures of Bethlehem, the birth and the Virgin Mary as I passed it. 'It must cost them a fortune.' Ward was changing the subject and I let it go at that. Time would probably answer my question. Meanwhile, there was the more urgent matter of why we had been followed. 'Who sicked those two on to us?' I asked.

'Aye, who did? Yer guess is as good as mine, Pete.'

'Gómez?'

'Ah'd imagine, yes.'

'But why?'

'That's what Ah don't know.' He leaned forward and pulled the map from the dashboard shelf, flashing his torch on it. 'The first town we go through is Huacho.' He spelled it out for me. 'About a hundred kilometres. There's a hotel marked. We'll stop there. Ah could do with a drink.'

'Maybe we could get something to eat.' I slowed as headlights blazed, dazzling, out of the mist. A great mammoth of an American truck went thundering past, forcing me on to the dirt shoulder.

'Pisco sour,' he murmured, settling himself on his seat and closing his eyes. 'Ah'm sure lookin' forward to my first pisco sour.'

The sea mist was thicker now, the road worsening with potholes in places. Roadworks came and went, unlighted piles of debris looming suddenly. 'What is pisco sour?' I asked him, but he was already asleep and I drove on to Huacho, wondering what sort of a man Gómez would turn out to be and why Iris Sunderby had broken her journey at Lima and driven up to Cajamarca. Was he really going to join ship as navigator? And if so, why had he paid those two to watch for us at the airport? What was the point of their following us?

I was still worrying about this when I pulled into the hotel at Huacho, the mist thicker than ever and my eyes so tired they felt as though they had been sand-blasted.

TWO

Pisco sour proved to be a local brandy whisked up with white of egg and the juice of fresh limes with a few drops of angostura bitters lying like dark bloodstains on the white bed of foam. I can't remember how many I had in the course of that meal, or what I ate. Ward was due to take over the driving and at the end of it I slumped into the seat beside him in a happy daze which insulated me from all sense of reality. I didn't care where I was going or what was going to happen to me. I just drifted away to the sound of the engine as we hammered our way up the Pan-Americana.

The rain hit us somewhere north of Huarmey, a solid wall of water lit by flashes of lightning. We were in desert country, the thick, cloying smell of fish oil from the port of Huarmey lingering in the car. There were oleanders and an untidy tumble of bamboo dwellings. The cloudburst switched itself off as abruptly as it had started, and the moon, peering momentarily out from an ink-black cloudscape, showed a coastal desert of pure white sand backed by low hills of chemical-green and violent reds, cactus everywhere and trucks parked on the dirt verge, most of them painted in livid crimson on white – *Optimista, Primero de Mayo, La Virgen.*

We rolled into Casma just after three in the morning, the stink of fish oil hanging over the port and an old adobe fort peering at us out of mist. The ugliness and poverty of the place is all I remember of it, and Ward saying, 'Ah'll drive as far as Chimbote, then ye take over.' He sounded half asleep and an approaching truck was flashing its lights. The green of sugar cane showed above dry yellow stalks as we crossed another river bed, the sound of rushing water drowning the engine. 'Light me a cigarette, will ye?' He fumbled a packet from the pocket of his anorak and I lit one for him with the dashboard lighter. 'We'll need to get gas somewhere.' He drew on the cigarette as though his life depended on it.

'Trujillo,' I said. 'Are we all right till then?'

'That's another hundred and twenty to thirty kilometres.' He was peering at the petrol gauge. 'Should just about make it.'

Chimbote was a dreadful place, litter everywhere and smelling to hell of oil. Miles of poverty with modern adobe dwellings either being built or falling into ruin. I took over and we lost our way where a blackened adobe town sprawled over a hill above a steelworks. Corrugated iron, cardboard, paper and sand were in constant motion as a wind came in gusts off the Pacific. We found a solitary gasolene pump and got the owner of it up from his couch of rags in a kennel-like shelter of tin and packing cases that rattled and moaned in the fitful wind. Fish oil chimneys and workers' shacks, fish boats lying at the quays, trucks and oil tankers as dirty as the town; only the central square showed a glimmer of respectability, with a hotel and flowers; but still the all-pervading stink, and there were pelicans scavenging in the blackened sand between the shacks.

Dawn broke as we reached Trujillo, the only decent-looking town we had seen since leaving Lima. There was a good hotel, too, but when I braked to a halt in front of it and suggested stopping there, Ward shook his head, muttering something about our still having two hundred miles to go and the coastal cordillera of the Andes to cross.

'What's the hurry?' I asked him.

'Iris,' he mumbled.

I was tired by then. We both were. 'Why the hell don't we stop here and get some sleep?' I think we were also suffering from jet-lag.

He sat up, rubbing his eyes and staring out at the mist that hung over the grey stone building. 'Drive on,' he said. 'We've got gas. No point in stoppin' now.'

But I'd had enough. 'I'm stopping here,' I told him, switching off the engine and opening my door.

I was just getting out when his left hand closed like a clamp on my arm. 'Shut that door!' He had swung his head round, glaring at me, his eyes hard as glass. 'What's the matter with ye? Ye haven't done a hundred miles yet. Now get movin'.'

'I'm staying here,' I repeated, my voice sounding obstinate, almost petulant. I don't know what it was, the mist, the way it hung, hot and heavy like a blanket, the weirdness and the exhaustion of the long night drive up the coast, but I suddenly realised I was scared. Scared of the country, scared of Ward. Most of all of Ward. I think it was then, with his powerful fingers digging like claws into my arm, that I realised how formidable the man was.

I turned away, no longer able to face the eyes that looked at me so coldly in the gleam of the dashboard light. He let go of my arm. 'All right, Pete.' His voice was quiet, almost relaxed. 'Off ye go.' He made a noise that was something like a laugh. 'Got yer passport?' And when I nodded, he said, 'Good! But ye'll need money. Quite a lot of money to get yerself back to England, if that's where ye're thinkin' of goin'.'

He let me think about that, a long, tense silence between us. He reached into his door pocket and pulled out the map. 'Pacasmayo,' he said quietly. 'No, San Pedro de Lloc. That's about another eighty miles. The Cajamarca road joins the Pan-Am a mile or so further on, at San José.' He looked at me, then nodded. 'Ah'll take over then.' He returned the map to the shelf in front of him and leaned back in his seat. 'Now fur fuck's sake drive on.'

Slowly I reached out to my open door and pulled it shut. I had no alternative. Maybe I could have had the hotel ring the British Embassy in Lima, but I was too exhausted, physically and mentally – particularly mentally – to face all the complications. We should have been over the pass by now and starting to look for the Hacienda Lucinda. Instead, we had only reached Trujillo and the mist had clamped down thicker than ever.

I glanced once more at the hotel, thinking of the comfort of sheets, the softness of a bed. Then I started the engine and drove back to where I had seen the Pan-Am Norte sign.

I suppose we were in that meteorological horror that is called an inversion, heat and humidity pressing down on us, numbing the brain and starting the sweat from every pore of the body. I didn't see the great walled city of Chanchán, only the mist and rain, the blur of the headlights and the windscreen wipers clicking endlessly across my vision. I had the strange feeling I was driving back in time, groping my way into a world of Inca and Chimú people, a world of great empires that built roads and temples and forts of mud on the coast and of cut stone in the Andes, stone that was dove-tailed to resist the trembling of its foundations when the earth quaked.

Finally the rain stopped. Miles of sugar cane, followed by miles of flat desert country, all seen through a damp haze so that nothing seemed real. Rice, too, in river outlets to the Pacific that were like oases of green in the waste of sand that fringed the coast. For a few minutes the sun glimmered through the mist to my right, a red ball just risen above the mountain. Then the mist closed in again thicker than ever.

Ward stirred and asked me the time in a voice heavy with sleep. No play-acting now, no switching of accents. He was still barely conscious and hadn't the energy to be anything but himself. I glanced at my watch, found I had forgotten to adjust it and read the time for him from the digital clock at the base of the instrument panel. It was 08.07. And then, more for the comfort of hearing my own voice than with any certainty, I said, 'We should get in to Cajamarca some time between ten and eleven.'

He gave a snort. 'We'll be lucky. It depends what conditions are like when we start climbin' up to the pass.' He reached for a cigarette and lit it. 'Want one?' He seemed to have forgotten I had tried to walk out on him fifty kilometres or so back.

I shook my head. The mist was now so dense it was more like a sea fog, the humidity very high and the sweat dripping from my forehead as I leaned forward, my eyes straining to see through the murk. I had the windscreen wipers on again and our speed was down to less than 30 k.p.h. Neither of us spoke after that,

Ward smoking in silence, and then, when he had finished his cigarette, he seemed to drift off to sleep again. Only the sound of the engine, and my eyes shifting from the mist and the road to take covert glances at his face; I knew no more about him now than when I first met him, except what he had told me on the flight down from Mexico. But that, unusual though it was, had been only the outline, the skeletal framework of the man. What his real nature was, what made him tick, I had no idea.

It is difficult to explain my state of mind. Fear, real fear, is something I had only experienced once in my life, and that, strangely enough, was not on the round-the-world race, but in my own little boat, and in my own waters off Blakeney. I had been following some seals in bright sunshine, stripped to the waist and taking photographs. I had no VHF then, only a transistor, and I was so preoccupied I missed the weather forecast.

Suddenly I was enveloped in one of those bitter North Sea murks and it was blowing quite strong from an easterly direction. I was off Cley at the time, so I lowered the main and ran for home. I never saw Kelling or Salthouse churches, or any sign of the coast at all, and I landed up sailing right over the ridge called Blakeney Overfalls, wind over tide, a filthy sea and virtually nil visibility.

That was the only time I had known real fear. Like most of my generation, I had never known a war, had never had fear rammed down my throat time and time again like the older generation. I was thinking particularly of my great-uncle George, the stories he had told, men pulled out of the sea half burned alive, the sudden explosions as another slow cargo vessel slid to the bottom, nobody stopping for survivors and the feeling of terror as the U-boats gradually picked the ships off until the one he was on was alone in the pattern.

He had been a gunner on three different merchantmen, first on Atlantic convoys, then on the Murmansk run. Twice he had been torpedoed, and each time he had finally been picked up; then on PQ17, when the destroyers left and they had been ordered to scatter . . .

He is dead now, but I've never forgotten his description of

how he had felt as the German bombers came in from Norway, picking the scattered merchant ships off, the sound of the bombs, and the cold, always the cold. Cold and fear. *It crippled your guts before you were even hit*. And all the time telling us about it in that slow, unemotional Norfolk voice of his.

Maybe my imagination was running out of control, but the weather, Gómez, the pass ahead, everything became distorted and magnified in my mind. Gómez in particular. *Ángel de Muerte*. By the time I was through San Pedro de Lloc and had reached the turn-off to Cajamarca at San José my mind had built the man up into some sort of a monster. I didn't believe what Rodriguez had said about the reason for that soubriquet. No man gets to be called the Angel of Death just because he tells his men to stand fast and fight. There had to be some more deadly reason than that.

Ward was still asleep when I turned right and headed eastwards towards the Andes, the mist a white vapour, the rice fields, the cacti, the occasional trees, all having a weirdness about them that matched my mood and added to my growing fear of what lay ahead, beyond the mountains I could not see. There were moments when the sun almost burst through the mist and I kept on driving, waiting and hoping for a first glimpse of the cordillera, my mind groping for some answer to the enigma of Iris Sunderby's behaviour. I think it was then I tried to work out her relationship to Gómez, but the complexity of it made it difficult to grasp. He was the son of a woman who had been a nightclub singer and briefly married to Juan Gómez, that was all my tired mind seemed able to grasp. That and the fact that Juan Gómez was her father, too. He had owned a big department store that had burned down, and he had then hanged himself.

So why had she gone rushing north from Lima to see this half-brother of hers? Why? Why? Why? Was he really coming with us as navigator? Winter in the Antarctic. Pack ice grinding. Bergs towering over us, thrashing through the pack, and that ghost ship seen by a frightened glaciologist . . .

'Look out!'

Ward's voice smashed into my consciousness and I slammed

on the brakes. A man had suddenly emerged out of the blinding iridescence of the mist, a vague figure standing in the middle of the road with his back towards us.

I only just stopped in time. Even then he didn't turn round, just remained there, motionless, staring straight ahead at the road, and there was a roaring that filled the inside of our vehicle with the solid, continuous sound of water on the move.

The road ran straight ahead of us until it disappeared in the mist, except that at the man's feet it was gone and there was a gap some fifty metres or so wide through which a brown torrent ran so high and in such furious waves that it almost lipped the broken macadam where the road had been swept away.

The man himself was small, with a brown and red poncho hung from his shoulders and a wide-brimmed hat of brown felt rammed tight on the lank black hair that covered his bullet head. He took no notice of us, just standing there, gazing at the swirling brown tide of water almost lapping his sandals as though lost in the wonder of such a happening.

'He is in the presence of his God,' Ward whispered to me. And when I asked him what he meant, he said irritably, 'Oh, don't be more stupid than you need be. He's lookin' at something too big for him to understand. And so am Ah,' he added, slapping me on the back as he got out of the car. '*Buenos días.*' He had to repeat his greeting twice before the Indian came out of his trance-like reverie and turned to face us.

'*Buenos días, señores.*' He had a broad, high-cheekboned face, a straight beak of a nose, and dark eyes that stared at us without expression. In fact, the whole face was expressionless, the only feature with mobility being the mouth, which was broad and thick, always seeming to be on the point of making a statement without actually saying anything. Having greeted us, he just stood there, gazing at us totally without curiosity or any sign of interest.

'What's the river?' I asked Ward.

'How the hell dae Ah know?'

'You had the map. I was driving, remember?'

I heard him question the Indian and I reached into the car for the map which he had left on his seat. The word 'Hecketypecky' passed between them, and when I eventually found it – the Rio Jequetepeque – I could hardly believe the spelling. 'Well, that's that,' I said. 'That mad flood of a torrent runs beside the road all the way up to the top of the cordillera.'

'Of course it does. That's why there's a pass.' He turned to the Indian again, asking questions in Spanish and getting nowhere. The man just stood and stared at him blankly.

'Why don't you phone Gómez if you want to find out whether Mrs Sunderby has arrived safely in Cajamarca?' He should have done that before instead of insisting on our groping our way up the Pan-Am Highway in darkness and bad visibility. 'Have you got his phone number?'

'No.'

'Then I suggest we go back to the hotel in Trujillo, get hold of his number and phone him from there.'

'Why?'

Why? I stared at him, wondering what was going on in that complex mind of his, what his real motive was in pushing north by car when we could have had a good night's sleep and flown up in daylight. The Indian had turned away, ignoring his questions and gazing across the swollen waters of that ridiculously named river. A wind had risen, the mist swirling and vague shapes of mountains looming through ragged gaps.

'If you're worried about Iris Sunderby surely the quickest way . . .' But he had swung round at the sound of a vehicle approaching. The ghost of what looked like a Land Rover took shape in the billowing curtain of the mist, emerging as a Japanese four-wheel drive rather like our own, with two people in it. A woman was driving and she parked beside our land-cruiser, nodding to us briefly as she stepped out onto the road and flung a series of questions at the Indian, half in Spanish and half in a more guttural tongue, which I took to be Quechua.

She was a startling sight in that setting, for she was immaculately dressed in riding clothes, her breeches almost white, boots black and so highly polished I could see the flood waters reflected in them. But it was the face that held me. It was a strange, very beautiful face, the mouth a broad gash of red, heavily made-up, the nose finely pointed with delicately arched nostrils, the eyebrows black like two thin pencil lines, and she wore a broad, flat-brimmed hat.

Her manner, the way she stood, everything about her suggested breeding. I couldn't help thinking she was like a racehorse, and when Ward started questioning her, she answered him with such haughty condescension, such arrogance, that his face went white and I swear he'd have play-acted the Gorbals slum kid and thrown a lot of four-letter words at her if he'd known how to do it in Spanish. She said the word Chepén several times, as though she was speaking to a particularly stupid servant, Tolambo, too, the Hacienda Tolambo, and at the same time she made a circling motion with her hand, ending up with her finger pointed at the road ahead and the jagged peaks of the cordillera disembodied in a ragged mist hole.

She said something to the man who was with her, a thickset, dark-featured fellow, who stood with his hands in the pockets of his anorak frowning at the flood water. He nodded, and then they were both moving back to their vehicle, the Indian drifting light-footed into the back. The woman paused before getting into the driving seat and said to Ward in near-perfect English, 'I think you're a bloody fool, but if you're determined to press on, I suggest you have a word with Alberto Fernandez when you get to Tolambo. He's the manager. He may be able to give you some idea what the road is like further on.' She suddenly smiled, a glimmer of warmth. 'Good luck, *señor*!'

'One more question,' Ward said quickly. 'There's a man named Gómez lives at Cajamarca. The Hacienda Lucinda.' Her face froze and he hesitated. 'D'ye know him?'

'I have heard speak of him.' She climbed in and slammed the door, the sound of the starter drowning Ward's next question. He watched as she backed and turned, then drove off, the grey curtain of the mist suddenly swallowing her up. 'Bugger the woman,' he grumbled. '*I have heard speak of him*.' He was mimicking her English. 'What did she mean by that, d'ye think?'

He took the wheel after that and drove at a furious speed back to San José, where he turned right on to the Pan-Am. 'Chepén,' he said. 'How far?'

'You're going on then?'

'Of course Ah'm goin' on. Ah've not come this far just to put my tail between my legs . . . How far is it?'

'I don't know,' I said, wondering what I could do to stop him.

'Well, look at the map, man.'

It seemed so pointless, the mist thicker than ever now. No sign of the cordillera, no glimmer of sun, and the Pacific invisible somewhere away to our left.

'Look at the map, damn ye!'

'All right.' My voice was taut with anger as I pulled it out of the shelf in front of me and opened it on my knees. Chepén. We were driving north and I saw it at once. 'It's the next town up the Highway.'

'How far?'

I told him I was trying to work it out. 'About thirty kilometres I would guess.' And I added, 'There's a minor road runs up over the cordillera via San Miguel and Llata to Hualgayoc where you can turn south to Cajamarca. It's a good deal longer, but there's no river marked, and it might be sensible –'

'No, we'll follow the woman's instructions. She lives here. She knows the country.'

He drove in silence after that and I fell asleep until the roughness of the road made me open my eyes. We were bumping our way between pale yellow walls of sugar cane. 'Where are we?' I mumbled.

'Tolambo,' he said. 'Sorry to spoil yer beauty sleep.'

My eyes were heavy-lidded with fatigue, and despite the jolting, I must have drifted off again, for suddenly we were stopped, everything quiet, only the sound of voices – Ward talking to a tall, dark man wearing dungarees and a sombrero. There was a narrow-gauge rail track stretching away through acres of cut cane, and in the distance a little tank engine panting wisps of smoke as a gang of men loaded its trailer wagons. They were talking in Spanish and I was only half awake. '*Adiós.*'

'*Adiós, señor.*'

The sun was burning up the mist as we drove on. 'Did he tell you what the road was like over the pass?'

Ward's reply was lost in the sound of the engine, and when I opened my eyes again we were bumping along the bank of what looked like an old Inca canal. The sun was blazing hot, the skin of my bare arm beginning to burn. Away to the left, black menacing clouds of cu-nim were piled up over mountains dimly seen through a haze of humidity. 'When do we hit the road again?'

'Soon.' Ward peered at the control panel. 'Another kilometre to go, according to the foreman back at Tolambo.' He was holding the bucking steering wheel with his artificial hand while he felt under the dashboard for his cigarettes.

'What about the pass?'

'He thought it might be a bit *peligroso*. Nobody has been through fur twenty-four hours and the telephone to Chilete, the last village before the summit, is out of action. So's the railway, of course.'

'And Cajamarca?'

'He talked to Cajamarca yesterday.'

Everything about us, the rocks, the yellow earth, the patches of vivid green in the valley, sparkled with moisture, the old irrigation canal half-full of stagnant brown water. Thunder rolled through the mountains, jagged forks of lightning splitting the black folds of the cu-nim. 'I think we should turn back.'

He didn't answer, lighting his cigarette one-handed, and I didn't press him. I was too tired, only vaguely conscious that we had come off the canal bank and were angling down across a steep slope of stony ground to the rice-green flatness of the valley floor.

Finally we climbed a bank and were on the road again, the smoothness of it lulling me into such a deep sleep that I never saw the barrier at the railway crossing, did not even hear them telling Ward the Jequetepeque had broken its banks a little further on. It was the violent jolting of our wheels on the sleepers that finally woke me to the realisation that Ward had switched

126

from the road to the railway line itself and was bumping his way along the track towards the gaping mouth of a tunnel.

I sat up then, suddenly wide awake. 'What the hell?'

'River's cut the road again. They say we'll see the break when we cross the bridge.'

'The bridge?'

'Aye. It's just beyond the tunnel. A girder bridge.'

'Anybody else taken this route today?'

'No.'

I was staring at him, at the set, aquiline face, the great beak of a nose and the hard line of the jaw, his features in silhouette. 'You're mad,' I said.

He nodded, smiling. 'Maybe, but right now Ah think the wind is southerly.'

'What's that supposed to mean?' The tunnel entrance had grown big, the stone arch of it rearing up ahead of us like the open jaws of some petrified monster.

'*Hamlet*, Ah think – *Ah am mad north-north-west, but when the wind is southerly* . . . Most times with me ye'll find the wind is southerly.'

A curtain of dripping water spat at the bonnet as the darkness of the tunnel engulfed us, the sound of the engine louder now and a sense of finality as the rock walls closed about us. It was like being in the adit of a mine, and I was driving into the bowels of the earth with a man who seemed hell bent on risking our lives for no apparent reason. I thought of the Weddell Sea, the ice and the ghost of that *Flying Dutchman*, visualising the friction that could develop in the close confines of a yacht. My God! I thought, the chances of coming out of that alive with this madman as the owner and driving force . . . It was crazy. Absolutely crazy.

The dark of the tunnel hammered the engine noise back at us, water drumming on the roof above my head. Ward switched on the headlights, glancing at me quickly, a tight little smile. 'Ye got to take a positive attitude. Ah enjoy this sort of thin'. Ah like excitement, the unexpected, shovin' against the closed door of the unknown.' He nodded ahead of us to where the tunnel showed an arched embrasure of light. 'Darkness is only fur ever when ye're dead.' He dipped the headlights and the far end of the tunnel seemed to leap towards us, bouncing up and down to the thump of our tyres on the sleepers.

Suddenly we were into daylight and right ahead of us the waters of the Jequetepeque ran brown and white, the river's level close under the rails of the girder bridge as it flowed, deep and very fast, through the gorge. The sound of our wheels changed to a hollow banging of wooden boards as we drove across. But then the stupid bastard stopped right in the middle of the bridge. 'What's the matter?'

'Nothing.' He switched the engine off. 'Just admirin' the view.' He was pulling the sun roof open and thrusting himself to his feet. The sound of the river increased to a roar. There was wind, too, funnelling through the gorge, whining through the girders and causing the whole structure to tremble. The sun came and went, thunder clouds growling and swirling up the valley.

I didn't like it. Twice the road had been cut and we hadn't even started the climb up to the pass. I could hear boulders grinding on the river bed and the grumble of thunder was like the sound of distant gunfire.

Ward slipped down into the driving seat again and slammed the roof shut. 'You're turning back, are you?'

'Of course not.' And then, as he started the engine again, he turned to me and said, 'If the sight of a storm in the Andes scares ye, what's yer reaction goin' to be when we're headed into the pack with a Southern Ocean gale up our backsides?' He stared at me very hard for a moment. 'Think about it, laddie.' This with a grin on a lighter note. 'There's no room fur cold feet on the sort of expedition we're embarkin' on.' He reached for the gear lever and we began to move slowly off the bridge.

I sat back, wide awake now and cursing the man for goading me so unpleasantly. But at least I had the sense to keep my mouth shut, and shortly afterwards we were able to leave the railway and get back on to the road. The surface was dirt, but despite all the water the going was good. It looked as though a grader had been over it just before the Amazonian rains had spilled over the Andes.

'Last night two Indians in a pick-up came down from Chilete.'

I didn't say anything, though the way he had said it made it clear he expected some comment.

'They went as far as the railway crossin' on the other side of the tunnel, talked to the man on duty at the halt there, then turned back. That was before the road was cut. They said things were bad up at Chilete with several houses already fallen into the river.' He looked at me, obviously annoyed by my silence. 'Well, say somethin', can't ye? Don't just sit there, sulkin'.'

'I'm tired,' I said. 'And I just don't see the point of pressing on through that muck.' I nodded towards the black murk of cloud that blocked off the valley and all but the lower slopes of the mountains. 'Apart from the storm, we don't know what the road is like, how bad it will be when we reach the pass.'

'It's not the road that worries me. It's those two men.' We were climbing now, the lower slopes of the mountains patched with the terraced green of small rice fields. We passed through Tembladera, a scattering of houses clinging to the mountain side. 'They knew about us, the type of vehicle we were drivin', and they instructed the keeper of that crossin' to tell us the road over the pass was open, that it was okay.'

'Why?' The question was wrung out of me by the absurdity of it. 'Why should they do that? How did they know about us?'

'Telephone. From our friend in Lima. They were both of them from Chimbote.'

That was the filthy coastal town smelling of fish oil where I'd taken over the driving. 'All the more reason why we should turn back.'

He snorted. 'All the more reason why we should go on.' And he added, 'Ah'd like to have a wee chat with those two, find out a bit more about them. Reach into the back, will ye, and open up that parcel of books. There's a knife in the pocket of my anorak.'

It was one of those all-purpose knives with a flick blade sharp as a razor. I slit along the seam of the cardboard wrapper where it had been taped over. Inside were three fat volumes of Mark Twain tied together with gold tape and a card with *Complemento de Librerío Universal* on which had been written in green ink *primera edición*. 'How ever did these get to Peru?'

He glanced at me sideways, smiling. 'Ah told ye it was useful when travelling to enter antiquarian as one's occupation.'

'First editions of Mark Twain! They must be worth quite a bit – in America.' But what was he going to do with them in this economically bankrupt country?

'Cut the gold tape and pull them apart. They're not quite what they seem.'

I didn't need to pull them apart. As soon as I had cut the tape the bottom volume dropped into my lap. The centre of it was a plastic mould in which the metal of an automatic gleamed snugly. The upper volume I had to prise loose from the middle one. It contained ammunition in three spare magazines, also a very light plastic armpit holster. Ward glanced in the rear-view mirror, then all round, finally pulling up in the middle of the road. 'Ye'll have to give me a hand.' He opened his door and got out, leaving the engine running.

I didn't move. I just sat there, my brain numb.

He was taking off his anorak. 'Well, come on, man. It's damp out here.' He was in his shirt sleeves staring through the side window at me. 'Come on, damn ye. Move it!'

I looked at him, feeling I had reached the end of the road. 'If you want to play cops and robbers,' I said, choosing my words carefully, 'you'll have to do it without me.'

He reached in and wrenched the little bundle of plastic bands out of my hands, and I sat there, silent, watching as he fumbled the bands into position with the little cup to hold the weapon under his right armpit. It took him a little while, but he got it fixed in the end, then held out his dummy hand for the gun.

I should have told him to go to hell. I should have flung the damned thing out of his open door so that it would bounce down the mountainside up which the road was climbing. Instead, I handed it over to him. I don't know why. Thunder rumbled high

130

above us, the clouds reaching down towards us, wisps of mist sweeping down the valley.

He had put his anorak on again, no sign of the gun, no bulge as he climbed in and we started on up the mountain road, windscreen wipers slashing back and forth. 'Getting quite chill out there.'

I didn't say anything.

'How far up d'ye reckon we are, a thousand feet?'

He was trying to ease my mind, to make me feel it was all right and quite normal for a man to have a gun in an armpit holster in Peru. '*Just in case.*' I could have said it for him. In case of what? 'Are you going to use it?' The words seemed dragged out of me, my voice subdued.

A pause, then very gently, 'Only if Ah have to.'

'And what constitutes *have to*?'

'Ah'll know when the time comes. Let's leave it at that, shall we?'

He drove in silence then and I closed my eyes, pretending I was asleep, my head nodding, and all the time my mind reaching forward to the future, trying to visualise what it would be like on the boat. That he'd use the gun if he had to I was quite certain. But why did he feel the need of a gun? What gave him the right to have it? And the way it was delivered to him, so neat, so innocent-seeming a package. Somebody had acquired it. On his instructions? Somebody had gone to considerable trouble and expense to acquire the books and have them hollowed out, then delivered to the car hire people just before our plane arrived. It all added up to an organisation, but what organisation? Who did they represent – a government, the Mafia, some drug ring? Cocaine? Was he mixed up in cocaine smuggling?

We never saw Chilete until suddenly we were in among the grey ghosts of houses, the road rutted now and full of mud. The sound of water, when Ward rolled down his window, was a solid roar that overlaid everything.

He pulled up and we could look down through the grey cloud-mist to the centre of the village where an old stone bridge and several houses were crumbling into the river. There was a little group of men gathered outside what looked like a café, Indians some of them, their faces dark and sombre as they stood arguing over the ruins of their village. 'Maybe they'll know if there's been any traffic over the road.' Ward got out and strode down the mud-sodden road to join them. I stayed by the vehicle, wondering what to do. But I knew the answer to that. There wasn't anything I could do and, knowing that, I was conscious of my own inadquacy, weighed down by a sense of helplessness.

Perhaps it was the village. There was something about Chilete and the cloud-mist drizzle of that dreadful morning that was utterly depressing. The last point of habitation before the pass and every dwelling a-gleam with water as though the whole place was deluge-cursed and waiting to fall into the river. I felt not only miserable, but strangely scared, as though the pass above me was in itself a terrifying manifestation of dark imaginings, like the entrance gate to the place where the dead wait in limbo.

'Two of them came in yesterday evenin'.' Ward was back, climbing into the driving seat. 'The word is that five or six miles further on we'll find the new road washed out. Apparently it's entirely blocked with mud and rocks.' He started the engine. 'But the old road is still passable. They've put stone markers at the intersection.'

'Who were they? The same two Indians who talked to the railway crossing keeper?'

'I guess so. The laddies back there had never seen them before. They thought they were probably road maintenance men from the Cajamarca region.'

The tumbled ruin that was Chilete disappeared almost immediately, swallowed up by the mist, as we drove out along the broad, freshly graded road, the walls of a valley gorge closing in. 'How far to the pass?' I asked him, but he didn't answer, peering into the grey void as the road doubled back on itself, climbing steeply. There were hairpin bends and soon we were lipping the edge of a two-thousand-foot drop, the river below occasionally glimpsed through ragged wind-torn holes in the cloud.

It was like that all the way to the intersection where the new road swung away to the right, the way blocked by stones placed in a line across it. They were not large stones, merely a warning. The old road ran straight on along the gorge edge. As far as surface was concerned, and even width, there was little to choose between them. Ward checked, a momentary lift of his foot on the accelerator, then he was powering straight on. 'Shorter this way,' he said. 'That's what they told me, anyway.'

'But less convenient,' I muttered. 'How long before we get back to the proper road?' More frequent glimpses now, through swirling cloud, of the river far below. Half a dozen parrots cut a brilliant green streak across our bonnet before disappearing into the looming darkness ahead. Lightning flashed, followed almost instantaneously by the sharp crack of thunder. 'What do we do if this road is blocked?'

He didn't answer and shortly afterwards he slowed for a right-hand bend, his body bent forward, the dummy hand clamped tight on the steering wheel. He took it slowly in four-wheel drive, the road much narrower here, the outer edge of it crumbling away. Round the bend it broadened out again with just room for two vehicles to pass, but ahead was the deep V of a side gorge with water pouring down it, spilling a flood across the road. He braked then, bringing the vehicle to a stop and sitting there, the engine ticking over. He wiped his face with one end of the brightly coloured sweat rag he wore round his neck, staring at the problem ahead. 'Know what Ah'd like right now? Ah'd like a nice cool pint of that Southwold brew.'

'Adnams?'

'Aye. Yer part of the world and one of the best bitters –' His words were cut short by a clap of thunder very close.

But it wasn't thunder. It was something else, more like a cannon, and before the echo of it had died away, there was a rumbling sound, growing to a roar. In the same instant Ward had revved the engine and rammed the gear lever home. The vehicle shot forward, and as it did so the first rocks from above came hurtling down onto the track just behind us.

Leaning forward I had a view of it in the side mirror, the bend we had just rounded obliterated by a great mass of avalanching rock and mud that went spilling down over the edge to disappear into the cloud vapour below. 'Christ!' My voice was barely audible above the noise of the slide and the sound of our engine. My eyes were on the far side of the valley where the track was clear and unbroken to the next turn above the main gorge. If we could make it through the torrent to the bend ahead . . . 'What is it?'

Ward had jammed on the brakes. 'Ye take her. See ye on the other side of the bend, if ye make it.' He was out in a flash, scrabbling for a foothold on the steep side of the track. Above him was a path of sorts trailing along the mountainside.

'What is it?' I asked him again, shouting to make myself heard above the grumble of thunder and the sound of water. 'Where are you going?'

His only answer was a wave of the arm, signalling me to drive on. He was climbing like a goat, moving with extraordinary speed. And then I lost him among the boulders and small trees that marked the course of the torrent.

By then the noise of the avalanche had died away, only the echoes of it reverberating across the valley, and when I shifted into the driving seat and looked back, the road behind us had ceased to exist. Where the bend had been there was now nothing but a piled-up, slithering mass of wet glistening rubble. I looked up the line of the torrent. No sign of Ward. He had disappeared entirely, leaving me to wonder what the hell he was playing at. I was on my own now, faced with that half-obliterated turn at the V-point of the side gorge where water pouring over the track was eating away at the surface.

There had been a bridge there once, or perhaps a culvert. I could just make out part of the stonework, though most of it was under water. I checked the four-wheel drive lever, eased off the brake and started forward. No good putting it off. At any moment the whole track might go.

When I reached the turn I found half of it gone already. The roar of the water coming down the gully drummed at my ears as I inched the Toyota into the bend. It was virtually a hundred-and-eighty-degree turn and very sharp, the culvert blocked with stone and the remains of a small tree, so that the full volume of the water coming down the gully was swirling across the track to disappear over the edge, thundering down into the main gorge of the Jequetepeque. There was only just room to scrape through between the roots of the tree and the edge.

I inched forward. Did I take it slow or fast? How deep was the water? Was it deep enough to sweep the vehicle over the edge? The nearer I got to it, the deeper it looked. And what was the track like underneath? Would it hold up for the half-minute or so it would take me to drive across? The devil of it was the vehicle was a left-hand drive, so that I was on the side that would go over the edge first.

I hesitated, and as I did so a big stone that marked the outer edge of the track began to move. I didn't wait. I let in the clutch and gripped the wheel, taking it gently, not using too much power and just willing the tyres to maintain a grip on the rotten surface below the water.

I was about half-way across when I felt the rear begin to swing sideways under the weight of the torrent. I gunned the engine then, slipping the clutch slightly, clawing for a hold. That way I had the power ready to hand and as the front wheels began to grip a solid surface and the snout of the Toyota reared up, I banged the clutch in with my foot hard down. Something clanged by the back axle, a rock presumably, and then, with the back still slithering sideways and the rear left wheel beginning to race as it fell off into space, the vehicle gave a sort of shudder and we were out, clear of the water and on a hard surface again.

That was when I saw it, right in front of me, a large lump of rock bang in the middle of the track. I stopped, the roar of the torrent drumming in my ears. The rear of the Toyota was only just clear of the water as I jumped out, checking to see if it would be possible using the low gear to push the rock over the edge. The inner side of the track was almost sheer at this point, brown broken rock glistening with water, and I could see at a glance where the rock had come from, a gaping hole oozing mud as though a giant molar had been extracted.

Lightning forked across the black belly of the clouds, and the rock that had moved as I was negotiating the bend had disappeared into the gorge below, the torrent running smooth as it lipped the broken edge of the old roadway. Still no sign of Ward, the cloud-mist hanging grey over the mountainside above. I felt very alone at that moment, stuck there on that track somewhere in the Andes, my body chill with sweat and my hands still trembling with the nervous tension of getting safely through the rutted mud of the bend.

I was just getting back into the driving seat when there was a shout and a figure emerged from the gully about fifty metres above me. It wasn't Ward. This was a much slighter man with a broad-brimmed hat and a poncho over his shoulders. He was moving fast down the side of the gully, Ward appearing suddenly behind him. 'Hold him!' The shout echoed in the rocks and at the same moment the man saw me. He checked, but only momentarily, then he had jumped down onto the track a knife in his hand.

There was only one thing for me to do and I dodged behind the Toyota. He went past me, running. But then he stopped. Ward was angling across the slope above to cut him off. I reached into the door pocket and pulled out the heavy wheel nut spanner. By then Ward was coming down onto the track, his false arm and dummy hand hanging limp at his side.

I think it was the realisation of his disability that decided the man to go for him first. He was already advancing up the track as Ward slithered down onto the flat surface of it. The knife flashed, a steely glitter as lightning struck again across the far side of the gorge, the crackle of it hitting the rocks and followed almost instantaneously. by a single shattering crash of thunder.

He went for Ward in a crouching run, and Ward just stood there, as though transfixed. 'Get out of his way,' I yelled and started forward.

But Ward didn't move and I was still several yards away when the two of them met. I saw the knife flash, a cold gleam as the man swung his arm back to strike at Ward's belly. Then, as the knife slammed forward, driving upwards for the heart, Ward's right arm extension came up, the glove-covered steel fingers of his hand open like claws. They closed on the knife blade, twisted it out of the man's hand, and then he was using the whole false arm as a metal club slamming down on the upraised arms, jabbing for the face, forcing the man back step by step until the edge of the track was only one more step away.

I think I called a warning, but Ward ignored it. I saw the man give a terrified glance over his shoulder, then that metal flail slammed into the side of his head. He was off-balance, his defences down as Ward drew back his right arm and slammed that gloved hand straight into the sallow face.

I can still see the blood starting from the man's nose, the way his arms reached out as his feet rocked back on to nothing, and still hear the dreadful high-pitched rabbit cry as his body disappeared over the edge. For all of a minute, it seemed, we could hear the sound of his body falling, the rattle of the stones it dislodged.

But when I looked over the edge there was no sign of him, or of the river – only the mist swirling.

I turned to Ward. 'You killed him.' My voice sounded strange in my ears. 'You did it deliberately.'

His only answer was to pick up the knife and hand it to me. Then he was climbing back up the bank he had slithered down and I watched as he walked in a leisurely fashion across the slope of the mountain to the gully. He seemed totally relaxed, and I felt the prickle of my fear. I had never seen a man deliberately killed before and I was more scared even than I had been before.

When he came back he was carrying something in his left hand. 'Ye seen one of these before?' He dumped it on the bonnet of the Toyota.

'Only in films.' It was one of those plungers that generate the electric spark for setting off blasting charges. 'Where did you find it?'

'Up there, where Ah expected.' He nodded to the mountainside beyond the gully and walked over to the rock that was blocking the road. 'Ye didn't think that fall behind us was an accident, did ye? But he then had to get across the gully and connect up the wires to brin' this lot down on top of us.' He waved his dummy hand towards the sheer rock above us.

'You didn't have to kill him,' I said.

'No?' He looked up at me, a quizzical lift of his eyebrows. 'Are ye happy with the thought of being buried alive under tons of rock?' He straightened up and moved to the driving seat. 'Well if ye are, Ah'm not. With luck they'll never know what happened to him. And that may worry them.'

'Who?'

But he had started the engine and he didn't hear me as he inched the vehicle forward in low gear. The wheels churned, the engine labouring, and slowly the rock that was blocking our way shifted. He forced it close enough to the edge to allow the Toyota to creep past on the inside. I got in, and as he drove on I was watching his face, fascinated. I had never been with a killer before.

Round the bend ahead the road ran fairly straight, a narrow ledge cut out of the mountainside. The clouds hung like a grey-black roof over the valley. He slowed at a view point, leaning out and examining the wet stone surface. 'There were tae of them,' he said as he drove on. 'Looks like his mate went off with the car. Ah couldn't see the little bugger clearly enough to be sure, but Ah think he was Indian. The guy who did the blastin' was a mestizo.'

'Why?' That's what I didn't understand. Why should we have been followed on our arrival in Peru? And now this crude attempt to kill us. The strong features, the massive head – the man radiated an extraordinary sense of inner strength.

'Why?' I asked again, and he said, 'That's what we're goin' to find out.'

'We?'

He looked at me, smiling. 'We,' he said. He drove in silence after that, leaving me alone with my chaotic thoughts, and at the end of the long straight slash across the side of the cloud-hidden mountain, we picked up the new road again, swinging right, away from the Jequetepeque. We were in cloud then, feeling our way again through a grey void. We had almost half an hour of this, then brown, wet walls of rock closed us in, the sound of the engine grinding upwards reverberating in a deep cut, the foglights accentuating the macabre theatricality of our struggle up the path through which Pizarro and his four hundred armoured hidalgoes had climbed to destroy the Inca Empire half a millennium ago.

Ward must have been thinking along the same lines, for as the road flattened out and the mist began to glimmer with a strange brightness, he said something about the Promised Land. The road dipped and we picked up speed.

'That's it,' he said with grim satisfaction. 'We made it,' and he slapped the gloved hand twice against the steering wheel. 'There was a moment, Ah'll admit . . . Look!' The thinning veil of cloud eddied in a gust of wind, and suddenly we were below it, looking down on to the flat roofs of a town spread out in a broad valley of rain-washed green. 'Cajamarca.'

'And the Hacienda Lucinda. Do you know where it is?'

'Past the Baños del Inca, out by a hill that's honeycombed with grave apertures. We'll have to ask.'

We seemed a million miles from the Weddell Sea and that ice-encrusted vessel, but I had a feeling now that this was all a part of the voyage to come. 'What are you going to say to Gómez?'

He smiled and shook his head. 'Nothin'. Ah think he'll dae the talkin'.'

'And Iris Sunderby?'

'We'll see.'

THREE

When you have travelled half across the world, with the background of the man you are going to meet gradually being filled in for you, a picture of him inevitably forms in the mind. There was the suspicion, too, that it was he who had arranged for us to be followed on our arrival in Lima, may even have planned our death by that gully on the old road up to the pass.

Twice I asked Ward about this, the first time just after we had come out of the cloud on the eastern slope of the pass and had caught our first glimpse of Cajamarca far away in the valley below, and then again when we stopped at the *Baños del Inca* to ask our way, the hot springs steaming beside the public baths. Each time he had given a little shrug, as though to say, 'We'll see', and left it at that.

But even if he had given me a direct answer, I don't know that I would have believed him. He had such a talent for self-dramatisation that I wouldn't have put it past him, on finding that plunger, to have invented the whole thing – except that I had watched in horror as he deliberately forced the wretched mestizo over the edge, thrusting at his face with that dummy hand until he had disappeared into the gorge below. I couldn't make up my mind about him, regarding him at times as some grotesque theatrical maniac, at other times as no more than a pleasant, if somewhat mysterious, travelling companion.

There was no such dichotomy in my mind when picturing Gómez. By the time we were enquiring for the Hacienda Lucinda he was growing in my mind as something wholly evil, as deformed and monstrous as Victor Hugo's hunchback of Notre Dame without the saving grace of simplicity. This view of him had been built up gradually, partly as a result of that interview with Rodriguez back in Mexico City, and partly from the bits and pieces of information Ward had let fall.

There were some Indians camped by a stream in a meadow of coarse grass below the sepulchre hill with its rows of necropolistic apertures. The whole hill had the appearance almost of a skull, the apertures like teeth exposed in a grin and black with decay. Ward got out and walked across to the Indians. They had been drinking chica and swayed as they stood up. A lorry rolled past us along the road, its crumbling body bright with painted pictures plastered over with dust. And behind it were two Indians riding a mule, brown ponchos draped over their shoulders, straw hats jammed on their heads and held with leather thongs under the chin.

'Straight on,' Ward said as he got back into the driving seat. 'Just over a kilometre there's a track to the left with an arched entrance gate.'

We were almost there and I wondered how he would behave when he was face-to-face with Gómez, what he would say. And Iris Sunderby, was she really with him in the Hacienda Lucinda?

We reached the gateway and turned in under the adobe arch with the name Hda LUCINDA plaster-embossed in large letters. A long driveway, with a lake on one side and flat, flowered meadows on the other, the dark shapes of cattle grazing. 'He's part Sicilian, part Irish,' Ward reminded me. 'Just remember that. And part God knows what else,' he muttered.

His words emphasised the racial element in the picture my imagination had formed of him. Angel of Death. The Disappeareds. A killer who was the son of an Argentinian playboy and a nightclub singer from somewhere near Catania. Christ! What sort of monster would he prove to be?

A few minutes and I was shaking his hand, completely dumbfounded by the physical perfection of the man, his elegance, his charm. There was a virility about him that showed in his every movement. He was like a Greek god, except that his hair was black and the nose had a slight curve to it that gave his broad, open features a somewhat predatory look.

He met us in the hacienda courtyard dressed in white shirt,

white jodhpurs and black riding boots. He had a riding crop in one hand and a clipboard in the other. He didn't ask us our names. He just stood there, a moment of shocked surprise as we got out of the Toyota. 'Yes?' He seemed at a loss for words, and Ward made no attempt to help him. Then he was smiling, coming towards us with the charm turned on. 'What can I do for you?' He spoke in English with only the trace of an accent.

'You are Mario Ángel Gómez?' Ward's voice was flat as though he were carrying out an official enquiry.

'Connor-Gómez. Yes. What do you want?'

'Señora Sunderby.'

There was a momentary hesitation, so that I half expected him to say she wasn't there. 'You wish to see her?'

'No. Ah've come to collect her.'

'You have come to collect her?' He was staring at Ward, his eyes gone hard, almost black in the sunlight. 'Why?' The broad, open face was no longer smiling. 'Who are you?'

'Ah think ye know that already. Ye know who we are, when we arrived in Lima, also that we left the capital drivin' north up the Pan-Americana.'

'You have come up from the coast then? How was the road?'

Ward told him about the two diversions below Chilete and the need to switch to the old road that ran along the lip of the gorge. He said nothing about the road being blocked behind us, or the man he had flushed out of the mist-shrouded mountainside and forced over the edge into the gorge below.

'Your name is Ward. Correct?'

'Iain Ward.' He nodded.

'And you are here about the boat, is it? The boat for this expedition. Are you the man who put up the money to buy it?'

'Ye know damn well Ah am.'

Nobody said anything for a moment, the two of them standing there, summing each other up. The silence was broken by the clip-clop of hooves as a horse was led from its stable at the far side of the courtyard by an Indian. 'And your name?' Gómez had turned to me, and when I told him, he nodded. 'You're the wood expert, right? So now we have all the crew of the boat gathered

142

here, except for the Norwegian, and I believe there is an Australian expected. Also we need a cook.'

'Ye have agreed then?'

'Agreed?'

'To act as navigator.'

Gómez hesitated. 'Per'aps.'

'So ye know the exact location of this vessel her husband saw. And ye have seen it yerself, from the air?'

He didn't answer that. Instead he said, 'How did you know where to find me?'

'Look, laddie, Ah'm askin' the questions. Just ye tell me now, have ye seen that old wooden ship down there in the ice, or no'?'

'And I asked you a question, Mr Ward.' It was said with studied politeness. 'How did you know where to find me?'

There was a moment of silence, the two of them facing up to each other, a clash of wills. To my surprise it was Ward who backed off. 'Rodriguez,' he said.

'Ah yes.' Gómez hesitated. 'You have met him, of course.'

'Aye. In Mexico City. Ah'm sure he will have told ye that on the phone.'

'And you have read his book, I suppose?'

'Of course.'

Silence again. Horse and Indian had now stopped close behind Gómez.

'There are many inaccuracies.' He shrugged. 'But what can you expect from a man like Rodriguez. It is sad to have to make a living by grubbing around in the dirt of a national calamity.' He gave another shrug. 'It is all –' he hesitated – 'what I think you call water under the bridge, eh? It is a long time ago and what matters now is the future. Always one must look to the future.'

'Aye. So let us talk about that old ship.' Ward glanced at the house, a low, one-storey building sprawled across the end of the rectangular courtyard. 'Can we go in?' He nodded towards the open door. 'We could dae with a clean-up. It's been a long drive. A little tiresome at times, too.'

'There was no need for you to come.' Gómez looked at his wristwatch, which was of heavy gold. The watch, and a gold signet ring on his little finger, glinted in the sun. 'This is the time I normally ride round the hacienda. We produce alfalfa, rice, cattle, and with mainly Indian labour it is necessary to oversee everything.'

Ward waited, saying nothing, and in the end Gómez said, 'Very well, come into the house.' The tone of his voice was distinctly unwelcoming. 'But when you have had a wash I must ask you to leave.'

'No harm in yer askin', laddie.'

They stared at each other, and I wondered why Ward had thickened his native Glaswegian accent.

'The normal courtesy would have been to phone ahead for an appointment.'

Ward nodded. 'O' course. Then ye could have prepared yersel'.' And he added, 'Now we are here, perhaps ye will send someone to inform Señora Sunderby.'

'No.' The frostiness of his tone had hardened. 'She is my guest here. And at the moment she is resting.' There was a pause, and then he said, 'I have no doubt she will be joining you at Punta Arenas, as arranged – when she is ready. *Alors*.' He gestured towards the front entrance to the house. 'The cloakroom is the first door on the right.' And he added, as he led the way, 'You both look as though you could do with some sleep, so while you are refreshing yourselves I will telephone to a hotel in Cajamarca where I know the owner will look after you very well.'

Ward thanked him, but said it would not be necessary. 'As soon as Ah've talked wi' Iris Sunderby we'll be on our way.' He was moving towards the house then, but suddenly he checked. 'Och, Ah almost forgot. Ah've a wee present fur ye.' And he turned back to the Toyota, reaching in to the rear seat and coming out with the blasting plunger. He held it out to Gómez. 'Well, take it, man. It's yers.'

For a second, it seemed, Gómez's eyes changed, a glimmer of some wild emotion mirrored in his features. But it was so fleeting I couldn't be sure. 'Not mine,' he said, staring hard at Ward.

'No, no, o' course not. A present. Ah told ye.' There was a long, awkward silence. Finally Ward said, so quietly I hardly heard him,

'Ah think we understan' each other now.' He chuckled softly to himself. 'Call it a souvenir, shall we?' He thrust it into the man's hands and strode past him, making for the open doorway set in the centre of the long white portico that ran the length of the house.

Gómez said something to the Indian, then hurried after him. A moment later the two of them had disappeared into the house, leaving me standing there in the sunshine, feeling suddenly weak at the knees. God! I was tired.

The horse was led back to its stable and I walked to the far end of the house, where there was a lawn of coarse-bladed grass, brown with the heat, some exotic-looking flowers in a stony border, and cushioned garden chairs standing bright in the dappled shade of what looked like a cherry tree. I adjusted one of them to the reclining position, lay back in it and closed my eyes.

I must have fallen asleep, for I dreamed that a girl was kissing me open-mouthed, the touch of her tongue light as a butterfly, and her hand caressing, and I woke suddenly to find I was thoroughly roused. There was a figure sitting in the chair beside me. Her face was in shadow against a shaft of sunlight, framed by hair that gleamed a brilliant black.

I sat up and she withdrew her hand.

It was Iris Sunderby. I could see her now that my eyes were in the shadow of a branch. Her lips were parted and her breath was coming in quick gasps as though she had been running, the breasts, looking naked under the light silk wrap, rising and falling. But it was her eyes that startled me. They were wide and very intent, the pupils dilated, and an expression of most extraordinary expectancy on her face. She wasn't looking at me. She was staring straight past me, sitting very still, as though waiting for somebody to come out of the house.

'What is it?' I asked.

But she didn't seem to hear me. I repeated the question, louder this time. There was still no response, no change of expression. It was as though she were in some sort of a trance, a pallid undertone to the sun-dark skin, the nostrils of that straight nose slightly flared; even the jaw seemed to have lost some of its determined thrust. 'Are you all right?' I asked.

145

'Yes.' She said it in a long, sighing breath, still staring, almost avidly, at the side of the house.

I turned then, for I could hear voices. There were open sliding glass windows at the side of the house and in the dim interior I could just make out two figures standing. Ward's voice was saying something about long distance aircraft, Gómez answering him more audibly, 'It's not possible. Not now.' They had moved towards the windows. 'Things are not the same. I am no longer a serving officer in the *Fuerza Aérea*. Why don't you get your people . . .'

I could see them quite clearly now. They were not looking at us. They were facing each other, Ward saying, 'We have nothin' that could make it there and back.'

'The Hercules. You have the Hercules at your Mount Pleasant base on the Malvinas.' And when Ward said it hadn't the range, Gómez replied sharply, 'But I think it has. It flies regularly to South Georgia and back for a mail drop to your garrison there. That is eighteen hundred miles the round flight. It is slightly less than that from the Malvinas to the region of the Weddell Sea where this ship is locked in the ice. So no problem. That cargo plane of yours has a range of three thousand, six hundred sea miles. That is with minimum payload.'

'They would need a bigger margin than that to mount a search down there at the bottom of the world. It's not exactly a Mediterranean climate.'

'Then why not refuel in the air? That is how I arrange it.'

'Aye.' There was silence then and I thought I saw him shake his head. 'No, we'll do it my way.' He turned to face the glass of the sliding windows and his mouth suddenly opened with surprise. 'Ah thought ye said she was restin' in her room.'

'*¿Qué?*' Gómez showed clearly then, peering over his shoulder, staring straight at us. Then he moved, brushing past Ward, and at that moment Iris Sunderby reached out, seizing me by the shoulder and letting out a scream as she fell to the ground, pulling me down on top of her. I finished up with a hand on her breast and my face within inches of hers. Her eyes still had that dazed, almost glazed look, but beginning to focus now, though not on me, on Gómez, and she was screaming all the time.

Suddenly she stopped, and there was a look on her face . . . I can only describe it as naked lust. It was as though she were in a sexual frenzy, completely transported by the excitement of her passion. Her lips stretched in a rictus smile, a satisfied look on her face, like that of a child who's got at the strawberries and cream, and Gómez was the cause of it.

A hand fastened like an iron clamp on my shoulder and I was flung off her, Ward bending down and shouting at her, 'Ye silly, stupid bitch!' His voice was thick with fury. And then he slapped her, twice on the face. 'Come on! Pull yersel' together, fur Christ's sake!'

I was lying on the grass, seeing it all from a low angle, Gómez moving in and Ward turning on him. 'Ye fuckin' shit! What is it? What have ye doped her with? Coke, I suppose.' He stretched out his dummy hand, and the metal fingers clawed at the man's arm. 'How did she take it – orally, or did she snort it?' The fingers were clamped tight and he was shaking Gómez back and forth, his features livid with anger. 'Or did ye inject it?' He was jabbing at the man with the clenched fist of his other hand, and Gómez, taken by surprise, was trying to hold him off. 'If it's crack Ah'll fuckin' kill ye, man.'

Gómez shook his head violently. 'Is not crack. I don't have any crack. I think perhaps it is the cocaine I keep for medical purposes, pure, straight cocaine. The best. I don't mix it with anything.'

'How did ye give it to her?'

'No, I don't give it to her. She must have got it from the room where I keep my guns. There is a box with all the things necessary in case of accidents. Cocaine is for anaesthetising against pain.'

Iris had got to her feet. 'Let him go.' Her voice sounded slurred and she was tugging at Ward's arm. She made an effort and pulled herself together, drawing away from them and saying with great dignity and a careful enunciation of her words, 'You must not q-quarrel, you two. We shall be a long time in *Isvik*. We will be living together in a very small space. You must be friends.'

'He's comin' with us then?' Ward was looking, not at her, but at Gómez again. 'Is that right? Ye're comin' with us?' And when Gómez did not answer, he swung round on her and said, 'Does that mean he knows where the ship is?'

She stared at him, her eyes gone vacant again.

'Does he, or does he not know where the ship is?' He said it slowly as though talking to a child.

'He thinks he can take us there.'

Ward stared at her a moment. By then I was on my feet and I could see her face, the cheeks marked by the slaps he had given her, the eyes showing signs of intelligence again. She seemed to have pulled herself together, but she didn't answer him.

Ward's head swung back to Gómez. He looked like a bull about to charge. But then he restrained himself and said in a quiet voice, 'Know anythin' about sailin'?'

'Some.'

'And ye've seen this ship we're goin' to look fur?'

There was a moment's hesitation, then he nodded. 'I think so. There was low cloud, white drifts of mist close down on the ice. But yes, I think I see it.'

'And ye pin-pointed the position?'

'Yes, I have the position.'

'Have ye given Mrs Sunderby the co-ordinates?'

Gómez did not answer, and Iris Sunderby said, 'No. He refuses to say.' And she added, cheeks suddenly a-flush and her voice wild, 'I tried very hard to get it out of him. Didn't I, Ángel?' She pronounced Ángel with a short 'A'. 'I do everything you want, but you don't tell me, do you? I crawl, I kiss your arse, do everything –' She had worked herself up into a state of almost incoherent fury, like a child in a tantrum, tears streaming down her face and her whole body shaking in a sort of passion as she suddenly flew at him, clawing with her nails.

He held her off, quite easily, standing there, smiling, and the look on his face was one of pleasure. He was a powerful, very fit-looking man, and he was obviously enjoying the mental distress he had caused and the fact that he held her powerless in his hands.

'Ye bastard!' Ward's voice was a harsh mixture of anger and contempt.

Gómez, still smiling, still holding Iris Sunderby at bay, said over the top of her head, 'That's one thing I am not.' He said it with extraordinary force, his face reddening below the dark skin and the eyes gone black again with anger.

Ward looked at him then with intense interest. 'Ye don't like bein' called a bastard?'

'No. Nobody likes being called that.'

'Och, that's not altogether true. There's some it doesn't upset the way it does ye. It's even a term of endearment to some people.' He gave a little laugh. He was suddenly relaxed, his voice almost casual. 'So yer mother and father were married, right?'

'Of course they were married.' The angry flush was still there on his face. 'So don't call me a bastard.'

'Ah'm sorry. My apologies.' Ward was smiling. He was enjoying himself so much he almost bowed. 'Very vulgar of me. Or perhaps Ah should say very stupid. Ah seem to remember it is all there, in that book by Luiz Rodriguez. Yer father married a nightclub singer. Then, when the family heard of it, they packed him off to Ireland, arranged fur the marriage to be annulled, and he married the Connor girl.'

'This is nothing to concern you.' Gómez began to turn away, but Ward stopped him.

'No, of course not. Ah was only makin' certain Rodriguez had got it right. A very tightly written little thumbnail sketch. If Ah remember rightly, he says the Gómez family already had Irish connections, so it was fairly simple fur them to find an impoverished landowner with a beautiful daughter goin' spare. That's where the Connor side of the name comes from, isn't it?'

Gómez nodded.

'All done in a hell of a hurry, with yer grandfather, Eduardo Gómez, obtainin' a special dispensation, or whatever ye call it, from the Pope.'

Gómez nodded again, waiting and watching, his eyes intent.

'And they were married in Ireland, at Rathdrum in County Wicklow, right?'

'Yes, but they returned to Argentina almost immediately.'

'So who is yer mother? Wasn't she the nightclub singer, Rosalli?'

'No, of course not. I am half Irish.'

149

Ward laughed. 'So yer mother was that Irish girl, Sheila Connor. Is that what ye're sayin?'

'Of course. I tell you . . .' But he stopped there, realising suddenly what that would mean.

'Sheila Connor – Mrs Juan Gómez – is also Iris Sunderby's mother.' Ward said it very quietly. 'That makes ye and Iris brother and sister. Ye realise that?'

Silence, and Ward turned to Iris Sunderby with a smile that was very near to a smirk. 'Ah just like to know the company Ah'll be keepin' down there in the Southern Ocean.'

Her face had paled. Hadn't she realised that her infatuation for the man was incestuous?

'Mother of God!' Ward was looking from one to the other. 'The tae of ye will need somethin' more than a dispensation from the Pope, Ah would think, if ye go on like this.' He turned back to Gómez, his head thrust forward. 'But perhaps ye have made a mistake and it is really the Sicilian woman . . .' He let it go at that, smiling to himself as he suggested to Iris Sunderby that she go up to her room and put her things together. 'We'll be leavin' just as soon as Ah've had a final word with our friend here. Ye go with her,' he said to me. 'Give her a hand with her packin'. It's wearin' off, but she's still a wee bit confused.'

She was more than a wee bit confused. I think, if I hadn't been there, she'd have gone to sleep right away. 'The bastard!' She said that several times, walking round the room. I wasn't sure whether she was referring to her brother or to Ward. Then suddenly she flung herself down on the bed and closed her eyes.

'Where's your suitcase?' I asked her as I began opening drawers to see how much had to be packed.

'Under the bed. Where do you think?' I had to kneel on the floor to reach it and her fingers fastened in my hair. 'You don't approve, do you?'

'What?' I had got hold of the suitcase and with the other hand I unclasped her fingers from my hair.

'How else was I to try and get the location out of him?'

'And did you?'

But now she had gone to sleep, or into a coma, I wasn't sure

150

which. I put the suitcase down on the other bed and began packing the contents of the drawers into it. It was mostly warm-weather gear, light cotton and silk dresses, blouses, skirts, jeans, tights, panties, bras, the whole lot smelling of her, a mixture of scent, talc, perspiration and her own peculiar body odour. By the time I had packed the things from the wardrobe and stuffed her toilet things on the top I could barely shut the case. I dumped it outside the door with her anorak and a crimson and gold coat on top. Shoes! I had left out her shoes. And when I had put these into a plastic bag that I found lying beside them under the dressing-table, I put my hand on her shoulder, about to shake her. Instead, I found myself staring down at her, remembering that moment alongside the *Cutty Sark* when our eyes had first met.

She looked so peaceful and relaxed, lying there with her eyes closed and no expression on her face, just the good bone formation and the smooth flesh with the bloom of healthy, slightly darkened skin, like a madonna, very beautiful. It seemed a pity to wake her. She was breathing so quietly I could hardly see the rise and fall of her breasts, and those lips of hers looking fuller than I remembered, the mouth wider, and the line of the teeth just showing very white. 'Mrs Sunderby . . . ! Iris!' I shook her gently. The eyelids flickered and the lips moved slightly. 'We're leaving,' I said.

'No.' The eyes were suddenly open, strongly blue and very wide. But no expression in them – just wide, and the blue very deep, almost violet. 'Not unless he comes.' She spoke slowly and with some difficulty.

'Come along,' I said, tightening my grip on her shoulder.

Her lips moved again and I bent down to her. 'What was that?'

'I said – he is not – my brother.'

I shook my head. 'I don't follow you.'

'That's what you think, isn't it?' She was suddenly sitting bolt upright, staring at me. 'You and that Iain Ward. I tell you, he is not my brother. He says he is, but he's not. I know that. I feel it – here.' She pressed her hand to her stomach. 'In my guts.'

I didn't know what to say. 'According to Rodriguez . . .'

'To hell with Rodriguez. I know. When I am lying with him, and he is inside me – that is the moment I know for sure.' She swung her feet off the bed. 'Now, let's get going, yes.' She lifted her feet, waggling her toes at me. 'My shoes. I'm not walking barefoot.'

I got her a pair of tough brogues from the plastic bag and all the time I was putting them on her she was looking at me with a vacant stare, her eyes still very wide, the pupils enormous. I took her things out to the Toyota. No sign of Ward, but I could hear the murmur of voices from the direction of the stable block. I called out that we were ready, but there was no answer, and when I returned to the bedroom I found her lying back full length on the bed, her eyes open and gazing up at the ceiling with that same vacant stare. 'You all right?' But I might have been speaking to a corpse, she was so pale and still and silent.

Somewhere somebody was playing a pipe, a sad fluting lament in the hot air. I pushed the sliding glass of the door to the patio further back to listen. There was no tune, but the notes had a pattern nevertheless that was very compelling. The primitive sound of it stirred something deep inside me as though it were Pan himself, not some Indian labourer, playing those haunting notes on that rude instrument.

I looked at Iris, wondering whether she could hear it. But she hadn't moved and I began thinking about how I was going to get her out to our vehicle.

The piping stopped abruptly and a horse neighed. I went out through the glass doors to the edge of the little patio. It was the same horse, the Indian holding its head and Gómez just swinging up into the saddle, Ward standing in the stable doorway. Gómez said something, smiling, his teeth white in the broad, handsome face. He looked young and carefree, almost like a boy.

A lift of his hand and then he had picked up the reins and, with a quick dig of his heels, went straight into a canter. Ward watched him, without any expression on his face, as he rode out through the arch, turned right and was lost to view behind the outbuildings that formed a part of the square courtyard. He turned then and came across to me. 'How's our little skipper?' He sounded in a jocular mood, no sign of tiredness.

'Come and see for yourself.' I said. 'We'll probably have to carry her.' And I added, 'How did you get on with Gómez?'

'Connor-Gómez. Please!' He was almost grinning. 'We understand each other now.' And then he said something that struck me as rather strange: 'He's made up his mind now. He's comin' with us. He's suddenly quite determined about it.'

'Why?'

'Ah. Ye tell me that, laddie, and it'd save me an awful lot of time.' We were back in the bedroom then and he stood for a moment looking down at her. 'Ye're right.' Her eyes were still wide open, a blind stare that was without any expression of intelligence. 'It's not speed,' he said. 'It must be crack. That's the worst way to cut the damned stuff. Ah wonder where he got the paraldehyde?'

'Is that what you mix it with to get crack?'

He nodded. 'Like cocaine it has anaesthetic qualities. Ye only need about three goes of crack and ye've got yerself an addiction problem. Och, well, we'll know soon enough.'

We picked her up then and carried her, dumping her, limp as a sailbag, on the back seat. 'Where are we going?' I asked as he began fixing the rear safety straps so that she wouldn't roll off the seat if he had to brake suddenly.

'Back down south.' He was fussing over her, arranging a sleeping bag under her head as a cushion. 'Accordin' to our hero, there's another road back to the coast by way of Cajabamba and Huamachuco. It's passable, he says, and it leads direct to Trujillo. We'll spend the night there, and then, if she's recovered, we'll go on in the morning through Lima to Tacna in the south of Peru. We pick up the plane for Punta Arenas at Arica, just across the Chilean border.'

He had it all worked out and he wasn't wasting any time. 'Ye drive,' he said and got into the passenger seat.

'Where's Gómez gone?' I asked as I started the engine.

'Doin' the rounds of his estate.'

'As long as he's not fixing for another of his boys to play around with this alternative route through the mountains,' I said.

'No, he won't try that again.'

'So what's the hurry?'

He was silent a moment and I thought he wasn't going to answer that. But then he said, 'Ah don't know. Just a feelin' that the sooner we're on board *Isvik* the better. Once he's joined us it'll probably be okay, but till then . . .' He paused. 'Ah'd just like to check her over, make sure nobody starts playin' silly buggers with the engine or the seacocks, somethin' like that. A fire on board . . .' He turned to the back seat as I swung under the arch and headed towards the Baños del Inca. 'Ah wonder if she has any idea what it is all about. Did ye ask her?'

'Ask her what?' I was trying to memorise the road.

'She comes up here, throws herself at a man who may or may not be her brother, but who is undoubtedly mixed up in a very unsavoury episode in his country's history, lets him persuade her to fool around with a very dangerous drug . . . Why? And why should he go to such pains to stop us comin' up here?'

'That's simple,' I said. 'A girl as attractive as Iris Sunderby, if you'd got her alone in your hacienda . . .'

'Ye mean ye'd be willin' to try and kill off her friends just to keep her to yerself?' He shook his head. 'That man is as cold-blooded as a snake. No, there has to be some deeper reason. And to suddenly decide he'll come with us . . .' He was looking at me, a hard, interrogative stare. 'What is it about that ship? He knows where it is. He's willin' to pilot us there. Why? What's he know about it that we don't? And when we find it, what then?'

I shook my head, my attention half on the road. There were quite a few people about, women as well as men, nearly all Indians, some of them on mules. Donkeys, too, and because it was hot, with only the faintest breeze, many of the men had their wide-brimmed hats pushed to the backs of their heads, held there by the leather thongs that were really chin straps. Occasionally a garishly painted truck passed us, raising a cloud of dust, and away to the west, hanging over us and clearly visible now that the clouds had lifted, the coastal range of the cordilleras towered pale and trembling in the heat. I think what attracted me most about the country round was its Englishness, meadows deep in grass and wild flowers, and willows wherever there was water.

It wasn't truly English, of course. It had a different feel to it, a different look, a different smell. And there was Iris Sunderby's recumbent body sprawled in the back. Nevertheless, the countryside reminded me of East Anglia, the willows in particular making me realise how far I was from home.

At Cajabamba we joined a slightly better road, and soon afterwards we turned west and headed up into the mountains through Huamachuco, climbing all the way. I don't know how high the pass was, but even with the sun casting long, black shadows, there was none of the fearsomeness of the journey we had made only that morning. No storm mist shrouding the slopes, no rain, no lightning stabbing, no thunder rumbling, the clouds all swept away as though by magic, the sky blue, the mountains looking quite serene now, almost kindly in the late afternoon light.

Inevitably the road worsened as we neared the pass, the surface rutted by trucks and still awash with water spilling down steep gullies. An abandoned truck, its snout rammed into the steep bank of a cut, caused me a moment's panic. Ward was asleep. I was climbing in low gear, my eyes searching the vehicle and the bank behind it for any sign of movement.

'It's all right.' He must have sensed my hesitation, his ears alert for any change in the note of the engine. 'Ah didn't tell him which route we were takin'. That truck has been there at least three days.'

'How do you know?'

'Use yer eyes. The road's dry under the chassis.'

He was asleep again before I had edged the Toyota round it. Shortly after that we came over the top of the pass and started down towards the coast. The sun was setting and there were moments when I, too, felt like 'stout Cortés' and thought I could see the Pacific. Perhaps here, from the vantage point of the Andes, I would see the green flash as the upper rim of the sun slid below the ocean horizon to leave a prismatic glimpse of the spectrum's final colour.

Twice I ran perilously close to the edge, my eyes dazzled and eyelids drooping. I was beginning to feel sleepy and I began to sing, softly, to myself. I was singing 'All things bright and beautiful . . .' I don't know why. I just felt that way. And then a voice from the back said, 'Where the hell am I?'

'We're taking you down to the Pacific for a bathe,' I told her.

'Like hell you are! Where's Ángel?' She was leaning forward.

I was on a tricky bend, the road falling away sharply and badly in need of a grader. I couldn't turn my head, but I could smell her, feel her breath on the back of my neck.

'Stop the car!' Her voice was shrill. 'I said stop the car. Turn round and take me back.' And then, when I said nothing and kept on driving, she said, 'If you don't stop, I'll jump out.'

I braked a little harder then and turned to look at her. Her face was still very pale, the skin shining with sweat, but the eyes were almost normal now, the pupils no longer dilated. I could see them quite clearly, the blue formed of all sorts of colours, like sapphires picked out in the sun's last rays.

'Where are you taking me?' She started to wrestle with the nearside door, but Ward had locked it and in the end she gave up, lying back again and muttering something about remembering now.

'Our little skipper more herself, is she?' The way he said it I knew he meant to goad her. She flared up on the instant, turning on him and almost yelling, 'You bought a boat, that doesn't mean you bought me. Now tell our pest control officer here to turn round and drive back to the hacienda.'

'Why?' Ward's face was suddenly contorted with anger. 'Why the hell dae ye want to go back there? Are ye in love with him? He fills ye up with coke, uses ye like a whore . . . And he's yer own blood.'

'How dare you!' Her face was flushed and angry. 'He's not my brother.'

'All right, yer half-brother then.' And he added, turning the knife in the wound, 'Christ almighty! Ye're a Catholic and you have an incestuous relationship . . .'

'I do not. I do not.' She banged her fists on the back of his seat.

'Okay, but what are ye goin' to say to the priest next time you go to confession, eh? How are you going to explain that ye're playing around . . .'

'He is not my brother,' she repeated. 'And I do not commit incest.' And then she went over to the attack again. 'Can't you understand, you great big stupid *asqueroso*, I was close to getting it out of him, the information I need to prove my husband is not imagining things. And I would have got it, if you hadn't come blundering in.'

'Balls! Ye'd never have got it out of him in a million years. Ye're besotted with the bastard. That's the real reason ye're holed up here in the mountains . . .'

'Oh, for Christ's sake, stop your play-acting.' And she added, maliciously, 'All right. He's a beautiful hunk of male virility, something you'll never be, and I enjoy playing around with him, as you so delicately put it.'

That was when I scraped the fender on a protruding lump of rock. It's not often you find yourself an enforced eavesdropper on two people screwing each other up with murder in their hearts. And when he said, 'Ye start playin' around with the bugger on board *Isvik* . . .' I slammed on the brakes, stopping with a jerk that almost threw her on the floor.

'Shut up!' I shouted. 'Both of you. The road's difficult enough without you yelling at each other, and I'm tired.'

An abrupt silence followed my outburst. I think they had both been so wrapped up in themselves they had quite forgotten my existence.

'We're all tired,' Ward said at length.

'Yes, but you're not driving.'

'Want me to take over?'

'How far to the coast?' I asked.

'No idea.'

'I'll drive till the sun sets,' I said. 'I want to see it drop into the Pacific.' I let the clutch in, jerking the vehicle into motion again, my driving suddenly vicious. I think I was scared again. I had every right to be if there was going to be this sort of hostility between the two of them all the way down into the ice. And Gómez? There was Gómez, a catalyst for disaster.

My mind went back to the scene in that bedroom and the sliding doors to the paved patio. I seemed to remember statuary and flowers – hibiscus or something flaming red, roses maybe, in great urns – and there were doubtless other bedrooms leading off it with similar softly sliding glass doors. I should have questioned her then. Still mazed with whatever the drug was she had taken, I might have got the truth out of her. Was he her brother, or wasn't he? She said not. She'd been very positive about that, not just here in the car, but she had said it to me in the bedroom while I was packing her things and she was still in a mentally uninhibited state. And if he wasn't her brother, what were his real origins? And was she in love with him? Well, not in love perhaps, but besotted. I remembered the charm of the man, that almost blatant virility. And Ward had said it was all fixed, he would join us on *Isvik* and navigate us to within sledging distance of the trapped vessel.

And then, suddenly, there was the Pacific, and the sun, a great crimson ball, like the tuning indicator on a giant music centre, dipping its lower rim on to the hazed line of the horizon. I stopped right there, where I had an uninterrupted view, and watched the rim of it flatten out, spreading fire along the ocean's edge.

It didn't take long. It just sank slowly and steadily below the ocean's horizon, and suddenly it was gone. No green flash, nothing, and the sky above fading from blue through green to the beginning of Stygian darkness. Suddenly a star showed.

'Venus or Mercury? Venus, Ah think,' Ward said, and I realised he, too, had been watching the spectacle in absolute silence. 'That was the star that brought Cook into the Pacific – the transit of Venus. Tae centuries ago.' He was silent then and I had the feeling he was thinking of all that Cook had done, first in *Endeavour*, then in *Resolution* and *Discovery*, ships not much longer than *Isvik*. And he had taken them down into the Southern Ocean, not as far as we were going, but far enough to be in amongst the ice, circumnavigating the whole land mass of Antarctica in waters no man had ever sailed before.

'Ah'll take over now,' Ward said.

III

RENDEZVOUS AT USHUAIA

ONE

'So what did she say about him?'

'Nothing,' I said.

'Ye were in that room alone with her. She must have said somethin'.'

I shook my head.

'Jesus Christ, man! Didn't ye ask her?' He was leaning forward across the table, staring at me with a sort of frustrated belligerence. 'Weren't ye curious?'

'I was packing her things.'

'Ah know ye were. But ye were there all the time Ah was talkin' to Gómez. Must have been quarter of an hour at least. Surely to God . . .' He stretched out his left hand and gripped my arm. 'Come on, ye had the opportunity, and after that extraordinary scene in the garden ye must have been bubblin' over with curiosity.'

'She was drugged,' I reminded him.

'Ah know that.' His voice had risen, his impatience spilling into anger so that other guests were beginning to watch us. 'Now just go back in yer mind to that room, tell me everythin' she said, or even how she looked in answer to your questions, that would help.'

'I didn't ask any questions,' I said. 'Not the sort of questions you want answered. I asked where her suitcase was and she said, under the bed, where else? Oh, and before that, before she collapsed on to the bed, she called him a bastard. She said that several times, walking round the room.' I didn't tell him how she had caught hold of my hair again when I was reaching under the bed. I could still hear her voice, the way she had said, 'You don't approve, do you?' As though my approval mattered to her.

There was no room service and we were breakfasting in the hotel dining-room at a table looking out on to a square adorned by several yuccas and some dusty oleanders. Iris hadn't surfaced yet. She had told Ward she didn't want any breakfast.

'Anythin' else?'

I hesitated, but in the end I told him: 'She said something about how else could she get the location out of him?'

'The location of the ship, d'ye mean?'

'I suppose so.'

'Tradin' her body fur the information?' His grip on my arm had tightened, his voice dropped to a whisper, suddenly quite menacing. 'That's what ye're implyin', isn't it? Or was it . . . ?'

I shook my head, unwilling to answer him.

'And did he give her what she wanted?'

His persistence annoyed me. 'Sex or information?' I asked. 'Which do you mean?' The way I put it was intentional and I think if we hadn't been sitting in full view of some dozen of the hotel's guests he would have hit me.

'The location,' he almost snarled.

'No. She was suddenly flat out.'

He stared at me a moment, as though he suspected I might be hiding something from him. Then he let go of my arm. 'Och well, Ah'll have to get it out of her myself.' He sat back, evidently considering how to go about it, then finished his coffee and got slowly, almost reluctantly, to his feet. 'Aye, Ah'd best have a wee talk with her myself.' He glanced at his watch. 'On the road at nine-fifteen, okay?'

He was just turning to leave the room when the door opened and Iris appeared. It was almost as though there were some telepathic understanding between them. Later I was to find this sort of coincidence recurring. They were after all, both of them, Sagittarians.

As she came over to our table I was amazed at the change in her. The olive colouring of her skin was back in full bloom, and though she was wearing little or no make-up, her lips, or rather her mouth, which, with her nose, was the most notable part of

162

her features, was bright red. Her cheeks, which had been so white the previous evening, now had colour, and instead of sagging with exhaustion she radiated the extraordinary vitality that had so attracted me at our first meeting on the *Cutty Sark*. 'Isn't it about time we hit the road?' She was addressing Ward, not me, and she glanced pointedly at her watch.

'Ah was just comin' to call ye,' he answered gruffly.

She ignored that and asked him whether he'd booked her a seat with us on the flight south from Lima.

'Ah was plannin' to drive down through Arequipa to the Chilean border.' His manner was slightly defensive. 'There are quite a few archaeological sites Ah'd like to have a look at while Ah'm here.'

'There's also a boat waiting for us down at Punta Arenas. We may find something wrong with her, items we need for overwintering in the ice. She's a long way from any source of supply and if there's something that has to be specially made, or is too bulky to fly out – a new engine, for instance . . .' They stared at each other for a moment, not exactly hostile, more two people measuring each other up. 'We can discuss that while we drive, no? Have you settled the *cuenta*?' Her tone was imperious, deliberately provocative.

I saw Ward hesitate, then he smiled and nodded. 'Aye, we can talk about it – while we're lookin' round the mud ruins of Chanchán.' He, too, was being provocative, quite deliberately making it a clash of wills, but still smiling as he told me to get the bags into the Toyota. 'And don't let that briefcase out of yer sight.' He nodded to the case, which was under the table, and strode out.

The route we had taken through the cordillera from Caja-marca had brought us virtually into the outskirts of Trujillo and we had put up at a hotel in the centre of the city, all three of us more or less out on our feet. Now, in the brightness of a cloudless morning, the air clear after a night of rain and surprisingly dry, we started out thoroughly refreshed. Certainly I felt, for the first time, that sense of anticipation, of excitement almost, at the prospect ahead of me – a journey down the whole coast of South

America, and then on to the very southernmost rim of the world. Even the digression up to Cajamarca now seemed in retrospect more like an adventure than something to send shivers down the spine.

But though my spirits were high, the shadow of that man, who liked to be called the Angel of Death, travelled with me, the memory of his good looks, his well-oiled virility, above all Iris Sunderby's apparent infatuation, constantly there in my mind.

Ward took the wheel as we left the hotel, but instead of heading south, he turned north, and when Iris Sunderby remonstrated with him, all he said was, 'Chanchán. Ah'm bloody well goin' to have a look at Chanchán.' Adding, by way of explanation, that it was the old Chimú capital. 'Pre-Inca and almost as powerful.'

Like Iris, I was impatient now to get on with the journey south and see the vessel that was to be our home, but when I saw Chanchán . . . It was incredible, so incredible, so lost in time that it did something to me – changed my perspective, my outlook, something strange that even now I barely understand.

To begin with it was vast, a huge mud city fallen into ruin, desolate, remote as the moon, and gloomy as hell, for a mist had rolled in, completely obscuring the sun. It was only a short distance off the Pan-Americana, all grey mud dust, the outer walls towering so thick, so solid, that, after the better part of a millennium, they were still standing eight or nine metres high, only the ramparts showing the erosion of time. It was virtually desert country, the irrigation channels blocked with debris, nothing that could be called a tree to be seen anywhere. Once inside those walls, it really was another world, more than fifteen square kilometres of streets bordered by the crumbling walls of houses, public buildings, cemeteries and reservoirs, some with bits and pieces of bone lying exposed where long-dead looters and grave-robbers had been at work. Looking back towards the Pan-Americana, the huge mud complex appeared ringed with peaked and desiccated mountains. Westward its bulwark was the Pacific. I could hear it, a steady, grumbling sound, like an earthquake.

I walked right through that fantastic ruin. It was the largest I had ever seen, split up into walled units, ten of them Ward had said, and when I reached the western limit of it I was face to face with the heaving bulk of the ocean. A big swell was rolling in, building waves like mountains in the mist and breaking with a thunderous and persistent roar.

There was a slight onshore breeze. I stood there with the salt spray and the mist damp on my face, and the vastness of it, and the antiquity of the desolate remains behind me, made all my life to date seem insignificant and of no account. I can't explain it, but it was as though I were transported outside of myself, on the verge of grasping the significance of being. In the atmosphere of the place there was something almost biblical, and yet this was a pagan world I had stepped into. How could it be so full of meaning? Was it the monstrous, heaving power of the waters confronting me, or was it my conscious awareness of the dead of a great city?

I don't know what it was, but I felt almost disembodied, ten feet tall and near to God. The impact was so great that the effect of it was to remain with me in the months ahead and give me strength when I most needed it.

I must have stood there for at least ten minutes, quite still as though transfixed. Finally I turned and started back, not conscious of anything, my mind still locked in on the impression the place had made so that I only vaguely heard a voice calling me. She was sitting in a gap in the outer wall, and as I approached her, she said, 'You look as though you've seen a ghost.' She smiled. 'What were you staring at?'

'Nothing – just the sea.'

She was looking up at me with an expression of concern. 'You are thinking about what lies ahead.'

I nodded. I was looking down at her, brown knees drawn up to her chin and the open V of her shirt showing the round of her breasts, even the pinking of the nipple circles. She patted the broken wall beside her. 'Does it scare you?' I didn't say anything and she turned her head away, facing the sea again. 'Well, it does me.' She said it in a whisper. 'It's so vast. That's what I find disconcerting. It goes on and on and on – ten thousand miles of

165

virtually uninterrupted ocean. And where we're going the winds come from right around the globe.'

I sat down beside her, both of us gazing out through the mist at the heaving, pounding water, the noise of it thundering in our ears, filling our whole world with sound. 'He's coming with us, is he?' I asked her.

'Ángel? Yes.' She nodded. 'He'll navigate us down into the ice, and afterwards he will act as our guide.' And she added, speaking quietly as though to herself, 'He knows where it is.'

'You trust him?'

She hesitated. 'No. No, I don't trust him. But he will take us there.'

'Why?'

She gave a hollow little laugh. 'Ah, if I knew that . . .'

I waited, but she didn't pursue the matter. 'Do you love him?' I asked.

She turned on me then, but not with anger, her tone one of contempt. 'Love! That is not something he would understand. You don't love a man like Ángel.'

'What then? He fascinates you, is that it?'

Her mouth was compressed into a tight line. 'It is none of your business. But yes, he is very attractive. Don't you feel it?' And she added slowly, 'He is as attractive to men, you know, as he is to women.'

I wondered about that, why she had said it. 'It's you I'm concerned about. I'm asking about you.' It was presumptuous of me, but I had to know, and now I had the opportunity. The atmosphere of the place, the mood between us, everything was right.

She nodded almost reluctantly. 'I suppose. It is the way we are made. He is a devil, but you cannot help what the gods . . .' Her voice tailed away in a little shrug of the shoulders that was like a shudder. 'And he is not my brother.'

'Not even your half-brother?'

'No.'

'Then who is his father?'

'How the hell do I know? I have barely seen him since my father died.'

'What about Carlos then? A cousin, you said.'

She ignored the question, turning to me and asking why Iain had brought us here. 'Why does he insist on Chanchán? All these mud walls – it is so depressing.' There was a pause, and she added, 'He never does anything without a purpose. The play acting, those accents, the changes of mood – all is intentional I think.' She was looking at me again, waiting for an answer. And I thought, my God! We're going to lock ourselves inside the fragile skin of a small floating home, and all of us, three of us anyway, at odds and full of motives I didn't understand.

She nodded as though she had read my thoughts. 'Looking at that sea, you have reason to be scared.'

'I'm not scared,' I assured her. 'Just a little concerned.'

'A leetle concairned!' She laughed at her mimicry.

'About Carlos?' I reminded her.

'What about him? He is all right. The police will sort it out, and if they have arrested the boy, then he will be released as soon as they realise the body is not mine, but that of some poor little Dockland tart.'

'But your handbag.'

'My handbag? Yes, of course. It suddenly came to me. If they mistook the body . . .'

'And the ring. Victor Wellington said there was a ring of yours on the dead woman's left hand.'

'I got very wet.' She nodded, smiling. 'Also I was a little frightened, and the water was filthy. There was nobody around. Nobody saw me, thank God. Poor little Carlos!' She glanced at me quickly. 'Why are you asking about him? You think they will blame him?' She said it almost eagerly.

'You recognised him when he followed us out of Greenwich.'

'Of course I recognise him. He is –' She stopped there. 'You ask too many questions.'

'I only want to know what his relationship is to Gómez. You said he was some sort of cousin.'

She was staring at the sea again. 'Per'aps he is. Per'aps not.' She shook her head, the dark hair glinting with moisture, her eyes turned to me and searching mine. 'I can talk with you, I think.' I was to learn that her English always tended to deteriorate when her emotions took hold. 'With Iain, no. I can't talk to him, not about private matters. I don't understand him. I suppose in a way I don't trust him. On practical matters, yes. He is a good man to have with us on this journey . . .' She shrugged. 'You ask about Carlos. I don't know what that boy is, except he is something very close to Ángel. His mother is that Rosalli woman, I think. But who his father is –' Again the slight shrug of the shoulders. And then she got to her feet. 'It is time we rejoin Iain and get going. We need to be in Lima tonight.'

'Where is he?' I asked as we turned our backs on the Pacific and began working our way back through the maze of walls and rubble.

'I left him examining what appeared to be the remains of a cemetery. He was armed with an archaeological book he had dug out of that bulging briefcase of his and was on his hands and knees sifting through a pile of discarded bones.'

We found him seated on a particularly high section of wall sketching the decoration of an inner chamber, and when I climbed up beside him I noticed his vantage point gave him a clear view of the Toyota. When we had parked there hadn't been another vehicle in sight. Now it had been joined by several cars and a coach was disgorging a gaggle of tourists. 'I see you're not taking any chances.'

I said it more as a joke, but he took it seriously. 'Would ye after what happened on the way up to Cajamarca?' I realised then that Iris had been right. It wasn't entirely his thirst for knowledge that had made him insist on driving north to Chanchán.

It was almost eleven before we left that great mud complex, driving back through Trujillo and on south across dull, desiccated country, a lot of it near-desert. The sun gradually ate up the mist until by the afternoon we were in a blazing oven under a burned blue sky. By the time we rolled into Lima it was dark and, though we had taken hourly turns at the wheel, we were all of us limp with exhaustion.

The following morning we flew to Tacna in the far south of Peru, crossed into Chile by taxi and flew on from Arica to Santiago. From there a delayed flight took us on to Punta Arenas where we arrived late in the evening.

I don't remember much about our arrival, only that the fourteen-kilometre drive from the airport was something of a nightmare with visibility almost nil in pouring rain mixed with flurries of hail and howling gusts of wind. It seemed bitterly cold after the heat of Peru. 'Ah doubt this fuckin' place has even heard o' primavera,' Ward said in his foulest Glaswegian, and that just about summed it up.

The house we were in was solid Victorian in style, both inside and out, except that it had a tin roof. Between the gusts, the sound of rain on the roof and water pouring off it was continuous. The place was owned by an old ship's captain. He gave us coffee laced with Chilean brandy. '*Es bueno. Hara dormir bien.*' He had been at sea on the Chilean coast most of his life, running cargoes between the isolated ports of the southern waterways, a marvellous-looking old man, big gnarled hands warped with rheumatism and a long wrinkled face, little lines running out from his eyes, which were slitted as though he were permanently peering out into fog. His hair was thick and iron grey, and the rather drooping moustache was curved round the mouth to finish in a little tuft just below the under lip. The effect was that he always seemed to be smiling.

I was half asleep when he showed us up to our rooms, Ward and I sharing one at the rear of the building, which, in place of beds, had a double-tier bunk in the corner. The wind in the gusts seemed directed straight at the small casement window, which rattled and banged. At times the whole house shook.

When I woke the sun was shining, everything very still. Ward had already washed and was getting into his clothes. 'Mornin'.' He was smiling. 'Ah think we can regard this as being the start of our voyage. D'ye think it's an omen?'

'What?' I was still half asleep.

'Ye'll see what Ah mean when ye get to the bathroom. It looks right out on to the Strait, and it's flat calm, not a breath, the

169

ships anchored off all standin' on their heads in marvellous reflection. And somethin' else –' There was an excitement about him that showed the boy behind the man. He looked so much younger with a mountain peak all covered in snow peering over his shoulder through the little window. 'Come on, stir yerself. Ye'll find me down on the quay looking at her. She's right there, right in front of us, and she's rusty as hell. But she's a good-lookin' boat all the same,' he added as he went out.

Thus my first glimpse of *Isvik* was from the bathroom window of a seafaring man, who had exchanged his small coaster for a house on the quay looking straight out on to the Magellan Strait. She was, as Ward had said, rusty as hell, but behind the rust she had a solid look to her. I just hoped he'd had a good surveyor on the job before committing himself.

By the time I reached the quay the water out in the centre of the Strait was darkening with little puffs of wind and the mountains west of the town were half obscured by cloud. My breath smoked and I began to feel the wind-chill even through my sailing jersey and the special anorak I had bought for southern latitudes. The quay was white and slippery with the granules of a recent hailstorm.

I was only a short time standing there, but long enough to take in the vessel's lines, the quite dainty sheer, her size and the layout of the masts and rigging. By comparison with a freighter, moored so close her black stern virtually hung over *Isvik*'s knife-edged bows, she looked very small, but viewing her from the standpoint of the maxi in which I had raced round the world, I guessed she was roughly the same size – at least twenty-five metres long with a good beam and what looked like a deep V-shaped hull. There was a low deckhouse amidships with an upper wheel and emergency tiller steering from a small cockpit aft. I thought at first she was ketch-rigged, but then decided she was more of a schooner. Her running rigging was in an appalling state, the ropes all frayed and tangled, but the standing rigging, which was partly of stainless steel, seemed to have been well looked after. The hull was presumably steel; it was this that gave her a rust-streaked look under the dirty coating of ice and snow.

The topsides and deckhouse, many of the fittings, were of aluminium or some smooth grey alloy.

A blackened pipe stood up out of the deck, just aft of the deckhouse on the port side, a heat haze dancing from the top of it and the ice on the metal supporting bracket dripping moisture. A delicious smell of bacon frying was wafted on a blattering down-blast of wind. I was suddenly very hungry. I went on board and from the open doorway of the deckhouse came the murmur of voices. 'Mr Ward?' I called his name twice, 'Are you on board?'

'Aye.'

But it wasn't Ward who poked his head up the companionway. It was a big, bearded man with a shock of blond hair on a round bullet head that seemed to have no neck. The shoulders were immensely broad, padded out by the grey and brown loose-woven rollneck sweater he was wearing. 'You are Pete Kettil, *ja?*' And when I said I was he held out a massive paw that gripped my hand as though in a vice. 'Nils Solberg. Velcome on board *Isvik*. The boss, he is already here. You come for *frokost, ja?* Bakkon, eggs, some seaveed, also fried lichen, what we call *lav*. Is *god. Kom* down.'

Ward was already eating. 'Nils is a bloody good cook,' he said with his mouth full. 'But Ah learned one thing already. Ye take a gander at the engines. She may look a ruin topside, but beJaisus, the engine-room ... Reck'n ye could've fried the eggs on the cylinder heads it's so bright and clean and polished. That right, Nils?'

'*Ja*. Engines okay.'

'So we need a cook. First priority. Nils may be a good cook, but his time will be better spent away from the galley. And we need to dae somethin' about the drive shaft.'

Apparently the retired sea captain, in whose house we were billeted, was willing to provide us with beds ashore, but nothing else. The deal was we made our own beds and fed on board.

'What about Mrs Sunderby?' I asked.

He looked at me with a quizzical lift to his eyebrows.

'I suppose she's sleeping it off.' I said it without thinking.

'Then ye suppose wrong.' He was grinning. 'She was down

before me, breakfasted and lookin' as though she was just off to complete a big business deal in the money centre of BA or wherever. In fact, she's over at the Yard now chattin' up some foreman or other she's got eatin' out of her hand. As ye doubtless noticed, there's work to dae.' He thrust his head forward as the big Norwegian dumped a plateful of an extraordinary mixture in front of me – a great wadge of fried bread, two eggs, two very thick rashers and the rest a mêlée of doubtful greenery swimming in bacon fat. 'Ah'm Iain, this is Nils, Mrs Sunderby is Iris – no, better call her Eeris, she responds to that much quicker – ye're Peter, or Pete for short, and what the hell we call Gómez we'll find out in due course. But Christian names from now on. Quicker to say, quicker to react to. And by God, where we're goin' we're likely to need quick reactions. Had a look at the riggin'?'

I nodded, suddenly realising what was coming.

'That'll be yer department. Ah know nothin' about sails, nor does Nils – he's a wizard of an engineer, that's all. And Iris, she's the managin' director. Okay?'

'And you?' I asked, my mouth stuffed full of lichen which was really much nicer than I'd expected.

'Me? Ah'm just old moneybags. But Ah tell ye this, laddie, Ah'm a helluva fast learner, so don't think ye can pull the wool or sit around on yer fat little arse doin' bugger all. Ah want that riggin' fixed and workin' inside of a week.'

'And the sails?'

'Iris is checkin' on that now. We've yet to find out if they've any sail-makin' facilities here at all. Ah suspect not, in which case we'll have to measure them up and have them flown out. Or we make our own. In a place like this there are bound to be some good seamstresses and Singers will surely have had their salesmen down here back in the days of the square-riggers. Iris will soon have some women organised. She's a great organiser, that girl.'

It was, in fact, Iris who found us a cook. He was a youngster of twenty-two just on the point of being invalided out of the Chilean Navy. Besides cooking, he seemed to have done most things, course after course. His name was Roberto Coloni and he had been in hospital following a bad fall in which he had broken his shoulder blade, forearm and two ribs, as well as suffering bad concussion, which had affected his hearing. It was because of his deafness, not his more obvious injuries, that he was being invalided out, and it was several days before he finally joined us and took up his culinary duties.

My immediate concern on that first morning in Punta Arenas was to learn all I could about the ship. Iain filled me in on the essential details while I was devouring that gargantuan breakfast. *Isvik* had been built in the Canadian Maritimes for an American millionaire who wanted to emulate Staff Sergeant Henry Larsen of the Royal Canadian Mounties who, in the years 1940–42, had sailed the schooner *St Roch* from west to east through the North-West Passage. He was the first to make the Passage except for Amundsen. And then he did it again in 1944, that time from east to west, the first man to make it across the top of Canada in both directions.

The design for *Isvik* was influenced to quite a marked degree by the Peterhead-type sailing vessels of the Mounties, also by a sketch made for him by that extraordinary Antarctic single-hander, David Lewis. 'Roughed it out fur him on the back of an envelope, a squeeze-up steel hull design with platin' thick as a tanker.'

It was, in fact, a much beamier vessel than the police ship, the hull fining up sharply towards bow and stern so that both fore and aft her deep, strong wedge-shape would cause the ice to squeeze her upwards in the event of her being caught in a series of pressure ridges. She was also much smaller, the police ship having been over three hundred tons. But it was from that and the scribbled design on the back of an envelope that *Isvik* had been pupped. Unfortunately her building was delayed by the failure of the small specialised steel company that was constructing the hull. Then the American millionaire had had a heart attack. He lost interest after that, his plan overshadowed by the oil tanker *Manhattan* making it across the top of America.

Lawyers handling his affairs had then dumped the boat on the market just after Wall Street had had one of its periodic crashes. Three years had passed since the time of her conception and she was still without spars and rigging and had not been fitted out internally. Her purchase by the B. J. Norsk Forsking of Larvik for seismographical work in the Bellingshausen Sea almost due south of the Horn was, as Ward put it, 'just about the very first good thin' that had ever happened to her,' even if it was a slightly clandestine operation.

He didn't say the vessel was jinxed, but after the sail plan and the interior layout had been redesigned and the ship completed for her new role in Antarctic waters, the B. J. Norsk Forsking, a drilling outfit operating in the Norwegian sector of the North Sea, struck a bad patch following a fall in the price of oil and abandoned the Southern Ocean project. They had acquired *Isvik* at a knock-down figure, spent about the same again completing the fitting of her out to their requirements, and Iain Ward had picked her up for not much more than they had originally paid for her. 'Ah tell ye this, Pete –' He was leaning across the table, his little steely grey eyes bright with a barrow boy's excitement at striking a bargain – 'it'd cost a wee fortune now just to build the hull. She's plated in the bows with steel eighteen mil thick. If we get caught up in the ice that means she'll pop up like a cork when the pressure's on. At least', he added, with a down-turn to the corners of his mouth, 'that's the theory of it.'

'What did your surveyor think?' I asked.

'Just that. In theory, that's what should happen. There the wee man goes and spoils it all by sayin' he's not an ice man and if we get ourselves into a really bad pressure ridge he couldn't say fur sure what would happen. The truth is, Ah suppose, if ye've got a berg sailin' down on ye and ye're trapped in the ice there's no thickness of steel that will save ye from gettin' crushed. That right, Nils?'

The big Norwegian shook his head, frowning. '*Jeg forstår ikke.*' I don't think he found Ward's accent at all easy, and anyway, like many foreigners, he found it easier to speak English than to understand it. 'Yu haf finish your café, Iain? Zen ve go look at *skrue* shaft, eh?'

There was an old pressure cooker half full of coffee simmering on the stove, a saucepan of milk beside it. I helped myself, and when I had finished, I went up on deck and began sorting out the rigging. Nils had already opened up the engine compartment, which was directly below the deckhouse, and he and Iain were sitting on the floor with their legs dangling over the big diesel, going through a list of requirements he had produced. As I stepped past them Iain had his glasses on and was peering at a diagram the engineer had roughed out in his notepad. 'Well, that makes sense, but if it means takin' the engine out and havin' engineers crawlin' all over the place so we can't get on with the job of takin' on stores and equipment –'

'Nei, nei, nei. We cut the shaft there. I do it myself. No need for Yard engineers. No need for anything, only gears and lever to disengage. And new dynamo – small one so we haf power off the *skrue* . . .'

'The propellor?'

'*Ja, ja*, the propellor.'

I left them to it. Engines didn't interest me very much. But rigging and sails did, and once I was on deck, coiling and sorting the ropes and making notes of what I would need, I barely noticed anything else, time slipping by and my mind so concentrated on the job that I barely felt the wind force rising, small frozen particles of snow driving almost horizontally. Periodically I went down into the warmth below, to write up my notes and check them over against the ship's design plans, which Nils had produced for me before going off with Iain to talk to the Navy Yard people.

We were almost into November now and I didn't need to be an expert navigator to work out from the charts, and the Admiralty Pilot lying open on the chart table, that to be into the south of the Weddell Sea in time to take maximum advantage of the summer loosening of the pack we would need to be away not later than end-November. It was a voyage of close on two thousand miles and, allowing for eventualities, it would be a month at least before we were within striking distance of the position where Charles Sunderby had had that brief sighting of the *Andros*.

And Nils was planning a major operation on our engine. Also the snowmobile ordered in England had not yet arrived.

That evening we learned the name the Argentinians had given their reconstructed East Indiaman – *Santa Maria del Sud*. And it wasn't Iris who told us, though she had known for some time that it had come through the Strait shortly after the *Belgrano* had been sunk. It was the old sea captain, in whose house Nils had billeted us, who told us. Iain had invited him over for a meal. The man lived on his own, except for a half-Indian woman who came in every morning. It was in the nature of a goodwill invitation, nothing more, none of us realising that he was the one man in Punta Arenas who had some idea of why an old wooden-walled East Indiaman, built like a frigate, should have been reconditioned and brought south by the Argentine Navy during the war.

Iris came aboard with him, wearing a long dress and in full warpaint. The *Contraalmirante* had invited her to dine at the C-in-C's residence. He was a Rear-Admiral, and as Commander-in-Chief of the Third Naval Zone, he was the most important man in Punta Arenas. The *Gobernador Marítimo* would be there, also the officer in charge of the Navy Yard. How she had managed it, God knows, except perhaps that beautiful and exciting women dropping in out of the blue at the bottom of the world were not very plentiful. 'It's important we get the co-operation we need.' She smiled and waved the formidable list of requirements I had helped her prepare.

The C-in-C was sending his car for her, and when it arrived, I saw her to the quay. By then it was blowing a full gale from the west, the wind slamming down off the mountains with kata-batic blasts that hammered the luminous white of the water with such fury that it splayed out like shot, a reminder that the heights west of the port were almost six hundred metres high, the first ski-run only eight kilometres away by car. She looked like a Cossack in jackboot-black sea boots, the skirt of her long dress looped up and tucked into the strap of a gold lamé handbag, the top half of her padded out by a fur-hooded anorak. It was sleet-ing, the ice-cold droplets driving past the light on the quay in a white mist, the freighter's stern glistening as though with salt spray. I was slit-eyed and shivering by the time she was driven off.

Our seafaring landlord was Finnish – Captain F. F. Kramsu. 'Like the poet. Ve haf a poet, same name, but different view of life, very full of miseries. The F is for Frederik, so you call me Freddie.' He was a little gnome of a man with intense blue eyes. 'F for Freddie. I am from Lapland. They don't speak my language here. It is English or nodding but their own sort of Spanish. So we speak English mostly and everybody call me Freddie – or something vorse in Spanish when they don't think I understand.' He grinned, baring rabbit teeth stained brown, his eyes crinkling with laughter as he reached for the drink Nils had just poured him. 'Then I get big laff with them because I am by then very fluent in Chilean Spanish.' He raised his glass, first to Nils, then to Iain, finally to me. '*Skool!*' He knocked it back in one gulp.

'It is pisco, I am afraid,' Nils said apologetically. 'Chilean brandy, not vodka. Vodka is difficult. So many foreign ships come through the Strait. The factory and freeze ships, they stay at sea, gobbling up krill and all the fish their boats bring them, and when they are full, they go straight back to Russia, Poland, wherever they come from, or if they haf trouble, they go to the Atlantic ports further north, in Argentine or Brazil. They are for them nearer to home.'

Captain Freddie's position in Punta Arenas was an unusual one and largely a result of the Falklands war. Being Nordic, and regarded as a neutral, he had come to be looked on as port representative for foreign ships passing through the Magellan Strait, a sort of consul. It was not official, of course. Nobody had appointed him. It was just that, since he had sold his coaster and settled in Punta Arenas, he had kept a log of all ships passing through. He had brought his telescope ashore with him and mounted it in the little dormer window high up under the eaves of the steep-pitched east-facing gable of his house.

In that log book, which he showed me later, was the name,

port and country of origin, of every ship that had passed through during the last eight and a half years, together with her age and condition, her destination, and of course the name of the captain and details of the cargo. As he pointed out to me, the port and other government officials, also the navy and military personnel, came and went, generally posted south for only a short period, whereas he was a permanent fixture. We learned later that he was paid an honorarium by the government in far-off Santiago, so that he was also in a sense their man in Punta Arenas, and it was, therefore, quite natural for him to cultivate us and be as helpful as possible.

He had a second book, started at the outset of the Falklands War, which though still in the form of a diary, was more of a journal. It not only covered ships passing to and fro through the Strait, but also included reports of Argentine air strikes, naval activity, including the sinking of the *Belgrano*, and even references to the British helicopter that had landed on the coast of the Magellan Strait almost opposite Punta Arenas, and had been destroyed by its pilot. He was full of all the gossip and rumours, most of it picked up from the ships he visited and seamen he talked to.

It was in this book that he was able to show me the first reference to the *Santa Maria*. The entry read:

On board the MV Thorhavn the first officer was from Helsinki. He told me they had put into Puerto Gallegos to land seven Swedish engineers with spares for Volvo and Saab equipment and had seen an old wooden square-rigger lying at the Navy Yard quay. She is the Santa Maria del Sud and had recently been brought down under tow from the Argentine naval base near Buenos Aires where she has been undergoing a complete refit. Captain of the Thorhavn, Olaf Peterson, tells me there were men aloft fitting aerials up the sides of two of the three masts and there was talk that the gun deck of this maritime relic, renovated just before the war as a museum ship, was now equipped with the very latest in electronics.

This is a translation, of course, the original being in Finnish. Then, shortly after the British Task Force arrived off the Falkland Islands, there was another reference to the *Santa Maria del Sud*:

> There is talk of the British landing on the coast of Patagonia north of Puerto Gallegos. But it is just rumour. I do not think it probable they will land. It would not make sense. At sea they have mobility. This, and the carrier-borne Harrier aircraft, are their great advantage. The only vessels in today are an Argentine tug towing what I presume to be the Santa Maria del Sud. She is a wooden ship, not unlike the old clippers we used to run for the grain trade before World War I, but she is at least a century older. She has been excavated out of the mud that preserved her in La Plata, they say, and virtually rebuilt. Now they have aerial wires attached to the masts and this made me think they must intend to use her for some sort of electronic surveillance.

It was about a fortnight after I arrived in Punta Arenas that he showed me his journal and I was able to take a translation of those entries. But that first evening on *Isvik* we had it from him direct. Iain asked him what he thought the electronics were for. He smiled and shook his head. 'I don't make any speculation. Not at that time. It is not wise because there are quite certainly agents of the Argentine Junta in Punta Arenas. I am well known here for the checkings I make of the movement of ships.' He pulled a battered pipe from his pocket and began to fill it. 'One time,' he continued slowly, 'I come back to my house to find it is rummaged, and they have taken out everything, all the drawers bottoms-up on the floor, also boards ripped up. I am telling the police, of course, but nothing happen, they don't arrest nobody. But they know. I am very sure they know who do it.'

He lit his pipe, drawing on it slowly, a Puckish smile lifting the corners of his mouth. 'Chile and Argentina . . .' He gave an expressive little shrug. 'You can see from the map how the frontiers between them here in the south are not made very good. So it is like a game of chess between them, eh? This country vile haf its own people in sensitive posts in the Argentine. They don't want them arrested for doing what they are trained for, so they don't arrest agents of Argentina. They live and let live. That is right, *ja*? You operate same vay, I guess. Anyway –' He laughed and slapped the table – 'they don't get what they come for. I start a new book just before they land on Malvinas, when those demolition men start work on South Georgia, remember? It was the begin of the war. I think what I say in that book may be sensitive, so I keep it always on my body, and in Finnish. The other books, of course, they leave. They are of no interest. That is what make me certain who they are.'

'They could have taken that book from you by force,' Iain suggested.

Captain Freddie shook his head. 'That is mugging, no? Ve don't haf too much mugging in Punta Arenas.' His smile was so elfin I was reminded of a troll and a performance of *Peer Gynt* I had seen at the Maddermarket in Norwich. 'If they are mugging me, then it is too much obvious. The police do not hesitate then, and it is more important at that time for the Argentine to have their observers here in freedom.'

'I understand.' Iain nodded.

'And even if they do take my book, they don't find nothing.' A crafty look had come over his face. 'After I go on board I don't write anything about my visit. Is too dangerous.'

Iain was leaning forward then. 'Ye went on board?'

'*Kyllä*, they invite me on board. That is when I begin to realise what the *Santa Maria del Sud* is about.'

Silence then, the sounds of the port coming to us softly through the night, partially overlaid by the persistent hum of machinery from the freighter moored ahead of us. Ward waited, but in the end it was only by persistent questioning that the details gradually emerged.

It must have been a very strange sight. Captain Freddie said he could hardly believe his eyes when he looked out of his bedroom window. It was like a 'ghost ship' – he used those words – the three masts standing black against the white of the low, snow-mantled line of the shore opposite and that enormously long bowsprit jutting out from the wooden hull of the ship 'like a lance'. He hadn't seen the tug at first because it was alongside on the far side.

The two vessels had laid there off the Navy Yard all that morning. Finally, in the early afternoon, he had been summoned on board the tug to try and resolve the 'liddle difficulty' that had arisen. The tow was on passage from Puerto Gallegos to the Argentine port of Ushuaia in the Beagle Channel. Just short of the entrance to the Estrecho de Magellanes they had encountered gale-force winds and off Cabo Virgenes the tow had begun to sheer violently and range up on the tug.

The tug-master had never, of course, towed a large sailing vessel before and had no experience of the windward effect of three tall masts in a gale. Periodically the ship had literally sailed up on to the tug, ramming her bows against the stern, and finally the towing hawser had ripped out the capstan to which it was fastened. All the tug could do then was to stand by the tow until the gale abated.

The towing hawser was finally reattached with rope strops round the bowsprit fastenings, and with this makeshift arrangement they had towed into Punta Arenas. What they were requesting was the co-operation of the Chilean Navy Yard in installing steel bits strong enough to ensure that the hawser did not again tear itself free. Also materials were required to effect temporary repairs to the starb'd bow where several timbers had been started by the ship riding up against the tug's stern. And they needed the loan of extra pumps because she was making water. The difficulty was that there was a naval lieutenant in charge of the tow and he refused absolutely to let any officer of the Chilean Navy on to the *Santa Maria del Sud* to assess the damage.

That was when they had sent for Captain Freddie, and after what he described as a long, sometimes 'vair ackermonious diskussion', and after a good deal of long distance telephoning, fax instructions had finally come through that allowed the Chileans to accept his decision as to what was required. That was how he had come to go on board the *Santa Maria del Sud*.

'It is a political decision, you see. *On poliittinen päätös, ymmär-*

rättekö. Everything politics. There is a war, but they still want friendly relations.' The fastenings for the steel bits would need to be on the gun deck, and it was on the gun deck they had some of the electronic equipment they did not want the Chilean officers to see. 'They don't want the purpose of the ship understood. I know nothing about electronics. *Olen vain vanha lastilaivan kapteeni, siksi olen turvassa.* Me know nothing, eh? Only old cargo boat captain.' He smiled, his eyes twinkling as he told Iain how he had had a glimpse of the lower decks, which had all been cut away in the centre and some sort of plastic covering installed.

He had been on board the *Santa Maria* some two hours or more working out with the Argentine naval lieutenant and the tug's engineers just what was required to get the tow safely down the short cut into the Beagle Channel and thence to Ushuaia. The pumps were sent out from the Navy Yard immediately. All the rest of the equipment, together with additional tools and a power generator, were sent out the following morning. Because they were effecting the repair work themselves it had taken longer to complete than if they had let the Yard do it, but even so the tow had been under way again shortly after noon on the third day.

That's all he could tell us. What the precise purpose was of installing complex electronics in an old sailing vessel he did not know for sure, and Iain did not press him. However, he did ask him about the crew, particularly those on the *Santa Maria*. 'Was there a man named Gómez among them?'

The old man shook his head. '*Ei.*' There had been two Argentine naval officers, one on the tug and the other on the *Santa Maria*, and he had seen at least six crew, but he did not know the names of any of them. Iain dipped into his briefcase and pulled out a photograph. It was a picture full-face of Mario Ángel Gómez in Navy uniform. 'Where did you get that?' I asked him.

His eyes flicked in my direction, but he didn't answer. 'D'ye recognise him?' he asked Captain Freddie. 'Was he one of the officers?'

The Captain stared at it briefly, then shook his head. '*Ei.* That man is not aboard the *Santa Maria del Sud*, nor the tug neither. Vy do you ask?'

Iain slid away from that, cross-examining him about the details of the electronic equipment. But all he could do was describe the look of the equipment on the gun deck. The rest was under wraps.

Iris returned, her eyes bright and her cheeks a-glow with the sudden transition from the cold outside to the warmth of the saloon. Everything was fixed, the Yard would do all they could to help. She had a private word with Iain in the after cabin, then put her anorak on over her dress and went off to bed, escorted by Captain Freddie. We had a final drink with Nils while he checked the list of his requirements for the prop-shaft alterations, then we went out into the night, walking quickly through the bitter blustering of the wind back to our billet.

That night I was woken by a thin, tinkling sound and sat up wondering where the hell I was. There was movement below me and I remembered that I was in the upper berth of a two-tier bunk and Iain had one of those wristwatches with a built-in alarm. I drifted off again only to open my eyes almost immediately to the sight of a head level with mine and arms reaching up. The wool of a sweater brushed my face. 'What the hell's up?'

'Nothin'. Somethin' Ah have to dae, that's all.'

An almost full moon filtered through racing clouds to give a pale light and I watched as he pulled on his rubber seaboots and slipped out of the room. I rolled out of the upper berth and padded down the corridor to the bathroom. I needed a pee anyway. It was 03.17 and I was just in time to see him climb into a waiting car and drive off.

It was almost five before he returned. But when I asked him where he had been all he said was, 'Go back to sleep.' He undressed and got quickly into his berth.

'You've been gone almost two hours.'

'Ah had to make a telephone call. Now shut up. It's cold outside and Ah want to sleep, even if ye don't.'

I didn't ask any more questions, just lay there listening to the wind. London. Via satellite. It had to be London. Europe anyway. Otherwise he wouldn't need to make the call in the middle of the night. But what was it about, and why now? What was the urgency? Questions buzzed around inside my head and I think there was a glimmer of dawn before I finally dozed off.

I don't know whether it was the overpowering sense of being imprisoned in a world of cloud and rock, the wild remoteness of it and the everlasting bludgeoning of the wind, but everything seemed to take longer than expected. And there were setbacks, of course. Coloni received a message to say his mother had been injured in some sort of political disturbance in Valparaíso, so instead of cooking for us, he decided to go home. Iris and Nils continued taking turns at the galley stove with the inevitable result that the dynamo that would run off the free-turning prop when we were sailing arrived by air from the States before the alterations to the drive shaft were complete. And then the ship had to be slipped, not once, but twice, first for the scraping, repainting and antifouling of the hull, then a second time for replacement of five defective keel bolts. Several items Iris had arranged to be flown in proved to have been wrongly listed and had to be sent back. About the middle of the month Nils discovered metal fatigue in two of the seacocks, the worst being the inflow to the heads, which meant that for all of a week, till we could slip yet again and fit replacements, we were using a good old-fashioned shit bucket. And all the time, work going on internally while I wrestled with rigging and sails, mostly on the open deck.

The one good thing was the Australian pair finally making up their minds to come, the wife's partners having agreed to her taking up to a year's sabbatical. *Will join ship end-November – Andy and Go-Go Galvin*, they cabled. And I had a piece of luck, too. The ship's library, in addition to all the necessary navigational books, a Bible, a Book of Common Prayer, accounts of Antarctic expeditions and a dozen or so lurid paperbacks, contained one or two self-help books, among them one on the rigging and canvassing of sailing vessels. It had been written for an age when wind was still the motive power for most of the world's shipping, so that, though technically out of date, it was invaluable for some of the work I was doing, particularly wire splicing, and if we were rolled over and had to jury-rig the ship it would be a life saver.

Re-rigging the ship for an Antarctic voyage inside of a week, after she had been lying idle for over a year, was quite impossible. A month at least was my estimate after I had sorted everything out. We were all working flat out and the only break we had was on the second Sunday when *Isvik* was on the slip and the Yard closed. For once the forecast was good. We took the semi-rigid rubber boat and went south towards Dawson Island, finally beaching it in a little cove of black sand and gravel on the shore of the Brunswick Peninsula just before the dog-leg that took the Strait north-west through miles of narrow channels to the Pacific. Moraine boulders were piled in rounded heaps and we walked inland through tufted heaps of tussac grass, climbing well up the scree-covered slopes to picnic in a spot where we had a magnificent view of the Strait and the channels and islands further west. The sun was shining, the water a deep indigo-blue and the air so crystal clear that it seemed as though I could stretch out my hand and touch the gleaming white of Sarmiento far to the south-east in Tierra del Fuego.

We had agreed not to talk about fitting-out problems and we lay in the sun drinking from the bottle Iain had humped up in his backpack. With the fish and cheese sandwiches Iris had brought the world seemed a different place, gentle and relaxed. And then she suddenly said, 'Carlos is arriving on Friday.'

Iain had been telling us how ten to fifteen thousand years ago early man had crossed from Mongolia to Alaska by way of the Aleutian chain of volcanic islands and then, over a period of some five millennia, had worked his way down through North and South America until finally he had reached Tierra del Fuego, living out the winters virtually naked except for the natural hair of his body. He talked about Fitzroy, the naval officer who had carried out the first detailed survey of the waters we were looking down on, and of Darwin, who had joined Fitzroy in the *Beagle* for a second voyage in which the survey had been completed, followed by the long voyage home via the Galapagos and other islands, including New Zealand. 'Five years it took them, the first tae of them spent in these waters, so Ah would guess Darwin's first tentative thoughts about the origins of species started here.'

The range of Iain's reading was a constant surprise to me; and he had that rare ability to remember what he had read so that he could pass it on. And then Iris, by that *non sequitur* announcement of Carlos's imminent arrival, showed that, far from listening to him, her thoughts had been on the voyage and what lay ahead.

'Why?' She must have given Iain some idea of the boy's background, for he didn't ask her who he was, just that explosive question – 'Why?'

'Why? I don't know why.' She was lying stretched out, her head against a pillow of lichen-covered stone, her eyes staring straight up at the incredible blue of the sky. 'All I have is this message.' She fished a crumpled sheet of paper from the pocket of her anorak and handed it to him.

Arriving Punta Arenas 1700 27 Nov – Carlos Borgalini. He read it aloud, then handed the paper back to her, and I thought what a pity it was to have to worry about that wretched boy on the one really good day we had had since our arrival. There was nothing much she could tell us about him anyway, only what we knew already. 'Ye're sure he's Gómez's cousin?' Iain had just bitten into a cheese sandwich and his mouth was full, so I don't think she heard him properly. He swallowed and repeated the question, adding, 'Ye're quite sure?'

'You have only to look at him to see he is some sort of a relation,' she said sharply.

'Borgalini. Who is Borgalini?'

'I don't know.' She said it too quickly and he glanced at her.

'Ah think ye dae. He is closely connected with that woman of yer father's, Rosalli Gabrielli. Accordin' to Rodriguez, that is, so why dae ye say he is a cousin?'

She didn't answer that.

'Is he a cousin? Or is he really somethin' closer?'

She shook her head. 'He is Ángel's cousin, not mine. That is all I know.'

'And Ángel is not your brother?'

She was silent, frowning.

'That's what ye told Pete. When he was with ye at the hacienda.'

'Did I? I don't remember.'

He was silent for a while, juggling with two small stones that were white like sugar cubes. At length he murmured, 'Somethin' wrong somewhere.'

'Wrong? What is wrong? I don't understand.'

'My information . . .' He stopped there, the click of the quartz-like cubes the only sound. 'Pass me the bottle.' He held out his hand and she gave it to him, watching him as he put it to his lips, her eyes fixed in an almost mesmerised stare.

'What is this information? What is it you are thinking?'

He had turned so that he faced her, his body propped on that deformed arm of his, the sleeve of his anorak empty, the metal fore-arm and hand stuffed incongruously into his pack. 'Let's get this straight, Iris.' He had reached over and was gripping her shoulder with his left hand, holding her so that her face was close to his. 'Yer father was born Juan Roberto Gómez. Following the annulment of his marriage to Rosalli Gabrielli he went to Ireland and married yer mother, Sheila Connor. After that he hyphened the tae surnames and called himself Juan Roberto Connor-Gómez. That right?'

She nodded, her eyes locked with his.

'Now, ye were born tae years after they were married. All very respectable. But our friend Ángel, when was he born? Dae ye know?'

She didn't answer.

'For God's sake!' His voice was suddenly high and sharp. 'What sort of a person are ye? Ye go up there to Cajamarca, behave like a whore, try and trade yer body fur information about the position of the *Santa Maria del Sud*, and now ye pretend ye don't know who the man is.' And he added, in a voice that would have done credit to an elder of the Wee Frees, 'If he is yer brother, then ye've been committin' incest. That's a carnal offence in the eyes o' the Church.' He paused. Then in a softer voice, 'An' if he's no' yer brother, then who the hell is he?'

The question hung there in the cool air of the mountainside, the whole world seemingly silent and listening. A bird slid past, wings soughing as it planed down towards the water below, darkening now with the beginnings of a breeze.

'Well?'

And then she went for him, her voice trembling, her eyes staring with sudden hate, all the Latin in her coming out as she ripped his hand from her shoulder. 'You big, filthy-minded shit. You spik to me like that again and you can go back to wherever is the name of that Glasgow slum where your drunken father spawned you.' She was almost screaming at him. 'All I wanted was to prove my husband right. I know Ángel has seen that ship. I know he has. I did get that much out of him. But he don't say where. He don't give me the position. So now I have to put up with him on the boat. And you throw it all in my face, calling me a whore, which I am not, and you know I am not. All I want is to show the world that Charles was not hallucinating.' And she added, quieter now, 'All right. Charles was scared. I know that. He was afraid of the ice. But there is nothing wrong in being scared. And there is nothing wrong with his brain. He don't hallucinate. That's what I want to prove.'

'And yer brother?' Iain's voice, too, was suddenly very quiet, very controlled.

'Ángel, do you mean?'

'No, of course Ah don't mean Ángel. Yer other brother, yer real brother, Eduardo. Don't ye want to know what happened to him?'

Her eyes widened, as though the reference to Eduardo was something physical like a blow, the fury quite gone out of her as she said, 'Why do you say that? Do you know something?' She leaned forward, gripping hold of him. 'What is it? What do you know?' And when he shook his head, she asked him in a voice fallen to a whisper, 'Who are you? Please, please tell me – who are you – what are you? I must know.'

And when he still didn't reply, she said, 'If you know something, for God's sake tell me.' The entreaty in her voice, the limpid, almost tearful look in her eyes . . . I suddenly had the feeling Eduardo meant more to her than anyone else in her life, even her husband. 'Do you know what happened to him? Do you?'

'No.' He said it abruptly. And then, almost in the same breath, his voice gone hard, 'What was the date of Mario Ángel's birth?' He was leaning towards her again, very tense. 'Ah have the date yer father married Sheila Connor. What Ah don't know for certain is what happened immediately before that. Was Mario Ángel already born then, or did Rosalli give birth to him afterwards?'

'Why? What does it matter?'

'Don't be a fool. Ye know it matters. He claims to be yer father's son. Now, dae ye know the date of Ángel's birth or don't ye?'

She was staring at him, her eyes wide, breathing quickly. 'I know when his birthday is. October 17.'

'And the year?'

'I don't think I can answer that – not for certain. You see, I never saw him till he came to stay with us in the school holidays.'

'You mean he was a schoolboy then?'

She nodded.

'And that was the first time ye'd ever set eyes on him?'

'Yes.'

'What sort of impression did he make on ye?'

Her eyes had a sudden dreamy look. 'He was different, totally different – different to any boy I had ever met before – quite . . . quite uninhibited.'

'How old did ye think he was then?'

'Oh, about ten, I think.'

'Did ye ever meet a man called Borgalini? Roberto Borgalini.'

'No. I never meet him. Why?'

'He was Rosalli Gabrielli's manager. He was also a member of the Mafia, and he was up to his eyeballs in drugs. Altogether a very nasty piece of work.' He hesitated, then got to his feet. 'He just could be Ángel's father,' he added, gathering up his things and starting back down the slope, scree-walking very fast over the first long patch of loose grey stones, swinging his pack, and the empty sleeve flapping against his hip.

TWO

It struck me as odd that Carlos should be turning up here in Punta Arenas after having been arrested for the death of a girl he had never seen. Odd, too, that neither Iris nor Iain seemed unduly surprised. It was almost as though they had expected it. Iris I could understand, but Iain . . . The trouble was, the more I was with him, the less I seemed to know him, and all my tentative questions about his contacts with the world outside Punta Arenas met with a stony reception. Increasingly the man was become an enigma to me.

Isvik was on the slip again and we were feeding ashore, at a little ristorante-cum-bistro just back of the dockyard. That evening after supper, instead of talking about Carlos, Iris began speculating once again on the role the *Santa Maria* had been intended to play in the Falklands war, asking, first Nils, then Iain, whether the Argentine Navy had intended to use her to penetrate the military exclusion zone. 'If she was intended as a sort of spy ship, she'd have been spotted in no time and boarded, or simply blown out of the water.'

'She is wood,' Nils said. 'She don't show up so well on radar.'

'If the British warships failed to find her, then the Harriers were bound to.' She was looking at Iain. 'Is that why you're so interested in the *Santa Maria*? You want to find out what her purpose is?'

He didn't answer, sitting there, his left elbow on the table, his shoulders hunched.

'It doesn't make sense,' I said. 'Those old ships may be built of wood, but there's still plenty of metal for the radar to pick up.

Guns, anchors, all the fastenings, the metal bands round the masts . . .'

'No.' Iris was suddenly quite excited. 'The bands round the masts, all the deck fastenings, they were plastic. Everything that was originally iron had been ripped out and replaced with specially moulded plastic equivalents.' She had been talking to the dockyard workers, asking them about the *Santa Maria*. One of them had told her about the deck fastenings and she had confirmed it with a naval officer who had been in Punta Arenas when the frigate was towed in and who was now on his second tour of duty in the Magellan port. She had Iain's attention now as she added, 'It must have cost a fortune to modify her like that. What did they do it for if not to use her as a spy ship? They never did use her, did they?'

He shook his head.

'Then how did she come to be down there in the ice of the Weddell Sea? Is that what you have come to find out?'

He smiled, shaking his head again. 'We don't know she's there. Not for certain. But if she is, and we manage to reach her . . .' He hesitated, still smiling, then gave a little shrug. 'Then we'll know her secret, won't we?' And he added, 'Ah'm inclined to agree with Nils. Ah think some naval officer with more imagination than sense dreamed up the idea of slippin' her inside the Navy's guard as a spy ship. And if that officer was high enough in rank . . .' He hesitated, then, still thinking aloud: 'Nobody could tell him it wouldn't work. It's never been tried, not as far as Ah know – a wooden ship with no metal anywhere and the electrics safely cocooned. Same principle as the plastic domes that protect our coastal radar defences. But, of course, the war was over so quickly.'

'But after the war,' she said. 'They sailed afterwards. I checked when I was making enquiries in Ushuaia.'

'Enquiries?' His head came up. 'What enquiries?'

'About Charles. I think I may be partly the reason Ángel was given facilities to fly down into the Weddell Sea.'

'He was testin' the suitability of a Fokker plane fur work in the Antarctic.'

'He found the *Santa Maria*. I know that. So he is flying two birds with one stone.' She gave a little giggle at her verbal mix-up. 'He had a test job to carry out and at the same time he can see if what Charles said is true.'

Iain was frowning. 'Ah thought he flew that test before there was any suggestion of an old ship caught in the ice down there. Did he tell ye when he flew over it?'

'No.'

'And if he flew over it before that plane yer husband was in crashed . . .' He left it at that, but the inference was obvious. If he had flown the test before the plane crashed, then he had had another reason to go looking for the *Santa Maria*. 'When did she leave Ushuaia?' he asked her.

'I don't know. I ask, but there is nobody there who had seen her leave.'

'But a ship like that, a centre of interest, can't leave a naval dockyard without her absence being noted and commented on. There must have been somebody there –'

'She was not moored at the dockyard. Nobody seemed to know where she was being hidden away. She was at the Navy Yard until just after the Falklands war ended, then she left, nobody could tell me where.'

'Right after the end of the war?'

'Yes, right after the war.'

'Are ye sayin' that was when she went down into the ice – right after the war?'

But she couldn't be sure of that. 'Some of them thought she was hidden away in one of the coves. There are hundreds of places she could have been beached or anchored. You have only to glance at the chart. All west of here is a maze of islands, channels and secret places.'

He picked her up on that. 'Secret places? Why do ye use an expression like that – any particular reason?'

She gave a little shrug. 'There was some talk. Rumours, you know. There are always rumours after a war. There was talk of an English commando unit. Marines. And of a camp.'

'What sort of camp?'

But she didn't know. It was just talk. 'And I was there because of my husband. I wasn't there to talk about the *Santa Maria*.'

'Did anybody happen to mention anythin' about the *Desaparecidos*?'

'I don't remember. Maybe. But it would have meant very little to me. It was Charles I was thinking of.'

The warmth of the bistro was making me drowsy. I must have dozed off, for the next thing I heard was Nils saying, '*Ja*, to make a good testing I need a full day.' And Iain's reply: 'Thursday then.'

'Okay. Ve start very airly so ve haf calm water. Then if the vind get oop is good again, so I test that *skrue* shaft with waves to throw her around.' He nodded. 'Thursday, but you take a telephone to the weather man first. I am not wanting flat calm all day. And no gale neither. A good weather mix I want. That is good for Pete and his sails, too.'

I came fully awake then. 'Sails? I haven't got any sails yet.'

'They are finished,' Iris said. 'I showed you the telex on Saturday. They are loaded on the cargo vessel *Anton Varga* and she left Valparaíso last Wednesday.'

'Sea trials on Thursday then,' Iain said, looking across at me. He got to his feet. 'And if the new sails haven't arrived by then ye'll hoist the old ones. Okay?'

I nodded. The old ones had been double-stitched and patched where necessary. They would be perfectly adequate to test the rigging.

He stopped at the cash desk to pay the bill, the three of us getting to our feet and shrugging our way into our oilskins. All through the meal the rain had been beating against the windows. Iris took my arm, a gesture of excitement, I think. 'Thursday and our first sea trials. Thursday is my lucky day. If everything goes right . . .'

But I was already thinking about all the things that still had to be done. There were the old sails to bend on, and because they had been with a retired dockyard worker, who had been employed making and repairing awnings and hatch covers, I had not yet been able to check the sheet leads. And then there was the problem of handling the sheets when under sail alone, and if it suddenly started to blow and we had to reef ... We were desperately short-handed, with Nils in the wheelhouse watching over his engine and only Iain available for deck work if Iris was at the wheel.

I tried to argue with them, but though they agreed it would be much simpler if we postponed trials until the Galvins arrived at the end of the month, Iain still insisted on Thursday. 'And if the weather's bad?' I asked. 'It's not just the sails. You both had a look at the chart. Somebody has to pilot the boat.' I had already discovered that I was the only one of us with experience in navigation. 'And if the wind comes at us from off the mountains, the gusts could be katabatic.' They both knew what that meant, vicious down-blasts hammering the water almost vertically so that a vessel with full sail up could suffer a knock-down. 'Just think what it could be like if we had to shorten sail in those conditions.' I talked to them about reefing then. There was no roller-reefing, it was rope down to the boom through the reefing cringles and tie-in reef pennants, and in the confines of the Strait I would have to be constantly taking bearings and marking up the chart.

'We'll take it as it comes,' Iain said finally. 'Ah want to see *Isvik* under way so we know what further problems we face. Okay?' He turned towards the door. 'No more argument, Pete. Trials are set fur Thursday, 09.00, and if the weather's bad, then we'll confine it to engine trials.' And he ducked out, shoulders hunched against driving hailstones.

I caught up with him, almost shouting to make myself heard above the drumming of the hail on tin roofs, the sound of waves breaking against the quay, as I reminded him how fickle the wind could be, how quickly it could get up. 'We could have full sail hoisted in relative calm and the next minute be roaring along with far too much canvas up and visibility about nil in a heavy rain squall. What do I do then?'

'Shit yer pants, Ah should think.' He had rounded on me, his voice cold with anger. 'Jesus Christ, man! Stop worryin'. Take things as they come.'

'But –'

'Shut up, blast ye! Ah don't want another word from ye on the subject. Thursday, 09.00. Sea trials. Got it?'

'It will be all right, Pete.' Iris had caught up with us, pouring oil on troubled waters. There was something to be said for having a woman along. 'He's right. Stop worrying.' I felt her hand on my arm. 'I'll get Captain Freddie to pilot us,' she added. 'I'm sure he would come. He would love it. There! Does that ease your mind?'

I said, 'Yes.' But it didn't really, and though I was tired, I couldn't sleep that night. Maybe it was the coffee, but for hours, it seemed, I lay awake, my mind going over and over all the deadly, disastrous possibilities. A young woman with only a rudimentary knowledge of sailing and a man who was not only one-armed, but mentally attuned to mechanics and electronics so that he hardly knew one end of a boat from another. And though *Isvik* was essentially a motor-sailer, she still carried a considerable area of canvas. She was schooner-rigged, the main mast aft carrying a huge stays'l for reaching as well as the main, and the foremast an upper and a lower squares'l in addition to a boomed stays'l and a full range of jibs.

I had three days, that was all, and the sails were sodden. We had been using the Yard facilities and they had been laid out in the loft while the old man worked on them. He had finished on the Friday, and because there had been a sudden demand for the use of the loft, they had been dumped outside in the open. Nobody had told me, and as a result, they had remained there all weekend. It had rained throughout the Sunday night. They said it was unusual for rain to last any length of time, but it did that night and the sails were so full of water they seemed to weigh a ton as we shifted them on a borrowed trolley from the Yard to the boat.

Fortunately, the weather was fine from noon onwards with a nice drying breeze. With Iris to help me, I hoisted the jibs, main and trysail upside down, an old trick that ensured the biggest area of sail was at the highest point on the mast. Even so, I lost a whole day, the sails slatting furiously as the wind increased out

195

of the west, funnelling north up the Strait and causing the heavy terylene to bang thunderously. The noise brought half the population of the port to the quayside. I don't think they had ever seen sails hoisted the wrong way up before, and anyway, they were as full of 'curtiosity' as a baby elephant, asking all sorts of questions, but particularly where we were going, when and how many of us. *Isvik* had been moored to the quay so long they had obviously come to regard her as a fixture.

The day was not entirely wasted, for I spent most of it staring at charts 1281 and 1337 and trying to memorise the more hazardous details, also the transit marks, bearings and all the courses we would need to steer going either south or north from Punta Arenas.

We had come off the slip first thing that morning, a Yard launch towing us round to the quay, and Nils had gone to work straight away, putting first of all the heads together, then connecting up the galley taps which were all pump action. As a result I had the deckhouse with its chart table virtually to myself. It was very different on Tuesday when Nils had the engine hatch boards off and the big Merc diesel thumping away as he ran a detailed check on the prop-shaft and the auxiliary dynamo, slipping the shaft clutch in and out.

Tuesday was my day for hoisting the sails the right way up, checking the sheet leads to the winches, the quick clamps we had had flown in from BA, reeving the mainsheet through the big titanium and carbon-fibre block, which was also new, and working out the reefing drill. Iain would be at the mast paying the halyard out on the winch, I would be hauling down on the rope rove through the lead cringle, running it through the quick clamp and cleating it down, while Iris did the same for the luff cringle and then worked aft along the boom, flaking the sail down and tying it into position with the reefing pennants. I took them through the drill time and time again until Iain finally lost patience and said he had other things to do.

'Well, just remember what you have to do when I yell *Reef*.'

'Okay, okay.' I don't think he had an inkling of what it could be like at night in a gale with a big sea running.

I stood there for a moment, looking at him. 'Something I think you should understand.'

He was on his way below then and he checked. He had caught the tone of my voice. 'Well?'

'You told me I was to be the ship's sailing master, right?'

'Aye.' He had his jaw thrust out and I had the feeling he was preparing himself for trouble.

'If I'm to be sailing master,' I said slowly, 'then the deck is mine. I'm in charge up here and you're under my orders, you and Iris, Nils, the Galvins, everybody. You do what I say without question or argument. If not – if it isn't to be like that, then I won't sail with you. It would be too bloody dangerous. You understand? It's got to be like that or we don't survive when the gremlins strike.'

There was silence, Iris standing on the wheelhouse roof with one hand still on the spoke of the upper steering wheel and Iain on the step of the wheelhouse entrance, just his head and shoulders showing and his eyes half-closed as though thinking it over. Finally he raised his head, looked at me and said, 'Fine. On deck ye're the boss. Ah accept that.' He laughed suddenly. 'Ye dae it right an' we'll work our arses off fur ye, but ye get too full o' yersel' an' by God Ah'll gi' ye hell down below an' on the ice. An' so will Iris – won't ye, luv?' He jabbed his finger at me. 'Ye're in command up here because ye know yer stuff, but just remember, this is me expedition. Ah pay the piper. And Iris – she's the cause o' the five o' us bein' here. So watch it, 'bor. Ah don't take very easy to people who like throwin' their weight about.' He nodded and swung himself below, saying, 'Just pray fur some good weather on Thursday.'

It was late afternoon by then and my patience had been exhausted. But what did they expect? On the last run-through there had been a sudden blattering gust of wind that had threatened to tear the ship from the quay, possibly break the mast or rip the main. Anyway, I was tired, we were all tired, and Iain letting go the topping lift when I had called for the main to be lowered . . . The thought of the damage that could result from inexperience sent cold shivers through me and I found myself hoping to God Galvin would prove a good hand.

I didn't have any coffee that evening and fell asleep at the table. It was Nils who woke me. The other two had left. He was still the only one of us sleeping aboard. 'The rain is taken away. You go to bed now.' I looked round the saloon with its big, gimballed table. It was like a carpenter's workshop, tools and wood shavings everywhere. But it was taking shape. The cabins and the heads now had doors and we had handholds conveniently placed all along the roofing timbers. 'Is good, *ja*,' he said, seeing me reach up to steady myself. 'We are all like apes swinging from one handhold to another.' He drank the dregs of his akavit and got to his feet. 'But is better with handholds, much, much better. We don't break many bones, eh?' And he showed his stained teeth in a cackle of laughter.

I was asleep again almost before I had climbed over Iain into my bunk and I did not wake until a shaft of sunlight streamed through the window onto my face. Immediately after breakfast I took them through the reefing drill again, Nils included, and then explained the gybe procedure for bringing the boat round into the wind in the event of one of us being knocked overboard. It is not easy to carry out man overboard drill with the vessel moored alongside a quay. I had them do a couple of dummy runs and left it at that, for there were changes I needed to make to the genoa leads, also the positioning of the main boom kicking strap needed adjustment, and the others also had things to do before we finally went to trials. And that evening I tried to tell them how to read a chart and lay off a course. Iain was very quick at picking it up, but even so, I was appalled to discover what an awful lot there is to learn on a boat of this sort, and we were going out into one of the worst sea areas in the world.

Next day, Thursday, I was again woken by a gleam of sun, but it did not last. By the time we had finished breakfast the sky was overcast, the tops of the heights to the west of us capped with dark masses of cloud and the wind beginning to funnel up the Strait. I tried to persuade Iain to switch the order in which we tried out engine and sails. He saw my point about the need for light winds, or said he did, but he still refused to take the sail trials first. 'If there's anythin' wrong with the engine or that prop-shaft the sooner Ah know about it the better. Engine trials first, then we'll get sail up and test out the shaft clutch and that new auxiliary dynamo. Okay?'

The Merc was already thumping out its hymn tune and ten minutes later we cast off from the quay and were away with Iris at the wheel and Iain laying off the course on the chart under my direction. I could have done with Captain Freddie at the wheel. His presence would have given me confidence, too, but unfortunately he had been called on board a Panamanian tanker so we left without him. The noise in the deckhousing made speech almost impossible. Nils had the sound-proof cover boards off and was sitting on the floor, his legs dangling over the noisy monster as we slid away from the quay. Out in the Strait we turned onto the southerly course we had run on Sunday in our semi-rigid inflatable, heading for the Brunswick Peninsula with wind over tide and the bows slapping noisily into a short lop.

Iris leaned away from the wheel, calling down to Nils, 'Everything okay?'

'*Ja.*' He nodded.

She looked at me, smiling. 'Everything's fine. No problems.'

I agreed. 'No problems.' So far. My mouth felt dry. The wind was increasing.

Nils was over an hour tinkering with his engine before finally asking me to get the sails up and turn downwind so that we could have the prop turning with the engine disconnected and test the dynamo and its drive. By then the wind had risen to something over force 5 and there were intermittent outbursts of storm rain. The sails went up with only one hitch, when I did what Iain had done two days ago, grabbed the topping lift instead of the jib halyard. I decided on Number 2 jib, and while we were still headed into the wind under engine, I had the mainsail lowered and a reef tied in. The result was that, when we turned downwind, we were under-canvassed, and with the engine disconnected there was insufficient power from the prop. It had to be that, for shortly after the dynamo had been installed Nils had gone up the ratlines and rigged the two-bladed wind prop to the upper crosstrees of the foremast and it had worked off that perfectly.

'Ye're being over-cautious,' Iain told me. 'We'll have to unreef the main and get a bigger foresail on her. And if that doesn't work, then we'll hoist the squares'l.'

In the end I agreed. It was a mistake, of course, but it was his boat and we had land on either side of us. By then we were cumbered with oilskins and safety harness and it took much longer than expected to change jibs and shake the reef out, so that by the time we turned downwind again we were well past Puerto Hambre and the end of the Brunswick Peninsula and were being set down on to Dawson Island, close to a mass of rock guarded by kelp.

I went about then, for it was blowing force 7 in the gusts with visibility cut to less than a quarter of a mile and snatches of heavy rain. Nils was aft, testing the quick-release system for the prop. Both prop, and the arm to which it was attached, could then be swung up through the slot in the transom to save the blades from damage by ice floes. I switched the radar on, thankful that our sailing speed now provided enough power from the dynamo to give a clear picture of the shore. The speed indicator, now that the wind was aft, was showing 10½.

Nils was gone a long time, so that we were well past Punta Arenas before he rejoined me in the wheelhouse. 'Is okay. It verk fine.' He peered down into the engine compartment, then he was at my elbow, flipping on just about every switch the instrument console possessed – echo-sounder, Decca navigator, Satnav, masthead, stern and navigation lights, the lot. There was enough power now to drive them all, the only exception being the search-light mounted on the deckhouse roof. When he switched that on all he got was a feeble glimmer.

'Okay?' I asked him.

'Ja. Okay.' He switched everything off and tried the little cooker Iain had insisted on installing to save fuel. It worked even with hot plate and microwave oven switched on.

'Okay, that's enough,' I shouted to him. I wanted the engine on again, for by then we were already abreast of Puerto Zenteno, which marked the turn eastward through the second, then the first narrows and out into the Atlantic The Strait was narrowing fast and already the Tierra del Fuegan shoreline was showing dangerously close on the radar. A moment later we could see it with the naked eye. There was kelp and rock there and I went about in a hurry, yelling orders, a course to steer to Iris at the helm, to Nils, particularly to Iain as he began hardening in on the jib sheet. I passed him the winch handle. At least he could work the winch one-handed. The main was flogging wildly, the noise deafening.

I got her round on to the port tack, heeled right over and water hissing along the side deck as we gradually pulled away from the shore. Suddenly we were in a void, nothing to see but mist and breaking waves, the boat heavily over-canvassed, and what scared the life out of me was that we were into the Segunda Angostura, the second narrows, being thrust rapidly sideways by the tide. If we were thrust right through into the expansion area of the Strait between the first and second narrows, we would be into the area where the Pacific and the Atlantic tides meet. The Pilot gave the tidal rate through the even narrower Primera Angostura as anything up to 8 knots!

The squall passed, the cloud-mist lifting to give us a visual impression of the grip the current had on us, *Isvik* moving sideways very fast, the shoreline slipping by.

I don't remember much about the next half-hour. Somehow we managed to get her reefed, but it took time and there were moments in the frequent squalls when I was afraid those old sails would be torn to shreds, even that we might break a mast. Twice we had to put about because she kept making up towards the Patagonian shore, and all the time at the back of my mind was the knowledge that if we were caught up in the first narrows we could be in trouble. There were four tides a day here, not two, and I had a horrible vision of our being forced to sail back and forth across this section of the Strait for the rest of our lives.

By the time the ship was properly reefed and we were motor-sailing, the tide was past its full force, but even so it seemed for ever before we had left those second narrows astern of us. I steered as close to the shore as I dared and suddenly we were out of the tidal grip. After that I think we all had an almost euphoric sense of satisfaction as we switched the engine off and beat back under sail alone.

A truck was waiting for us at the quay, the driver fuming as we bungled the first attempt to come alongside and tie up. Another freighter had come in and it was not easy berthing in the small space left between them. The truck had been there over four hours. It contained the first consignment of stores Iris had ordered and we had to turn to, unload the truck and hump the stores on board without even a break for a cup of tea.

We had that some two hours later when all the boxes and containers had been transferred from truck to deck and roped down under a tarpaulin we had obtained for use in emergency. By the time Iris had a meal ready for us we were almost past caring about food, and at the end of the meal Iain served us coffee heavily laced with an almost black Jamaican rum.

I slept like a log that night, surfaced late, and then, when I crossed the quay and went down to breakfast, there was another man sitting eating at the saloon table. He half turned as I entered, and Iris, standing at the stove, said, 'Carlos.'

I recognised him then. He had jumped to his feet, holding out his hand. 'Carlos Borgalini.'

I ignored the proffered hand, muttering my name and going straight to my usual seat. 'Carlos came in on a special charter flight early this morning,' Iris explained. 'We are to pick up Ángel at Ushuaia.'

'Ushuaia! But that's in the Beagle Channel, down by Cape Horn.'

'I know.' She passed me my breakfast and turned back to the stove. 'Coffee or tea this morning? You have a choice.'

'Coffee.' I said it automatically, prodding a sausage and biting into it on the fork. 'It's out of the question. Ushuaia means going out through a maze of rocks into the Pacific, then turning back into the Beagle. Not the way we want to go at all, headed straight into the prevailing wind.'

'I can read that much from the chart.'

'But why?' I turned to our visitor. 'Tell him to meet us here.'

'No. As I have already told the *señora*, he will meet us in Ushuaia. Not here.'

'Us? You said *us*.'

He nodded, smiling, and I thought I saw a little devil peeping out of his eyes. I may have been mistaken, for the gleam of wickedness was gone in a flash, but I was convinced his presence here on board meant trouble. He was dark and very Sicilian, smooth-faced and handsome, almost too good-looking to be true. But the way he moved his hands, the little smile that indicated pleasure at the violence of my reaction, everything about him suggested a vicious streak of effeminacy.

'He wants to come with us,' Iris said.

I began to argue, but she told me to wait until Iain was here, then we could all of us discuss it together.

'I've done quite a bit of sailing. I can give you a hand on deck and I'm a good helmsman.' His English was almost perfect, barely the trace of an accent.

'What sort of sailing?'

'Dinghies mainly, but some cruising out from Buenos Aires after the war.' He meant, of course, the Falklands war. 'My family has a small cruiser-racer.'

'You were cruising with your father?' It seemed unlikely from what little I had heard of Rosalli Gabrielli's boyfriend, but perhaps he was referring to another member of the Borgalini family.

He smiled and shook his head. He was very beautiful when he smiled. 'You're short-handed so I think you find me useful.'

I nodded and got on with my breakfast. It did not really matter who he had sailed with. The point was that he had the best range of experience, dinghy as well as cruising. By then Nils had joined us and we were all sitting, drinking our coffee, when Iain came in. He was in a foul mood. He already knew about Carlos. The woman who looked after Captain Freddie and his house had told him. Carlos had knocked her up shortly after six, and because he had said he was related to the *señora*, she had made up a bed for him in the little box-room at the back. 'You.' Iain stood glowering down at him. 'What the hell are ye doin' here?'

Carlos had got to his feet. Apparently he didn't have to be told who Iain was. 'Carlos Borgalini.' He held out his hand.

Iain ignored it. 'Ah ken who ye are. Ah asked ye a question.'

Carlos was smiling, full of charm as he began to explain.

'Ushuaia! Why Ushuaia?'

'Mario said you would understand.'

'Mario? Our Connor-Gómez friend, ye mean, eh – Ángel?' Iain stared at him a moment, then turned to Iris. 'Gi' me some coffee, fur God's sake. It's been a bad mornin'.' He didn't say why it had been a bad morning, but Nils had already told me he had arrived on board early, got some papers from his briefcase, which was locked in the security drawer at the back of the chart table, and then gone up into the town where he had found some-body with a fax machine. 'Oh, an' the snowmobile has been unloaded by mistake at Puerto Gallegos, God knows why. Ah've been tryin' to sort that out, too.'

Much to my surprise he seemed to accept that we would start off by heading west and ducking down into the Beagle Channel. And when I told him it didn't make sense poking our nose out into the Pacific, then facing Cape Horn, just because Connor-Gómez preferred to join ship at Ushuaia rather than Punta Arenas, he turned on me and told me to mind my own business.

'It is my business,' I answered angrily. 'A raw crew –'

'Shut up, will ye!' He had grabbed hold of me with that gloved steel claw, thrusting his face forward, his eyes gone cold. 'Ye dae yer job, Ah'll dae mine. We pick him up at Ushuaia if that's what he wants.'

'You mean he's *persona non grata* here in a Chilean port?'

'Ah told ye, mind yer own business.' The claw bit into my arm. 'Okay?' He let the silence round the table hang a minute, finally releasing my arm, his face relaxing into a smile. 'One good thing, the *Anton Varga* is due in around ten-thirty. Yer new sails should be off-loaded shortly after midday.' Iris handed him his coffee and he sat back. 'The first thing is to get all our stores listed and stowed. Then ye can go to work checkin' the sails. Carlos can gi' ye a hand.'

To my surprise the boy proved very useful. He might look

204

effeminate, but he had plenty of energy, and he was intelligent. In no time at all he had learned the ropes, so that the following day, when all the stores had been correctly stowed in order of use and I was free to deal with the sails, I found I could rely on him for quite a lot of the hard pulley-hauley and winching as we hoisted them one by one, testing them out as best we could with the wind coming at us round the bows of the freighter moored astern.

Thrown into his company like this, I took the opportunity to try and clarify his connection with the Connor-Gómez family. It seemed unlikely I would get as good a chance again, for once we were all of us living on board, privacy would be at a premium with seven of us cooped up together, eight if he came as well. My main concern was his relationship with Iris and the reason for his apparent determination to join the expedition. Remembering the look on his face as he had peered down at us through the *Cutty Sark*'s skylight there had to be something between them.

I tried a straight question first – 'You're Iris's cousin, I understand?' But he just laughed. 'Some cousin she is, going off, pretending she's dead and leaving me to pick up the cans.' He wouldn't say much more than that, and when I asked him what his connection with the Connor-Gómez family was, he answered that if Iris hadn't told me by now, he was damned if he was going to.

Later I tried another tack, complimenting him on the speed with which he had mastered the intricacies of *Isvik*'s rig and saying he must have had a good sailing instructor. 'The best,' he said, his eyes lighting up.

'Who?'

He glanced at me, a sudden wariness. 'Mario, of course.'

'Mario? Mario who?'

'Mario Borgalini.'

But when I asked him whether Mario Borgalini was his father, he shrugged and turned away, muttering over his shoulder, 'I never know who my father is, only that I am a Borgalini.' He said the name almost pretentiously as though he were proud of being a Borgalini.

'You mean you don't know who your parents are?'

'No, I do not mean. My mother's name is Rosalli. She is a singer, to the guitar mainly – a very passionate, very remarkable woman.' His eyes were alight now with a luminous warmth. 'She is also very beautiful, even now, though she is more than forty when I am born. And very talented,' he added. 'You have not heard her sing? She is Rosalli Gabrielli. All those records . . .'

'Yes, of course.' I was suddenly remembering an advertisement in a King's Lynn shop. Not my sort of music, but vaguely I recalled a very Romany face with a large open mouth full of teeth and very black hair. So that was his mother. A woman who had briefly been married to Juan Gómez. And Mario was Ángel Connor-Gómez's first name.

'It was Ángel who taught you to sail, Ángel Connor-Gómez. Is that right?'

He nodded, turning away again. 'At home we always call him Mario.'

'So he is your half-brother.' He had to be since Rosalli Gabrielli was his mother also.

'Per'aps. You want me to get the fisherman up? Shall we try that next?'

'Did you see a lot of him?'

'Of Mario? No. I don't see enough of him.' He said it almost petulantly. 'It was only during that one year, in the holiday. I was at school, you see, and he was at school, too, in a way, at the *Escuela Mecánica*. And then, of course, we were often away from our home in Buenos Aires. My mother's engagements took us all over America.'

'How old were you when he taught you to sail?'

'Fourteen, I think. Why?'

It was an impressionable age and I was beginning to have an uneasy feeling about their relationship. 'What about Iris?' I asked. 'Did you see anything of her?'

'Of course not. Why should I?' He said it with what I thought was a touch of venom, adding by way of explanation, 'As you can imagine, the Connor-Gómez and the Borgalini families don't mix.' He banged back the hatch on the foredeck, disappearing down into the sail locker, and that was the end of it.

Just after dawn on the Sunday the cargo vessel astern of us pulled out into the Strait and I had *Isvik* warped round while we had room, so that she faced into the wind, and then once again I had the sails hoisted one at a time, Carlos and myself working as a team. Unfortunately, I did not dare test the set of the upper and lower squares'ls, having to be content with setting them flying. The fisherman stays'l, too. And there was another sail I didn't quite understand. It was huge, with a hoist on both masts and filled all the space between, the foot of it reaching back almost to the rear of the deck housing. A block just aft of the upper squares'l boom that I had not understood now made sense. Carlos went up the foremast, rove a long nylon line to it, and with this round the belly of the sail, we were able to scandalize it into a roll as we hoisted it.

Thankfully all the sails seemed to have been cut correctly, the luffs exact as to length and only the main requiring some adjustment to the leach. Also I decided to have the lower panels and batten pockets double-stitched.

'Lucky we are not junk-rigged,' Carlos said, smiling at me as he stood on the stern looking up at the flogging sail. The wind was gusting quite strongly now and I dared not sheet any of them in. 'You ever sailed in a junk rig? I do it once. Only in the Río de la Plata. It is the lazy sailor's dream of a rig, but too many battens for us, too much sewing. Do you have a machine for sewing on board this ship?'

'Yes,' I said.

'Good. Then I sew for you. I do that on the boat I sailed in from Rhode Island to Plymouth when I come to study in England.' It was then that I managed to extract one further piece of information from him. It was in connection with some wild plan of his to purchase a boat and sail round the world. 'Alone?' I asked him, and he laughed and said no, not alone. 'With Mario, of course.'

'You mean he plans to sell that hacienda in Peru?'

'No, of course he don't sell the Hacienda Lucinda. But when

we get the money from the insurance people ... There is a lot of moneys owed to us for the fire at the Gómez store.'

'Won't that go to Iris?' I asked.

'No.' He smiled. It was a nasty little vicious smile. 'Mario has seen to that. She gets nothing. Her father made all the shares over to Mario, and some to me. It is enough to buy several boats.' He said it boastfully, his eyes as intense as a cat looking at a bird caught in wire netting. 'And nothing to Eduardo. Or to Iris.' The undertone of viciousness was back in his voice.

I came to the conclusion then and there that, however good a hand he turned out to be, I wasn't going to like the boy. And that's how I thought of him, as a boy, though there couldn't have been more than a few years between us in age. There was something immature about him, as though he had grown up outside of parental control and was mentally an undisciplined kid.

However, I was certainly lucky to have somebody else on board who was not only hooked on sailing, but had transocean experience. And then, the next day, he suddenly announced that he was going climbing. The kit he had brought with him included a rucksack and into it he stuffed his oilskins, some cold weather gear, heavy socks, food, and strapped to the top of it a waterproof sleeping bag.

'I am studying too much, then in a police cell –' He was looking at Iris as he said this, but smiling still. He didn't seem to bear her a grudge. 'I need to harden up.' He slapped his stomach.

'Where are you going?' she asked him.

'Up there.' He waved his hand vaguely towards the north. 'There is some sort of a track leads back of the town and up over the top of the Brunswick Peninsula. Maybe I hitch a ride up to the ski slopes. That will save me eight kilometres. Once on the tops I will be able to have a look at the Seno Otway and all the rest of that sweep of water that makes an island of Riesco. *Seno* means womb, and that's what it looks like on the chart – a secret place.' He was looking at Iris, smiling. 'If I don't return the day after tomorrow send out a search party please.'

He borrowed the lightest of our four ice picks, also a little plastic handbearing compass from the chart table drawer, which he slung round his neck. We were both on deck to see him off, and as his slender, boyish figure disappeared behind the sheds, I said to Iris, 'I don't understand him.'

'No?' She was tight-lipped, her voice cold.

'He talks about "us" and "we" all the time. He seems to think he's coming with us. Is he?'

She didn't answer.

'You'll decide at Ushuaia, is that it? When your brother arrives.'

'I have told you . . .' She stopped there, turning away towards the wheelhouse.

'Why does he want to come?' I called after her. 'Does he need to prove something?'

She looked back at me then. 'Per'aps. We'll see what Ángel says – what their relationship is.' She said this slowly, standing there, looking worried. 'That boy –' She shook her head, beads of moisture gleaming like diamond dust in the blackness of her hair. 'You ask if he need to prove something. I think per'aps he need to prove he is a man.' She smiled fleetingly. 'I don't think his life has been an easy one.' She turned then and went below.

That night, I don't know why – possibly it was because the arrival of Carlos brought it home to me that we were very near to the point of departure – I started thinking about the purpose of life, my life, and why I was risking it on this crazy search for what would probably turn out to be a non-existent ship. What was the point? Was *I* trying to prove something?

I looked back down the years, so little of achievement, not even the commonest of all – a home, a wife, children. Was that what I wanted?

I thought of the ice ahead and almost laughed aloud. I wouldn't find those sort of satisfactions down there. So why was I going? What the hell did I want? That question went rattling round in my mind until it merged into a welter of ice, and myself standing gazing up at an image of Iris stretched out like one of the carved angels on the hammer beams of a Norfolk church.

No, more like the figurehead on the bows of an old sailing ship. She was staring down at me, bare-breasted and her hair flying, and the bows were bedded in ice, the long bowsprit reaching up into scudding clouds. She was trying to tell me something. I could see her lips moving, but I couldn't catch the words. And then the figurehead changed into my mother, watering cans in her hand, and she was calling to me to help her with the flowers. But there were no flowers, only a great berg of ice hanging over the broken stump of a mast and the gaunt figure of a man staring at me out of a bearded face. And all the time there was the tinkling sound of crystals falling.

I woke then to the stillness of the night and Iain's wristwatch alarm ringing like a cracked musical box. 'What is it this time?' I mumbled as he heaved himself out of the bunk below me.

'Got to catch a plane,' he replied.

'Where to?'

There was a long pause. Then he said, 'BA. Then Montevideo.'

'Checking up on the *Santa Maria del Sud*?'

He didn't answer that and I dozed off. He woke me just before he left to say he would be away three days, possibly more. 'Tell Iris, will ye? And as soon as Galvin arrives to give ye a hand, take *Isvik* out again and give those new sails a thorough trial. Don't worry about the engine. It's the sails and the crew we need to concentrate on now. Ah don't want any balls-up reefin' as we beat our way down towards the Beagle Channel. Okay? Ah want everybody knowin' exactly what they have to dae on deck in any eventuality.' I could just see the lift of his hand in the meagre light that came from the uncurtained window. 'And don't put the ship ashore, understand?' Then he was gone, and a minute later there was the sound of a car pulling away.

Shortly after dawn it began to blow very hard from the west with intermittent outbursts of driving sleet. We wondered how Carlos was faring after his first night out as we finished tidying up below, sorting gear out ready for the arrival of the Galvins that evening. It was the end of November now, and though the intention had been to sail mid-December, the customary time for expeditions to leave for Antarctica, we now had to allow for the switch to Ushuaia as our point of departure. Also, the Chilean Met. people were muttering about the ozone layer and an earlier than usual break-up of the ice.

Darkness fell and no sign of Carlos. Or the Galvins. Their flight had been held up by bad weather. However, the wind was beginning to fall away and by the time we started in on our evening meal the sky had cleared and the almost full moon was peering up at us out of the Strait, where the waters had suddenly gone still and as black as polished obsidian.

It was stew again that night – we were eating plenty of fresh meat and vegetables while we could – and I had just passed my plate to Iris for another helping when there were thumps on deck and the sound of shod feet, then a voice called, 'Ahoy there! Anybody home?' The call came again, this time from the wheelhouse above our heads, the voice a soft drawl with the faintest of nasal twangs.

'The Galvins!' Iris jumped to her feet. 'Come on down!'

The man who entered was tall, almost lanky, with a narrow, slightly freckled face, sandy hair and the brightest of blue eyes shining like sapphires in the glare of the saloon light. 'Andy Galvin.' And as we shook hands, he said, 'And this is my wife, Go-Go.'

She was still on the companion ladder, just the crimson slash of her pants showing. A bulging valise was heaved down, then in a flash she was beside her husband, and we just stood there gaping at her. All I remember of that first sight of one of the most extraordinary young women I have ever met was the white gleam of her big teeth, the brilliance of her smile of greeting and the way her mouth was made to appear even broader by the scarlet of lipstick that matched her pants almost exactly. Her skin was the colour of a golden coffee blend, the nostrils broad, the eyes black and her hair even blacker, frizzed out so that she bore a startling resemblance to an adman's idea of a golliwog.

I saw a flicker of anger cross her husband's face. So did Iris, for she recovered from her sense of shock quicker than either Nils or myself, stepping quickly forward and giving the girl a warm hug. 'Welcome aboard. I'm Iris.' She hesitated. 'Do we really call you Go-Go, or would you prefer us to use your proper Christian name?'

'No, Go-Go – please. Just look at me. I can't remember anybody ever calling me anything else.' She was laughing, a deep, infectious chuckle.

She had a warmth that almost at once enveloped us all, so that the saloon became a brighter, more cheerful place. They had fed on the plane, but they needed no pressing to help themselves from the stewpot. Later, in the more relaxed atmosphere that followed coffee plentifully laced with rum, Andy admitted that he had not been as open as perhaps he should have been about his wife's origins. 'I thought if I told you she was quarter Aborigine it might crook the whole deal and I very much wanted to be on this expedition. So did Go-Go once her firm had agreed.'

It was Andy, not Iris, who had brought this up, but now that it was out in the open I could see she was worried. 'Two things.' She reached across the table impulsively, taking hold of the girl's hand. 'I'm thinking of her, Andy, not the expedition. She comes from a hot climate.'

'So do I,' Galvin cut in.

'Not genetically you don't. You're a Nordic. Just look at your skin.'

'And she's quarter black, is that what you mean?' His tone was defensive, almost belligerent.

'No, it is not what I mean. The colour of the skin is immaterial except in so far as it indicates an affinity with heat rather than the sort of cold –'

'She's used to the cold, Mrs Sunderby. Her father's an Orkney man, and when she left veterinary college, she started work up in the Snowies. That's where I met her. In any case, the Abo background is the desert, in the case of her mother's tribe, the Simpson, a place where no white man can exist without an airlift of supplies, and they lived there in complete self-sufficiency, hot as hell during the day and bitter cold at night. Try that with no clothes on, Mrs Sunderby . . .'

Iris held up her hand, laughing. 'All right, Mr Galvin . . .'

She was mocking him with a matching formality. 'Just so long as she can take it. I don't want her to get hurt just because of your determination to join us.'

'She won't get hurt. I'll see to that.' He was leaning forward, his eyes fixed on Iris across the table. 'Now, you said you had two points. What's the other?'

'Her sailing experience!'

'Virtually nil. I told you that in my letter. We've been married less than a year and after buying a house all I could afford in the way of a boat was an old racing dinghy. She's been out in that quite a few times, so she knows port from starb'd, how to tack and gybe, and though she's a bit pint-sized, I can assure you she makes up for it in quickness, and in toughness, don't you, mate?' He grinned at her, at us. 'And I speak from experience.' Then, more seriously. 'She's also a bloody good vet, which means she has experience of dealing with most bone injuries and knows the difference between a tumour and a pregnancy.' Again that little gleam of humour. 'Sort it out for yourselves and let us know in the morning what you decide.' He had got to his feet. 'Right now we'd be glad to get sight of our berths and kip down. What with the weather and some trouble with the air crews, we've been three days getting here and we're just about all in, both of us.'

They were sleeping on board, so Nils and Iris agreed we'd breakfast at nine, which would give them an extra hour's lie-in. But when I went across in the morning, they were already on deck. 'Couldn't wait to look her over.' He was bright and chirpy, and his wife was standing at the upper steering position, her appearance quite changed by a bright red woolly cap with ear-flaps. 'Got it taped now, squares'ls, everything, except one or two strings aft of the foremast. You set reaching sails between that and the main, do you?'

I took him briefly through the handling of fisherman and reaching stays'ls, then we went down to breakfast. As we passed through the wheelhouse he paused at the head of the companion-way. 'Good gear you got there.' He nodded to the radio equipment banked behind the chart table. 'A nice little amateur network outfit as well as single sideband HF. Anybody on board got a licence?'

I hesitated. 'Iain might have.' With him anything seemed possible. 'But I don't think so.'

Andy looked at me, that crooked little half-smile on his face. 'Reck'n it won't matter much anyway where we're going. Nobody's going to arrest us 'cos we ain't got a licence, not in the middle of the Weddell Sea! I'll check it over this evening, make a few calls. But it's all good gear and it looks okay.'

Next morning the weather was fine with cirrus high up and very little wind. 'We'll take her out as soon as we've had breakfast,' I said. 'Give you a chance to get used to the deck layout.'

It was incredible what a difference it made to have the back-up of somebody really experienced, and he was right about his wife. She was very quick, very sure-footed round the deck, and she learned fast. Before the wind began to get up shortly after midday, we had tried out all the sails, not once, but several times. We had lunch hove-to, coffee and sandwiches in the wheelhouse so that we could watch for any change of wind and keep tabs on any traffic bearing down on us.

By the time we packed it in for the day I was beginning to feel I had the makings of a crew, that we really could sail down into the pack ice of the Weddell Sea. We had been so concentrated on sail handling that I think all of us had quite forgotten about Carlos, but he was waiting for us on the quay as we came alongside. He had a bottle of that rough red Chilean wine you could get in the bar-ristorante. I recognised it by the label and he waved it at us as we came alongside. He had made it over to Seno Otway and was very full of himself, which he had a right to be, for it was a hike of some fifty miles there and back. 'I was lucky, I had a moon both nights. A lot of shooting stars, satellites, too. The clarity of the sky was incredible.' His voice was a little slurred. 'And the birds. I should have taken that book you've got on board. Now, of course, I can't remember all the details.' He was talking mainly to Andy. He seemed fascinated by the lanky Australian, who had just seated himself at the chart table, the earphones on the back of his head and his long fingers playing over the controls of the single sideband. 'You interested in birds?'

Andy nodded vaguely, his attention on the radio.

'You were at the Davis Station, I hear.'

'Yeah.'

'Did you see Emperors there?'

'No. Lots of King penguins, Adélies, too.'

'But no Emperors?' He turned to me. 'Will we be calling at South Georgia?'

'I don't know,' I said.

'There are several Emperor rookeries there.' He had turned almost eagerly back to Andy. 'They're all of three foot tall, beaks level with your belly button, and they can break a man's arm with their flippers. I was reading all about them on the plane, an old book on South Georgia. It said they slide belly-down on the ice and then tip themselves upright with their beaks like those little weighted dolls you get in Christmas crackers.'

He went on like that, his tongue running away with him and constantly asking questions till Andy turned on him. 'Shut up, will you, for Christ's sake! I'm trying to listen.' In the sudden, almost shocked silence Iris's voice called up to us that the evening meal was ready.

It was stew again, but with a lot of deep-freeze cauliflower and some fresh seaweed in it, so that it was like a thick soup. And just as we had started to eat Iain came in. He looked tired, and after he had said hullo to the Galvins, he just sat there, saying nothing, even when Iris offered to get him some stew, merely shaking his head.

He didn't show any surprise at Go-Go Galvin's appearance, seeming to accept her presence as though he had known in advance she was part Aborigine. But Carlos wasn't going to let the opportunity pass. And that little devil was peeping out of his eyes as he leaned forward, staring at Go-Go and quoting, 'A damsel with a dulcimer in a vision once I saw'. There was a cruel little smile on his lips as he went on, speaking slowly and deliberately, 'It was an Aborigine maid and on her didgeridoo she played, singing of Mount –'

215

'Belt up!' Andy's voice was quiet, but menacing. 'You're drunk, but that doesn't excuse you, mate.'

Iain thrust his head forward, smiling and addressing Go-Go. 'There's a bottle in the cupboard behind ye. Pour me a slug, there's a dear.' Then he turned to Carlos. 'A neat little parody. Very clever of ye. But ye dae that again –'

'You don't like poetry, no?'

Iain stared at him, the silence suddenly electric. Then he smiled, and speaking slowly took up the quote, *'Could Ah revive within me, her symphony and song, to such a deep delight 'twould win me, that with music loud and long, Ah would build that dome in air, that sunny dome!* What comes next, boy?'

Carlos was staring at him fascinated, a poodle confronted by a bull mastiff.

And Iain went on, *'Those caves of ICE! And all should cry, Beware! Beware!'* He looked round the table, eyeing each of us, emphasising the warning. 'So beware,' he repeated gently. 'This is a small band of human beings headed into the unknown. Start a quarrel and you have a disaster. So, gang warily, and mind yer tongues.' He downed the drink Go-Go had passed him in one gulp and got to his feet. 'Ah'll bid ye all goodnight. God willin', we sail the day after tomorrow.' He turned to me. 'How long will it take us to get to Ushuaia?'

'Depends on the weather,' I said.

''Course it does. But what is the probability?'

'It could be bad in the Cockburn. That's the channel that runs almost due west, straight into the prevailing wind, with the whole weight of the Pacific ahead. Storm-force winds would almost certainly stop us dead. I don't dare think what it would be like out there.'

'And if it's only force 5 and we can keep goin'?'

'Then we ought to be able to make Ushuaia in three days, provided nothing goes wrong, of course.' And I added, 'It's a bad area, and after Ushuaia we'll have Cape Horn ahead of us. It's bloody stupid making our final departure from Ushuaia. If we left from here –'

'He insists on Ushuaia.'

'Just look at the chart, man. Tell him –'

'Ah've told him. Ah can read a chart, too. So can he.'

'And he still insists?'

'Yes. Ah phoned him as soon as Ah got in to Montevideo. Ah thought it safer from there. He refused to discuss it. He would join us at Ushuaia, or not at all.' He paused, looking round the table. 'So, the day after tomorrow, unless anyone can show good cause . . .'

'That's Sunday,' Iris said.

'Aye, Sunday. What's the difference? We're not a bunch of Wee Frees and even the Catholics allow football in the afternoon, provided ye genuflect in the mornin', of course.' He looked across at me. 'If we left, say at 06.00, that would make an ETA of 06.00 at Ushuaia on the Wednesday mornin' a reasonable bet, right?'

'DV,' I said.

He nodded. 'DV. Aye.' He looked at each individual face in turn, and when nobody else said anything, he nodded. 'Good! Then Sunday it is. Pete will give ye the precise time of departure tomorrow after we've got the weather forecast.'

It was Carlos who asked when Mario would be arriving at Ushuaia and Iain told him Wednesday. 'Wednesday of next week, Ah said – by the latest. And he agreed.' Then, suddenly relaxed and smiling, he added, 'A wee gift from the gods to cheer us all up. Ah've been on to our base at Halley Bay. The ice information is still good. It could be an early break-up.'

217

THREE

Ushuaia is only just inside the Argentine boundary with Chile. You would, I think, have to go to Africa to find a demarcation line between two countries more arbitrary and ridiculous than that which gives the tip of the Tierra del Fuegan 'boot' to Argentina. Patagonia finishes at the very tip of the northern entrance to the Magellan Strait, the border then jumping a slice of the South Atlantic to reappear, quite disjointedly, at the Strait's southern entrance point. Hardly to be wondered, therefore, that there is constant friction between the two countries that share the very bottom of the South American continent. Ushuaia, like Punta Arenas, has a barracks and a strong naval presence. Also it has an airfield with a single runway laid out on a north-south axis. Thus all take-offs and landings are at right angles to the prevailing wind and that much more uninsurable.

We arrived at Ushuaia shortly after midday on the Tuesday, having had what really amounted to a very successful shake-down cruise, logging altogether two hundred and eighty-three nautical miles. We were lucky with the weather, the wind a light westerly on the Sunday, so that we were reaching, even broad-reaching, on the starb'd tack right down to the start of the Cockburn Channel, which we reached shortly after midnight. By then the wind had died away and we were motoring.

There is a series of channels between the Cockburn and the Beagle – the Brecknock, the Aguirre, the Burnt, the Ballenas or Whaleboat and the O'Brien, all of them intricate and all of them requiring maximum vigilance on the part of the navigator. Thanks be to God it was a wonderfully clear, starlit night, and when the moon rose it was so bright we no longer needed the radar. The long stretches of water, and the hills all round, reminded me of the fortnight I had spent sailing with a school friend on the west coast of Scotland.

The wind came in from the west again shortly after dawn and we then had a fast passage rock-hopping through the out-islands on the edge of the Pacific. The passage was well marked with lit buoys at almost regular intervals and, with the sort of visibility we were blessed with, the navigation was easy. So was the sailing, for the wind held at a fairly steady force 5 on the starb'd quarter. By Monday evening we were approaching the Beagle Channel and the wind had become variable, the sky overcast, with sudden squalls of rain, sleet and hail, so that I had a wretched night of it, constantly on watch, or being called, and in the dawn, well into the Channel, and with the wind aft, we had everybody on deck and for the first time hoisted our squares'l rig. And it worked. It worked a fair treat, well enough to give us speeds of over 10 knots, a third less with the prop rotating in reverse and generating power on the alternator.

We were still in the narrows, just abreast of Fleuriais Bay, when the wind began to increase very rapidly. We could have put in there. We had the 559 chart and it would have given us a comfortable night at anchor. But at the speed we were going, and with a strong tidal current under us, we were past the entrance to the Bay before I had even thought of it. The wind was 'right up our jacksie, mate', as Andy put it, and, with the land close on either side, it was funnelling through the Channel at what seemed almost double its true speed. The square sails were designed to be handled from the deck so that there were a lot of strings, and bellied out as they were, taut as a couple of drums, we had a hell of a job getting them down. It was the first time we had had to lower them running before a strong wind. It must have been force 7 at least, the surface water being lifted and spilled forward in the gusts. We didn't bother to lower the yards, but got the small jib up and went careering into the night at 4½ knots on that one sail. The wind decreased slightly in the early hours and when Andy relieved me at 04.00 we decided to set the number 2 jib. It needed two of us up for'ard and somebody had to be on the helm, so he called his wife, and after we'd set it I managed to get a good three hours' sleep.

It was shortly after I had relieved him at 08.00 that the volatility of Carlos's Latin temperament suddenly displayed itself. It was a dark morning with a lot of heavy cloud, low and black in the rainstorms. I had climbed the ladder to the top of the wheelhouse and was at the upper steering position when I heard the sound of voices, very faint. For a moment I thought it was the after-effects of tiredness and stress. I had been navigating in the dangerous waters between the Cockburn and the Beagle Channels all the earlier part of the night and thought I must be hearing things. But then I traced it to the voicepipe that connected with the wheelhouse below. I had been testing it out with Andy before he went to his bunk and had left the cap off.

I started to put the cap back on, but then realised there was an argument going on in the wheelhouse. ' . . . spying on me.' It was Carlos speaking. 'Why were you phoning him?'

'Ye told Mrs Sunderby yer father had sent ye.' Iain's voice was quiet, but with what seemed to me an undercurrent of menace. He had completely ignored the boy's question. 'That was a lie.'

'I want to come with you.'

'Ye can't, an' tha's that.'

'But I must.' The boy's voice was getting wilder.

'Why?' And when Carlos did not answer, he asked, 'How did ye know where we were? Did Connor-Gómez tell ye?'

'*Si.* I was at the hacienda about a week after you were there. He told me then that he is going to join Iris Sunderby on this ship of hers and navigate for her. I said I was coming with him, but he said, No, he didn't want me on board with him. His only interest is that woman.'

'What dae ye mean by that? What are ye tryin' to say?'

There was a long silence and I thought perhaps Iain had gone back to his bunk. He had hardly left it since his return to Punta Arenas. I was just about to put the cap on when Carlos's disembodied voice announced on a rising note, 'I don't care what he say, I'm coming with you.'

'As far as Ushuaia, that's all.'

'No. All the way.' Carlos was almost screaming now.

'Ye leave at Ushuaia.' Iain's tone, though still quiet, was very determined. 'Is that understood?'

'No, no. I must come with you.'

'Why?' he asked again.

'Why do I want to come?'

'Yes, why? It will probably be a tough, uncomfortable voyage. And a long one if we have to winter over, so why dae ye want to come when ye should be continuin' yer studies?'

'I have to – please.' His voice was suddenly pleading. 'I must know.'

'Know what?' Iain's voice had sharpened with sudden curiosity. 'What dae ye have to know?'

Another long silence, and then: 'Nothing, nothing. But I must come.' And then Carlos added, the words coming in a rush, 'I can hide on board at Ushuaia. He need not know till after we sail. Or I can stay ashore and jump ship just as –'

'No. Ye are no' comin'.'

The argument went on for a moment longer, Carlos first pleading, then insistent, his voice rising uncontrollably, a trembling contralto of urgency. Then suddenly he shouted, 'All right. If I don't come with you, then you don't go. I see to that.'

'Stop being childish.'

'Me? Childish? It is you. Please. One last time. Let me come with you.'

'No.'

'Okay.' There was a sudden rush of movement, impossible to define through the voicepipe. I heard Iain's voice shouting 'Carlos', and a moment later the for'ard hatch banged open and he erupted on to the deck like a man gone berserk, the ice axe he had borrowed gripped in his hand, his eyes wild and a frenzied look on his face.

For a split second I was rooted to the spot, not realising his intention. Then suddenly I understood. We had tanks below for almost three thousand gallons of diesel. They were right down in the ship's bilges. But the paraffin for cooking and the petrol for the semi-rigid inflatable and the snomobile was all in drums securely lashed along the bulwarks. He made straight for the petrol drums alongside the foremost ratlines.

I shouted at him to stop, but he didn't even glance at me, his eyes glazed now and his face set in an intense grimace. Somebody else yelled at him just as I started down the ladder. I heard the ring of the axe pick biting into the metal of the drum as my feet hit the deck, and then I stopped. Andy, in nothing but his pants, was rushing in on Carlos, barefoot and with only his hands to grapple with him. I saw the ice axe swung high, shouted and stubbed my toe as I flung myself forward. But then Andy had hold of the axe, had wrenched it out of the crazy loon's hands and tossed it aside.

I thought that was the end of it and I stood there in some pain as the two of them began to circle each other on the foredeck as in a ritual dance. Carlos reached into the pocket of his anorak, came out with something gripped in his hand, and then there was a flash of steel in the masthead floodlights that Iain must have switched on. The boy was moving forward in a crouch, the six-inch blade of a flick knife pointing at Andy's stomach.

I was shouting again and moving at the same time, vaguely conscious of the jib slapping furiously as we came up into the wind. I had almost reached them when a dark whirlwind in red pyjamas flung herself on to the boy's back, her hands fastening on each side of his neck, thumbs digging in. Carlos gave a wild scream of agony. The knife clattered to the deck and he stood there, totally paralysed and still screaming.

Andy bent down and picked up the knife. 'Yours, mate?' He was smiling, tight-lipped and holding it out to the boy. 'Do you want it? 'Cos if so, I'm going to plunge it right into your sodding little testicles. Well, do you?' He looked over Carlos's shoulder. 'Okay, let him go now.'

His wife released her grip on the pressure points either side of his neck and he stood trembling uncontrollably. 'Well, do you want it?' And when Carlos dumbly shook his head, he tossed it casually over the side, took his wife by the arm and the two of them disappeared down the for'ard hatch without a word, except that as his head disappeared Andy nodded up at the slapping sail and called to me, 'Better get her back on course or we'll be into the kelp.'

Iain was out on deck now, the smell of petrol strong as he wrestled with the lashings that bound the drum to one of the guardrail stanchions. I got out my own knife, sawing through the wet rope so that we could up-end the container. 'Now then, laddie, what was all that about?' Carlos was still standing there, apparently in a daze. 'Why the hell are ye so urgent to come with us, eh?'

I don't know whether Carlos answered him or not. The fores'l was making a hell of a din and I was already on my way back to the wheelhouse. By the time I had got *Isvik* sailing again the two of them had disappeared below and for a time I had the deck to myself. It was a strange, wild world, the long ribbon of water stretching out ahead, leaden under the louring overcast. The great mass of the Darwin Cordillera was behind us now and though heavy banks of cloud obscured the towering peak of Sarmiento I could feel the menace of it in the sudden wind shifts, the violence of the gusts. It made me very conscious that I was now at the bottom of the world, Cape Horn ahead and the Screaming Fifties; after that the frozen wastes of the pack, the icebergs, the whole mass of Antarctica with its blizzards.

I suppose I was tired. Certainly I had been under stress with almost two days of very concentrated pilotage. Fear began to build up inside me. I was thinking of Scott and the long trek to the South Pole, of Amundsen, and Shackleton, particularly Shackleton. All that ahead of me. But for the moment I was here, in the comparative safety of the Beagle Channel with Ushuaia the last port of call. One last chance to duck out.

'Are you cold?' Iris was suddenly beside me. 'You're trembling.'

'Am I?' I had been so engrossed in my thoughts I hadn't seen her come up, hadn't realised I was shaking almost uncontrollably.

'I'll take her now. You go below, get yourself some hot coffee.'

I nodded. I could smell it now and I stepped back from the wheel, automatically giving her the course. 'What's the matter with Carlos?' I asked. 'Why is he so set on coming with us?'

She gave a little shrug.

'Why doesn't he want Connor-Gómez to know he's on board?'

She turned to me then, the knuckles of her hands white with the tightness of her grip on the wheel. 'You ask him. No, better you ask Ángel when he comes on board at Ushuaia. See what he says.'

But Ángel Connor-Gómez didn't come aboard at Ushuaia.

We snugged into a little gap between a patrol vessel and a stern trawler, and before we had even made fast Iain had jumped ashore and was hurrying along the quay to the port office with the ship's papers. He was back inside of half an hour, and without consulting Iris, or any of us, ordered Nils to get the engine going. 'These are the co-ordinates.' He thrust a piece of paper into my hand. 'Mark the position on the chart, will you?' And he told Andy to cast off.

'But what about Ángel?' Iris asked. 'It is essential we don't sail without him, otherwise . . .'

'He's joinin' us further along the coast. On the north side of the Channel, Ah imagine, since that's still Argentine territory.'

'But why not here? It is arranged that he join us here – tomorrow, Wednesday. That is what you said.'

I didn't hear his answer. The engine had come to life, Nils at the helm and Andy tossing the warps on to the deck and leaping for the guard rails as *Isvik* gathered way.

The position indicated by the co-ordinates was almost at the mouth of the Beagle Channel, just past the bay called Almirante Brown and almost opposite Puerto Eugenia on the Chilean shore. Iain was peering over my shoulder, and when I had pencilled in a little cross to mark the spot, he nodded. 'Like I thought.' He picked up the magnifying glass and began searching the area inland. 'Have ye got a larger scale chart?'

I took the *South American Pilot Vol. II* from the bookcase at the back of the chart table. I had already put a marker in at the Beagle Channel page. It was the next number to the one that was out on the table. 'Chart 3424.'

'Have we got it?'

I checked through the chart drawer, found that we had and spread it out on top of the Ushuaia chart. Again he didn't seem interested in the approaches or the soundings in the little bay indicated by the co-ordinates. His mind was concentrated on the hinterland, the magnifying glass following the contours very slowly as though he were trying to visualise the terrain. But Admiralty Charts are not like geographical maps. They concentrate on the foreshore and seabed. In the end he gave it up, flinging the magnifying glass down and muttering something to himself about waiting till we got there. 'What's the state of the moon? Almost at the full, isn't it?' And when I told him it would be full in two days' time, he nodded and said he hoped it would be a fine night.

'We'll be picking him up during the night, will we?'

'Not this night. Early Thursday mornin' – 0200.'

'So why the hurry? We could have stayed at Ushuaia, topped up with diesel and had a meal ashore. Got drunk maybe.' I was thinking of the long weeks, possibly months ahead.

But all he said was, 'Give me an ETA at that bay as soon as ye can.'

'I can give you that right now,' I said, measuring off the distance with the dividers. 'Sail or motor?'

'Sail. The wind is westerly and we need to conserve fuel now.'

With the squares'ls reset we found we were logging a comfortable 6 knots. 'Should be there shortly after midnight,' I told him.

He nodded. 'Have the inflatable ready to launch as soon as we're anchored. Ye'll come with me. Okay?' And he disappeared below.

The wind force varied considerably during the latter part of the evening, reaching force 5 at times and veering north-westerly. The result was that we arrived well before midnight. There was still just a little light in the sky astern of us, but shoreward visibility was fitful with about seven-tenths cloud. We got the sails down and felt our way in under engine, the moonlight coming and going with the clouds very black in contrast.

There was a little beach with a stream pouring like a white streak across it, but the kelp forced us to anchor some way off in a depth of over thirty metres. Once the ship was settled, and the engine silenced, a sudden peace descended, only the racing, ink-black clouds to indicate that it was still blowing quite hard. Close in, we were under the lee, and the stillness, and the emptiness of the land, the sense of being at the world's end – it was almost spooky. And the kelp moving all the time, a slow, voluptuous lifting and falling as the waters of the strait heaved sleepily.

Iris wanted to come with us. I think she sensed a purpose behind Iain's haste to get ashore that in some way concerned her. 'Ye'd only be in the way,' he said almost brutally. Her reply was drowned in the noise of the engine as he started it up and we headed for what appeared to be a passage through the kelp. It did not reach as far as the beach and just as we entered it a pile of wind-driven cloud swept over the face of the moon so that one minute we could see the kelp moving lazily either side of us, the next all was utter darkness.

Iain cut the engine and we drifted in an eerie stillness that was punctuated by strange grunts and sucking noises as the sea moved the weed and sloshed among the stones and rocks of the beach. The inflatable was stopped almost immediately, and while Iain tipped the engine up on its bracket, I got hold of one of the oars and began to paddle. In the Stygian darkness we had nothing but the sound of the water streaming down the steep slope of the beach ahead to guide us, and it was hard work, for we were literally sliding the boat over the long streamers of kelp.

I had just started to pole our way through the shallows when the moon swam out of the blackness overhead, and there was the beach, with the stream gleaming white barely twenty metres away. It seemed afterwards as though the circumstances of our arrival set the scene, preparing us for the shock of what we were about to find. Iain had brought a torch with him, but he hadn't used it, so that the eeriness of that little beach was exaggerated by what I can only describe as the stage lighting. It conditioned me, instilling a degree of nervous tension, as though at any moment those naked, half-savage Onas of the old land of Tierra del Fuego would come storming out of the darkness, intent on clubbing us to death to provide them with the plumpest, best-fleshed meal they had had in years.

We stumbled ashore through ankle-twisting boulders, hauling the inflatable up a beach that looked like, and probably was, the moraine of an old glacier. I stopped to wrap the painter round a large stone so that Iain was ahead of me when the lighting suddenly dimmed, the moon sliding behind the ragged edge of a cloud. I could see the vague shape of him picking his way over the black debris of fallen trees that marked the tide line and the edge of the stream.

'Beaver,' he said as I fought my way up to him. The tide line had once been treed, but now they were fallen, rotting sticks, all lying higgledy-piggledy as though destroyed by the whirling vortex of a tornado. We struggled on for almost a hundred yards, picking our way through the mad, ankle-twisting debris of crumbling timber. 'Some bloody fool of an Argentinian thought it'd be nice to import a few Canadian beaver to Tierra del Fuego.' He swore as his foot slipped from under him. 'Ye saw the black debris of the tide line as far back as the Cockburn Channel. Nobody hunts them, so they've multiplied like mad.'

Away from the stream, there must have been a change of soil. Suddenly there were no tree stems lying around and we were wading in among hard, wiry stems of some sort of low-growing vegetation that could stand the cold of the winter at the bottom of the world. Away to the left there was a patch of tussac grass standing like the solid woolly heads of a little army of golliwogs. He found a path of sorts that climbed steadily up the shoulder of a bluff, the top of it just visible, a vague outline humped against the half-lit sky. And then the moon popped out again, the stage lighting switched on and the bluff was smooth as Sussex downland. We reached the top and looked down on to a rolling plain. 'Sheep country,' Iain whispered quite unnecessarily, for there, right in front of us, was a whole flock of them standing bunched and motionless, staring in our direction. 'The Dark Tower,' he murmured, nodding away to our left where a huddle of dilapidated huts crouched against the side of a stony hill.

'I don't see any tower,' I said. 'More like the quarters of some military outpost.'

'*Childe Roland*,' he murmured, and the way he said it sent a shiver through me, for I too had read my Browning. 'Ushuaia was an Argentine penal settlement at one time, did ye know that?'

'No.'

The going was easier now. We were walking on firm, close-cropped grass, the huts getting steadily nearer. 'Is this an old prison then?' I asked. 'Did you know it was here?'

He made no answer, striding on ahead. We reached the first of the huts and the moon slipped behind the black bulk of a cloud. The wind rattled the panes in a broken window, a door creaked – stage effects that included the winged shadow of a bird taking off into the night. There was a padlock on the door, but the hasp was broken and Iain pushed his way in, the beam of his torch stabbing out to show rusting iron beds stacked against the far wall. The only windows were either side of the door through which we had entered. At the far end was a shower cubicle and a tin washbasin, also a stack of galvanised iron buckets. The beam swept across the walls, hesitated and steadied on the single word 'HOY' scratched into the cement just to the right of a curved pipe that had presumably been the smoke outlet for a stove that had been removed. I heard him sigh. 'The poor bastards.'

'What's it mean?'

'Today,' he said. '*Hoy* means today.' He led the way out of the wind-shattered door and into the next hut. The huts were in three lines, four to each line, every hut alike and all in the same dilapidated condition. There was no barbed wire, no guardroom or jailers' quarters, no watchtowers. And in every one of the huts we found wall scratchings: lines of poetry, cries to God – *Que dios me salve* or simply, *Salvame* – demands for justice, the names of loved ones, and always, somewhere, a calendar. Not a proper calendar, no dates, but the weeks and the months recorded and the days scratched off as they passed. *En desesperación*. That word *desesperación* appeared again and again. 'No way out, nowhere to go – "desperation" about sums it up.' Iain's voice was muted, a sadness in the way he spoke.

'You knew this place existed, didn't you?'

As before, he didn't answer my question. He was probing with his torch, briefly checking each piece of graffiti.

'You looking for something?' I asked.

'Try and remember some of the names,' he said. 'Somebody, somewhere, must have a list.'

I started to write some of the names down on a scrap of paper, remembering now that Iris's brother Eduardo had been one of the Disappeareds. But Eduardo is a common enough name, and though I found quite a few Eduardos, either they did not add any surname, or else it was the wrong one. 'It's like a concentration camp,' I muttered as we were walking into the next row of huts.

He nodded. 'That's probably what it was.' And he added, 'Let's go and see if we can find their grave.'

'Is it the *Desaparecidos*?'

He led the way out, tramping in silence across the sheep-cropped grass as we circled the derelict camp. But there was no communal grave such as had been the last resting place of the gassed victims of Hitler's concentration camps, only a few lone headstones, a wooden cross or two, that was all.

'So where did they go?'

He shrugged, standing there in the wind, the racing clouds black overhead, gazing down at the huts. Finally he turned to me. 'You're not to mention this to anyone. Least of all to Iris – or to Connor-Gómez when he arrives. Ah don't want him to know we've seen it. Ye understand?'

I nodded, and after staring at the huts in complete silence for another minute or so, he started back towards the beach. We were in a clear patch of sky then, the moon very bright and still, the clouds all gone and the wind getting stronger. Away to our right, clearly visible in the stark brilliance, the line of an old track slanted up across a stony hillside.

The question in my mind, of course, was why Connor-Gómez had chosen to join ship at this Godforsaken place rather than at Ushuaia. Was it because he was *persona non grata* throughout Argentina? Then why send us all the way round the west side of Tierra del Fuego when, if he had joined us at Punta Arenas, we would have had a downhill run to the Falklands and South Georgia? I did my best to get an explanation out of Iain as we retraced our steps to the beach, but he just shrugged his shoulders. And when I pressed him for an answer, he finally turned on me and said, 'Keep yer mouth shut and yer eyes open, that way ye'll get at least some of the answers.'

The moon had disappeared again as we reached the beach,

but he didn't use the torch and we stumbled about in the dark looking for the boat. There was more movement in the water now, the kelp sloshing about and waves actually breaking on the beach. We got pretty wet launching the inflatable and once we had poled and paddled our way out into open water we had a rough passage to the ship. 'Remember what I said,' he whispered to me as we made the inflatable fast and started below. 'Ye'll be on yer own tomorrow when ye go in to pick him up. No questions. Ye understand? Ye take everythin' fur granted, and ye don't provoke him – either then or in the future. Okay?'

Sleep eluded me for a long time that night. It was blowing force 6 or 7 and the halyards frapping against the mast were a constant irritant. In a sense they matched my mood, my mind going over and over the voyage ahead, the problems that must inevitably arise with such an ill-assorted crew. And there was the question of navigation, for I had already discovered that we were at the very limit of Satnav. The satellites for this are in fixed positions directly over the equator and they move with the rotation of the earth, so that they are always conveniently sited for the big concentrations of shipping in the northern hemisphere. Down here on the edge of the Southern Ocean I was having to check the accuracy of every Satnav reading by star sights taken with the navigator's old, reliable standby, the sextant. *Isvik* had all the necessary tables, of course. What I didn't often have was a clear sight of the stars I needed.

It worried me. But what worried me still more was the imminent arrival of Connor-Gómez and the memory of that ghastly little huddle of huts standing derelict and forlorn in the intermittent moonlight.

I could hear Andy snoring, or was it Go-Go's broad nostrils reverberating up for'ard? They had all been asleep when we came back from our recce ashore, but just after turning in I thought I heard Iris questioning Iain. But it was probably my imagination, the ship's frames creaking and groaning, the halyards frapping and banging. I made a mental note to rig some lizards. I had seen some of these elastic fastenings in the store.

There were other things I tried to make a mental note of, for one thing we had gained out of the voyage from Punta Arenas through those wild inshore waters was that it had shown up all the various things that needed to be put right, particularly the stowage of some of the gear, the stores too. It had been as good a shake-down cruise as I could have wished for.

It rained all the following day, cold, driving rain that made work on deck a misery, and it didn't start to ease off until late afternoon. The wind died, too, but the cloud level remained low so that even the smallest hilltops were obscured, and there was a lurid sunset. By then we were all set to go, and shortly after 23.30 I lowered myself into the inflatable. Iain leaned down over the rail. 'We up anchor and leave the moment he's on board.'

'What about Carlos?' I asked.

'He'll stay below.'

'You mean he comes with us?'

He turned away, but I thought I saw his left eyelid flicker as he said, 'Remember – keep yer mouth shut.'

I didn't bother with the engine, and as I was settling myself to the oars, I caught the flash of a torch from the beach. He had said midnight so he was dead on time.

Glancing over my shoulder, as I pulled into the pathway of open water between the kelp, I saw his figure standing solitary in the moonlight. There was nobody with him, but he must have had help getting his gear down to the beach, for there was quite a considerable pile of it stacked beside him.

He greeted me by name as though we were old friends, apologised for having caused us to detour south to the Beagle Channel and hoped we had had a comfortable passage. 'What was the wind like?'

'All right,' I said as we began humping his gear into the boat.

'And the ship? What is she called – *Isvik*? How was *Isvik*?'

'Okay.'

'A good sailer? No breakings?'

'No.'

The moon was only just risen, a baleful orb of orange red that peered at us beneath a ruler-straight line of low cloud, casting a livid light that made his face look older. Or was it strain? I flicked my torch on to him, then on the baggage. There were half a dozen cases that looked as though they were plastic. 'Put the torch out!'

'Why?'

'Somebody may see. Put it out!'

I started to tell him he didn't have to worry, that the area was deserted, but then I thought better of it. The cases had buff-coloured labels stuck across their tops. I was just moving forward to examine one of them more closely when the torch was whipped out of my hand and switched off. But not before I had noticed the label on one of the cases was torn to reveal the upper half of some stencilled lettering – SEMTEX. Also the letters D A N and what looked like I V E S.

I had also caught sight of his face, and though it was only a glimpse, I had a distinct impression of tiredness round the eyes and the skin had a muddy look. But he still managed to look elegant, even in anorak and sea boots.

We finished loading the cases and his gear into the inflatable, and while hauling it out into water deep enough to float it, a wave slopped over the top of my sea boots. The water was ice cold. I scrambled in, picked up an oar and began to punt our way out through the kelp.

It was hard work getting out to the ship for the wind had risen again so that the big Seagull was slamming us into a steep, white-capped sea. It was a wet ride, with the ship riding stern-on to us in silhouette against that low band of livid light. As soon as we were alongside Connor-Gómez leapt on board, not waiting for my orders, not even taking the painter with him. I had to toss the stern rope up and a wave slopped over the fabric side as the boat swung round. Iain was busy greeting him and it was Iris who made fast. Carlos was down below, of course, and Andy busy talking again to a 'ham' he had contacted on the Falklands.

Standing there in the bouncing inflatable, clinging to the ship's rail, I heard Iain inviting the man below for a welcome-aboard drink. 'A splendid idea,' I called out as they started to move aft to the wheelhouse door, 'but first let's get the gear on board.'

Connor-Gómez turned immediately. He had caught the note of censure in my voice. 'So sorry, my friend. Of course.' He was smiling, the tired eyes crinkling, all the charm switched on so that his face was transformed, the mask of youthfulness back in place. Go-Go suddenly appeared to give a hand. They met at the rail and I saw him check, his face hardening abruptly, his body coming erect as though standing on tiptoe, racial dominance in every line. And then, as I introduced them, he smiled and I saw a touch of the devil I had seen in Carlos.

'Her husband, Andy, is our radio operator,' I said quickly, for I had seen her stiffen, the eyes dilating, the nostrils flaring. The instant flash of sexual awareness that passed between them was like an electric spark, and she was hating herself for it. There was something else, too, something age-old, primitive even, her body gone so taut I could see her trembling. And all the time he smiled, savouring the moment. He held out his hand. 'So we sail into the ice together, Mrs Galvin.'

'I'll call Andy.' She turned quickly away, and as she hurried to the wheelhouse, she said to Iris, 'We'll need everybody on deck to stow the inflatable and lash it down.'

We had the welcoming drink in the main saloon, a bottle of champagne Iain said he had brought back with him specially for the occasion. 'To our voyage.' Ángel – it was Ángel now he was one of us – raised his glass. 'And to our ship's company.' He smiled first at Iris, then at Go-Go, pointedly toasting the women. His features had smoothed out and there was colour in his cheeks. He looked suddenly handsome again, almost debonnaire.

The bottle empty, Iain gave me a nod and took Ángel aft to show him his quarters. I changed quickly into dry socks and followed Andy up to the wheelhouse. Iris was already there, the engine ticking over and Nils up forward starting to take the slack up on the winch as we motored gently into the wind. She looked at me, a nervous smile on that full mouth of hers, but the light of excitement in her eyes. 'Well, this is it, Pete.'

I nodded, butterflies flickering in my stomach as I asked Andy for the latest forecast. 'Wind,' he said. 'Gale force. But decreasing shortly after dawn – perhaps.' His voice was tense, a cover I thought for nervousness. Then, on a note of almost forced gaiety, he said, 'But I've just got an ice report you'll like, mate. I been talking to an ice-breaker down by the BAS base at Halley Bay. They report they're in open water and they've got print-outs from the Met. station at MPA of sat-pics that show a line of open water extending half-way round the southern end of the Weddell Sea.'

'What's an ice-breaker doing down there?' I asked.

'Thickness of ice tests. The SPRI – that's the Scott Polar Research Institute – have been carrying out tests in the Arctic for some years. Now BAS are doing it down here in the Antarctic.'

'With what result? Do they think it's melting?'

'Correct. According to the sparks feller on *Polarstern* – that's the ice-breaker, not one of yours, German, a big 'un, too – they've been running tests for several years using sonar buoys. Testing for the effects of the destruction of the ionosphere and the hole in the ozone layer. The ice is thinner than they thought. In fact, he says the fellers at British Antarctic Survey's Halley base reck'n it won't be all that long before the Weddell Sea becomes open to the fishing fleets, the eastern side of it anyway.' He gave a little laugh. 'But that's for the future, mate. Right now we're dealing with the present and it looks like a dirty night.'

'But you say we could have it fine tomorrow when we'll be clear of the Beagle Channel and out of the lee of the land meeting the big seas that have rounded the Horn.' I said it casually as though I were referring to a Channel crossing, but that wasn't at all how I felt, for this would be a close encounter with the Horn. Very different to the Whitbread when we had been thundering along the 57th parallel, virtually in the middle of the Drake Strait.

'Yep, they'll have the whole weight of a globe-circling ocean behind them.' He laughed a little wildly. 'Guess I'll go to my scratcher, get some shut-eye while I can.'

I told him to stay and give me a hand with the squares'ls. The wind was west-sou'west, the direction indicator in front of me swinging between 220 degrees and 240 degrees. With Iris on the helm, both sails went up in quick time, and immediately afterwards Andy dived down the for'ard hatch so that after I had relieved Iris I was alone at the wheel. I cut the engine and suddenly everything was quiet, only the sound of the bows slicing through the water. I switched to autopilot and reached for the log to write up the time and position at which I had shut down the engine. 'Where do you anchor next?' It was Ángel peering over my shoulder at the chart.

I finished my entry and shut the log. 'We don't.' I saw the surprise on his face, the look of shock almost, and felt pleased. 'Next stop is the Ice Shelf at the bottom of the Weddell Sea.' I got Chart 3176 out of the drawer and opened it on the chart table. It covered almost all of the Weddell Sea, including part of that finger of Antarctica which thrusts north towards Graham Land and the Horn. 'Now that we're on our way perhaps you'd pencil in the position you want us to head for.'

He didn't say anything, just standing there beside me, breathing rather deeply as he stared down at the chart. 'I did not understand you would be leaving like this, so immediately.'

'Ice reports indicate the pack is melting early.'

'Yes, I know.'

'If we had left direct from Punta Arenas –'

'Of course.' He straightened up. 'You are in charge of the sailing, I understand. When do you want me on watch?'

'After breakfast. You'll then be able to get used to handling the ship in daylight before you face a night watch.'

He nodded. 'Then I think I go to my bunk now.'

I held a pencil out to him. 'Mark in our destination and the position of the *Santa Maria*, will you, please. Then I can work out a rough ETA, read up on the ice conditions again and have another look at Shackleton's *South* before we're out of the Beagle Channel and into the rough stuff.'

'The rough stuff! It will be bad you think?'

'We'll be jumping off the deep end as far as our sea legs are concerned.' I tried to make my voice sound casual, but my imagination was leaping ahead to the moment when we were out of the Beagle Channel, facing the tail end of the gale that was forecast, and I had to decide how close in to Isla de los Estados and the toe of Tierra del Fuego I dared go. 'The position,' I said. 'I need to know now while conditions are quiet.'

But he shook his head, backing away from me. 'I get some sleep now.'

'Don't you know the position? Is that it?'

'Of course I know the position . . . But that chart . . . It does not cover the extreme south-west corner of the Weddell Sea. So I cannot mark it in for you. Tomorrow perhaps. You find me a chart that covers the whole area . . . Now I am tired. I don't have much sleep for several days. Okay?' And with a smile and wave of his hand he disappeared below.

A blip showed on the radar, in the passage north of Piedra that we would be taking to Cabo San Pio and our entry into the Southern Ocean. I watched for a while until I had confirmed it as a vessel steaming towards us, then I told Nils, who was in the helmsman's chair, to wake me at 03.15 and curled up under a blanket on the couch at the side of the wheelhouse. I was thinking about Ángel's evasiveness over the position of the wreck, his reaction to our quick departure, and about those cases. I heard the sails banging as a gust came in from the beam, wondered whether I should get up and trim them, and the next thing I knew Nils was shaking me. 'A quarter after three, Pete. That ship very close now. Green to green, ja?'

She passed us at a distance of about four hundred metres, the sound of her engines coming to us quite loud across the water. She was a medium-sized tanker, her lights blurred by a rain squall. I stayed awake until Andy relieved Nils and we were into the passage between the island and the Argentine mainland, then I went back to my couch, telling him to wake me when we were approaching Cabo San Pio, or when Iain relieved him, whichever was sooner.

In the event it was the violence of the movement that woke me, the rolling gradually becoming so bad that I had to get up and rig the canvas leeboard to stop myself being pitched on to the deck. The first pale streak of a sickly dawn showed over the bows. We were coming out of the Beagle Channel now and already beginning to feel the effect of the gale building up round the Wollaston group of islands that terminate in the Horn. By the time Iain came on watch it had become very rough indeed. Andy and I got into our oilskins, took down the upper squares'l and hoisted the largest of our three storm jibs to steady her. Water was beginning to surge for'ard along the deck and we could hear the grumbling roar of breaking seas above the scream of the wind. It would be bad off Cabo San Pio, much worse probably when we reached Los Estados island and San Juan, the final tip of South America and our point of departure.

I warned Andy he was on call and to keep his oilskins on. He was pale and I wondered whether he suffered from seasickness. The movement was unpleasant and I was beginning to feel a little queasy myself. 'You all right?' I asked Iain.

'Aye. The good Lord gifted me with a cast-iron stomach.' He smiled at me, a good colour in his cheeks as he sat, seemingly relaxed, in the swivel chair, his hands holding the wheel, not tight, but firmly. 'What about ye?'

'Okay,' I said, though I wasn't all that sure. 'What's in the cases we brought off from that beach?'

'Why d'ye ask?'

'Semtex is an explosive, isn't it? The stuff the IRA get from Czechoslovakia. One of those cases –'

His hand banged down on the wooden ledge of the console. 'I told ye. Keep yer thoughts to yerself. Ye're the one person –' He checked himself. 'Nils had been paintin' the back of the for'ard heads. Ah've slapped some of that on it. Ah don't mind ye askin' me questions. Ah reck'n Ah know ye now. Yes, of course it's Semtex, and there's a case of detonators, too. We may need to blast a way out of the ice and Ah couldn't bring the stuff down through Chile.'

He checked the swing of the bows as a breaker went surging beneath us, slamming the ship violently to port. He was a quick learner, or else at some time in his chequered career he had handled a vessel in rough seas before. 'Remember what Ah said – keep yer eyes open and yer mouth shut.' Another breaker, white water all along the deck and the bows swinging. But he anticipated it this time and checked the swing almost before it had begun. 'Gettin' a wee bit frisky, isn't she?'

'It'll be worse when we're abreast of Cabo San Pio.' The black outline of the cape was just becoming visible low down on the horizon ahead.

'Very probably.' He grinned at me and I realised he was actually enjoying himself. 'Ah wonder how our Ángel is takin' it. He was a bit upset at bein' whisked off like that. Felt as though he was bein' hi-jacked.'

The smell of bacon frying came up from below. It was past seven, but the cloud, even between the rain squalls, was so thick and low that there was still no more than a drab glimmer of daylight. I went below, thinking that Iris or Nils must have started breakfast, but to my surprise it was Carlos. 'Thought you might be getting hungry.' He smiled at me and I thought, my God, the boy's a natural sailor. He handed me a plate that was almost too hot to hold with two thick rashers, a fried egg and a hunk of bread. 'You want it fried? I have enough fat.'

I shook my head, the heat and the movement making me wonder whether I could cope with what he had given me. But I was hungry, and after I had eaten I felt better. 'You found your sea legs pretty quickly.'

'Sea legs? Oh yes, sickness at sea is never any trouble with me.'

I was just considering whether it was the moment to go to the heads, always a struggle when you've got oilskins on and the ship is trying to bounce you off the seat, when Ángel appeared wearing, of all things, a red and green Paisley-patterned silk dressing-gown. His hair was tousled and he was yawning.

'I could not sleep, also there is a good smell.' He stretched, running one hand through his hair, holding on tight to the corner of the cupboard with the other. 'Where is Iris?' He was moving towards the stove, his eyes half closed. 'I like my eggs sunny side up. And the bacon . . .' He stopped there, his eyes widening as Carlos turned towards him. 'You! *¿Qué diablos haces aquí?*'

'I am signed on as one of the crew.' He was smiling an ingratiating, nervous little smile. And there was something in his eyes . . .

'You are coming with us? Is that what you are saying?'

'*Sí. Vengo contigo.*'

'No.' The word shot out of Ángel's mouth as though something had exploded inside the man. He turned and shouted for Iris. And when she appeared from her cabin aft, a scarf tied hurriedly round her head and her fingers still pulling at a heavy grey sweater, he told her we must put back immediately and land Carlos at the first possible place.

'Why?'

He didn't answer that, the three of them standing there, staring at each other. 'Please,' Carlos murmured.

'I tell you, no. You will be put ashore, somewhere, anywhere. You are not sailing on this ship.' And to Iris he said, 'How could you be so stupid? He is not a good sailor and he is due back at college.'

'Please, no.' It was a cry of despair almost, and I was shocked to see the blatant look of adoration in the boy's eyes. There was also a strange undercurrent of excitement radiating from him. 'I am staying here.'

The crash of a sea and a surge of water overhead caused the saloon to swoop, then roll, throwing us off balance so that we were suddenly in a huddle on the starb'd side. Iain descended slowly from the wheelhouse above. 'What's the trouble?' And when he was told, he said, 'Are ye serious? We're approachin' Los Estados and y' want me to put back into the Beagle Channel?'

The other nodded, saying that if we didn't put Carlos ashore he would not continue with the expedition. Another wave broke on board, the movement increasingly violent. I dived for the companionway, realising he had left the helm on autopilot.

'Wait. Take our friend with ye, let him see what it's like out there. We would never make it back into the Channel against this wind.'

'Then turn north after Cabo San Juan, go through the Estrecho de le Maire and drop him off at Rio Grande, anywhere along the east coast of Tierra del Fuego. You will be sheltered there.'

'It will be down-draughting off the mountains,' I said. And Iain told him bluntly that there would be no turning back. 'Dae what ye fuckin' like,' he said furiously when Ángel reiterated his non-co-operation threat. 'We're no' turnin' back, man.'

'The Malvinas then. You can land him on the Malvinas.'

'The Falklands? Aye, we could have done that if ye'd joined ship at Punta Arenas. But from here our course is east towards South Georgia, then south into the Weddell Sea as soon as we get a favourable report on the state o' the pack ice. Anyway, the boy's a good cook an' a useful hand. Ah should have thought ye'd be happy to have him –' I lost the rest of it, for another sea came slamming over the stern with a noise like an express train hitting the buffers. I heaved myself to the top of the companion-way, staggered across the wheelhouse and disconnected the autopilot. Then I settled down behind the wheel to ease her run before the wind-driven break of the waves.

The apparent wind speed had risen to 36 knots, 40 plus in the gusts. Our speed through the water was 7½ knots, and since we were running with the wind almost dead astern, the true wind speed was something approaching 50 knots, or storm force on the Beaufort scale.

Iain didn't return, finally calling up to ask if it was all right for him to stay down for breakfast. The trouble over Carlos seemed to have died down. Iris relieved me about half an hour later and I asked her what it had all been about. I had to shout to make myself heard above the roar of the wind and sea. But all she said was, 'Nothing very much. You get some sleep now. You've been up all night.'

I didn't argue. The clouds had lifted a little, the light was stronger and I thought I could see the end of Tierra del Fuego and the entrance to the Le Maire Strait. I called Nils up to stand watch with her, entered our Satnav position in the log, and after pencilling it in with the time and date on the chart, went below to my bunk.

I was so tired I went straight off to sleep, regardless of the violence of the movement, and when Iris finally woke me I was shocked to see it was 12.47. 'Everything all right?' I asked in a sudden panic.

'Of course. You're not the only one who can navigate.' I thought she meant Andy, but no, she was referring to Iain. 'Andy and Go-Go are both sick, and Carlos has taken to his bunk, looking very pale.'

'And Ángel?'

'He had his breakfast – two eggs and a lot of butter with his bread – then retired as though he was a paying passenger on a luxury cruise ship.'

Apparently he had finally accepted the fact of Carlos's presence on board. 'Why did he object?' I asked. 'Is he afraid we may never get out of the ice?'

She shook her head. 'Of course not. He doesn't think of him in that way at all.'

'What way then?'

'I don't know. It is something personal, something that concerns him. I don't understand. All I know is that wretched boy is in love with him.' She said it quite viciously.

I sat up, staring at her. She was still leaning half over me and just for a second I caught a glimpse of something akin to hatred in her eyes. 'You're in love with him yourself, aren't you?' I was thinking what a hell of an emotional time bomb we had been landed with.

'No. No, of course I am not. How dare you suggest –' She turned quickly, knowing her protest had been too vehement. 'It is not a question of love.' She knew her voice had given her away. 'It is . . .' She stopped uncertainly, biting her lip. 'You were asking about Carlos.'

'Yes. How much do you know about his background – the Borgalini family?'

'Very little, except that Roberto Borgalini either lives with, or is married to, that woman who keeps him. They are both second generation Sicilian.'

'The singer, Rosalli Gabrielli?'

'Yes.'

'And she is Carlos's mother?' And when she nodded abruptly, beginning to turn away, I went on quickly, 'When did you first meet Carlos?'

She frowned. 'I was trying to remember that the other day. I think it was when Ángel took me sailing. It was the only time, and Papa was with us. Carlos must have been about fourteen or fifteen. He was still at school.'

'And he's Borgalini's child?'

There was a fractional hesitation before she said, 'I suppose so. I've never really thought about it until now. Seeing them together again . . . They're very alike, you know.'

'You mean –' But I was suddenly conscious that the movement of the ship had changed. It was less abrupt, more a long, slow roll with a twisting swoop followed by a crash drop and the surge of water along the deck. But the whine had gone out of the wind. 'The wind has dropped.'

She nodded, her face crusted with salt. 'Barely 20 knots now. And the sky is clearing. We are opening up the Le Maire Strait and can see the island of Los Estados quite clearly.'

I swung my legs out of the bunk. 'What's our speed?'

'Four and a half.'

I nodded. We needed more sail. 'Give Andy a shout, will you.'

'I tell you, he is seasick.'

'I don't care. I can't get the main and the upper squares'l hoisted on my own, so get him on his feet somehow.' I was pulling on my sea boots, feeling slightly dizzy myself. Now the wind had dropped, the great wave trains marching up astern of us from the Horn were rearing higher, the toppling crests hitting our stern, flooding the deck right to the bows. Water was splashing down the wheelhouse ladder and there was a drip over my bunk.

'What is the trouble?' Ángel was standing at the entrance to his cubicle wearing nothing but a pair of pink and white striped underpants, his torso tanned, the muscles of his legs taut against the movement of the ship. He looked hard and very fit. 'Anything I can do?'

I told him and he said, 'Okay. I give you a hand.' He was back, fully clothed, almost before I had got my oilskins on. 'You tell me what to do.'

I didn't argue with him. I just nodded, wondering whether I could do it with just him to help me. I refused to let Iris go out on to the deck, and Nils had been up all night watching over the engine. Anyway, he was the engineer, not a deckie.

Going for'ard that morning was like a balancing act on the bows of a roller-coaster, but I suppose if you have ridden horses all your life muscle and nerve are tuned to that sort of movement. At any rate, Ángel just stood there as though he were part of the deck fittings, everything slatting and banging about us, the water sometimes up to our waists and the ship heaving wildly on the break of the great seas rolling under us. When I yelled above the tumult for him to pull on this rope or winch in on that, he literally jumped to it, so that once he got the hang of what was required he was doing it often faster than I could.

It was my first real introduction to a man who was to prove a remarkable addition to the ship's company whenever there was need. Arrogant, emotionally and socially disruptive, vain, self-conscious and supersensitive to the behaviour of those around him, he had an extraordinary flair for rising to any occasion that would offer him the opportunity of demonstrating his superiority. 'A very dangerous man,' Iain had said to me after we had watched him greeting the various members of the expedition on his arrival. 'Just ye watch it, Pete, or he'll charm the pants off ye an' leave ye stark naked in the ice.' It was said jokingly, but the broadness of his accent made it clear to me that the warning was a deadly serious one.

With both squares'ls set on the foremast and the main sheeted half in, *Isvik* steadied down, heeled slightly to port and rode the waves with a great swooping surge of power. At times we were surfing and had over 14 on the clock, which was a lot for a heavily-built boat loaded below her marks with a year's stores and the gear to cope with a winter in the ice. I remember Andy, white-faced in the wheelhouse doorway, breathing in great gulps of air and saying, 'We could get pooped running downwind like this in the Roaring Forties.' And when I reminded him we were into the Fifties now and anyway you could get pooped in the North Sea, he nodded a little wanly. 'But down here we don't have any lifeboat stations handy.'

'There's the Falklands.' I was laughing then with the sheer exhilaration of our speed as *Isvik* was lifted on a breaking comber and went careering wildly through the seething water of the crest. And Iain, his head appearing like a jack-in-the-box at the top of the companionway, said, 'There's an ocean-going tug at East Cove, where there's two fishery protection vessels, a Marr trawler and all sorts of foreign krill and squid fishers, plus the Navy, of course, so don't get the idea there are no ships around but ourselves.'

He heaved his bulk into the wheelhouse and was promptly

flung against the gyro column. 'We won't be fully on our own till South Georgia is behind us and we're enterin' the pack.' And he added, 'There's even drillin' rigs in the sea area between Patagonia and the Falkland Exclusion Zone, and then there are the various Antarctic bases. Argentina has about a dozen, the three nearest Marambio, San Martin and Esperanza.'

It was like that most of that first day, the cloud lifting steadily and the visibility becoming so clear we had the highest parts of Tierra del Fuego in sight hour after hour despite our speed. That was what impressed me most – not the great wave trains and the steady weight of the wind that drove us, but the wonderful, breath-taking clarity of the unpolluted air. And the sky. Sunset that day, and the next, was a roaring furnace of red that changed gradually to horizontal streaks of cold blue and white, then translucent green. And when night finally came and the stars grew like lanterns being switched on, they were so brilliant they were unbelievable in their beauty and their nearness.

Once we had cleared the land and the seas were less disturbed, the movement was much easier. It was still a roller-coaster of a ride, but gradually, as the eight of us found our feet again, the routine of shipboard life asserted itself. Andy raised his 'ham' contact on the Falklands and got a repeat of the weather situation. Ángel was in the wheelhouse at the time and in due course it was borne in on me that he almost always contrived to be around when Andy raised either the Falklands or the mainland of Argentina or Chile.

It was just after dawn on the fourth day that we raised South Georgia. It was almost two hundred miles away, broad on the port bow, and it showed as a mirror image of pale white peaks upside down on the horizon. Nils was at the helm and he called me to check that it really was South Georgia. The image was gradually paling with the dawn, but there was absolutely no doubt. The phenomenon, and the inversion, was on a bearing of 67 degrees, which agreed precisely with our Satnav position, and for a time it was so clear I could actually identify the Allardyce Range and the great nine-thousand-foot peak of Mount Paget.

There happened then something so bizarre that for a moment

I couldn't believe it. We were all of us on deck, or in the wheelhouse, for I had called them up to look at the extraordinary sight of the great volcanic mass where Shackleton is buried, standing on its head and gleaming white like an upside-down wedding cake. There was a sudden, sharp crack, as though a piece of ice had broken away, and I turned my head just in time to see the albatross that had been following us for the last day and a half fold its left wing and veer away. I saw its beak open, heard its cry, and then it collapsed into our wake, its eight-foot span of wings folded, the left held awkwardly and trailing in the water.

I was so surprised, so shocked, that I just stood there, South Georgia forgotten, staring at the bird that we had identified from the book on board as a young specimen of the Great or Wandering Albatross. For almost two days it had been *Isvik*'s aerial escort, riding the wind so effortlessly I had come to think of it as the spirit of Antarctica, and now to see it down in the water, ditched and unable to rise.

Heads turned abruptly to stare upwards, towards the upper steering position. I rushed out of the wheelhouse, already guessing what I would see. It was Ángel Connor-Gómez standing there with his .22 laid across his arm, a thin wisp of smoke curling out of the barrel, and he was smiling down at us, pleased at the effect his action had had.

'You bastard!' I said, instinctively choosing the one word that I knew got through to him. 'Don't you realise – ?'

'I know the legend, yes.' His smile broadened. 'But see, I don't kill the bird. I only wing him. In the joint.'

'Why?'

He shrugged. 'Why not? It is to prove my shooting is still good and the gun accurate.'

'You could have used something else for a target.'

'It was following us.'

Nobody said anything then, all of us staring up at him. 'What do you mean?' somebody breathed.

'Nobody, nothing, not even a bird follows me.' He said it so quietly I barely heard him. 'Not where I am going.'

Was he mad? His gaze had shifted to the horizon, a far-away

look in his eyes. South Georgia had disappeared and the sun blazed a golden glitter across the waves. I looked astern, but the albatross was lost to sight. Andy turned away. To him it was just a bird, nothing more. But for Go-Go it was different, her eyes staring blankly at nothing and tears welling up as though somewhere in the recesses of her partly Aborigine mind she saw it as a manifestation of the Dreamtime.

That little episode seemed to epitomise the whole nature of the man. But when I said that to Iain, he just shrugged. 'One shot, a crippled bird and he had yer attention, everybody gawpin' at him. Aye.' He nodded slowly, then turned away. 'He likes an audience,' he muttered as he headed back down to his cubicle.

Late that evening I think we must have crossed the Antarctic Convergence, the line where the surface layer of cold polar water dips below the warmer waters to the north. The sea became very confused and there was a sharp drop in temperature accompanied by an increase in both cloud and wind. By evening the Satnav positions indicated a 2-knot drift to the north-east, and the following morning, when we were midway between South Georgia and the South Orkneys, we were into the cause of that drift current, the south-westerly gales that blow almost continuously from the horn-like peninsula of Graham Land.

For the better part of three days we had a wild, broad-reaching run. Conditions were so bad at one point that we were almost broaching on the breaking crests and in danger of a knock-down. If the crew had been stronger I think I might have put a sea anchor out and hove-to under bare poles. She was going so fast at times it seemed she might pitch-pole end over end, for every so often a real giant of a wave would rear up like a mountain on our starb'd quarter.

Down below, of course, it was chaos, everything that could break loose flying all over the place, and Carlos as well as Andy so sick they were useless, Andy in particular retching his guts out with nothing more to bring up, just black bile, so that I feared for his lungs and the walls of his stomach. Fortunately Go-Go had a natural balance that enabled her to adjust very quickly to the unpredictability of the boat's movements. She was the one person who seemed totally unaffected by the swoops and jerks, the poundings, the crash of the bows, the roar of the water and the constant, high-pitched, demoniac sound of the wind tearing through the rigging. All the rest of us were affected to some degree, and in the circumstances, I soon learned who I could rely on in an emergency. Nils was like a rock, steering the boat through the worst of the seas hour after hour. Angel slept through it all. At least, he kept to his bunk, firmly strapped in, but his breathing and his colour were normal and whenever I looked in on him he would open an eye. But he didn't say anything, and I had the feeling he was still resenting my having called him a bastard.

Iain also kept to his bunk, his face drained of blood and feeling the cold so badly that his body shivered uncontrollably. Twice I saw Iris get up and make him a hot drink. She hadn't a cast-iron stomach, but she had the will to force herself to wedge her body into the galley and produce mugs of soup for us and thick wodges of coarse brown bread spread with Marmite.

In those three days I learned a lot about the people I was sailing with, their good and their bad points, their weaknesses and their inner strengths. Gradually I realised we were moving out of the area where great mountains of water spilling white crests reared up behind us to come crashing down on our stern. The wave trains were still there, but the rogues were gone. I had altered course the previous day to the south-east and we were no longer getting the full weight of the wind roaring untrammelled round the southern globe; we were coming under the lee of the land and the attendant pack ice. It was bitterly cold.

As conditions quietened, the strain eased, and with miraculous speed our bodies recovered. Suddenly there was energy and warmth in the big central saloon-cum-galley, everybody in good humour and looking to the future, to the moment when we should close the pack and the seas would be diminished by the weight of it. The clouds lifted and the sun came out.

We were then right in the centre of the triangle formed by South Georgia, the South Orkneys and the Sandwich Group. Gradually I had been altering course further to the south so that we were now headed straight down into the Weddell Sea. It had been a fast run so far, and with the sunshine and the lengthening days there was an undercurrent of excitement and anticipation on board. Or am I writing that because it was the way I felt?

Forgotten now was the impersonal way I had been fired from my job, the months I had spent trying to build up a business of my own. All I could think of was the ice getting nearer and that lost ship, the mystery of it, the loneliness. We were broad-reaching at 9 knots in force 5, the bow wave sparkling in the sun, and there were whales, three of them dipping and spouting across our wake. Birds, too – petrel, terns, a solitary sooty albatross.

Next morning, as the sun lifted off the horizon, we caught the first glint of the iceblink, a pale translucence reflected in an overcast sky far to the south and south-west. Nils produced akavit from his own secret store and we stood out on deck, with the night's coating of ice dripping from the rigging, and drank a toast to the unknown ahead. None of us had any experience of pack ice, so the excitement of seeing it mirrored there, just below the southern horizon, was tinged with the sense of danger ahead. Ángel, I noticed, was the only one of us whose face did not show some reflection of the excitement I was feeling. Instead, he stood there, the drink in his hand, his gaze fixed on a point somewhere off the starb'd bow. His teeth seemed set, his lips a tight line, and there was something in his expression – fear, desperation, a steeling of the heart against things out there that had to be faced? I couldn't tell. But it has stayed in my mind that just for that moment he was a changed man. He looked older, less sure of himself. But it was only for a moment, then the mood was gone and he lifted his drink, knocking it back in one gulp. He must have sensed I was watching him, for suddenly he was looking straight at me, his eyes narrowed. 'You are wondering – what? How we face the ice!' He smiled. 'We see what that does to us, eh?'

There was something in the way he had smiled that sent a cold shiver of fear down into my stomach. Why was he here? Why was he so anxious to reach the ship? Those, and other questions, rattled round my head as I lay in my bunk that night, listening to the sound of water against the hull, so close to my ear, to the creaks and groans, the frapping of ropes against the mast, the occasional slat of a sail. And what was I doing here? Why hadn't I gone back home while I had the chance? It was crazy, lying here, frightening myself with wild imaginings, images of *Flying Dutchmen* and *Marie Celestes* flitting through my tired brain, and all the time thinking of Ángel and the dilapidated rows of huts just back of where I had found him waiting for me.

And in the morning Iain got him into the wheelhouse, stood him in front of the chart and said, 'Now then, Mr Connor-Gómez – where is it? Ye say ye know the position, that it's in the ice in the Weddell Sea and when we're down there ye'll give us the co-ordinates. Well, we're in the Weddell Sea now and there's the ice, so the time has come fur ye to show us where it is on the chart.'

At first he said we must wait until we were actually in the ice. He'd have to see what the rate of drift was. 'I know where I saw her, but that was almost eighteen months ago. The ice will have carried her to the north since then.' How far he didn't know. 'There is a northerly drift on the west side of the Weddell Sea. Your man, Shackleton, in his *Endurance* drifted over four hundred miles in nine months. That is a daily drift rate of about one and a half miles. But this is an unusual year. I don't know what the drift rate will have been.'

Iain accepted that. The man had done his homework and couldn't be expected to pinpoint the position of the ship now. 'Aye, well – let's go back to that test flight of yers when ye actually saw her. Ye mark in that position on the chart and we'll take it from there.'

Ángel hesitated. But in the end he gave in with a little shrug. He didn't have to refer to a notebook. He had the co-ordinates in his head and using the big perspex ruler he marked in a little cross at the bottom of the Weddell Sea. And when Iain said immediately that it was quite a way to the west of where the *Endurance* was beset, I realised that Ángel wasn't the only one who had done his homework. 'Eighteen months, ye say.' Iain reached up to the bookcase and pulled out Shackleton's *South*, turning immediately to the map at the end which showed the drift of the *Endurance*. 'If yer vessel experienced the same sort of northerly drift, then by now she would be free of the ice and somewhere off Graham Land.'

'Or grounded on the coast,' Ángel said.

'Aye. Or crushed by one of the bergs breakin' off from the Ronne Ice Shelf.' He pronounced it 'Ronnay'. 'Or wrecked, or sunk,' he added, 'or just crushed to pieces by the layerin' of the pack. So, just how dae ye propose to find her?'

Silence then and Ángel standing there, head in hand, staring down at the chart, deep in thought.

'Well?'

'You leave it to me. I will find it.'

'But how, man – how?'

'That is my problem.'

'But ye'll find her, ye're sure of that?'

And when Ángel nodded, Iris chipped in with the question that was on the tip of my own tongue, 'You know where it is, don't you? That's what you told me.'

He hesitated, then suddenly turned on his heel and walked out on to the deck, Iris calling after him, 'If you know, why don't you tell us?' The sliding door slammed shut and she turned to Iain. 'What do you think? Does he know, or is he just leading us on, playing some sort of game?'

Iain shrugged. 'Yer guess is as good as mine, m'dear, but if he does know, then it can mean only one thing, the wreck is in a fixed position, held in ice that's grounded against the coast. That right?' He turned to me. 'D'ye agree that if he knows where it is he must be damned sure the ice that's holdin' it isn't driftin'?'

I nodded, and he added, 'And if it's not driftin', then it's bein' held by somethin', and that can only be the shoreline. Ye agree?'

'Yes,' I said.

He turned back to Iris. 'So, we wait and watch. Keep yer eye on him, both of ye.'

IV

ON ICE

ONE

We entered the pack on the second day of the New Year in the company of two humpback whales. We were then under fore-and-aft rig, having handed our running gear and lashed the yards along the gunn'ls. Sailing south now and well over to the eastern side of the Weddell Sea, the current, which runs clockwise, was still helping us, and with the stars diamond-bright in the shortening periods of darkness, I was able to get a whole series of fixes, thus establishing our position without any doubt.

The previous day we had been lucky enough to have perfect iceblink conditions, which had given us an upside-down view of the open water leads through the pack that stretched ahead of us. We had chosen the largest of these, a gap well over a mile wide, the ice on either side already so degraded by the long daylight hours it was virtual brash. Sailing conditions became superb, a steady force-3 breeze from slightly north of west and virtually no sea, just a long, slow swell. *Isvik* revelled in it, chuckling along at between 6 and 8 knots, and all of us on board in a very relaxed mood.

From north to south the Weddell Sea is the better part of a thousand miles, and sailing the course dictated by Ángel, not direct, but jinking from lead to lead, often with one of us balanced on the foremast yard brackets to con the ship, we managed to make steady progress along a line 192 degrees, which cut the coast well to the west of the BAS base at Halley Bay, even to the west of Vahsel Bay on the Leopold Coast, and not a hundred miles from where Shackleton's *Endurance* was beset on 18 January 1915.

More and more, as we made our southing, our movements were controlled by the ice, which gradually became thicker, less degraded, and the leads between fewer. There was a storm on the 12th, a real Antarctic blizzard with driving snow, wet and sticky, so that it clung to the wheelhouse and masts, and during the cold of the short night had to be chipped off with ice axes. With all the cargo we carried on deck, there was always a danger of the ship's centre of gravity being so badly affected that she became top-heavy. The thought of being rolled over in these waters in the dead of night with the black, snow-laden wind gusting 70 knots was not attractive!

Once the storm had blown itself out, the sky cleared, and our whole icebound world became still and beautiful. This summer interlude lasted four days, and with no wind we had to motor, the lanes of open water always enabling us to steer a generally southerly course. But conning the boat was a strain, the ice so dazzling white that the sun's reflection seemed to burn into our eyes, even through dark glasses.

The two girls took advantage of the brilliant sunshine, and armed with bottles of sun lotion disappeared behind a canvas screen they rigged for'ard of the mainmast on the port side. I forgot about this at one point when an open lane, narrowing to what appeared to be a cul-de-sac, forced me to run up the ratlines and search ahead for a way through. In fact, the lane we were in was not a cul-de-sac. Instead, it bent sharply round to the east, to an icebound lake, a polynya, from which several dark threads of open water led southwards again.

Once I had satisfied myself that the way ahead was still open, I stood there for a moment, balanced on the yard brackets, enjoying the endless vista of broken ice, the sun and the breeze of our passage. I was watching the slow emergence and submergence of a couple of *Orcinus orca*, the so-called Killer Whale, the white of their bellies looking almost muddied by contrast with the brilliant whiteness of the world that was their playground. A seal surfaced almost alongside us, and as I watched it heading for the bow wave on our port side, I found myself looking straight down at the two figures behind their canvas screen, their skin glistening with suntan oil. They were lying buttocks-up on their stomachs, one darker than the other, but there was a beauty and an innocence in the way they lay there, stark naked and totally exposed to my gaze, so that I held my breath for fear even my breathing would break the beauty of the scene.

Then one of them stirred. It was Iris and she rolled over on her back, her eyes open and staring straight up at me. She smiled and waved, and I hurried back down, feeling embarrassed by the way I was suddenly swelling up. I think by then I was slightly in love with her myself.

Perhaps because of the nature of my thoughts it did not shock, or even surprise me, when, late that evening, I saw Ángel walk up to Go-Go and put a hand on her buttocks. I was on the port side, helping Nils pump a canful of paraffin out of one of the deck drums. The sun had just set, a bright orange flaring, the sky streaked with lines of thin white vapour interspersed with cold, translucent green. It was very beautiful and, the can full, I straightened up, standing there, staring at the wonderful Turneresque colouring of it. Go-Go was taking in some washing she had pegged to the guardrails, her body bent down, the fabric of her pants stretched tight across her bottom. Ángel appeared as a black cut-out in silhouette against the evening light, his hands reaching out to caress her.

She reacted quick as a flash, straightening up and brushing his hand away. She said something, I couldn't hear what, but he took no notice, reaching out both hands to grasp hold of her. She seized one of them and for a moment I thought she was pulling him into her. So did Ángel. He laughed, and in that laugh was the excitement of conquest. He had, I think, a firm belief that he was irresistible to women. But then she suddenly bent down, jerking his arm forward and at the same time twisting it. The effect was startling. With a cry of pain his body was bent sideways and he went sprawling over her shoulders to land up flat on his back on the deck.

Before I could move Iain had erupted out of the wheelhouse. Go-Go was standing there, looking down at her tormentor. I couldn't hear what she said to him, but her voice was tight with fury. Then she turned, almost colliding with Iain, who, to my surprise, ignored the figure slowly picking himself up off the deck and addressed himself only to Go-Go. 'Ye're a bloody fool, girl.

Suppose he'd caught his head on a steel deck plate or the corner of the hatch there?' He left it at that, adding, 'Don't flaunt yerself or we could end up on a voyage without a purpose. Find yer husband now. Tell Andy Ah want to see him in the wheelhouse.'

'Why the hell are you blaming her?' I demanded as she ran, crying, for'ard along the deck.

He glanced down at Ángel, with an expression of something near to contempt on his face, then turned to me. 'Think it out for yerself,' he said and went back into the wheelhouse.

You would expect a man losing face like that to cover it up with a show of anger, at least retreat into his shell. But not Ángel. He got up off the deck with a quick, lithe movement. 'Some girl, that!' He winked at me, then walked away with his head held high and a little smile on his face as though he'd enjoyed the experience of being thrown on his back. And that night, at dinner, he seemed as easy and charming as ever. It was Go-Go who sat silent and watchful, a sulky, withdrawn look on her face.

It should have been a happy occasion, for at sunset, with no wind and surrounded by ice, the sea so still the surface of it looked like burnished pewter, we moored *Isvik* to a floe and went below. It was the first time since Ushuaia we had all sat down together for the evening meal. Nils had opened a bottle of red Chilean wine, but even that did not lift the brooding tenseness that hung over the table. At the time I put it down to the realisation that we were nearing the point at which we would have to take to the ice, might even be beset and locked in for the winter. But in retrospect I think it went much deeper than just a matter of nerves. Each of us had our own personal and very different reasons for being seated there at that table in the quiet of the saloon on a ship moored in the midst of a world of ice.

We were like the cast in some strange theatrical drama, sitting silent at that table listening to the sound of the sea sucking at the ice floes, grinding them together as the current shifted them, and conscious all the time of something waiting in the wings. There was little or no conversation, all of us, including Nils, seeming to be locked in on our own thoughts. Go-Go and Andy had their own personal problems. I had already come to the conclusion that he was tiring of her. She was, I guessed, sexually very demanding. He often looked washed out, or as Iain put it more crudely, 'The laddie's clapped out, so ye just watch him.' And he had added, 'Also he's scared, and so is she.'

By now we all knew that she had only come because she couldn't bear to let him go on his own. She was desperately in love with him, and he was for ever trying to escape into a world of his own, the world of air waves and disembodied voices that made no demands on him. And Ángel, looking at her hungrily across the table, smiling a relaxed smile, while Carlos watched, his eyes eager and full of jealousy. Periodically I glanced across at Iain. Iris was sitting beside him, her eyes on her plate, both of them silent. And when she got up to get him a second helping of seal meat and rice, I found myself looking right through the scarlet of her polo-necked sweater and navy-blue trousers, imagining her as she had been when she rolled over and I had found myself looking down on her naked body sprawled on the deck below me. Christ! It made me ache for the feel of her.

'Make certain, Pete, ye get an accurate fix tonight.' Iain smiled at me and I had a feeling he knew exactly what had been in my thoughts. Later, as we stood together in the wheelhouse, he said, 'Women are the devil on board ship.' He was jotting down chronometer times and angles as I took the star sights and called out the sextant readings to him. 'Aye, but it's not for very much longer.'

'How do you mean?' There had been a note of finality in his voice.

'Ye'll see. Soon as we reach the Ice Shelf and get to the point where our progress along it is blocked . . .' He left it at that, and in the small hours, as the light increased with dramatic suddenness at the imminence of sunrise, our windspeed indicator at the mainmast top began to spin with a nice little breeze from the north-east, so that Andy and I were able to get the ship under way again.

Ángel should have been on watch by then. I left Andy at the wheel and went down to rout him out. He was always doing that, lying in and waiting for the watch on duty to call him. His bunk was on the port side aft and the door across the cubbyhole that did for a cabin was slid to. I flung it back, annoyed at having to come down to call him when he had a perfectly good alarm clock and I had sounded the change of watch on the ship's bell. 'Time you were on watch,' I told him, and I shone the beam of the powerful deck torch I had with me full on him. His face was turned away from me, only the back of his head visible. I stood there, staring, for there were two heads on the pillow and it was Carlos who slowly turned and looked up at me, smiling softly like a cat that's been at the cream.

Abruptly Ángel flung the duvet top of his sleeping bag back and swung his legs across Carlos, reaching with his feet for the floor. They were both of them naked and I swear the boy winked at me, that little devil peeping up at me from out of moist, slightly pink-looking eyes. I cut the beam of my torch and left them in darkness, feeling oddly shocked, which was silly of me really since I knew very well Carlos was a homosexual. But it's one thing to guess at somebody's sexual appetite, quite another to see him practising it. And with Ángel, who was just old enough to be his father. Christ almighty! The thought was there in my mind, quite suddenly, quite unbidden.

There was, of course, no indication of anything untoward when Ángel came into the wheelhouse fully clothed and took the helm, repeating the course Andy gave him in a quiet, matter-of-fact voice.

It was a pity I didn't have the satellite pictures I was shown later by one of the Met. officers at Mount Pleasant. They were basically weather maps, and it was possible, when the cloud was thin, to see the extent of the pack ice, even the degree to which it had degraded into brash. Some of the bigger bergs, too, that had carved off the Ice Shelf – I was told there was one over seventy miles in length, a 1986 Landsat picture showing some thirteen thousand square kilometres floated off, the Belgrano base gone and the Filchner with a new front where the great Chasm had been. But the weather maps did show the darker patches at the base of the Weddell Sea that meant open water. These were quite large in the east, but gradually thinned out towards the west till, beyond the Filchner, they were little more than an intermittent thread of dark at the eastern end of the Ronne Ice Shelf.

Had we had one of those satellite weather maps on board we

might have found the nerve to push on through the dangerously narrow leads to the next open water patch and even beyond. As it was, having sighted the Ronne Ice Shelf on the 21st through flurries of snow, and sailed right up to the sheer front of it the following day, we hesitated about pushing our luck much further. The open water was gradually thinning. Soon we were motoring through thread-like passages no wider than twenty feet, with the distant Ice Front gleaming white like chalk cliffs in the crystal sunlight on our port side and bergs of all shapes and sizes huddled in fascinating, sun-eroded shapes to starb'd. We could see bits of the Ice Front carving off in great chunks, rolling and tumbling into the water and tossing us about in the waves it created, and whenever we were in broader waters there were always growlers and bergy-bits to contend with, so that we gradually became exhausted with poling off to keep the bows clear of the much larger expanses of ice hidden beneath the surface.

We got as far west as 61° 42″ before being stopped by a tabular berg that looked as though it had broken away from the Ice Front quite recently. Between it and the Front the pack had layered, great up-ended shelves of ice lying higgledy-piggledy. It was no place to venture, we thought, even though there was a slender line of dark water stretching away north that looked as though it might lead round the berg and out again into the flat ice prairie of the pack.

We dared not risk it, and so we laid out four mooring lines with grapnels on the ends to the surrounding floes and shut down the engine, relying on wind power, of which there was then plenty coming straight off the Ice Shelf, to keep our batteries fully charged. That was on the 25th and Andy managed to get a weather forecast from the *Polarstern*, or maybe it was from the BAS base at Halley, I'm not sure which. The outlook was fairly good for the next few days with winds from south veering through west to north-west. Strange, but I still found it difficult to accept that the Coriolus effect makes a veering wind in the southern hemisphere indicative of low pressure conditions, causing them to vortex clockwise, not anti-clockwise as would be the case north of the equator. Most of my previous navigational experience being in northern waters, my instinct was to regard wind shifts that followed the clock as blowing from out of a high pressure system.

'Well?' Iain was standing in the wheelhouse facing Ángel who had come up to listen in on Andy's conversation with the Halley people. 'How far is it? We're west now of the 192 degree bearin' ye gave us way back. How many miles d'ye reck'n we got to trek across the ice?'

'Not far now,' Ángel replied.

'How many miles? That's what Ah asked ye.'

Ángel shrugged. 'You know as well as I do that the ice here is shifting northward all the time on the current. I know where I saw the ship. I have the co-ordinates and we are now very close. But how many miles she has drifted . . .' Another shrug of those square, well-proportioned shoulders. 'How fast is the current – 0.5, 0.75, 1 knot? You tell me, then I tell you where is your ship.'

Iris had joined us and she started to insist on an answer, but Iain put his hand on her arm and said, 'We'll discuss it tomorrow. It's late now.' The hands of the chronometer stood at six minutes past midnight. It was already 26 January.

Next day dawned bright and very still, no wind at all, which enabled us to take the ship over to the north side of the polynya and moor alongside a floe that was secured to the remains of an old berg. We then rigged a block and tackle to the mainmast yard and hoisted out the snowmobile. Iris, who had spent some months in northern Canada, insisted on calling it a skidoo. After swinging it across on to the ice, we rigged a small cargo net, loaded it full of all the stores and gear we needed and swung that over on to the ice. The outboard for the semi-rigid inflatable started up almost immediately we pulled the cord, but the snowmobile, despite being cocooned in heavy-duty plastic sheeting, appeared to have got water in the engine. It refused to give even the slightest cough. In the end Nils began stripping it down, but long before he had cleaned it thoroughly and checked the fuel lines a hand-chilling wind had come in from the south, and by the time he had got it assembled again it was blowing a good force 6.

The temperature drop was considerable and he had some difficulty in putting the engine together again. Still it would not start.

There was more water in the carburettor. We knew what the answer was then. Why we hadn't examined the tank in the first place I cannot think. Doubtless we were tired. We were also excited, anxious to get everything ready in the shortest possible time.

The tank had water in it and I thought of Carlos lashing out with that ice axe. I jumped back on board, checked the drum from which we had filled up. 'You bloody, stupid little fool,' I yelled at him. 'You did that.' I was pointing to a round, jagged little hole I had found near the top, half-concealed by the rope securing the drum to the bulwarks. He shook his head, glancing quickly at the others, who were all standing round in an accusing semi-circle staring at him. 'I didn't . . .' I think he had been intending to deny it again, but his voice faltered and in the end he said, 'I w-was not m-meaning to make any damage. It was not – not intentional.'

By the time Nils had thoroughly cleaned out the snowmobile's tank and refilled it from a different drum, and I had dismantled the fuel line and thoroughly cleaned the carburettor again, the wind chill had seeped through to our bones and we were shivering with cold. But the fact that the engine started at the first pull of the cord cheered us, and just to make sure everything was all right, we hitched the loaded sledge to the snowmobile and gave the machine a test drive of a few hundred metres under load, each of us taking a turn at driving it.

The floe ice here was flat, so there was nothing difficult about it, but Go-Go stayed on board. She was preparing lunch, she said, and Andy was in the wheelhouse. The snowmobile had been adapted for travelling on water, so that it was our recce vehicle as well as our sledge-puller. If that hadn't worked we would have had to use the smaller sledges which we put together that afternoon, just in case. There were two of them and a second inflatable, all rubber, which we got out of its pack, testing it out in the water between the ship and the floe.

Just before noon it started to snow, hard, driving stuff that was more like hail and hit one's face hard as bird shot. We went back on board where Go-Go had pasta and a pot of piping hot seal stew waiting to thaw us out. Slowly the snowmobile, with its attendant sledges all packed with gear, were transformed into white mounds that merged with the background. Seen dimly through the driving white of that mini-blizzard, they made a wretched tableau, reminding me of Scott and all the difficulties Shackleton had faced. I was no Worsley, and the prospect of being lost in a whiteout, and having to find my way back, filled me with dread. The ship, buried in snow and ice, would present such a very small target in the vast wastes of Antarctica.

But then the snow stopped and the wind died as quickly as it had got up. Suddenly the sun was shining and it was warm again. We took the stores off the towing sledge, wrapped them in tough woven polyethylene plastic sheeting and strapped them on to the sledge again. Then we slid the whole clumsy-looking package into the water. To my surprise, I must admit, we had got the weight right; it floated. We hitched the ungainly contraption to the snowmobile and towed it back and forth several times across the polynya, then unpacked it and erected the small tent, a dry run for the ice trek ahead. Everything inside the plastic was dry. No water had got in, though in the last run Iain had driven the snowmobile at full throttle.

We were ready to go then. Iain would accompany Ángel. That was the plan. I would be in charge of the ship in his absence. In the event of difficulties, or any disaster, he had a VHF set with a fully-charged battery on the snowmobile. I would be in command of any relief party.

Iris, of course, wanted to go with the two ship-seekers. But no, Iain wouldn't agree to that. 'If ye have to come after us,' he said, turning to me, 'Iris, as expedition leader, will have to take charge of the ship. Andy stays on board. He's needed to man the radio. Nils, too. Ye'll need him to handle the engine,' he told Iris. And then to me again, 'That leaves Carlos. If we dae get into difficulties, then it's ye and Carlos to come to our aid, and make sure ye're able to maintain contact with the ship at all times. There's tae spare VHF sets, and across the pack they should have a range of anythin' up to a hundred miles, that is, so long as ye're not tucked in behind a berg.'

Iris tried to argue with him, but in the end she gave up. I think she realised that, however determined she was, the two men would still travel faster on their own. Everybody turned in early that night. The forecast was good and the starting time was fixed for shortly after first light. I set my alarm for 03.00 sun time. Breakfast would be at 03.30 and DV the start time was fixed for 04.30. For navigational purposes our chronometer, and my own quartz digital wristwatch, were on GMT, or Zulu time, a difference of over four hours since we were over 60 degrees west of the Greenwich Meridian.

I woke once, hearing movement and the sound of voices. That was at 01.17, but I thought nothing of it and turned over and went to sleep again. In a boat like *Isvik*, with its semi-open plan, there was always somebody moving around. The ice was creaking and there were the usual ship noises as she strained at her mooring ropes, shifting to the lift and roll of the slight swell.

My alarm went off at 03.00 and I slid out of my bunk into a raw, cold draught from the wheelhouse. Somebody must have left the door to the deck open. I was struggling into my fur-lined boots when I heard Iris's voice and the sound of feet on the deck above. 'What's that ye're sayin?' It was Iain's voice, much fainter, and then he laughed. 'What the hell did ye expect?'

I grabbed my anorak and went up into the dawn. The sky was shot with cloud, the sun painting it a virulent orange. Iain and Iris were out on the ice and the snowmobile was gone, the big sledge too. The twin lines of their going, imprinted on the flat white surface of the floe, ran away to the north-west. 'Don't worry,' Iain said to her. 'He'll not lose us.'

It was Ángel, of course, and I would have expected Iain to be furious that the man had gone off with our only powered ice transport and a sledge piled with stores. Instead, he seemed quite relaxed about it, even smiling slightly as he turned his head and saw me. 'Have a look, will ye, and see if Carlos is in his cabin.'

When I returned to the wheelhouse he and Iris were back on board and the Galvins were on deck. I told him, not only were both cabins empty, but they had taken most of their cold weather clothing with them, also skis, snowshoes, glasses and camera.

'Carlos is with him then.'

I nodded.

'The little fool!' Iain shook his head. 'Ah'm sorry about that. The boy could be in trouble.'

He took Iris's arm and the two of them came in out of the cold, sliding the door to behind them. 'We'll have breakfast now, then we'll load up the two small sledges. Soon as that's done, Pete and Ah will get goin'.' He said this to Iris. I think he was expecting her to continue the argument she had started the previous day, insisting that she should go with him, not me. There was a sudden tightness about her mouth, her eyes narrowing under a frown. But she didn't say anything, merely turned away and went below.

Now we were in colder regions we were having porridge in the morning. It was warm and comforting. I was thinking there wouldn't be much in the way of comfort as we ploughed our way north parallel to the line of the Ronne Ice Front, each of us hauling a sledge. 'You were expecting it, weren't you?' I said as I passed Iain a steaming mug of coffee.

'Expectin' what?' he almost growled, burying his face in the mug. For some reason he didn't want to talk about it.

'That he'd steal a march on us.'

And when he still didn't say anything, I added, 'Why?'

'Yes, why?' Iris echoed. 'Why would he be so anxious to find the ship?'

He banged his mug down, starting to get up, and I thought he wasn't going to answer that.

Andy nodded. 'That's something I've been curious about ever since Go-Go and I joined ship. What's the magnet that's pulling you all?'

'Curiosity,' Iain said. And he got to his feet. 'Come on.' He tapped me on the shoulder. 'Time we got ourselves organised.' He told Nils to have a seal meat stew, good and hot, waiting for us when we were ready to leave. 'Some spuds, too. That'll give us plenty of body warmth to go on with.'

'*Nei*, beans is better. I put in plenty of beans for you.'

'Ye dae that and we'll be wind-propelled. Potatoes. Okay?' He looked at me. 'Everythin' ye load on to yer sledge ye'll have to pull. Just remember that, and what won't go on the sledge goes on yer back. So keep it light.' I asked how many days he reckoned and he shook his head. 'How the hell dae Ah know? Depends on the ice. If we run into old pack that's been layered, or a gaggle of bergs that have run amok . . .' He gave an exaggerated, almost Gallic shrug. 'Better load a prayer mat.' He was trying to keep it light-hearted, but it was a warning all the same and I saw Iris watching him, her face tense.

It was, in fact, beans, large butter beans Nils had soaked overnight. The spuds were beginning to shoot, he said. And there was treacle tart to follow. We left immediately afterwards. I remember Iris standing very still with her raven hair falling in wisps across her eyes, the full lips shut tight and an expression on her face that I can only describe as forlorn. Her eyes were fixed on Iain, and she didn't speak. What she was thinking I can only guess – there were just the four of them left with the ship and I think she had come to rely very heavily on him.

A wave of his hand and we were off, that casual salute his only farewell. He didn't say anything, didn't add to the instructions he had already written out for her, and he didn't look back, not even briefly – just put his face to the tracks we would be following and trudged off, hauling his sledge behind him.

I did look back. Iris was still standing there, quite still and staring after us, and behind her *Isvik* stood out very stark against the sun-sparkling light of the icy background, the water black around her. The Galvins watched us from the door of the wheelhouse, Go-Go's scarlet anorak and trousers looking like an advertisement for some ice-cold Italian drink. Nils was nowhere to be seen and I couldn't help feeling it was not a very strong party, two men and two women, to be left alone in such a remote, icebound part of the world, responsible for handling a largish vessel whatever the weather conditions.

It was just after noon when we left, and six hours later we were still hauling in conditions that had become almost a whiteout. As a result the first we knew of open water ahead was a slight movement and bending of the ice. The tracks we were following went right to the edge of it. There was nothing for it but to inflate our rubber dinghy, load the sledges on to it and paddle across, a laborious exercise requiring two journeys. To add to our difficulties, the slight breeze that had been on our backs most of the way was getting stronger and producing little whitecaps on the water.

Iain went first, and when he got back, he reported that the wind was drifting the light covering of snow and ice so that he had had difficulty picking up the tracks. By the time the two of us were safely across, with the second sledge and the remainder of the stores, the tracks were virtually obliterated, the surface of the pack drifting like icing sugar and making a strange, monotonous rustling sound.

We got going again, pulling wearily. It was almost nine by then, the sun a blurred circle of opaque light reaching down towards the Ice Front. We were moving slower now, our feet dragging and the sledges seeming heavier, the harness cutting into our shoulders. The wind shifted gradually into the south-west, increasing in strength, the rustling surface of the ice drifting like white water round our boots, obliterating the tracks. Suddenly they were gone and we were hauling on a compass course, our heads down, earflaps buttoned tight and the sting of tiny ice crystals on our cheeks.

It was a hailstorm that finally decided us to call a halt. Also we were moving into an area of old ice where there was a certain amount of layering and the going had become much harder. Even so, Iain was quite reluctant to pause, which was odd, thinking back to the moment when we had first discovered the snowmobile had gone, how remarkably laid-back he had been, almost as if he had had us pack the towing sledge as a bait for Ángel to take. 'It's that boy,' he said, when I asked him about it. We were unpacking the Arctic sleeping bags from our sledges and I suddenly had a mental picture of the two of them in that bunk together.

'Seems perfectly natural,' I said. 'In the circumstances.'

'What circumstances?' The words were snapped out, and he stood there, his thick waterproof sleeping bag in his hand, staring at me. And when I told him, he said, 'Good God, man! Ye should've told me.'

'Damn it!' I said, 'You could see Carlos worshipped the man – his behaviour, all his actions, right back to the way he followed Iris down to Greenwich and later into the Isle of Dogs.'

He stared at me a moment longer, then he nodded. 'Aye. Ye're probably right. Ah should've remembered.'

It was shortly after that, just as I was about to work my way into my bag, that he wanted to know if I knew anything about firearms. I asked him what sort – 'I've done some wildfowl shooting. Why?'

For answer he pulled a longish, plastic case from the unstrapped pile of stuff on his sledge. Out of it he slipped the dark gunmetal shape of a deadly looking weapon. 'Ye may as well know how this thin' works. Just in case.'

'What is it, a Kalashnikov?' I asked as he unfolded the skeletal metal butt and handed the thing to me. I had never handled a Kalashnikov. In fact, I had never handled any firearm more lethal than a shotgun. I could just read the maker's name as he ran through the safety and firing mechanism for me. It wasn't a Russian name, or English, or Italian. The name stamped into the metal was Heckler & Koch. 'German?'

He nodded.

'How did you come by it?'

'Ah saved up my petrol coupons.' He grinned at me, then went on explaining how to handle it when firing. There was a single shot mechanism and it was fitted with a small telescopic sight. It was only later I learned, quite by chance, that the Heckler & Koch sub-machine-gun was a weapon favoured by the SAS. 'Are you expecting Ángel to be armed?' I was feeling suddenly chilled and a little tense. Shooting birds and rabbits was one thing . . .

'Aye. He'll be armed all right.' And he added, 'Also he's haulin' tae, possibly three of those cases of Semtex he brought on board with him.'

I think that shocked me more than the thought that he might be armed. 'You mean you loaded them on that sledge yesterday?'

''Course Ah didn't load them. But as soon as we found he'd gone Ah checked the forepeak, where we had stored them, and tae of the cases were definitely missin'.'

It was not a comfortable thought to go to sleep on, but I was so damned tired I fell asleep immediately, not even bothering to eat the bar of chocolate, nuts and raisins we had dug out of the stores. I woke once during the night, my face wet with snow. I shone a torch out into the twilight. The wind was blowing and it was snowing big, sticky flakes, so that all I could see was a moving curtain of white, and Iain, lying beside me, was just a snow-covered hump. It was very warm in my waterproof bag. I tucked my face down into it and fell asleep again immediately.

I woke finally to a blindingly white world and a sun like a great blazing orange resting its lower rim on a crystal horizon, everything very clear, so clear in fact that I couldn't gauge the distance off or the height of the bergs that seemed to litter the endless ice field ahead. I couldn't even guess how far it was to the Ice Front to our left. It just stood there, a long wall of white blocking us off from the sight of anything further to the west.

Iain was already out of his bag, sitting hunched on the untidy heap of his sledge. He had a little plastic compass in his hand and between his knees was a small radio. 'You trying to get a forecast?' I asked him.

He shook his head, holding up his hand for quiet. He sat there for several minutes more, head bent, and listening with great concentration as he made small adjustments to the position of the radio, periodically raising the compass to his eye and aligning it in the same direction. 'Okay,' he said finally, and put the radio carefully back in its case. 'It's fainter than it was last night, so Ah reck'n they're already on the move. We'll eat as we go.'

We wore skis that morning and I was glad he had made me practise for a few minutes the previous day, for he set a fast pace. 'We'll start closin' up on them soon. Those bergs will hold them up. The ice will be bad there. Could be the snowmobile won't make it if he has to go through to the other side.' He wanted to be much closer to them at that stage. 'If they get behind the berg Ah may not be able to pick them up.' Apparently he had fixed a homing limpet to the snowmobile and the little radio was a direction finder.

All that day the sun shone and the bergs seemed to get no nearer. The snow clogged on the skis, the going hard. We tried snowshoes, but those were worse, and with the snow almost a foot deep, it was incredibly tiring to haul in just our boots. The bergs were flat-topped, obviously carved off the Ice Shelf, and judging by the jagged layering of the pack around them we presumed them to be grounded. 'Shouldn't be. We're way off shore.' And when I muttered that we still had the Ice Front in sight, he laughed and said, 'That's the ice cap pushin' seaward. If those bergs are grounded, they're on some sort of an underwater reef, the top of a submarine volcano even.'

The fact that we were gradually able to make out more and more of their detail was the only indication we had that we were slowly getting nearer. The ice field around them was very broken as though the sea crashing against their massive bulks had suddenly frozen into solidity.

We shed layers of clothing as we trudged, and time passed. It was quite hot when the sun reached its zenith, blazing straight in our faces. It was a day for dark goggles and white sun cream. I couldn't see myself, but Iain looked like some crazy clown out of a comic movie. Every two hours we stopped for a breather and he checked the bearing of the tiny blips given out by the homing limpet. This was when we ate, quick snacks of concentrated food, an apple each, and on the march we sucked an occasional barley sugar.

It was after our fourth stop that our line of march cut obliquely into the snowmobile's tracks. They were sharp and clear, obviously made since the night's snowfall, so that we were now only a few hours behind them. By then we were also very close to the first of the bergs, so close that suddenly we could see individual pebbles and boulders embedded in the ice, a yellowish band low down near the pack. There was a small polynya just to the east of it. A seal's head surfaced in the centre and we realised that it was a blowhole and we were right on top of it. In the blinding white of the light our eyes played tricks.

Nothing moved on the berg, or on the surface of the ice around it. We could see the twin line of the tracks passing to the west of it. The ice was flat there and relatively undisturbed, as though the berg had acted as a breakwater. All to the east it was a jumbled mass of layered chaos where wind and current had thrust the pack against the sheer wall-like side of the berg, certain proof that the solid mass of glacial ice was grounded.

'Ye said ye had read what Sunderby wrote about the ship, his description of it.' Iain was speaking to me over his shoulder. 'Can ye remember whether he said anythin' about bergs?'

'I don't think so,' I replied. 'At least I don't recall a reference to icebergs. He wrote that there was something that looked like the figure of a man standing at the helm and the masts were all broken off short, just the stumps left. But I can't recall that he made any reference to the ice around the vessel.'

Iain had his glasses out and was searching the flat area on the shoreward side of the stranded mass of ice.

'You're thinking bergs like these might have acted as a break-water, protecting the vessel from the moving pack, is that it?'

'Aye. It's the only explanation. The current runs northward up this side of the Weddell, and if the ship had been caught in the pack, it would have been carried up the coast, almost certainly smashed to pieces. It could be this group of bergs, or another further on that's saved it.' He put the glasses down. 'Well, it doesn't matter much. Our Ángel came lookin' fur it in that air-craft he was testin' and he found it. He knows, so we've only to follow him.' He reached down, burrowing into the pile of gear on his sledge. 'D'ye think his name is really Connor-Gómez?' He came out with a silver flask and held it up with the sort of smile a magician wears when he has accomplished a clever trick. 'Ah thought per'aps a wee dram wouldna come amiss at this point.' He took a swig, wiped the top of it with his hand and passed it across to me. 'It's the real malt – Glenmorangie.'

It was smooth and warming. 'Well, what's in a name? But just suppose he's not the lassie's brother, but the product of that whore Rosalli Gabrielli and that pimp of hers, or perhaps some unknown, a one-night stand.' He smiled. 'Interestin' thought, eh?' And he added, suddenly leaning forward and stabbing his finger at me, 'But a bloody sight more interestin' is the thought of what the fuckin' bastard has been up to with a ship and a pack of poor devils, Disappeareds from out of that ghastly huddle of old prison huts.' He reached for the flask and swallowed another mouthful, then slipped it back into its place on the sledge. 'Och, well, better get goin' now. All will be revealed, eh?' But he didn't move for a moment, just stood there, staring towards the stranded iceberg, a shut, taut look on his face. 'Ye remember Iris's brother was one of them – Eduardo.'

'One of the Disappeareds, yes. Or do you mean . . . ?' I saw him nodding and I said, 'In those huts, is that what you mean? I didn't see his name there.'

'No, ye weren't lookin' for what Ah was, or in the same place.' And he added, 'Ah knew what to look fur. A lot of prisoners write their names on the walls of their cells before they are taken out to die. I suppose they think it's the only monument they'll get, and man in his vanity likes to leave something for posterity.'

'You say Eduardo Connor-Gómez's name was there?'

'Not his name, but . . .' He leaned down, tightening the fastenings of his sledge. 'Ah didn't show it to ye. Ah didn't want her to know.'

'I wouldn't have told her.'

'No, but she might have asked, and if she had, Ah was afraid she'd read the answer in yer face.' He reached down with his dummy hand, picked up his sledge harness and began shrugging his massive shoulders into it. 'If she had even guessed he had been on that ship, she'd have insisted on comin' with us, and Ah didn't want that. Yon man –' He nodded to the north along the line of the tracks – 'if ye can call him a man, more a devil, Ah think – if he thought she knew, he'd kill her. He'd kill anyone who discovered his secret.' He broke his sledge out and began pulling.

'Us?' My mouth felt suddenly dry. 'You mean he'd kill us?'

'Why do ye think Ah brought that gun with me? Aye. If we find the ship, and there's still evidence on board of what happened to the human cargo . . .' He left it at that and we trudged on in silence, my thoughts running back over the whole sequence of events since he had ducked in through the door of the *Cutty Sark*'s saloon.

We didn't stop after that until we were abreast of the berg and could see the tramline marks of the snowmobile tracks running clear-cut across flat floe ice to the frozen chaos of what looked like a huddle of some five or six bergs. One of them was so long it stretched right across our line of march, out into the infinity of the Weddell Sea, where the flatness of its top merged with the pack. By then the sun was lipping the distant wall of the Ice Front, shadowing the face of it, so that it showed as a black line along the north-western horizon.

Darkness came on the black wings of a storm cloud. We just managed to get our sleeping bags out and wriggle into them before it hit with a violent rush of wind that was suddenly full of hailstones the size of peas that drove at us almost horizontally and poured along the ice with a rustling sound. It was as though the contents of a container full of ball-bearings were being flung across our cowering bodies, covering them in an armoured shroud.

I don't suppose the storm lasted more than ten or fifteen minutes, but it seemed to go on and on for ever. And when it did stop, it was as though a fairy godmother had waved a magic wand: there was sudden and absolute peace, not a sound anywhere, the stars showing bright in a shot-silk sky of deepening purple.

My father, towards the end, became addicted to the *Rubáiyát of Omar Khayyám*. He liked to read extracts of it aloud to anyone who would listen. It was natural for him in the circumstances of his illness, but for a kid of fifteen, which was all I was when he died, it was not exactly appropriate, dealing as it did with death and the meaning of life. However, there were times when the words stuck in my memory and one particular passage came back to me now.

We had stopped where the surface of the ice was no longer flat, but had shattered and ridden up against the old shore ice in great jumbled slabs. The sun had vanished below the horizon, the sky beginning to cloud over again so that it was getting quite dark. We had placed our sleeping bags in the lee of one of the up-ended slabs of ice so that we were out of the wind, which was blowing from the north-west about force 4, enough at any rate to drift the surface snow in exposed places. We had with us a small spirit stove and it was after we had brewed up a mug of tea, very strong with a lot of sugar, and were drinking it – the first hot drink we had had since leaving *Isvik* – that I recited those two lines to Iain: '*And that inverted bowl we call The Sky, Whereunder crawling coop't we live and die –*' I hesitated, my memory failing me.

'Fitz,' he said. 'Unmistakable.'

'Something about it rolling inexorably on . . .'

He shook his head, frowning. '*Lift not thy hand* . . . Aye, that's it. *Lift not thy hands to it for help –*' And then I took up the rest of it with him: '*For it Rolls impotently on as Thou or I.*'

He sat, cross-legged like the servant of some god, nursing his offering in a tin mug. 'The Rubáiyát. Very appropriate,' he mused, his accent broadening. 'Sin an' forgiveness, death an' what comes after – aye, and Ah hope it's no' too appropriate. *Who is the Potter, pray, an' who the Pot?*' The faraway look was suddenly gone as he leaned across to me and said grimly, 'Life an' death, good an' evil – ye jus' remember, boy, in the case o' Ángel there is no good, only evil.' And he added, 'Ah recall a doctor tellin' me once – a country doctor – that inbreedin' could produce progeny that were throw-backs to primeval man, worse still – monsters. Ah can hear him sayin' it now – *Monsters; there's no other word fur it.* An' he then went on t' tell me the terrible story o' a wee laddie that was left an orphan an' adopted by a kindly couple who had no children o' their own. That little bastard grew into a monster thàt bled them white o' all they had saved in a lifetime o' hard work, an' then he killed them fur no other reason than he wanted the roof their lovin' kindness had put over his head, wanted it all to himsel'.'

He paused there, pouring himself more tea. 'That's the sort of man whose trail we are followin'. Scrape away the surface charm and underneath the man's all evil.'

I asked him then about the names we had seen scrawled on the walls of those prison huts to the east of Ushuaia. 'Are you saying he shipped them out in an old square-rigged ship and murdered them?'

'Ah think so.' He nodded.

'But why? What was the point?'

'Ah don't know why. Does there have to be a reason? Ah tell ye, the man's evil.'

273

'It doesn't make sense,' I muttered.

'Does it have to? Not everybody is reasonable like yerself. Some people act on instinct, or on emotion – on the spur of the moment, no reason at all. Killin' for killin's sake. Ah've seen that. And torture, too. Women as well as men. Ah've met a woman, a very beautiful woman . . .' He paused there. 'There are also people who are schizophrenic. But Ángel is no schizo. He's just evil, paranoid perhaps, but evil through and through.'

I wondered how he could be so sure, but my eyes wouldn't stay open and I drifted into sleep, to be woken, almost immediately, it seemed, by a seal barking. Anybody who has lived and sailed on the North Norfolk coast of England cannot possibly mistake that sharp, grunting sound. I sat up, the sun blazing like a great balloon low in a cold green sky, the pack reflecting the glare of it in a spill of liquid fire. The seal barked again, and I turned my head to see Iain's body sprawled on a raised platform of ice as he searched the route ahead through his glasses. Behind him a great slab of the pack was raised almost vertically, the surface of it smooth and white like the marble of a grave stone and blinding with reflected light.

'Any sign of them?' I asked him.

He turned and shook his head. 'The goin' looks bad, bits of open water full of brash ice and the pack is badly layered right up to the first of the bergs. After that it's not so bad where the bergs have created somethin' of a windbreak.' He handed me the glasses as I climbed up beside him. I could see the blowhole then. It was almost right below us, a small pond of ice slush. But no sign of the seal. 'Did you see it?'

'See what?'

'The seal. It was barking.'

'Of course Ah saw it. But Ah'd not got my gun so Ah couldn't grab ye a nice juicy steak fur breakfast.' He pulled himself up on to his hands and knees and began lowering himself down to the flat patch where we had laid up for the night. 'Porridge,' he said. 'We'll have a big bowl of hot porridge to keep us goin'. Ah've a feelin' in my guts it's goin' to be a long day.'

We were on our way a little after five, up-ended slabs of ice and pools of partly frozen sea causing us endless detours. Mostly we followed the trail blazed by the snowmobile, but as we neared the stranded berg, with its flat top crenellated by constant melting and freezing, the going became so bad it was almost impossible to drag the sledges through the chaos of disintegrating ice slabs. Twice my own sledge turned over on its side and once we were faced with a slush pool so large that it was really a polynya. They had floated their way across it and we did the same. But for us, with the need to unload and inflate our dinghy, it took a great deal more time, so that it was almost noon before we resumed our march on the far side.

By then the sun was virtually at its zenith, still shining out of a clear sky, and with hardly any wind, it was hot work dragging the sledges through the broken-up pack ice. We were so close to the berg now that, though I doubt whether it was more than sixty or seventy metres high, it seemed to tower above us, a cliff of ice that varied in colour from cold, translucent blue, through white, to a dirty yellow, the face of it pock-marked by the black of cave holes. And near its base the degraded ice had formed arches in which the salt sea water gurgled noisily, slapping large chunks of ice around.

It was here that we found the snowmobile abandoned. They had gone on, dragging the sledge between them, manoeuvring it by brute force through the built-up tangle of ice slabs until, close under the berg's western side, they had finally been forced to leave it behind, taking only what they could carry.

Shortly afterwards we were forced to do the same. Progress with the sledges had become too slow, too exhausting.

'Ah think we're gettin' close,' Iain said. 'Why else would he risk leavin' everything behind?'

That was his explanation for deciding that we, too, should travel light. We had two shoulder haversacks with us. We loaded these with the bare essentials, and he took his gun. Then, before leaving the sledges, he took compass bearings on various parts of the berg, calling them out for me to write down with a description for identification. He was using one of those little French plastic compasses you hold to your eye. It was hung by a cord round his neck and he took it off and handed it to me so that I could check his bearings. 'We can't take those sleepin' bags along with us. Too heavy. But Ah'm takin' no chances of our not findin' them again when we need them.'

It was exactly 14.17 when we set off once more. I noted it down in the pocket diary where I had entered the bearings. Even without the sledges, it was tiring work clambering over the disordered entanglement of layered ice. Dangerous, too, in places, for it was very slippery and there were black crevices where it would be easy to twist an ankle or even break a leg.

Then, just after four, we reached the lee of the berg's western side and gradually the chaos subsided until there came a point where we could look ahead to relatively undisturbed floe ice. And there were their footprints stretching away ahead until they lost themselves round the flank of the berg where it protruded in the convoluted shape of a frozen waterfall, the face of it glistening with moisture. Iain went round this ice-smooth shoulder, keeping to the flat. He was in a hurry now. I decided to try a short cut, having seen a way I could clamber over the lower part of it. My boots had small studs in them and I made it quite easily to within a few feet of the top, but the last part was in full sun and had melted smooth as glass. It was a hands and knees job, clawing my way upwards till suddenly I was there, looking across to a vista of bergs huddled in a semi-circle. And within the shelter of that glittering wall the floe ice, ribbed by old layering, had melted and frozen again into a smooth pattern of mounds, so that it looked like an area of white desert full of wind-eroded tumuli, and in the middle of them was the ship.

I yelled to Iain, but he was still fighting his way through the jumbled ice off the north-western tip of the berg I was on and could not hear me. I could see the footprints we had been follow-ing stretching all the way to the frozen outline of the ship's bulwarks, but not in a straight line, for they had had to work their way around numerous pools of brash ice.

I must have been sprawled a good fifty feet up, so that I had a grandstand view of the whole spread of the grounded bergs. It was a staggering sight, an almost complete wall that glittered like sugar icing in the bright sunlight and was topped by fairy ice castles carved by the action of sun and wind out of the solid berg tops. And almost dead centre, in the middle of that harbour of ice, the whited sepulchre shape of the sunken ship lay embalmed in ice.

That we had found it in the middle of this infinity of frozen water seemed almost unbelievable, and the beauty of the scene, the strange deadliness of it, held me spellbound for a while, so that I didn't call to Iain again until he finally came into my field of vision. Even then I felt reluctant, lying there thinking about what we might find, wondering where the poor devils were being taken, why their ship had landed up in this extraordinary situation.

'Ye all right, Pete?' Iain's voice floated up to me, strangely disembodied in the still air. Looking down at him, I realised the ship was so buried in ice and snow he hadn't seen it yet. I slithered down and joined him, the description of what I had seen pouring out of me: 'It's unbelievable. Those bergs are like a harbour wall, and there it is, frozen in, yet from up on the berg she looks almost like she's anchored there in the middle of that ice harbour.'

He didn't say anything, just quickened his pace until he was near enough to see the outline of her. He stopped then, standing suddenly very still and sniffing the air. 'There's a smell.'

I hadn't noticed it before, but now that he mentioned it I could smell it, too. Something bad. 'What is it?'

'Putrefaction.' He had his glasses to his eyes, sweeping either side of the ship. 'A carcase. Or carcases.' He dropped the glasses on to their neck strap and took the gun from off his shoulder. 'Ye wait here.' And he started forward, moving cautiously, his head thrust out, his eyes searching.

Had Ángel really got a gun? I thought it unlikely. There was no wind, and the sun blazing down from the north out of a picture-postcard sky was literally quite hot, warm at any rate, the whole icescape so sparklingly brilliant it hurt the eyes. It was very, very beautiful, very peaceful. But there was an underlying coldness that gave it a brittle quality, so that at any moment I felt the whole wonderful panorama might shatter into the howling blackness of an Antarctic blizzard.

I stayed there until Iain had reached the icing-sugar outline of the vessel's bulwarks. When she had struck that underwater reef or bank, whatever it was the bergs had grounded on, she had been swung round, her bows towards the distant glimmer of the Ice Shelf. The stern was turned towards the north-east, so that the current had piled the floe ice so high against her port side she was almost invisible from where I was now standing. The bulwarks, and whole section of her topsides, seemed to have been ripped out of her, the deck line so jagged and humped that it was difficult to tell what was heaped-up plates of ice and what the iced-up side of the ship itself.

While I was trying to sort this out, there was a sudden sharp sound, like the cracking of ice. I glanced quickly round, but nothing seemed to have changed, no gap opening up. Then it came again and I saw Iain start forward, struggling through broken ice till he was almost at the stern, where he grabbed hold of what looked like a rope ladder and hauled himself up with one hand till he was on the quarterdeck. For a moment he stood, quite still, only his head turning slightly as he searched the deck and the ice on the far side.

Nothing moved. There was no sound. Nothing had happened, the whole world seeming to stand still. Then suddenly he was gone, the icebound deck swallowing him up as he disappeared below.

I picked up my haversack and followed him, the ship's side gradually growing higher as I neared it. From a distance, the hull had seemed just about buried in the ice, but close-to the tops of the bulwarks were at least ten feet above me and I wondered how Ángel and Carlos had got on board; or had the rope ladder already been there when they arrived? There were nine rungs of it hanging vertically above me, all of them encrusted with smooth ice. It made for a slippery climb, and the deck itself was like a skating rink.

I called to Iain that I was on board, but there was no answer, the silence and the frozen state of the vessel very eerie.

I didn't follow him below. Not then. Our interests were different. It was the ship itself that attracted me, the hull and the bits and pieces of rigging buried under layers of old ice, the carbon-fibre blocks, the broken spars, the barrels that had been stove in, and up in the bows the remains of the great bowsprit lying in a tangle of heavy rope with the flukes of a massive anchor sticking up in the middle of it.

It took me several minutes to work my way the full length of the ship. Not only was it difficult walking, but I was stopping all the time, fascinated by the things I was seeing. I guessed her date of building as quite early in the 1800s, the first half of that century at any rate. She had an almost flush deck, and in clambering on board I had seen the outline of a gun port. She was either a naval frigate or an East Indiaman built on similar lines, in which case the National Maritime Director was probably right in thinking it was one of the ships John Company had had built at Blackwall close by the naval yard.

The bows confirmed it, for the 1830s had been a period when both naval and commercial interests, and not only in our own country, were going for speed and manoeuvrability. That meant more sail, particularly fore and aft sails, and the place to hang them was up for'ard, right out beyond the bows. The bowsprit on this vessel had been massive. With its jib-boom it must have been almost as long as one of the masts, and it had been cocked up at a sharp angle, the weight of it held by thick rope rigging to the foremast. The crans irons were still lying there under a coating of snow and ice, but when I kicked them free, I found they were not iron, but some form of plastic. Even the flukes of the anchor were not the original iron, and when I leaned over the side to see if anything had been left attached to the dolphin striker, I could just see through the glazed ice covering that this, and the martingale stays, which acted as braces against the upward pull of the jibs when under sail, had also been converted to a man-made fibre.

I was straightening up with the intention of checking on the chain-plates, remembering what Captain Freddie had said about the installation of aerials and electronics, when my eye was caught by a movement on the ice below me, right close under the bow overhang where a heavy rope anchor cable hung down. A figure lay huddled close against the ship's side, the feet so buried in slush ice that it looked at first sight like a discarded anorak. But then I saw the hands stretched out towards the hull. The head, in its fur cap, lifted slightly, the fingers scrabbling at the black paintwork. A tremor ran through the body, the legs kicking out in a nervous reflex.

It was Carlos. I recognised the clothing and I called down to him. But there was no movement now, his body lying still. He must have pitched over the bows. But the drop was only a dozen feet at most. Not enough to knock him out. 'You all right?' My voice sounded strangely disembodied in the lonely stillness of the icebound ship. 'Carlos! Are you badly hurt? What happened?'

No answer, no movement, the young man's body lying there as though he were dead. I straightened up and made my way back aft, calling to Iain. My voice remained a solitary and disembodied sound, as though I was a ghost on board a ship that wasn't real.

I didn't like it. No sound anywhere. It was as though I were the only sentient person alive. And the sun shone with unreal brilliance in a sky that was powder blue, almost green, the visibility infinite, an endless vista of ice that sparkled like crystal. 'Iain!' There was a note of panic in that cry for help and I got a grip on myself, shutting my mouth and making for the rope ladder, hurrying down it, out on to the ice and round the stern of the ship to get to the bows on the starb'd side where that body lay.

It was still there, just as I'd first seen it, and it was Carlos all right. He hadn't moved, his hands still stretched out towards the black of the hull planking, his head face downwards in the ice. 'What happened?'

No answer, and I reached down and tried to turn him over. But in the shade there his clothes had already frozen to the ice. With an effort I managed to get his shoulders free and turn his head. There was blood at the corner of his mouth, the skin of his face gone pallid and his eyes closed. 'Carlos!' I shook his shoulders. 'Can you hear me?'

I felt a tremor run through him. It was as though he had the shakes. And then his eyes flicked open, a vacant stare that had no recognition in it. 'It's Pete,' I said. 'From *Isvik*. Remember?' His lips moved and I bent closer. 'What was that?'

He seemed to be trying to say something, his body shaken and a froth of pink blowing like bubblegum from his mouth. There was a gurgling sound and I bent closer to hear a horrible stuttering whisper of urgency – 'I w-would – n-not have – t-t-tell anyone. You – know – th-that.' The voice died to a liquid gurgle in the larynx, then suddenly quite loud – 'Why? Why you d-do it? Why you –' But that was all. His words were stopped by a gout of blood that burst from his mouth.

How do you know, instinctively, a person is dead? I had no real experience of death, and his eyes had been blank all the time. Yet I knew. I muttered something to myself, a prayer maybe, then I rolled him right over on to his back and saw the wound. It was a gaping, bloody hole where the wall of his chest had been blown clean out.

'Shot in the back, the poor wee laddie.'

Iain was leaning out over the bulwarks above me.

'Ángel?' I asked.

'Ah'm no' sure.'

'What do you mean?'

He leaned further down towards me. 'He was tryin' to say somethin'. Did ye hear what?'

'I think he mistook me for Ángel. *I wouldn't have told anyone.* That's what I think he said. And then he asked me why I had done it.'

'Why ye had shot him? Is that what ye mean? Believin' ye were Ángel?'

'I think so. But why? What was it that he wouldn't tell anyone?'

Iain straightened up. 'Come. It's not a pretty sight, mind, but Ah'll show ye all the same.' And he added, 'Just ye watch it, that's all. There's the tae of us, and there's that murdering bastard. As for the rest . . .' He gave that Gallic shrug. 'There's others, ye see, on board of this dreadful vessel.' He banged his dummy hand on the iced-up remains of the bulwarks. 'Christ! The fuckin' bastards – their own people, too.' His head disappeared. 'Come on up an' Ah'll show ye.'

TWO

The only way for me to get back on board was by the rope ladder, which meant traipsing half round the ship. It was slow going, for the ice was very broken. The gun ports were just above the level of the ice and most of them were open. I was conscious again of that smell. I had forgotten about it in my excitement at exploring the ship and then finding Carlos lying there under the bows, but now it was so strong and all-pervading that it was no longer possible to ignore it.

At one moment it seemed to come from the interior of the ship. I caught a whiff of it from an open gun port. But when I reached the stern, which still had some of its gingerbread intact, the gold paint of the carving protected by a thick layer of ice, I realised where the stench was coming from. A little wind had sprung up from the north-west, and from the far side of the ship a beaten track stretched out in that same direction to where a fire-blackened mound of garbage had been built up on the ice. And beyond it was a white adobe of ice like an igloo beside a round pool of open water.

'What is it?' I asked Iain when I had swung myself up the rope ladder on to the afterdeck.

'The smell, is that what's worryin' ye?' He nodded towards the pile of garbage. 'It's what archaeologists would call a midden.' He looked at me sharply. 'Tell me, dae ye remember when the people at Ushuaia said this ship had sailed?'

'They weren't sure,' I said. 'They thought it was two, two and a half years ago. That's what Iris said.'

He nodded. 'That's about right, Ah reck'n, fur one man livin' here alone. Mebbe tae, but not more than tae.'

'What are you talking about?'

'Ah'm talkin' about that pile of shit and bones and putrid meat. Out there on the ice there's no way ye can get rid of the filth ye produce. Give him his due, he's tried. He's had fires down there. Looks like he burned a hole in the ice first go, then built a hide in the hope that seal, or somethin' even bigger, would use it as a blow-hole.'

A midden, he had called it, and I stared at it, fascinated by the thought that somebody had been living here ever since the ship had become icebound. 'Who is it? One of the Disappeareds?'

He nodded. 'Or one of the guards.'

'And he's on board – now?'

'Look around ye. There's nowhere else he can be.'

'And Ángel?'

But he had turned away. 'Come below and Ah'll show ye how he's been living this past tae years and more.' He led me down the companion ladder to the gun-deck below, moving cautiously, a step at a time, probing the gloom with the powerful beam of his torch, the machine pistol ready in his hand. All the time we had been talking, I had been conscious of his eyes fixed on the long sweep of the ice-encrusted deck, watchful for the first sign of movement.

At the bottom of the ladder the smell was very noticeable and I made some comment about it seeming to have followed us. He laughed. 'That's not the midden ye're smellin'.'

'What is it then?'

'Bodies,' he said.

'Bodies? D'you mean dead bodies?'

'Aye. Dead bodies.' And he added, 'Dead sheep, dead humans. Carcases rottin' in the hold.' There was a note of sadness as well as disgust in his voice. 'Ah'll show ye in a minute. First Ah want to check again how this man's been livin'.' He turned aft then, away from the half-light of the open gun ports. There were doors here, officers' cabins with wooden bunks. He pushed open the central door just aft of the thick rudder post. There was sunlight here, slanting rays pouring in through the cracked glass of five big stern windows.

The place was lived in. So much was obvious at a glance. There were clothes draped over the back of a chair, the table laid ready for a meal – plate, knife, fork and spoon, a dirty brown lump of something that looked like bread. A big iron stove stood just behind the door jacketed in asbestos with a pile of sawn pieces of the ship's timbers in a basket beside it. The bunk was also on the starb'd side and had several dark skins spread over it; fur seal, by the look of them, and one that was bigger and might be leopard seal.

'What's he hunting with?' Looking around the cabin I couldn't see any sign of a weapon.

For answer Iain took me over to a big wooden chest in the corner and lifted the lid. Inside, neatly resting in their racks, were all sorts of weapons – rifles, machine pistols, a revolver, several automatics, two shotguns. 'Quite an arsenal.'

He nodded. 'Ye'll notice there's one of the racks with nothin' in it.'

I had noticed. That, and the single place setting at the table, suggested it was just one man on board, one man, besides Ángel, prowling about somewhere in the ship, and he was armed. 'Dae ye no' sense a weird feelin' here?' Iain's accent was more pronounced and there was a nerve twitching at the side of his jaw. 'If it weren't fur the fact that he's got a weapon wi' him, Ah'd be worryin' me head about ghosts an' sich like. Och aye, Ah would that. But a man wi' a gun is summat Ah understan'.'

He reached down into the chest and picked up one of the machine pistols. It was an Uzi, he said. 'The magazines are over here.' He went to another, smaller chest, that was full of ammunition. 'Put those in yer pocket.' He handed me several mags, fitted one of them on to the pistol and thrust it into my hands. 'Just in case.' He smiled, but the nerve was still twitching along the left side of his jaw. 'Now Ah'll show ye what this is all about. Better prepare yerself fur the worst, because it's no' very nice.'

I followed him and we went for'ard, past the rudder post and the ladder to the deck, past what appeared to be the stowage for hammocks and bedding, out into the long, open run of the gun-deck. No torch was necessary here, enough light coming in through the open gun ports in low, slanting rays. The guns themselves were not run out, of course. In fact, they were not real guns at all, but made of some black plastic that looked real enough so that the whole deck had an air of waiting, as though at any moment the call for action stations might ring out. The breeze was blowing a draught of air from one side to the other across the deck and it was bitterly cold.

'Down here.' He led me to a grating in the centre of which was a lift-out section with ropes attached to the four corners. It was roughly spliced into a single strand, which ran up to a block in the deck beam above. He hauled on the tail end of it, swinging the section of grating aside to reveal a black hole. 'That's where the East India Company's merchandise was stowed in the long passage from London to Bombay. But the hold has a different cargo now. Take a look.' He shone the beam of his torch down into the darkness, moving it slowly across the ice, first for'ard, then aft.

'My God!' I murmured.

'Aye, an' ye can thank him also that the water there is frozen solid.'

For'ard, the bodies were all human, lying just as they had floated up when the ship struck and water flooded the hold, a horrible jumble of cadavers, the outline of their bodies blurred by the thickness of the ice that had virtually mummified them. Amidships there was a partition wall of timber, a sort of half bulkhead, and aft of that the iced-up hold appeared to be full of sheep. It was one of these that was the cause of the smell. The surface of the ice had been hacked into broken fragments, and as I stared along the beam of the torch, I saw that there had been a method in the way the ice had been broken up, one of the sheep chipped out, dragged towards the partition, where it lay on its back, its upthrust legs standing like matchsticks, the stomach, no longer in the deep freeze of solid ice, bloated with trapped wind.

I was moving closer, peering down at the ice-glazed huddle of human bodies, when I felt that gloved hand of his grab hold of my arm. 'Ah wouldn't go any nearer if Ah were ye.'

'Why?'

He shook his head. 'How many dae ye reck'n there are down there – thirty, forty? What did they die of, all together like that? Ye don't know, so we'll get the hatch cover on again.'

'And what about you, do you know?'

He didn't answer, and I stood there, utterly appalled, half petrified with the horror of it. To see death like that – it reminded me of pictures I had seen of Belsen and Auschwitz, or of death in the Ethiopian desert. Except that this wasn't a picture, this was the real thing. 'Why?' I asked him again. 'And the sheep – why sheep? What did they all die of?'

'That we'll find out in due course. At least, Ah hope we will.' He hauled on the rope and I helped him swing the heavy section of grating back over the hole, lowering it into position. He switched off his torch, his eyes searching the gun-deck, adjusting to the change of light. 'We'll go back to the main cabin now an' await developments.' But he didn't move immediately, his head cocked a little on one side, listening. 'Did ye hear anythin'?'

'No,' I whispered, my nerves tensing as I realised how exposed we were. Was this what Carlos had seen? Was that why Ángel had killed him, shooting the poor devil in the back as he stood there on the foredeck?

Iain had turned his head to face the fore part of the ship, still listening, his eyes watchful. 'Wonder why he's got that hatch open?' The beam of his torch flashed out, the gun in his hand levelled at the for'ard end of the deck.

'What is it?'

He shook his head, puzzled. 'That's been raised since Ah came on board.' The light was shining on a section of the deck that had been swung up into the vertical by block and tackle. It wasn't a grating like the one we had just lifted. It was a solid section of decking so that it had the appearance of an over-sized trap door. 'Why would he want it open?' He was voicing his thoughts aloud, the question rhetorical. He switched off the torch again and turned to me. 'D'ye think that's what he intends to dae? Fittin', don't ye think? Very fittin'.'

I stared at him, a thought crossing my mind, so that I felt

suddenly as though I was caught up in a nightmare. 'Fitting?' My voice sounded hoarse, little more than a whisper.

'Aye. What would ye dae? Ye've seen the crime that's been committed.'

But my mind had gone off on a tangent, to the fact that the man was armed and we were standing here in the open on the gun-deck, our bodies, in silhouette against the light from the open gun ports, a perfect target. But when I suggested that we were in danger of getting killed, he just laughed at me and shook his head. 'He won't be troubling us, not just yet.' And he added, 'What will be worrying him right now is that there is a man who's been on board here ever since the ship struck, a man who knows the answer to what happened, how all those bodies were done to death. One of the rifles is missing so he knows the man is armed. If he fires at us, then he reveals his position. He needs to get his bullet in first.' He turned then, muttering something in French. '*Incroyable!*' Catching his repetition of the word, I thought he was referring to the scene in that frozen hold. Then, as he headed aft, he said quite distinctly, 'She couldn't have known, surely.' He was talking to himself, not to me. And he added, his accent broadening, his voice barely audible, 'What the hell state o' mind will the poor bugger be in?'

He didn't bother to soften the sound of his footsteps, but when he reached the door he kicked it wide open, his gun ready in his left hand. As I followed him in, the thought uppermost in my mind was that phrase he had used before. He had been referring to that cargo of Disappeareds, not to Carlos. How the hell did he know Ángel was responsible for that ghastly hold full of refrigerated bodies? But when I put the question to him, all he said was, 'Ye'll see. Ah'll be proved right.' He looked round at me, smiling. 'Want to bet on it?'

That sudden glimpse of callousness shocked me. 'You can't be certain of that. Not until you know what they died of.'

'Don't worry about Ángel now. Concentrate yer wee mind on the person who's been livin' on board this antique hulk fur the last couple of years or more. Who is he, d'ye reck'n? And what's happened to his mates? They won't have sailed with the hold half full of political prisoners without some sort of a guard. Who disposed of them, eh?' He reached for the catch of a door just beyond the stove, motioned me aside and yanked it open. A pantry, the shelves almost empty, but still a sack with some flour in it, a collection of rusty tins, some sugar in the bottom of a deep jar, and strips of meat hanging from hooks in the beams above. 'Olive oil.' Iain was shaking a can marked *aceite*. 'Strips of smokey seal meat, homemade bread, an occasional delicacy from out of one of the tins, with a wee bit of mutton now and then. Reck'n ye can exist on that fur quite a time. But no green stuff. Nothin' to keep the scurvy at bay.' He put his hand into an open cardboard case. 'Ugh! Look. It's crawlin'.' He held out his hand to me, biscuits all crumbled and full of weevils. 'This is the sort of diet they used to live on in the old days, and fur months at a time, the whole ship's company dyin' of lethargy with ulcered gums and their teeth droppin' out.'

He stepped back, closing the pantry door as though to keep the maggots from invading the big cabin. 'Take that safety catch off,' he said, pointing to the Uzi I had placed on the table. He showed me how to work it and told me to hold it ready. 'An' don't shoot me in the back if Ah'm lucky enough to flush some-body out.' He then kicked open the doors of the four smaller cabins, one by one, his gun ready and probing with his torch.

But they were all empty, the heads, too, and the little cubby-hole of a galley with its simple paraffin stove where the officers' food had been prepared. The main galley, he said, was up for'ard, also the main storeroom, where the fresh food had been kept. 'But that's empty now. Rats have been at it, and what they haven't taken he's moved here.' He motioned me back into the main cabin, shut the door and pulled up a chair facing it, but a little to one side, the gun on his knees. 'It's just a matter of waitin' now.' His haversack was on the table and he pulled it across, rummaging inside. 'Here yer are.' He produced a slab of choc-olate, broke it in half and tossed one half across to me.

It was nut chocolate with raisins, and as I bit into it I suddenly realised how hungry I was. 'We'll have a brew-up later. Could be a long wait.'

'You think he'll come – here?'

'Och aye, of course he'll come. He'll want some food, same as us. And he'll be curious, wonderin' whether he's got to shoot us, or if this is the moment he's been prayin' fur all these years, the moment of release. How many years is it, Ah wonder, since he was a free man – five, six? D'ye remember when it was Iris said her brother disappeared?'

I shook my head. 'Do you think it's him – out there? Is that what you mean?'

He didn't say anything for a moment, chewing ruminantly on his chocolate. Finally he said, 'Ye're sort of a scientist, aren't ye? Ye've spent all yer life since leavin' school playin' around with chemicals and such deadly liquids and powders that kill pests, woodworm, deathwatch beetle, and that worm ye find in tropical waters, what's it called?'

'Teredo.'

'Aye, that's it.' He fell silent then, staring at me, as though wondering whether to continue, and I sat there, just across the cabin from him, waiting, until finally he laid his gun on the table, leaning forward. 'Does Porton Down mean anythin' to ye?'

'What's Porton Down got to do with it?' And then I remembered his telling me Iris's brother had been there. Or had Iris told me herself? I couldn't remember. It seemed so long ago, another world. 'You're not suggesting the men in the hold here were killed by poison gas, are you? Porton Down is a government research station specialising in chemical warfare. A poison gas in the confines of a ship would make the air so toxic –'

'Not if the killers had masks.'

'I haven't seen any gas masks.'

'No. They would have got rid of them, thrown them overboard. But Ah wasn't thinkin' of anythin' toxic like poison gas.'

He was silent then, his eyes turned towards the stern windows. The sun had set a little while back, the polar twilight darkening the cabin. He got slowly to his feet, went to the door and opened it. 'Thought so. Could do with some oil. Thought Ah remembered the hinges creakin' when Ah first opened it.' He pushed it to again and went through into the pantry. 'What would ye like? Some bully beef? There's two very rusty tins of it left. He's probably savin' them fur Easter. He'll be a Catholic, so he's sure to starve himself over Lent. Not that he would have had much choice. There's water here and some oats. The oats look all right, so we could cook up a mess of porridge, or we could cut a piece off a strip of the seal meat. What can Ah get ye?'

'You said there was some tea there? Is there a tin opener?'

'Tea we have, but we're fresh out of milk, and there's no lemon or sugar. There's coffee, just a dreg that looks more like a dark brown paste at the bottom of the jar.'

'What about a tin opener?' I heard him pulling drawers open and got up and joined him. He had a cupboard door open and was bent over an olive-green haversack full of stones. 'Tea,' I said.

He didn't seem to hear for a moment, staring intently at the whitish fragment he held in his hand. 'Aye, tea.' He nodded and replaced the stones in the haversack. 'Or would ye care for some coffee?' He dumped the haversack back in the cupboard, closed the door and straightened up.

'It doesn't look very appetising, the coffee, I mean.' I was wondering what the stones were doing there.

'No, it doesn't. And we don't want to upset our stomachs, do we?' He grinned and held up a bent and very rusty tin opener. '*Voilà. Thé au naturel* and *bully beef à la Frégate Ancienne*. How's that suit ye, *mon ami*?' His humour sounded a little macabre in the circumstances, but perhaps it was an attempt to conceal what he really felt.

'You were talking about Porton Down . . .' I had sat again, conscious now that I was very tired.

'Aye.' He was sawing away at the rusty can of bully. 'But not over such a gourmet meal. Wait until we've finished.'

But by then, of course, I was virtually asleep, my eyes leaden, my nerves dulled, no longer seeming to care who came in at that door, what he did, or whether I would even wake in time to know. I heard his voice as though from a great way away, heard him say something about an island. 'Gruinard.' He repeated the name several times, leaning forward and tapping my knee. 'Haven't ye ever heard of it?'

'Yes,' I murmured. 'I think so.' But I couldn't remember in what connection, or even where it was. 'What about it?'

'Wake up, man, ye're half asleep and Ah want to talk to ye.' His voice was sharp, a note of impatience.

I opened my eyes, but it was so dark he was no more than a dim shape in the gloom. 'Is there any more tea?' I asked him. Tea might revive me.

'Christ almighty! Ye want tea and ye've let the mug Ah brewed ye go ice cold.'

'It's cold in here and I'm feeling sleepy.'

'Ye've been asleep fur the last tae hours and more. It's after one in the mornin'.'

'The witching hour,' I mumbled.

'Aye, the witching hour, and any moment he'll be here.'

I sat up then, the whole ghastly situation flooding back into my memory. 'What makes you so sure?'

He laughed. 'So that got through to ye. Any moment now.' And when I repeated my question, he shrugged and muttered something about his water. 'A gut feelin' in other words.'

'You mentioned an island.'

'Ah was just talkin' to myself.'

'You were talking to me.' I could feel my temper rising. 'You were talking to me.' What the hell was the man on about? 'Gruinard. That's what you said. You asked me whether I'd ever heard of it.' And then, suddenly, it dawned on me. 'That island! In the Inner Hebrides. The one nobody has been allowed to set foot on since World War II.' I couldn't remember why. 'Some poison, wasn't it?'

But he was silent now.

'Porton Down,' I said. 'You were talking about Porton Down. That wasn't only chemical warfare, was it? They were into biological warfare . . .' There was a sudden percussion sound, not loud, more muffled – a shot? I couldn't be sure. It reminded me of the sound I had thought was the cracking of an ice floe when Iain had gone on ahead of me to the ship.

I started to get to my feet. But he told me to sit down. 'Wait!' And as he said it, there came a fusillade of shots. No doubt about that, it was an automatic. 'AK47,' he whispered. Then came a single shot, followed by a cry of pain.

Silence after that. A long silence. The shots had come from the fore part of the ship. I could see the door now, my eyes having accustomed themselves to the gloom. It was slightly ajar as Iain had left it. Any moment now, he had said. The sound of voices, very faint. Like ghosts, they seemed to echo through the timbers of the ship. A sudden scream that went on and on, then was cut off short, very abruptly. But almost immediately it started up again, muffled now and a different sound, a cry for help rather than a scream of pain. It rose and fell on a pleading note. A thud, like the sound of timber falling on timber, and after that no sound at all, just silence.

'What was it?' The silence was more frightening than the shots and screams. My eyes, fastening on the dim-seen edge of the door, felt unnaturally wide. But it wasn't the door I saw, it was that section of the gun-deck up for'ard. A trap door. That's what I had thought it looked like, and Iain saying it had been hauled up into the vertical since he had come on board. The door of a trap. And that thud. The silence. 'Jesus Christ!' I murmured, and if I had been of the old faith I would have crossed myself. I was thinking of the man down there amongst those frozen bodies, an abominable, unholy incarceration. 'We've got to do something.' I was on my feet.

'Sit down!'

'No. You listen to me. You've got to –'

'Sit down, damn ye, and shut up!' His voice was very quiet, very compelling. 'Just think of all the poor devils who died down there. Ah just hope to God it's the right man who's gone down to join them.' Almost against my will I found myself seated again as he added, his voice fallen to a whisper, 'Now wait. And not another word.'

So we waited, and the wait seemed endless. My eyes, accustomed now to the dark, could see the shape of his head outlined against the faint luminosity from the stern windows, the metal of the gun barrel gleaming faintly. He had it resting on his knees ready for instant use. In front of him, on the table, he had placed that indecent little pottery votive offering given him by the Indian we had released on the Pan-Am Highway north of Lima. He kept fingering it, his touch almost a caress, as though the wretched figures were good luck talismans.

I thought his dummy hand would make it difficult for him to use his automatic pistol effectively. I stretched out my hand for the gun he had given me lying there on the table within my reach. 'Let it be. And sit tight.' His voice was a fiercely breathed whisper, tense in the stillness.

All very well to sit tight, but what if it wasn't the man we were expecting? What if it turned out to be Ángel? An AK47, he had said. Did the Kalashnikov have a distinguishable firing sound? And if it did, how did he come to be able to recognise it? Which brought me back to the same old question – who was he, what was he doing here, who had sent him? Questions, questions, questions, my mind running round in circles. And then the hinges of that door creaked.

I turned my head. The edge of the door was shifting, the crack widening. Suddenly Iain's voice, very quiet, very restrained: '*Tengo un mensaje de tu hermana, Eduardo. Ella esta abordo del* Isvik, *un pequeño barco expedicionario mandado para rescatarte.*' Then, switching to English, he went on quickly: 'My name is Iain Ward. Also in the cabin here is Peter Kettil, a specialist in the preservation of old ships.' He paused there, waiting for a reply. But there was silence, the door quite still now, no creak of the hinges, only the distant sound of ice falling from a rotten berg.

'If you *are* Iris's brother, Eduardo Connor-Gómez, please signify.' There was a note of tension in his voice now as he repeated the request slowly in Spanish.

Still no reply, and I looked at the table where the Uzi lay. But if it had been Ángel he wouldn't have stayed silent like this. A man so full of braggadocio would have needed to explain himself. He would have wanted to talk himself out of the present situation while he thought up some safer way of dealing with us. So it had to be one of the Disappeareds. Not necessarily Eduardo, but one of the poor devils incarcerated on this hulk. I was thinking then about what must be going through his mind as he stood there, just the other side of that door, with somebody inside the cabin, where he had spent so many months alone, talking to him in English and halting Spanish. The shock of it would be enough to strike any man dumb.

'*Eeris*.' The name stumbled from his mouth. 'You say – Eeris is – with you?'

'She is with the boat.' Iain spoke in English, I suppose with the idea of distancing himself from any possible connection with the man's captors.

'*El barco*.' The voice was hoarse, like the croak of a frog. 'Where is – this boat?' It was obvious he was quite unaccustomed to the sound of his own voice, the English coming very slow and hesitant.

'Three days' march across the ice,' Iain answered slowly, sticking to English. 'South of here.' And he named the three people who had been left on board with her. 'Ah take it you are Eduardo Connor-Gómez?'

There was a long pause, then – '*Si*.'

'What is her married name?'

'You think I am lying?'

'Just being careful. Ye tell me her married name and Ah'll be satisfied.'

Another pause, and I wondered whether he had forgotten it in all the years he had been in captivity. 'It is – Sunderby.' And he spelt it out, slowly.

'Okay, Eduardo. There's my gun.' His weapon clattered to the floor close to the half-open door. 'Pete, throw that Uzi down, too.' And when I had done so, he said, 'We are unarmed now. Ye have nothin' to be afraid of. So come in please. Ye must be very tired. It has been a long night fur ye. And fur us,' he added.

The door was suddenly pushed open wide and out of the dark rectangle came the same voice asking us if we had any matches. 'There is a lantern in the stores room. Light it please and put it on the table so I can see you.'

I relaxed then, for that, more than anything, convinced me he had preserved his sanity, despite the loneliness and the terrible cargo he had had to live with. But when the lantern was lit, and he advanced out of the darkness into the cabin, I wasn't so sure.

He was quite a small man with sad, wild eyes that peered at us myopically out of a tangle of hair. He looked so much older than his sister, and yet he couldn't be much over thirty, perhaps less. He looked almost senile, his body stooped, his hair gone grey, thin on top, but reaching to his shoulders in greasy wisps. An unkempt beard tucked into the open neck of a threadbare blue uniform shirt. And he stank. That was the thing about him that struck me most forcefully. He stank of stale sweat, excreta and something else, a fishy smell that I gradually identified as coming from the sealskin jerkin draped over his thin shoulders.

He pulled up a chair and sat down facing us. His skin was dark as a gypsy's, what little of it showed through the matted hair. He didn't say anything for a while, his hands trembling slightly as he listened to Iain's slow, careful explanation of how we came to be here, his high forehead creased in the effort of trying to understand and adjust to the fact that this was the end of his ordeal, the door of his Antarctic prison finally open.

Iain told him how his sister's husband, Charles Sunderby, had caught a glimpse of the ship just before his plane crashed, how that was the start of her determination to mount an expedition to prove that the ship really existed. 'She didn't know about ye. She thought ye were dead. It was yer brother who led us here.' Iain was leaning forward then, his eyes fixed on the man as he told him how Ángel had flown a plane on a test flight, searching out the ship's position, how he had persuaded Iris to let him join the expedition, and in the end had led us here. 'What are ye goin' to dae about him? Ye can't just leave him to die of starvation –'

'My brother!' The words burst from him. 'You call that man my brother?'

'Step-brother then.'

'No!' It was an explosion of wild fury. And when Iain pointed out, very quietly, that his name was Ángel Connor-Gómez, the man shook his head furiously. 'No, I say. Is not my brother. Is nothing to do with me.'

'Then who is he?'

'There was a woman – Rosalli Gabrielli.'

Iain nodded. 'Yes, Ah know about her.'

'Then you know there was a marriage. It last a very short time. She was already pregnant. The father of that boy is a very evil man, a Sicilian, Roberto Manuel Borgalini. Ángel is no connection with me, or Iris, or with my father.' He had become very excited, waving his hands about. His nails were very long and very filthy, the smell emanating from his clothing almost over-powering.

'Aye, Ah thought it was somethin' like that.' Iain leaned further forward, tapping the man on the knee. 'But we can't leave him there.'

Eduardo stared at him, his mouth open.

'Ye dropped the trap on him. Ye shut him in, down among the dead men.'

The other nodded. 'Of course.'

'Well, ye can't leave him there. We'll go for'ard in a wee while and let the poor devil –'

'You don't understand.' The tone of his voice was almost hysterical.

'What don't Ah understand, laddie?'

'Nothing. Nothing. You don't understand nothing.' That was when Eduardo began to talk. Iain had finally got through to him. He had broken through the crust of over two years of total isolation, and once Eduardo began to talk he couldn't stop, even though he was using a language other than his own. It poured out of him, the whole appalling story, from Porton Down and Montevideo, through the solitary confinement cell at the *Escuela Mecánica* to the prison huts east of Ushuaia and the start of the *Andros* voyage. Wellington had guessed correctly. This was the *Andros*, and the voyage the reconditioned frigate made to the Southern Ocean must rank with one of the most extraordinary and dreadful any vessel has been forced to undertake.

Eduardo had been seized in Montevideo, and it was only after he had been taken on board the frigate that it gradually dawned on him why he was there. The men incarcerated in the prison huts we had stumbled on were all left-wing activists, men who had fallen under the Ché Guevara spell, the hard core of the Disappeareds. Many of them were apparently shot and dumped into a deep bog in the mountains behind the camp. A total of twenty-seven had been kept back, and it was these who had been embarked on the *Andros*, in the fore part of the hold. Sheep had already been packed into the after part. He remembered their incessant, pitiful bleating. 'Is like the cry of lost souls.'

He had not been put in the hold with the others. He had been taken to the cabin we were in now. That was when he discovered that the man organising the whole thing was the one who had masqueraded as his brother, who had set fire to the Gómez family store in BA and who had murdered his father. 'I have no proof, you understand, no absolute proof, but that is what I believe happened. Not suicide. He kill my father.' And he added, speaking very slowly, 'But that is not why you cannot let him out of that hold. Now listen. It is something quite different.'

He got suddenly to his feet, very agitated, speaking fast again, and his voice high, on the edge of hysteria. 'He is a dead man now. That is why. And so are you if you go near him, so are we all.' And, still on that high note, he switched to something he had seen as a child in the Opera House in Buenos Aires. 'It was light opera, very English, and it has a phrase in it, something about fitting a punishment to the crime.' He laughed then, quite wildly, staring towards the stern windows, at the blur of white that was the starlit pack ice. 'Down there with the dead, that is very right, that is the punishment to fit the crime.' He swung round on us. 'I tell you now what his crime is. It is a much more terrible crime than when he kill my father, for he is one of those that were the cause of so many disappearing. But worse than that, much worse. You know about anthrax? There is an island where they try it out during the last great war.'

And then he was telling us how, when he was brought into the cabin here, Ángel Borgalini was waiting for him. 'Because I was his "brother" – he is smiling when he say that – my life is to be spared. All I have to do is administer antidote serum to those who are spraying the anthrax spores into the hold, then monitor their condition until they make their escape from the Falkland Islands.'

The wickedness of the plan was almost unbelievable, yet knowing a little about the effects of chemical poisons and biological infections on insects, I knew it would work. The object was to make the Malvinas uninhabitable for sheep and for humans. Anthrax would do both. Having lost the war, these men, who had been involved in the seizure and disappearing of people for years past, saw it as a most suitable fate for the islands they had coveted so long and could not have. Anthrax would be infinitely more effective than the plastic-encased mines their forces had scattered in such profusion.

He was being given a death sentence. He knew that. The ship's after guard consisted of a captain, who was ex-*Escuela Mecánica*, a navigating officer, a sailing master, who had been involved in the sea training of young naval entrants, and six crew. He would ensure their health until such time as the cargo of humans and sheep had been let loose on the Falklands and the ship was aground. It was a condition that both officers and crew had insisted on, and once they had got safely away, in good health, he would be free to go ashore himself. That was the deal he was offered, and he had accepted, hoping that somehow, in the three or four days it would take to reach the islands, he would have an opportunity to save the twenty-seven men battened down in the hold below the gun-deck.

But no such opportunity occurred. He was shown a medicine chest. It was in what we had thought of as the pantry for the big cabin and was well stocked with everything a doctor would require to deal with ordinary shipboard ailments and any straightforward accidents. They had taken it for granted that, as a chemical and biological scientist, he would know how to use them. The cylinders containing the anthrax spores under pressure were on the floor there, and the antidote serum, in case something went wrong, was in a heavily sealed metal box on the shelf above. The Captain himself had shown it to him and specifically asked whether he knew how to administer the serum, and when he had said he did, he had been asked to repeat it in front of two other officers and the crew.

By then Borgalini had gone. At no time did he refer to Ángel by any name other than Borgalini. Perhaps it was the way he said it, but somehow Borgalini seemed to fit the personality of the man.

They had sailed that same night with the moon in its last quarter, a clear sky, and a light breeze from the west. The vessel had no engine, of course. It had been stripped of all metal furnishings and equipment in the hopes that the radar station on Mount Alice, in the south-west of West Falkland, would fail to pick them up. If they were stopped, then they would co-operate and proceed to Port Stanley, or East Cove, wherever they were ordered to go. By then, of course, both the sheep and the human cargo would have breathed in the anthrax spores.

'Do you know what that means? Do you know what sort of a death it is?' He was standing up now, the lamplight making his eyes shine wildly out of black, shadowed sockets, his beard, now lying loose on his chest, giving him the appearance of some Old Testament prophet. And when we just stared at him in silence, he went on, very agitatedly, 'It is a spore-bearing bacillus – *Bacillus anthracis*. Breathe it in and it will attack the lining of the lungs, destroying them. It is like a septicaemia. You can get it by contact also, through cuts, abrasions, any breakage of the skin. In the case of the lungs, or of the intestines, death is very painful. There is a tough envelope around the bacilli that makes them very resistant to changes of temperature and humidity and to disinfectants. The result is that they are almost indestructible. That is what is down there in that hold. Without the serum you cannot go down there. You cannot breathe the air Borgalini is now breathing. Anthrax septicaemia causes you to spit blood. You die like you do with pneumonia, only worse, and there is vomiting, diarrhoea. Terrible pain like you die when you have eat that Death Cap fungus *Amanita phalloides*.'

At that stage I was wide awake, visualising the horror of it, the way those wretched men had died. The last of the Disappeareds – what a way to go! But I was so damn tired, and the man going on and on, constantly digressing, my eyelids closing; each time they closed I would jerk myself awake to hear him digressing into his family history, how the Portuguese side of the family had come to South America over a century and a half ago, Pedro Gómez being a young fisherman from Setúbal, just south of Lisboa, talking about the shipping business this great-grandfather of his had founded, the way their sea connections had continued, so that there had always been sailing vessels of some sort. 'They had become yachts when I was born. We had a succession of them, you understand, so I grew up knowing about the sea and how to handle big sailing boats. That is how I am connected with the Navy when I am a kid.' He was explaining how he was able to navigate and keep the *Andros* going when he was on his own.

I had been drifting in and out of sleep while he had been explaining how he came to be the only man on the ship left alive. The result is I am a little vague about the details, though the rough outline of what happened is reasonably clear in my mind. I asked him to fill in on the details for me later, of course, but he wouldn't talk about it then. Nor would Iain. What I am least clear about is his relationship with the Captain and the rest of the crew.

They had cleared the entrance to the Beagle Channel and were abreast of Isla de los Estados by noon the following day, and with all sail set were making something over 12 knots. Because they knew he had experience of sailing ships, he was allowed on deck, and the navigating officer even permitted him to follow the course on the chart. 'You see I am the only other man on board who has experience of navigating the old way so he let me have the stop-watch and fix the exact time when he is taking a sun sight. The same at night, too, with the stars. They have no Satnav or any electronic means of fixing their position. It don't seem to matter very much at the time, a massive group of islands like the Malvinas not being something you can easily miss.'

They lost sight of land shortly before dusk and by the time it was dark the sky had become overcast, the ship ploughing a lonely furrow over the long wave trains sweeping up from the Horn. They had already shortened sail, the wind being then south of west and increasing. The Argentine weather forecast, which they had picked up on their portable radio, gave the wind as strong to gale, possibly severe gale, and this was confirmed by a Chilean forecast.

Daylight was beginning to seep into the cabin. He leaned back in his seat, passing a hand across his face, suddenly silent. 'Is that when they decided to dae it?' Iain's voice was weary, but insistent, and I knew he would go on questioning Eduardo Connor-Gómez till he had all the facts. Then what?

'Do it?' The man's eyes were open and staring. Now that it had come to the point, and he knew that he was going to be pressured to remember the details, it was obvious he didn't want to talk about it.

'When did they pump the spores into that hold?'

'That same night.' He said it reluctantly. But then in a rush – 'There is a conference, here in the cabin, and they call me in, the Captain wanting to know the time it would take between spore inhalation and death. I tell him it will probably vary – three, four days maybe, but the lassitude will begin during twenty-four hours, maybe thirty-six. At the speed we are running we have only another twenty-two hours before we are level with Cape Meredith. That is the most south point of West Falkland. After that it is only about six hours to Bold Cove.'

They had chosen Bold Cove, he said, because that was where the English had first landed in 1790. He even remembered the name – Captain John Strong of the *Welfare*. 'They thought it very right, you know, the close-by settlement of Port Howard being one of the largest sheep stations in the Malvinas.' The plan was to ferry most of the infected sheep, and some of the humans, ashore in the wooden barge they carried amidships. The rest of the infected cargo would then be towed in a big rubber inflatable across Falkland Sound to Port San Carlos – again, something they regarded as appropriate. One of the very few bits of metal they had had on the ship, apart from the cooking stoves, was the big outboard for the inflatable.

He leaned back, closing his eyes. 'That Scotch island – you know, where they make an experiment during the Hitler war. I have forgot the name –'

'Gruinard,' Iain said.

'Yes – Gruinard.' He nodded. 'Is sealed off for over forty years and cost half a million sterling to decontaminate. There are some thirteen trials made in 1942. There was even a bomb full of spores released and sheep tethered downwind of posts where other tests had been tried. I remember a paper I studied –' He leaned forward, frowning. '1969, I think. There were annual inspections, but in 1969 they stopped because the soil and vegetation is still infected. There were other tests carried out in America, I believe, but it is only this test that I studied, and that because I was at Porton Down. So, you imagine what it would be like in the Falkland Islands, which is as big as your area of Wales – the sheep driven ashore, infecting other sheep, roaming all over the territory, and the humans nursed in isolated settlements where they don't know what the illness is and all inhale the infection. The whole of the Malvinas would be no-go.'

'So how did ye stop them?' It was the question I had been about to ask. 'Ye had a plan?'

He shook his head, slowly. 'No. It is God, I think, who have the plan. The wind is rising, you see, and the movement is becoming more violent all the time as we head out from the Estrecho de Magellanes. So they decide to do it right then, before conditions get worse.'

Weapons and ammunition had been issued and all of them had donned chemical warfare protective clothing and gas masks. They had then gone for'ard on to the gun-deck, spread a heavy-duty tarpaulin over the gratings and opened up the big trap doors at each end of the deck. It was the humans that had woken first, crying for water. But when they saw the plastic-coated, masked men coming down into the hold with their guns and their spray containers, a sudden hush had fallen over the crowded hold. The only sound then had been the seas breaking under the ship, the straining of her timbers and the sheep 'bleating like new-born *bébés*' – those were his words.

302

He had known when they had started releasing the compressed air from the spore-impregnated cylinders because of the sudden outcry from the humans up for'ard. Two shots had been fired. After that there had been silence, except for the cries of a man who had been wounded. But when the crew began coming up out of the hold again, drawing their ladders up after them, the outcry from the humans had drowned out the sound of the sheep until the thud of the heavy trap door muffled the terrified uproar.

He got as far as that in his story, his voice getting more and more choked as he recalled the details. Then suddenly he broke down completely, his shoulders wracked by sobs he could no longer suppress. 'I knew – you see. I understood, how they would die.'

There was a long silence. Embarrassed, I turned my head away from him, towards the stern windows. The glass was cracked and dirty, boarded up in places, but through them I could see the north-eastern sky tinged with the first pink of sunrise. 'Ye said somethin' about God,' Iain prompted him.

Eduardo nodded.

'Ye had no plan yerself?'

'No.'

'And God? How does God come into it?'

'Who else?' He suddenly crossed himself. 'Who else but Jesu Christ would have so touched them that they had to get drunk.' And he added, his voice stronger again, 'I think if it is just a matter of shooting it would not have concerned them so. They were hand-picked, the toughest, the most unimaginative and brutal . . . They were trained killers. But air from containers – that is something they don't understand. To them it is like hand-ling dark magic, a thing that is cursed. So they want drink. They want to dull their senses and forget that hold full of men. The Captain in particular. He is a very hard-bit man, but he is not a fool. He know very well what he has done. There is twenty-seven men down there –' He suddenly grinned at us, and the change in his face sent a cold shiver through me. 'They put me on the helm, you see. They gave me the course and left me there. That is what I mean about God.'

Every now and then either the Captain or the navigator had come up to check that everything was all right. And then time passed and nobody came. In the end he had left the wheel and gone below. They were still drinking and some were already feeling the effects. He told the Captain he needed a glass of water and went into the pantry. The sight of an open case of vodka dumped on top of the medical chest had made it easy for him. He had screwed the top off one of the vodka bottles, then emptied into it the contents of nearly a dozen ampoules of sodium amytal – at least, I think that's what he said, and Iain had nodded – 'What we call Amy. Of course.' He had screwed the top back on, given the bottle a good shake, then walked out into the cabin with the bottle held behind him in such a way that the Captain was bound to see it. 'There is a roar and I am seized from behind, the bottle wrenched out of my hand, and he is shaking me and calling me names so my teeth want to jump out of my mouth. That is how God came into it.'

Two hours later he had gone below again to find the bottle empty and all of them slumped unconscious on the floor. He hadn't thought it through, of course. It had been done on the spur of the moment. He could have dragged them up, one by one, and pushed them overboard. Instead, he roped them together with their hands tied behind their backs, inflated the rubber dinghy, and then, when they came round, had given them the choice of going down into the hold in place of the men he was about to release or taking a chance in the inflatable. Inevitably they had chosen the inflatable.

To get it launched over the side he had released two of them, men he regarded as less dangerous than the others. But when it was in the water the Captain had claimed they could not climb down with their hands tied behind their backs. An argument had followed and one of the men he had freed had finally made a rush at him. 'So I shoot him. What else can I do? I did not mean it to be in the stomach.'

After that he had let them go, one by one, the Captain last, and when they were all in the boat he had thrown off the securing lines. He asked us then whether they had made it to the Malvinas, and when Iain said, 'No, not as far as Ah know,' he had given a little shrug, pointing out with a horrible stuttering defensiveness that he had given them every chance. He had even had the man he hadn't shot lower the big outboard and a plastic container of fuel to them.

'It was the gale, I suppose.' Again that little shrug as he went on to describe the conditions that had made it impossible for him to raise either the trap door to the hold or the grating. He had tried, having first inoculated himself with the serum antidote, but the ship was by then moving so violently that it was almost impossible to stand, let alone work, on the gun-deck. The shambles, he said, was impossible with the gun carriages broken loose and charging the ship's sides at every plunge and roll. 'It is like riding a great horse that is run away from you.' There had seemed to be nothing that wasn't moving to hold on to, and even when he had managed to rig the block and tackle, he was unable to shift the trap door. The timbers had jammed. And all the time he was having to rush back to the helm to save the *Andros* from broaching-to.

His plan had been to head for the southern shore of East Falkland. It had taken him all the rest of that day to rig tackle and trim the sails so that he could head her up towards the islands, and by then the wind had shifted into the north-west. The ship was over-canvassed and making considerable leeway, at times being thrust so far over to starb'd that waves were breaking right across the deck. The barge was the first to go. It had broken loose from its rope fastenings and gone careering around the deck, acting like a battering ram at the base of the mast. Finally it had been swept overboard.

'By then I am so exhausted,' he said, 'there is nothing more I can do.' He thought the wind force had reached perhaps 100 k.p.h. 'The sails begin to go, and I don't care any more. I am too dam' tired. I don't remember how it was I strap myself into a bunk. All I remember is waking later to a terrible banging against the hull, the crash of seas and broken timber, the howling of the wind. Also, a feeling the ship is held down, as though she is sinking. And I don't care. I don't care about anything. I just want to cover my head and sleep for ever. I am like an animal creeping into a dark corner to die. You understand? I want the womb again. I am finished.'

How much of his story I learned in the small hours of that strange night, and how much in snatches on the long trek back over the ice to *Isvik*, I cannot be sure. The masts, all three of them, were overboard, still tethered to the ship by their rigging and banging against the hull with such force that he was afraid she would be holed. It was several days before the storm subsided and he found the strength to cut the wreckage free with an axe. Finally he was able to go down to the gun-deck and rig tackle to raise the trap door. The black horror of that hold was almost unbearable, the stench of excreta, both human and animal, so overpowering he said he would have been sick if he had had anything to retch up. There were bodies lying all over the place just as they had been thrown in the weakness of approaching death. There was nobody alive, and anyway if there had been, there was nothing he could have done to save them at that stage.

I found it very difficult to assess the damage he himself had suffered as a result of his terrible ordeal. The dirt and stink of the man, the unkempt hair and beard, the eyes seeming to stare at nothing, the way he went on talking and talking . . . I suppose we should have realised that nobody could have lived on top of that heap of frozen bodies without his mental stability being impaired; particularly as we saw evidence that he had been down there chipping away at the ice to get at the sheep, and since they were easier to get at, he had also been hacking in to some of the human limbs.

But to survive two and a half years, alone, with little or no hope of rescue, must be accounted a very remarkable achievement, whatever the means employed. It was for this reason, rather than the probability of political repercussions, that I agreed to Iain's suggestion that we say nothing about the ship's grisly cargo.

This was after Iain had opened up the hold and found Ángel Borgalini dead. He had shot himself. At least, that's what he told me. But how can I be sure? Somehow I did not think Ángel the type to commit suicide, and I had been in the pantry, checking over the stores with Eduardo, at the time Iain had gone down to look into the hold. If there had been a shot then, I don't think I would have heard it.

Whatever the truth, one thing was abundantly clear. His death would save everybody a great deal of trouble, and it was on this account that I agreed to keep quiet about the real nature of the *Andros* voyage and the cargo she carried.

Before we left, Iain produced a mini camera and began taking close-ups of Eduardo and the great cabin where he had lived for over two and a half years, also some quick snaps of the iced-up deck, and then he had gone down on to the ice, taking pictures of the *Andros* from all angles, some that would show how the stranded bergs had boxed her in. Finally – 'fur the record,' he said – several shots of Carlos's body lying there under the bows, even unzipping his anorak and pulling up his sweater to get close-ups of the wound that had been the cause of his death. Then, after a hot meal of porridge and seal meat, which was the best we could rustle up, we started back round the shoulder of the southern iceberg, through the tangle of up-ended and over-laid pack ice, to the spot where Ángel and Carlos had abandoned the snowmobile.

It was a hard struggle, the going very bad and Eduardo having to be helped over the worst sections. He showed no curiosity about where we were taking him, or the fact that, after we had located our own abandoned sledges, Iain was constantly pausing to listen out on his little receiver for the direction signal from the bug he had planted on the snowmobile. It seemed as though the sudden transition from an eternity of loneliness, and the inevitability of a cold, hard death, to companionship, and the imminent return to the world of people, had triggered off an intense mental reaction. In a sense, he had switched off, words still pouring out of him, but a lot of them without meaning, and there was a growing helplessness, which contrasted alarmingly with his behaviour when faced with the abrupt appearance of a man he must have hated.

Those shots we had heard, the way he had hunted Borgalini

through the ship, finally forcing him down into that hold full of the bodies of those he had caused to be murdered, the cautious way he had approached us in the dark of the great cabin . . . All of his actions had been those of a man who was mentally alert and in full command of his faculties. And then the rush of explanation, the unaccustomed sound of speech, words tumbling out of his mouth. It shocked me to remember how the whole outpouring had gradually become jumbled and confused until it had deteriorated into near-incoherence, the clarity of his mind blurring and his brain's command of limbs and actions falling away till he was like a man-size rag doll, dependent on us for movement and motivation. It was quite horrible to see the deterioration in him, the way his mind tended to slip back into the dark corners of his memory. I had never seen anything like it before and I hope I never shall again.

With childish insistence he had clutched hold of that haversack full of stones as though it was some sort of talisman, and as the hours passed, I became increasingly petulant at the useless weight of it and Iain's willingness to humour him. By the time we reached the snowmobile it was almost dark and I was exhausted, both mentally and physically, by the babbling weight we were half carrying over the up-ended slabs of layered pack. There was almost no wind now, just a light breeze from the north-east, and it was surprisingly warm. Eduardo was very weak by then. We got him into a sleeping bag, had something to eat, and after that I slept, the sort of sleep that comes when you have had all you can take.

I woke to dark clouds driving low out of the north and the incredible noise of pack ice breaking up, floe riding on floe, great slabs of ice, big as houses, rearing up. This was all happening to the north of us, barely a mile away, the din appalling, and the whole scene so frightening I felt an urge to run. We hitched the sledges to the snowmobile, strapped Eduardo to one of them, and headed south towards the greater security of the Ice Front.

V

PORT STANLEY

ONE

The storm lasted two days, so that by the time we got back to *Isvik* it was the last day of February. Fortunately we had the power of the snowmobile to help us, for by the third day Eduardo was not only mentally deranged, but so physically weak that he was just a half-conscious body strapped to a sledge that had to be pulled. As soon as we were within VHF range, Iain had informed Iris her brother was with us. But though he did his best to prepare her for the condition he was in, it still came as a dreadful shock to her.

We were used to it by then, of course, but after that first wild, garrulous outpouring, he had withdrawn into a mental shell that isolated him from the world. And when they met, he didn't even seem to recognise her. In fact, if we hadn't had the use of the snowmobile from the point where Angel had abandoned it, I doubt whether we would have got him to the ship alive. The going was very bad, with a lot of wet snow, the air temperature rising so sharply that the melt was producing large areas of slush ice, and new polynyas were appearing all the time, so that we were on water more often than on ice.

It was this melting of the ice, which, according to the British Antarctic Survey at their Halley base, had been going on for several years now, that had enabled the *Andros*, after she had been dismasted, to find open water throughout her drift along the eastern and southern perimeter of the Weddell Sea. In addition, of course, once past the South Shetlands, driven first west, then south through the sixties and into the seventies, *Andros* had had the advantage, not only of the prevailing wind, which shifts from west through north into the east, but also of the current, which follows the wind pattern, running clockwise round the Weddell Sea at a rate of anything up to a knot. It had, in fact, taken her less than two and a half months to drift down to the Ice Shelf and then along the Ronne Front until she was blocked by those stranded bergs and sealed in for good.

As soon as we reached *Isvik*, Iain went into the wheelhouse, talking urgently into the Inmarsat boom mike. We had been away over a week, and in advance of the storm that had pinned us down, they had moved the vessel some twenty miles to the south, where the water was more open. Even so, they had been badly squeezed and, for a short time, the bows had been forced right up on to the ice. Now, with a southerly wind, she was afloat again, in open water that was steadily expanding as the pack ice was driven northwards.

I had the details of what had happened while we were away from Andy Galvin, a nervously excited rush of words. Our absence seemed to have made him even more turned in on himself, so that he was now so self-centred that other people's experiences barely registered with him. He asked very few questions and seemed more relieved than anything else when I told him Ángel and Carlos were both dead.

Iris had taken charge of her brother as soon as the sledge to which he was strapped had been floated across to *Isvik*. Nils produced hot soup that was so thick it was more of a stew, also the remains of a bottle of rum. Afterwards I went up on deck, had a quick look round to make certain the ship was in a reasonable state of readiness for any sudden change in the weather, then I turned in. The forecast was good, but with the altered wind direction, and the sun already set, it was much colder, so that a thin film of ice was beginning to form round the hull.

I woke in a sweat to the sound of Eduardo's voice shouting in his sleep, and a wonderful smell of coffee. The sun was already high in an opaque, milky sky and to the north of us a whiteout was forming where the warmth of it was lifting a fog of moisture from the ice.

There was a slight heel to the ship, the creaking of spars and the sound of water rushing past the hull. By the time I had cleaned myself up and put on some fresh clothes, it was past midday and they had been under way since first light. I hadn't heard a sound.

Iris was sitting at the saloon table. She got up and handed me a mug of coffee. There were dark rings under her eyes, tiredness showing in the wan smile she gave me. She looked utterly drained. 'The ice-breaker that was at the BAS base at Halley Bay left three days ago,' she said. 'Iain was on to the MoD. The best they can do is have the RFA supply vessel rendezvous with us in the vicinity of the South Orkneys. They want an ETA, of course, as soon as possible, and if the weather is right, they could have their helicopter meet us and winch him off.'

That was what finally happened. We had a rough time of it off the Filchner Ice Shelf, with strong, gusting winds, almost katabatic at times, coming down on us from the interior of Coats Land. There was a lot of ice about, but we always seemed to find a way through, and when we were finally able to head north, we sailed into open water. In fact, we didn't run into any more pack ice till Iain insisted we tried to short-cut it across to the rv point. It cost us the better part of two days, and when we did get clear of the pack, we lost the wind and had to motor.

By then Eduardo was in a bad way. Partly it was the violence of the movement, partly reaction. Also, of course, he was suffering badly from vitamin C deficiency. But it was his mental state Iris was chiefly worried about. The shock of his return to a world and people he had thought he would never see again was traumatic enough, but added to that was the knowledge of what he had been through, all that had happened on the *Andros*, the bodies in that hold. That was what was eating at his mind. He had shut himself in with the demons of recollection.

In a way, that was fortunate. Iain and I kept our own counsel, so there was nobody to tell the others. I think it probable Iris guessed at some of it, but not the full horror. And I kept a guard on my tongue on the numerous occasions when she questioned me, till in the end she avoided the subject.

That was after we had had a blazing row in the wheelhouse on a night watch. She had suddenly turned on me – 'You don't tell me, do you? Whenever I ask about how he lived for all that time, what exactly there is on board for him to eat, what he said to you when you found him – always, you and Iain, you avoid my questions.' And she added in a choking voice, tears of anger and frustration in those strangely blue eyes of hers, 'What is it you are hiding from me? For God's sake, Pete, tell me. I am not a child. If it is something dreadful, and you are keeping it secret, I can hold my mouth shut. Tell me, please,' she pleaded. 'I am his sister. I have a right to know.'

What could I say? I didn't answer her, and in the end I simply turned away. After that she spoke to me only when she had to, avoiding my company as far as she could.

The odd thing was she made no attempt to subject Iain to the same emotional pressure. He told me that himself. Perhaps she sensed it would be a waste of time. Instead, she had fastened on me as more likely to give in to her pleading.

We were well into March now, and even in the open sea, we were motoring through a paper-thin crust of newly-formed ice during the early hours of each day. By then our course was west of north as we coasted the edge of the pack with the great north-pointing finger of Graham Land to give us something of a lee, so that there was hardly any swell, the sea at times glass-calm. We had two days of this, and each day we were in touch by radio with the RFA ship.

She had left Grytviken, South Georgia, on 11 March and we were now closing each other at a combined speed of 24 knots. The next day she flew off her helicopter, and shortly before four in the afternoon it was hovering over us like a giant dragonfly. By then the wind had picked up and was strong in the gusts, which made the winching operation difficult, the waves having become steep and breaking and the mast wavering around errati-cally to the plunging, rolling movement of the ship.

I had never been right underneath a chopper while the winch was being operated, and this was a grandstand view of it, for I was at the upper steering position, on top of the wheelhouse, trying to keep the ship as steady as possible. I was dead scared the winchman would reel in the wire at the wrong moment and tangle the gyrating stretcher with the mainmast crosstrees. It seemed an age that the helicopter hovered there, but they got him up safely in the end, and as I watched Eduardo's stretcher-bundled body manoeuvred into the helicopter fuselage, the tautness went out of my muscles and I began to relax.

I was expecting the side door to be closed and the machine to wheel away from us and head back to its mother ship. Instead, the winchman's head reappeared above me and he was waving to me urgently as he lowered the wire again. Somebody yelled at me. It was Iain, standing just below me on the side deck, but I couldn't hear what he said. He was muffled up in full cold weather gear and he had a suitcase with him, also a sailbag crammed so full he hadn't been able to tie it properly, and that olive-green haversack slung over his shoulder.

He looked up at me, then smiled and shook his head as he realised his words were being drowned by the down-rush of air and the chop of the blades. I can still see that beak-nosed face of his, brown and wrinkled with ice glare, the heavy jaw and the tight line of his lips as he smiled. He raised his gloved hand and turned aft, calling to Andy to give him a hand.

It was only then I realised he was leaving us. No warning, no goodbyes. I saw Iris stop in her tracks as she was leaving the afterdeck, her eyes widening in unbelief. So he hadn't told her either. He hadn't told anyone. They just stood there, staring at him.

Andy was the first to move, taking hold of the sailbag and slinging it into position as the cargo net came down towards us. A sail began to slat and we yawed wildly, a broken wave rolling under our hull. I dived back to the wheel, forced now to go through the whole process again, holding the boat steady long enough for Iain and his baggage to be got into the net and the whole thing winched up clear of the masts.

'Did you know?' It was Iris. She had climbed the port ladder to join me as I stood there watching the helicopter put its nose down and begin driving forward, northward to regain the fleet auxiliary. 'Did you know?' she repeated in a strangled voice.

'No,' I said, and for a while we stood there in silence, watching

315

the helicopter dwindle to a speck, watching until, finally, we could not see it any longer.

'What a strange man!' she murmured. 'Never a word to anyone about leaving. Just bang, I'm off. And that's it. He's gone.' She turned, groping blindly for the gap in the rail and the first rung of the ladder. 'Jumped ship, that's about it, isn't it?' She smiled at me, and the way her lips trembled on that forced smile I knew she was very near to tears.

Partly it was the abruptness of his departure. We hadn't expected it and the sudden removal of such a dominant personality left a gap that all of us felt in our different ways. But for Iris and myself it was much more personal. We had been through a lot together these last few months, and always he had been there, providing the motivation and the driving force.

However, we had little chance to brood over it. The wind was steadily increasing, and as the clouds swept lower, darkness closing in, we shortened sail. No squares'ls now; we were close-hauled on the port tack and barely able to lay South Georgia, let alone the Falklands.

It took us eleven days to reach Port Stanley, eleven exhausting days of extreme discomfort. Once past the South Orkneys, we felt the full impact of the great Southern Ocean waves that circle the globe and at Lat. 60° S have to squeeze themselves through the narrow gap between the Horn and Graham Land that is named Drake Strait. It was against a dawn sky of incredible clarity that I got my first glimpse of the Falkland Islands. Nils had called me up to identify a small pyramid of rock just lifting above the north-western horizon. It was Mount Kent, fifteen hundred feet high and almost fifty miles away.

Once under the lee of East Falkland, we were able to motor-sail, and something I shall always remember is the sudden transition to peace as we passed the lighthouse on Cape Pembroke and entered calm water, with the wired enclosures of old Argentine minefields on the slopes above us. We dropped anchor for the night close to an old dredger, with the steeple of Port Stanley's red brick cathedral bearing due south, and went straight to our bunks.

We had reported in by VHF, of course, and they let us sleep through till midday before coming out in a launch to deal with the formalities of entry. The media came out to us, too – the *Penguin News*, the little *Tea-Berry* paper, the local and forces radio stations. They knew by then we had located the wreck of a wooden sailing vessel down at the southern end of the Weddell Sea, but islands that boasted more wrecks and hulks of old square-riggers than any other place in the world were less interested in the discovery of another than in personal accounts of our voyage and the ice conditions we had experienced. They knew nothing about the deaths of Carlos and Ángel Borgalini, so there was no necessity to parry questions.

Customs had already told us the vessel that plies the triangular route, Stanley-Montevideo-Punta Arenas, was leaving that evening. Since it would be over a week before they would have another opportunity, Andy and Go-Go decided to take it. They got a lift ashore with some local people who had come out to us with cans of beer and kind offers of hospitality. Then, just as it was getting dark, a police launch came alongside with a note from Government House requesting Mrs Sunderby's presence at 4 p.m. next day.

There were now just the three of us left, and after we had fed, Nils produced a bottle of vodka he had secreted against the moment of our return to civilisation. We toasted the boat over our coffee, then each other, finally Iris raised her glass to absent friends. No mention of Eduardo's name, nor of Iain's, just absent friends. And after that, Nils went off to his bunk muttering something about being too old 'for gallivanteering around the Veddell'.

Iris got up at the same time and went aft. I started to say goodnight, but she waved me to stay put. 'No, please. Stay there. I won't be a moment.'

I sat down again and poured myself another drink. I thought perhaps she was going to the heads, but she was back almost immediately, a large brown envelope in her hand. 'More coffee?' She put the envelope down on the table and reached across for my mug. 'We have to talk, about money.'

She poured the coffee, sat down again and helped herself to another vodka. She had on an emerald green shirt that was cut low and had a very silky sheen. The top button was undone. I don't think that was intentional, for her mind was on the envelope, which she kept on fingering. 'How much money have you got? I am sorry. It is not a proper question, but I need to know.'

I told her and she gave a little half-smile. 'Not enough even to get you back to the UK.'

'No.'

She pushed the envelope over to me. Scrawled across it was the one word *Yours*. No signature. No address. Nothing.

I looked across at her. 'Iain?'

She nodded. 'After he is gone I find it lying on my bunk. Have a look inside. No letter – nothing personal. Not even a note.'

The envelope contained a thick wadge of traveller's cheques, all countersigned with an illegible signature and ready for encashment. Also *Isvik*'s registration certificate, together with deed of ownership, both in the name of Iris Sunderby. 'You own the boat then.' I was staring at her, all sorts of possibilities rushing through my mind. 'You own all sixty-four shares in *Isvik*.'

'Yes.' She shook her head slightly, still with that little half-smile. 'I didn't like it, but he insist.' She hesitated, then leaned forward suddenly. 'Pete. Who is he? Why doesn't he want his name on that certificate? And the traveller's cheques . . . That is not his name.' She shook her head again and reached for my hand. 'What do I do now? I have this boat. But what to do with it? And he won't come back. I know that. He is out of my life altogether.' She stared at me a moment, then picked up the ship's papers and put them back in the envelope. 'And these.' She waved the traveller's cheques at me. 'I suppose I cash them?'

'Of course.' There was Nils to pay, work to be done on *Isvik*, repairs, replacements, stores, all the incidentals that go with the running of a boat. And there was her brother. 'You'll be going to England, will you?'

She nodded. 'Yes, I must see that Eduardo is all right.' All we knew was that he had been airlifted out on the first available

Tristar flight to RAF Brize Norton, and Iain had gone with him. 'Will you stay here till I get back?'

I hesitated, my mind switching to the house in Cley, to my mother and her flower festival, to the search for a job and the struggle to set up on my own. I think it was then that I realised I had changed. I was a different person. And here was a whole new world, over three hundred islands full of sheep and rock runs, penguins, upland geese and albatross, a land spun off from the bottom of Africa that I would certainly never get the chance to see again once I returned to Norfolk.

'Yes,' I said. 'I'll be here.'

She reached out and touched my hand, at the same time raising her glass. 'To *Isvik* then!'

Forgotten now was the horror trapped in that icebound wooden frigate, my thoughts reaching out into the future. 'To *Isvik*!' I said.

All Pan books are available at your local bookshop or newsagent, or can be ordered direct from the publisher. Indicate the number of copies required and fill in the form below.

Send to: **CS Department, Pan Books Ltd., P.O. Box 40, Basingstoke, Hants.   RG21 2YT.**

or phone: 0256 469551 (Ansaphone), quoting title, author and Credit Card number.

Please enclose a remittance* to the value of the cover price plus: 60p for the first book plus 30p per copy for each additional book ordered to a maximum charge of £2.40 to cover postage and packing.

*Payment may be made in sterling by UK personal cheque, postal order, sterling draft or international money order, made payable to Pan Books Ltd.

Alternatively by Barclaycard/Access:

Card No.

———————————————————————————————————
Signature:

Applicable only in the UK and Republic of Ireland.

While every effort is made to keep prices low, it is sometimes necessary to increase prices at short notice. Pan Books reserve the right to show on covers and charge new retail prices which may differ from those advertised in the text or elsewhere.

NAME AND ADDRESS IN BLOCK LETTERS PLEASE:

....

Name ————————————————————————————————

Address ——————————————————————————————

————————————————————————————————————

————————————————————————————————————

————————————————————————————————————

3/87